CINDERWILD

Coranna Adams

Published by Coranna Adams

ISBN: 979-8-9896915-1-7

For my father, who made history come alive.
And for my mother, the wisest godmother witch I know.

CHAPTER ONE

The Lily Speaks

April, 1634

Spain

The sea witch, Violante, hides on the Catalonian coast like a knife in its sheath, cloaked but dangerous. I search for weeks, to no effect, until rumors of unusually soft waters make their way to my ears. I track those whispers to the hidden caves near Begur, where villagers offer repeated admonitions not to climb the cliffs.

Heedless of their fear, I scrabble along the tall sheets of rock that brace the sea, searching for an entrance and peer between two large boulders, sweating and swearing, preparing to wedge myself between them when someone speaks softly in my right ear. "Hola."

I jump back, banging my head on a nearby rock. "Zounds." I shut my eyes against the pain.

When I open them again, the sea witch stands before me, barely five feet tall, tanned with a long, lined face. Under a mass of uncombed curls, her left eye roams wild, while her right stares directly forward, a fact made more chilling because the orb is almost fully white.

"Violante Aramburu?" I ask.

The witch nods. She wears what can only be called a sack, so old and gray that it's impossible to determine the fabric, and a necklace of white shells and tiny, bleached starfish.

"You're a difficult woman to find."

Violante says nothing in response, stroking the gray wisps of hair that dangle from her chin.

It is no surprise Violante hides far away from the Spanish King and his Catholic army. The Catalonian coast might even be its own kingdom, so far removed as it is from Madrid, and a water witch as powerful as Violante must work to remain unnoticed.

"I have come to ask for your help," I go on. I try to smooth my brown wool riding dress, worn without a bustle, the stomacher laced loose enough to climb. "I, Marina Mullenheim, witch of the Black Forest, speak on behalf of Madame Mablean and the godmothers of the Strasbourg Hearth."

"I have heard of your Hearth," Violante croaks. "What help do you want?"

"Your skill with the waves is unmatched. Even those who know nothing of magic recognize its effects." I don't flatter, merely speak the truth. If the sea witch can stop aid from reaching past the Spanish King to the Catholic Emperor, then perhaps all fighting will stop, and our wild places remain untouched.

"Between my home and yours, we witches burn, and at the hands of soldiers, the forests dwindle. The storms of winter come soon. Surely no one will suspect if the water rises up and the ships sink."

The sea witch ignores my words and strokes her hairy chin, watching the waves break against the unbending shore.

"Will you sink the Spanish fleet?" I ask.

"Why would I do such a stupid thing?"

The answer is obvious. "Between the pyres and the war, no witches will be left if we don't work together. We owe it to our sisters to protect the source of our magic. Surely in this, we're united."

Violante turns her white eye in my direction, and although it must be blind, I still feel watched. "We all die, in the end. Witches. Commoners. Kings. Why should it matter if it's sooner or later?"

Not even I am such a fatalist.

"If the Catholic nobles decide to burn down all the forests to the East, they can. Their soldiers plunder and pillage without care, but we *must* protect the Black Forest. It is the last of the wild woods, the source of many remaining witches' power." I hope this truth tugs at the sea witch's salty heart.

"They could cut down the wood. But they won't." Violante watches the ocean below. "And if every ship in the Spanish fleet sinks, they'll surely suspect magic and come looking for me. I care not for your Black Forest, Marina Mullenheim. Below the waves, the sea remains wild as ever. My power, unlike yours, is safe."

This is how elemental magic works. Witches draw from aether, earth, air, fire, or, as Violante does, water.

"No witch is safe these days," I argue, carefully weaving the thread so that the sea witch sees our shared interests. "Kings mark trees and land and water as money, Violante. Gold. Opportunity." I grab at a rock and come away with a handful of sand. "They don't know that without the wild, we have no magic."

"Hidden here, I'm safe. Safe enough." Violante turns to look me in the eye, that is with her good eye. The milky white eye roams now, as if I've been judged no longer of interest.

"So you'll not help us then? You leave your sisters to suffer?" I shouldn't press her when we've only just met. But my legs ache from climbing, and I've come so far from the city I call home.

"You think I've not suffered too?"

Violante's humped back forces her to walk slowly, and her fingers appear gnarled, as if broken in several places, probably from torture.

"The villagers speak well of you." I lie. They speak of her not at all.

"Because I've taught them to fear what they do not understand." Violante cuts me off, shaking her head. "They fear me. Even the creatures of the sea fear me, as they should." She whispers this last to herself.

"Have you ever seen a mermaid, Marina?"

For a moment, I do not believe that I heard the sea witch correctly. Mab warned me not to be drawn into Violante's orbit, but the sea witch speaks words I waited for my whole life. "Not in the flesh," I shake my head, disbelieving. "Have you?"

Violante already makes her way down a small path I hadn't noticed before now.

By the time we arrive at the hidden beach, the sun touches the edge of the horizon. Violante warns me to stay quiet by putting her finger to her whiskered lips, but there's no need for the warning. To my witch's sight, the air glitters gold with magic.

Below us, two mermaids swim, their hair long and beautiful. One, dark-haired, wears a shirt woven from lacy seaweed, but the second wears nothing except the finery of her blue-green tail. Her red curls hang heavy over a plump mouth and bare breasts.

"Sisters," Violante whispers. "They visit the mouth of the river to eat the tender fish who breed in the rocks."

The dark-haired sister slaps her powerful tail on the top of the water and preens, sluicing sand against her arms, while her sister hunts.

Unable to stop myself, I creep closer, using the sea grass and the downward wind from the dunes to hide my scent. "I thought there were no more," I whisper. "Will you show me a dragon or a unicorn next?"

"All the dragons died long ago. The old ways pass, and with them, the creatures who belonged to that world," the sea witch says. "These few may be the last of their kind."

A movement from the far end of the beach catches my eye. A third mermaid, submerged except for her beautiful face and black curtain of hair, swims near the mouth of the cove, watching a ship anchored off the coast.

She sings, each note pure, familiar, and the sound unties my heart. Before I can stop myself, I'm stumbling into the sand on my knees, tears running down my face.

"No!" Violante whispers. She has her fingers in her own ears. "Fool, the song's not for us." She drags me back to the rocks, pointing beyond the cove.

I look out at sea and notice for the first time a figure unmoving on the ship's deck. He faces us, as if he too can hear the song.

"Idiot!" Violante says, and stuffs a wad of linen in my left ear. "Here." She hands me a second handful for my right.

I can still hear the sound through the fabric, but its effect lessens enough that I remember myself.

"Surely this only makes my point for me. Help us sustain the old ways. Keep the forests wild as the world beneath the waves, so that our magic stays strong. Then these creatures can return to our lands. We can protect them."

The ship shrinks as it sails toward the horizon. The mermaid brings her song to a close. Eventually she swims back toward her sisters.

I plead. The mermaid is a sign I am in the right place at the right time. "Help us end this war, Violante. If the fleet cannot deliver supplies, then the Catholic war dies. And we can return to this." I point down to the mermaids.

"No woman, not even a witch, can stop the tide from coming in. And even creatures such as those are no longer content to live and die in the wild as they should." Violante reaches down to pick up a shell. She holds it out to me. "Beautiful, no?"

The spiral makes a perfect, geometric pattern that repeats in miniature again and again. "Yes," I nod, hearing a loud splash when it drops in my palm.

In seconds, the mermaids disappear.

"You frightened them." I frown.

Violante makes a rude noise with her mouth. "The ocean has no mercy, Marina. And neither do I. No one can keep the witches alive when God and the King want them to burn. Certainly not me. Certainly not by sinking a few ships."

I am not too proud to beg. "Please, Violante, your power is greater than many of the witches who are left, even many of our godmothers cannot claim to rule the elements as you do. If you will help us…"

"You fight against forces so strong you cannot win. Go back to your Madame Mablean and tell her no."

"But the mermaids…"

"Those beauties become the foam on the sea itself when they die." Violante climbs up the cliffside path. "They do not have a soul, and so they cannot suffer as we do."

"Such a song could save us all," I plead, still feeling the mermaid's magic moving within me—even the memory of its beauty is too much to bear. "It is a sign." But Violante's gone, scrambled up the mountain quick as an old goat, and I am not fast enough to stop her.

I must find another way to save the wild woods.

Two months later, after visiting several more abbeys and covens, I stop in the small Spanish city of Tossa de Mar. The city's Moorish tower watches over the sea here, while several pre-Romanesque shrines dot the silver-leafed hills behind the city, reminding me that the King's control over this land feels relatively new.

Prince Domingo passes along the Wild Coast too, on his way to be appointed viceroy of Catalonia in place of his older brother, Ferdinand, and gossip about a silent, beautiful girl flies alongside him, faster than the wings of a termagant.

The castle here appears small by royal standards, but easily houses the many servants and courtiers with whom Domingo travels, including the unknown girl to whom he's taken a liking. The unmarried prince gives the young woman leave to sleep outside the door of his bedroom, a privilege that should be salacious but is described to me with awe instead.

I resolve to meet this girl before I continue back home, thinking she may be another Spanish witch who can offer aid. I find an apartment near the castle through one of Madame Mablean's many high-born contacts, but at first glance I recognize the same little mermaid who sang her song of love, a creature of the sea no more.

Even on land, Amalia moves with the languid sensuality of water, her heart-shaped face surrounded by curls of jet-black hair, features almost identical to her mermaid sisters. Everyone who stands nearby senses the power of the sea rising within her, though they cannot name it.

Amalia's fixation with the prince never wavers. I daren't call it love. The girl accompanies him everywhere.

I finally manage to separate the pair when the women are invited to visit a nearby convent. After an hour of hand gestures and silent communication, I pull the girl from the group of courtiers into a quiet corridor.

"I know your true nature, child, but I don't understand how you come to be here. And more, why you no longer sing?" I put a hand on the girl's thin wrist and smile encouragingly at her.

Amalia frowns and pulls away. Her face flushes, and she shakes her head *no*, preparing to follow the others away.

I put up my hands in entreaty. "No, don't go. I'm a witch, yes, but I mean you no harm. Let me show you. Sit. There."

Suspecting that the girl's silence is not by her own design, I point to a low-slung couch near a large stained-glass window, looking for something that will help me work the magic I need. On the table nearby, a vase full of lilies stands, the flowers deep-throated and white.

I pull one from the bunch and push it into Amalia's hand. Then I take a length of green ribbon from a hidden pocket and unravel it, binding it three times around the flower's stalk and then three more loosely around the girl's throat.

"Go ahead. Speak through the flower. Tell me who has done this to you."

The voice of the lily is so small and whispering that I have to bend close to hear through its sobs.

"Violante."

I pull back and stare into Amalia's liquid brown eyes. "The sea witch? What did she do?"

This answer needs no speaking at all. Amalia opens her mouth to show me that her tongue has been cut from her mouth.

Sacrificial magic works a spell powered by the girl's pain.

"If I can convince my prince of our love, then I become human, just like you." Amalia smiles, her eyes so full of hope that I feel my stomach squeeze.

"But you're already…" I point down to Amalia's perfect, tiny feet.

"Illusion," the flower whispers.

I shake my head *no*. "More than an illusion. You walk. You dance. To hold such a spell in place for so long must be painful. Not even losing your voice can compensate for this." There's more I don't say: how can your prince fall in love if he cannot hear your voice, if he cannot see your true form?

Amalia nods. "It hurts," the flower admits. And now tears glisten and fall on Amalia's plump cheeks.

Every step the little mermaid takes feels as though she walks on cut glass.

"This is dangerous," I tell her, brushing the tears away. "And not because it's painful, but because the very essence of love is freedom, and yet you are already bound."

"Violante should never have mutilated you in such a way. She is older and presumably wiser." I take the little mermaid's small, shaking hand. "Do not worry though. I will help you before I turn toward home. I must."

Amalia nods and squeezes my hand.

In the days that follow, I devise a plan to reach the little mermaid's goal, and in the way of a godmother, I craft it to serve both the girl and the wild from whence she came.

"There's a stream which wends its way into the mountains behind the city. Take the prince there and dip your feet in the water. Encourage him to take off his boots and wash his feet. While you are both in the water, you must kiss him so that the knowledge of your value may nourish the root of love that grows in his heart."

Amalia smiles, and her eyes shine like light over water.

I don't tell the little mermaid that with the help of the castle's laundress I've finagled a strip of fabric from the clothing of each of the lovers, knotting the cloth together along with the dried rind of an orange the two shared. Another hefty bag of coins ensures that the love spell is secretly placed under the prince's bed.

"I will come along as your chaperone," I promise, and Amalia nods.

There's a pang of guilt at the words. Mab wants me to return quickly, already more than the month we planned for has passed, but Violante's ruthless spell promises only pain to the mermaid. I feel bound to offer aid to the creature, by my calling, and even without that, I know how dangerous this world is for those made of magic.

And once Amalia and the Prince are married, I can ask for any favor. A royal favor is something Mab will want to have.

The knotwork begins to release its power as soon as the bowl-shaped hills capture us in their palm. Olive trees dot the hillside here. The land feels protected. Private. Domingo ties both his and Amalia's horses, allowing the beasts a drink, and just as we planned, the mermaid takes her boots off and wades into the nearby stream.

She gestures to the Prince to join her.

Domingo hesitates. He knows such behavior signifies courtship. If the two are discovered, such play is tantamount to a declaration of love.

Amalia begins to dance. Each step cuts the girl to the bone, but she smiles and moves in a rhythm perfectly in tune with the water's gentle burble.

The magic begins to take hold.

"Come play in the water with me."

Domingo sits, transfixed. He pulls off one boot and puts a toe into the cool water.

Amalia beckons to her love again.

The Prince responds by removing his second boot. He slips deeper into the stream, and the two grasp hands.

Time slows.

I crook my index finger, directing the water to push the two lovers together. The current twirls suddenly, and Amalia is thrown against the Prince, her dark hair mixing with his lighter locks.

The Prince falls back in surprise, losing his footing, and slides thigh deep into the pool. Water splashes up onto his shirt and face.

But instead of laughing and loosening, Domingo frowns and wipes water off his dripping nose. He pushes Amalia away and scans the horizon. "Amalia, you do your virtue a disservice by playing like a child. No child looks as you do, with those…those…"

The pious, Christian prince cannot bring himself to say *breasts*. He moves away and climbs back to shore.

Amalia follows, and the two silently mount their horses, Amalia sidesaddle as is the custom of the land.

When we return, I discover that the Prince's manservant found my knot. My attempt at protection makes the situation worse. Now, the courtiers and servants whisper about a witch in the household, and Amalia is cast in suspicion.

That night the mermaid is not permitted to sleep outside of her Prince's door. Unsettled, I walk the hills near the castle and find a blood offering in a crumbling Roman shrine. I trace the mermaid's path down to the sea, where her body washes up against the sand, her false legs covered with the slimy sheen of fish scales. Amalia's halfway transformed back to the creature she once was, beautiful in death no more.

With my witch's sight, I see something move above me, a dark shimmering of moonlight over fish scales, surely a trick of the air.

"Marina…." Amalia's angry voice whispers. "I hear the sea, but I cannot return to it. Why am I not where I belong?"

I nearly jump out of my skin. "No," I argue against Amalia's misery, as if it were my own. I'd hoped to help the girl. Even if all the forests burn and the witches' power wanes, I wanted one girl in the world to have the thing her heart most desires. I lost such a chance long ago, and I thought the mermaid offered me a chance to make my loss less. "How can this be?"

The hidden part of Violante's spell locks into place. The little mermaid, caught between the animal and the human world, joins the realm of air.

"I am trapped," the mermaid shrieks. "*You* did this to me."

"No. I would never do this." I nearly trip trying to walk back along the beach path, trying to get away from the memories that threaten to spill out of me.

The mermaid's death stacks another consequence on top of Violante's refusal to help the Hearth and the witches of Strasbourg. Now I've found no favor from Domingo or his father—twice I am unable to keep the Black Forest free.

Worse, I have gone against the godmother's code and caused more harm than good for this poor creature. She is not even as protected as an apprentice of mine would be.

As if she hears my thoughts, Amalia's voice comes again, full of suffering, empty of song. "Ma-ri-na, you failed me."

My haunting begins.

CHAPTER TWO

Little Ashes

May, 1634

France

Two cobblestone streets lay before me, identical in every way. Two black-coated merchants stroll past. Washerwomen, both red-faced and angry, tow a pair of shouting children.

I take a step forward on stones that shift under my feet and stumble into the glove maker's stalls, getting a face full of leather and lace.

I'm drunk. And seeing double.

The Strasbourg Cathedral bells ring nine o'clock mass.

I'm late to meet Madame Mablean. I straighten and try again, this time staying upright. I weave and bob past the cafe and storefronts on my left until I find what I am looking for. My stomach turns as two handles resolve into one solid brass knocker before me.

I push open the door to the dressmaker's shop.

A fire witch pushes past me, sparks visible only to my witch's sight trailing in her wake. The shop bell rings as I follow. I ignore bolts of fabric and the matronly witch keeping watch and lurch past. At the far wall, I pass through a door into the cool, dark room beyond the storefront, gooseflesh rising on my arms, even as two Moors, Black witches I don't recognize, bustle past me toward the street beyond.

This innermost circle of the witches' council is called the Hearth for it is where the fire of our women burns brightest, but the name lies. I'm not fire. I'm ash. I am the bearer of endings, not beginnings.

"You're late," someone calls from the large inner room.

I turn my head to see who speaks, but they duck and run. A witch can disappear at will, it is said, but that is bullshit. The coward hides.

"Arschgeige!" I curse and try to wipe the smell of brandy and gutter piss from my blue wool dress.

Safe from the street's prying eyes, I climb the stairs on my left, listening for whispers or claps, any sign that I don't travel alone, but other than my stomach offering a groan of protest, I hear nothing.

My hands feel numb in my skirt pockets. My heart is…I feel into the space where the organ should be but find nothing. I am a cup overturned. I am stained like spilled wine. My eyes prick hot and full, until my gut lurches.

I'm going to vomit.

On the second-floor landing, I spy a large decorative pot and retch hot, sour liquid into it. "Gah…gar." I make miserable sounds and try to hold my silver hair out of the way.

"Oh, Marina," someone says softly, her beautiful voice sad. "What have you become?"

I jerk around, but the landing stands empty.

Tears threaten to rise. Something stirs in my chest.

"No," I growl and push the feeling down. I will not draw the mermaid's spirit any closer, not here.

The hinge on Mab's door creaks upon opening. I settle into a large chair by the fire before Mab looks up from the table where she sorts herbs and consults an ancient, curling spell book.

"I'm haunted," I say.

Mab holds up one crooked finger in the air to silence me, consulting the page before her, but I ignore the gesture.

"Spirits of the air never die, do they? They travel the mournful earth, ever restless."

Wise, Mab returns my query with one of her own. "Is this a theoretical question, Marina? Or just hysterics?"

There's no looking glass in this room, but through Mab's eyes, I sense how I must look, my nice blue wool dress punctuated with leaves and dirt from the flight home, foul stains from the city streets at the hem. My silver hair coming unbound. And after so much vodka and crying, my eyes feel clouded and red-rimmed.

"So the journey did not go well then?" Mab asks, when it becomes clear I don't intend to answer her question.

Nearly seventy, Mab stands unbent before me, slender and beautiful, with silver-white hair that falls to her waist. Dressed in blue silk, she appears the pinnacle of everything a godmother and witch should be–wealthy, well-mannered, well-placed. Through careful, clever subterfuge, Mab protects the witches of the Hearth and makes sure this building remains a sanctuary for us all, the lower floor storefront masked as a modiste's shop.

I sigh, shaking my head before the double-vision can return, and press my hands on my eyes to keep my tears inside.

"Violante never meant to help us, Mab, no matter what you hoped. The sea witch won't sink the Spanish fleet. She refused."

Mab curses like a sailor. "By God's heart, Marina. The sea witch could be the key to the lock our world finds itself bound by, and you can't make her turn? One woman. Meanwhile our magic grows weaker and weaker and more of us die." She crushes a few leaves in a mug and pours water from a kettle hanging over the fire, handing the mug to me in passing.

Mab goes on. "If Strasbourg falls, then the augurs have said that the Black Forest will burn. Then the last bit of wildness will be lost, the very source of our power."

I know this. We all know this. Still, the Catholic Emperor harasses every nobleman from Rome to Barcelona for arms or ships, and slowly the battlefront inches closer to our city.

"Don't lecture me, Mab. Violante does not care if witches burn across all of Europe and the forests with them. She said as much and then reminded me that death comes for us all."

I take a sip of the foul drink and curse, wishing I could escape this conversation, but for me, there's nowhere to hide. Lately every time I close my eyes, I see the little mermaid, dancing before her prince, smiling to hide her pain. "She plays her own game." A game I stumbled into by chance, and now am bound to play by rules I did not create.

A breeze rustles the damask curtain, and suddenly, I smell the stench of the nearby witch pyres, burning hair and greasy flesh.

"How many were burned last night?" I ask, struggling to keep myself from retching again. "And not one of them with true magic?"

Mab arranges her gown around her as she finally sits across from me. She pulls on a green wrap the color of new-made leaves. Her beautiful face does not indicate she smells anything foul. In this way, she and Violante seem similar, both able to conceal what lies behind their masks.

"I've found a new girl," she says.

It's much easier to talk about living witches than dead ones.

"No." I try to put iron in my voice, but I'm too drunk. I do not say what I think which is that I cannot lose another beautiful young thing to the cruelty of this world. "Do you remember my godmother ceremony? Do you remember what we saw?"

My questions go unanswered. "If vinegar does not work, honey might," Mab says. I've heard her say this more than twice, and I hate it every time. "If the sea witch won't help us keep war from the city, we must find another way."

I take a sip. And another. My stomach settles as Mab's concoction does its work.

"Who is she and what are her powers?" I ask, before I can help myself. It's been some time since we've found a new witch in our midst.

"A merchant's daughter. Her mother died when she was young. Monsieur de Boer travels a great deal. The family's monied enough, at least for our purposes. And reports are the girl skipped the first magic and masters the elements. She's powerful, Marina. Very powerful."

"So she's had no training, with her mother gone," I clarify. "And will be little help to us when we have to keep the war away."

"Honey, Marina," Mab reminds me, *tsk-ing*. "There are several noblemen who own lands near the Black Forest. At least two are in need of a wife."

"We're witches, not village matchmakers, Mab." I stand up, but then sit back when the room starts to spin. "And there's an army of well-trained witches in the city. Choose one of those. Why do we need another?

"Pah! The land between Württemberg and Offenburg lies in the crucible of the battle. We need someone we trust in that crucible. A hidden figure. And who's more hidden than a nobleman's wife?"

I hear a soft clapping, applause. She's here. Of course she's here, and the mermaid approves of Mab's cleverness.

My stomach twists. I'm too old for this game. I'm a piece of fabric unraveling. And the truth of our circumstance is the opposite of my words: so many witches lie dead. There are very few left in all of Alsace, certainly no army.

Mab tsks, looking down her nose at me. "What is this drunken protest about? Who better to apprentice Elina de Boer, especially if she's powerful?"

I try to speak, but Mab interrupts.

"You're a monster, Marina. All over the city, mothers keep little children awake with tales of the magic you can work." Mab smiles with the pointed teeth of a predator.

I glance around the room with my witch's sight.

There.

Amalia floats in the air behind Mab showing a mirage of watchful black eyes and pointed teeth.

"I will not do it. I can't." I stumble backward and nearly trip trying to find my way to the door. "I should go home. I am too drunk."

"Find her tomorrow then," Mab flings the words at my back like stones. "Once you sober up."

Mab knows I cannot stifle my goddamned curiosity. That's why I search the rubbish outside of the de Boer estate first, prowling through barrels of vegetable clippings and sifting their burn pit.

There's not much of interest until I find a pair of slippers, hidden in an old wooden crate under a burlap sack in the garden shed. They are beautifully made, white spun silk thin as porcelain, and so lovely that some servant was unwilling to torch them despite an obvious order to do so.

I steal the shoes, tucking them inside my carrying bag, and knock on the back door, stooping my back and making my voice quaver. "Oh dearie," I say, not looking up. "I've been walking all day from Gengenbach. Lost my way. Would you offer me a cup of tea?"

"I shouldn't," the girl at the door replies, showing a too-thin face blackened by soot. She wears stained rags, and I realize, with a shock, that she's been cleaning the chimney, risking life and limb climbing up the thin column to scrape the insides clean with a broom.

"Madame de Boer will be angry if I let in the rabble." She tries to close the door on me, too gently, so I wing my way past her, huffing and making conciliatory sounds.

"Out," the cinder girl says again, eyes green as moss. This time she almost sounds like she means it.

"I won't go. Not 'til I've had a cup of watered down wine and put my feet up by..."

Both of us stare at the cold hearth.

"This won't do." I look around for a source of heat and see the ovens burning. From there, I make a simple spell of transference, snapping my fingers and beckoning a fire to the dry logs in the hearth.

"NO!" the cinder girl replies even more firmly. She betrays herself by her lack of surprise. Then I'm surprised when she snaps her own fingers, and just like that, cook's bread bakes again. "Madame de Boer does not countenance magic in the house."

"So she knows you have a bit of magic then?" I ask, wondering why the girl calls her stepmother by her formal name.

Elina de Boer reveals more of her jawline every minute. The sharp point strains and pushes like the lead on a stubborn horse. She refuses to answer.

Finally, caution. Good. Such a display sends her to be burned at the stake in the wrong company.

Wordless, she steps over to the fresh bread cooling on the cook's counter, ripping off a section and hands it to me. "You must be hungry though, Madame. Go ahead. I will tell them I took it."

I bite into the warm loaf, savoring the yeasty smell. Chewing, I plod back to the hearth, lifting the newly plundered slippers from my bag and setting them beside me.

"Those are mine," Elina says, and hands me a cup of mulled wine that I hadn't noticed her pour. I look down and see that the silk slippers appear to be a pile of knitting now. The girl weaves a serviceable glamour in moments.

That solves the question of who kept such fine things from the burn pile. The girl calls fire and can reach into the aether too. Mab's source spoke true. Elina de Boer already touches the elements.

"Cendrillon!" Madame de Boer, the stepmother, hurries into the room. Literally, she calls the girl, *little ashes*. "Cendri!" Madame wears a green satin day gown that turns her complexion sallow. "Have you finished? I'm cold," she whines and, turning, catches sight of me.

"Out," the shrew says, without a thought to my obvious age and bent back. "We do not open our doors to every wandering charwoman. Out."

I huff, and bare teeth as sharp as any wolf's. "No, Fraulein." I stand, unmoving, and Madame de Boer's face tightens.

She yells over her shoulder, "Johann!" and turns back to screech at the girl. "If you've given your lunch to a beggar, then you'll get no more food today, child."

It's late afternoon, hours after lunch. Where is the girl's father, that his daughter is so mistreated?

I have no time to follow that thought because a great clod of a man stomps into the room, grabbing my arm tightly enough to bruise. He pushes me out the door and slams it closed.

I go to the lead window and peer inside. The slippers revert back to their original form on the hearth, which means the girl can't keep hold of her magic with her stepmother in the room. Thankfully Elina notices the transformation and slides the shoes behind her back, as Madame de Boer lectures her.

"The chimney must be clean in an hour, or I'll light a fire with you still inside it." Madame de Boer pinches Elina's arm as she leaves, careful to wipe the soot on one of the cook's clean towels.

I've seen her kind before. All of this woman's messes belong to someone else.

Quick as a cat, Elina wraps the slippers in another scrap of fabric looking for somewhere else to hide them.

I borrow a stiff wind and fly to the roof to clear my head.

The girl's strong, but her connection to the elements unpredictable. Fear and abuse damage even the strongest witch, and I don't need more work.

I need another drink. I need to lose myself in a game of dice. I need Kasimir Leiningen whispering love words in my ear, even if all the forests of the world burn, but instead I'm stuck here, doing Mab's bidding.

You failed me, Marina, a voice whispers, the same quiet voice that spoke in my ear at the Hearth. Even here, Amalia's ghost haunts me.

I need to be free of my mistakes.

"Yes, I did," I say aloud. "And I may fail Elina de Boer too. Have you thought of that? Perhaps it's a better mercy to leave her here?"

I lean against the nearby chimney, taking stock of the city I love so well. Mab's warning rings in my ears, dragging me back from the ledge. If Strasbourg falls, then the forest will burn, and we witches will be no more.

"Did you come for me?" The girl's voice unravels like a thread from inside the dark chimney cap, looping around me.

I nod. "The godmothers got word of your power somehow, Elina. You must be more careful from now on."

Her coal-marked face peeks out a few seconds later—Cendrillon indeed—as she clambers up with the slippers wrapped in her arms, but to my witch's sight, I see only the bright power within her glowing green and gold and the black weed that wraps around it, threatening to choke off the girl's connection with herself. "No one has called me that since my mother died," she says. "You may call me Cendrillon, instead. That is my name now."

We seek a weapon, something with which we can push back the war and the men who fight it, but can this creature be shaped to serve the godmothers' needs, especially crippled as she is by lack of love?

I can't face another failure, so I speak plainly. "Your power likely can't overcome the damage that that beastly woman does to you. You'd have to be free of her to make the most of your magic. No, I wish you the best, *Cendrillon*, but I should not have come."

I know better than anyone that there are no happily-ever-afters, not for witches.

With that, I let the wind carry me down to the alley below, already imagining the taste of cold vodka on my tongue.

CHAPTER THREE

Rabbit & Hawk

The next morning I write Roland, my son's, name in water on the mirror he gave me for my fifty-fifth birthday. The finding spell conveniently also offers me the chance to check my face, no longer swollen from alcohol and grief.

Among all witches, godmothers are the most long-lived and age with grace and beauty—that is so long as they aren't burned at the stake.

After washing and changing, I set out to find my family, wearing a clean skirt and stomacher in which I can comfortably walk.

Roland occupies Sylvie along the banks of the Grande Île. His daughter hums and sings as she moves, talking to the water and the sky as if they are the closest of friends, a sign she may, in fact, be a witch one day.

I catch their attention and join. We stroll in silence until we find a smooth grassy spot far enough away from the water to make sure Sylvie's safe.

"Back so soon?" Roland asks, brow creasing in worry.

I feel a pang of guilt, recognizing that he grows used to my long absences.

"Everything did not go as planned." Platitudes cover a bevy of sins. I don't talk about my magic often, but Roland knows what I am.

Among witches, it's a great honor to rise to the calling of godmother. That is what they tell us, and I believed them for the first thirty years. Then I realized that if the elders told us the truth, how many would be lost, how many would be hurt at our own hands, no one would ever answer the calling.

And now I am an elder charged with telling others these lies.

I glance over at Sylvie, her dark tuft of hair short and spiky as any young, growing thing. She fashions a wooden knife from a bit of log and begins lopping off dandelion heads with fastidious skill. "And you, and you, and you," she says. "Not you, because you're the strongest one."

The tallest flower stays standing, unbowed by her wrath. Children recognize simple truths: brutality is an effective form of management.

"Sylvie," Roland calls as she roams further afield with her weapon. "Please leave some of the flowers for the bees."

"Aaaaeeeeeee." She screams.

Roland and I both jump and run toward Sylvie who points down at something below the edge of the trunk. I pull a branch back and find a small hare, bleeding and sticky.

"What happened?" Sylvie asks, watching from behind her father's knees.

I inspect the slash in the animal's belly, pink skin of the gut lining poking out. The little rabbit lies one step away from death and breathes so hard its heart might stop even before its guts fall to the ground.

"A hawk caught it," I say, marking the length of the cut for Sylvie and pointing into the sky where the bird circles. "See."

"Can we save him?" Sylvie asks. She comes forward to lean against me, curiosity making her bold. In her hand, she still holds the sword stick, and judging from the involuntary twitching of her fingers, she wants to poke the tiny animal.

"No," Roland protests. "Sometimes it's better to let a suffering animal die."

"Maybe it won't get caught next time," Sylvie says, her child's logic forgetting the finality of death. "The blood's pretty, but the bunny doesn't feel good, does it, Mimi?"

"No, it doesn't." I stroke my finger down the bunny's long ear, wanting my granddaughter to know nothing of blood and pain and death.

I weigh the risk. Healing an animal, or human, by draining the life of another living thing, even the flowers and grass is verboten. *Forbidden.* But I'm so sick of death. If I could go back and find Amalia before she died, I would bring her back to life.

Beneath my hand, the soft creature jerks once, twice, and then moves no more.

I was too slow to act, again, and now there's another death on my hands.

Sylvie flings herself into her father's arms. "Is it gone?" she asks in a muffled voice.

"The body's still here," I say. "But his spirit moves on."

Move on. I pray the mermaid listens.

"Moves on to what?" Sylvie asks.

"To a field greener than this one," I comfort. "Come on. Let's bury him, Schatzi." We find a stick and dig a shallow grave. I mark the spot with a red rock we find by the water's edge.

"He was too weak. Too hurt. Remember, we only keep the strongest ones," I say to Sylvie, gesturing to the rolled heads of dandelions dotting the green brush of grass. I turn sideways and plunk down.

Sylvie's finally comfortable enough to sit on my lap. She puts her legs over my own and grabs my hand, slapping it in rhythm playfully.

"But when someone's hurting, we help," Sylvie says.

"If we can, yes. We must try," I nod, and turn my face away as hot tears surface.

I failed the mermaid, but there's another girl I could help. Cendrillon de Boer may be powerful but without training, she may not survive long enough to learn how to hide her power. Nor how to use it well.

I watch the hawk circle above us, a predator looking for its prey. Power is its own drug, interesting to be sure, but compassion?

Compassion is a trap that catches me every time.

Every witch knows that alcohol dulls the senses, making it much harder to hear or see spirits, so that night I drink in a dark bar at the south end of Strasbourg, where the sound of drunken laughter hurries better people home.

The city at the crossroads, Strasbourg is called, and the St. Catherine's crowd trues the name. Two Jewish cloth merchants sit at a nearby table, flanked on either side by Swedes and Bohemians who trade in fur and linen. Several men local to nearby Gengenbach perch near the door, uneasily eyeing a number of recently arrived Portuguese Moors. A few women circulate, servants or prostitutes, I can't tell which.

I wave the barmaid away after ordering another drink.

"What play you?" I ask of the table closest to me.

"A simple game of Pair and Ace." A toothless gentleman speaking almost unintelligible French shakes the dice cup, marking a space on the small table around which a crowd gathers. He rattles the knucklebones one more time. "Let me show you how it works, Madame. Make your throw. Roll, Monsieur." He prods the blond Swede to his right.

The man takes up the cup and shakes it, rolling out three knucklebone dice, made from sheep's bones.

I count their numbers–a three, a four, and a six.

The Swede grumbles and turns away.

"And the lady?" The racketeer takes back the cup, waiting for my call. "Would you like to wager?"

I spy a dark-haired, broad-shouldered man across the circle, his skin warm brown. Newly arrived, the man's doublet and boots appear to be worth twice that of this establishment's regular patrons. The man watches me with admiring eyes that betray nothing of the thoughts within.

"Come on now," the racketeer urges me. "Join the game."

"I will wager a silver thaler," I nod. "But he must call it." I point to my well-heeled admirer.

Our small crowd quiets, and the shifty-eyed racketeer frowns. "What's this?"

"Do you not recognize the bastard Kasimir, half-brother to Count Leiningen-Leiningen?" Another man pipes up, one of the locals, I think.

"Is that his name?" I chime. "He's handsome enough. Maybe Fortune's Wheel will smile on the Bastard tonight. Roll the dice, mon bon Monsieur."

"Non. Non." The racketeer shakes his head.

The handsome man's mouth twitches, as if he stills a smile. "Come now. Hand it over," he says, and the racketeer relents.

In the Bastard's confident hands, the tin cup rattles with the sound of three dice turning. Everyone, the Jews, the Swedes, the Bohemians, the locals, and the Moors all pause as if listening to the sound.

Kasimir turns the cup over, and the knucklebones roll onto the wooden surface. "A pair of sevens and the ace! He's won. He's won." Several at our table cheer, and the Gengenbach locals boo. Across the room, the establishment's owner shouts for us to calm down.

"The game's fixed. The game's fixed!"

The win and its protesters garner me too much attention, so I stand, intent on leaving, and sway, watching the room spin for a moment.

"Where will you spend your coin, mistress?" A voice behind me, familiar to my ear, asks.

"At the baker's, or dressmaker's," I joke, turning to the Bastard. He draws soundlessly closer. "My mind's full of feathers at the moment, but I do love a ruff made of fox fur."

"I will give you that and more if you come home with me tonight." He stands more than a head taller than me. The man's unbound curly hair hangs to his shoulders, showing brown with a few threads of gray. He loops his hand through the crook of my elbow, anchoring me without a true feeling of weight.

"Are you propositioning me, Sir," I gasp and feign distress. "Do I look a whore with this neckline?" —unfair because I *am* partial to low cut dresses, and I only wore this high-necked lace-cursed ruff to act the part of a granny in the day's earlier farce.

"No good woman throws dice," he admonishes me.

We step out of the tight walls of the bar onto the cobbled street.

"I assure you," I answer, turning to run a hand over his shoulder, feeling the muscles beneath my palm bunch. "They do, and more would if the customs here constricted less."

He laughs, showing me his straight white teeth. "Let me take you home, Marina. My bed is cold, and your skin is very, very warm. Haven't you finished visiting your family?" He turns to wrap his arms around me, speaking into my ear so that only I may hear.

"I saw them this morning," I admit.

"You're strung tight as a bow, and the best cure for that is lots of sex. And the best cure for too much sex is sleep, and you will sleep better with my arms around you." He slides his fingers through mine and tugs me close enough to feel the heat of him.

"I can't. I have something to do," I say.

The forest?" he asks.

"I've told you too many of my secrets." I kiss Kasimir silently, not stopping until we both pull away for air.

"I've not been to the wood since I returned from Spain. My power wanes. Tonight I must walk among the trees." Maybe there I will find escape from my mermaid.

"Fine. Tomorrow," he kisses down my neck again, pressing his lips through the lace of my blouse.

I sigh, wanting to stay but knowing I can't. "I'll be back in the city when I'm done, and not a moment before. Now take this. After all, you won it fairly." I press the coins into Kasimir's large palm.

"But I've offered no services yet, madame?" he teases. "Surely you should test your pleasure before you pay."

I laugh at the ribald joke and feel the wind ruffle my hair. It's the first time I've laughed in weeks, and I instantly feel guilty. How can I play when the mermaid lies dead, never to kiss her love again?

"Goodnight, *mon amour*." Sensing my change of mood, Kasimir kisses my hand and walks to the end of the street, heading toward his townhouse alone.

I put my hands out and beckon the wind to me, flying into the city's shadows.

A quarter moon winks at me from above as Strasbourg falls behind, the smell of shit and rotting vegetables gone. Air rushing past, I feel the cold kiss of moonlight, the only kiss I will have tonight, for I fly alone.

And the forest awaits.

From the air, the Black Forest is a thing of beauty. Curving and indelicate, the sash of trees rises for miles along the downy cleft of the Rhine Valley. The trees at its center are so old that the forest barely recognizes the movements of man.

Here, the leftover scent of cheap vodka is sacrilege, and I apologize silently that I've brought any contagion into the purifying woods. Breathing deeply, I follow the tinkling voice of water.

The creak, the trip of a branch breaking, alerts me to the fact that I'm not alone.

"How long have you been following me?" I ask and whirl around to face little Cendrillon de Boer.

"Are you married to that man you were kissing?" Cendrillon asks, leaning against a tree and inspecting her filthy nails. In the shadows, she's nearly invisible, dark and mottled as it is by the cinders she's still not washed clean. Maybe she never washes? Maybe she prefers to stay hidden in that mean, downtrodden home?

"I've been married twice. And that is surely married enough. Not that it's any of your business, Mademoiselle."

"You're a witch, just like me."

We still do not know one another well enough to boldly tell the truth.

"I'd beg you not to slander me so," I frown. "I go by the title Godmother, Cendrillon."

Now it's the girl's time to fall silent. "I have a godmother," she finally says.

I nod. "Not the magical kind," I promise. "Who taught you to fly? Tell me. Your mother?"

"I taught myself," she says. "Why are you here—so far from the city?"

"To dance naked in the moonlight," I joke, and the girl gasps.

I laugh. "Surely you don't believe such bullshit. I'm looking for the stream. I need to bathe." I follow the sound of water, ignoring my unwanted companion. When the small pool comes into view, I strip, and the girl turns, uncomfortable with my freedom.

The pool measures to my knee, too shallow to dive within, so I wade and let the moonlight bathe me first. I take fistfuls of dirt and scrub the smell of the city away and then I lean down and submerge all of me that I am able. When I'm clean, I use the outermost robe of my dress to dry off.

"You next," I say. "If you want to walk the sacred woods, you should at least be clean."

Cendrillon de Boer may dislike following my orders, but I can see by the slits of her eyes that she wants to do this thing.

And why not? Reclaiming one's wildness relies on small acts of courage. Being comfortable in her own skin is a birthright Cendri must decide to claim.

I walk to the far part of the clearing and sit with my back to the girl. In a moment, there's the slip of fabric off her too thin frame and then the splash of water. For a time, we are both silent and only the Stillness speaks.

"Why are we here?" she finally asks, climbing up from the water.

"This is the heart of the world. There's nowhere safer, especially for a woman such as you, because all magic comes from the earth and the elements and nowhere are those things stronger than in the wild wood."

The girl is no alchemist, nor a poet, but she considers my words.

"Did your mother never tell you that if you feel your power waning, or you are tired and undone, get thee to the forest?" I ask.

"My mother died when I was young," she says. "She taught me nothing about magic."

"Well, those words are not said in jest. I'm exhausted, and so I come to the source of my power to rest."

The girl must be part cat for she leaps onto a nearby fallen trunk and scrambles up it, rubbing her hands along its edge. "My stepmother says that beasts hide in the dark. She will not let her daughters anywhere near a forest."

"Your stepmother is a wise woman," I reply. "She's right to be afraid of that which she cannot control. That's why she is afraid of you, I think."

"Afraid of me? I don't think so." Cendrillon laughs nervously, and the sound is so untested I try not to give any sign that I heard it.

"Why do you call yourself a godmother? Why not a witch?"

"Have you never learned that it's easiest to hide a thing in plain sight? Among a small number of witches, the title of godmother names one who is pledged to keep other cunning women secret and the wild places safe."

An owl calls, a friendly sound. The forest approves of the girl. She's shown much skill following me here.

"So you will keep my secret?" Cendrillon asks.

"Yes, and maybe more. Now, if you're staying, we best get to it." I try not to think of my mermaid and how she died a mere month ago in a forest much like this one. "It's time to administer the tests."

CHAPTER FOUR

Trial of the Trees

"There are three kinds of magic," I explain to Cendrillon de Boer, as we walk through the woods.

"The first is cunning magic, spells made from household items, candles and ribbon, salt and wine. We will take time to learn these the longer we are together."

"The second is elemental magic, taken from the Leap. Only the most powerful witches can work elemental magic from birth, but with time, all may be trained how to use it."

"So I'm powerful?" Cendrillon's voice tells me that she already knows the answer to this question.

"Yes, you're one of the most naturally powerful witches I've ever met," I admit. It's probably the only reason the girl survives her stepmother's abuse. She carries the proven knowledge of her own value inside herself, a shield against her stepmother's meanness. "And tonight we will learn more about the elements with which you share the closest bond."

"And the third magic?" Cendrillon asks.

"The third magic is born from need and desire. It comes from the Stillness, which is hidden from all. Dangerous and wild, the third magic takes what it will and offers a witch only the chance to know the mystery."

"Teach me that!" Cendrillon nods. "Teach me to do the third magic."

"No one can *teach* the third magic," I answer. "We listen for it. Dance with it in some way, maybe, if we're lucky." I trip over a root and nearly fall flat on my face.

"Are you powerful?" Cendrillon's voice doubts my skill.

"Powerful enough," I snap, standing and looking around me. Yes, the burbling stream flows nearby, and I count the trees in the clearing. Yes, we are surrounded by at least six rooted sisters here.

"Come close, girl. Remember my words: in the beginning, there was the Stillness and the Leap. The Stillness was known to no one, but the Leap spoke to us in the language of form." I snap my fingers and flames burst into life.

"The Leap is made of five elements: earth, air, fire, water, and the hidden one, aether, the one most akin to the Stillness. Tonight, at least one of the elements must be present to witness your passage, for if you're to become a witch, we must know which of these are your sisters, to come when you call, to feed your bond to the magic when you need."

"I have no family," Cendrillon snaps. "No sisters." The abandoned child is back. Her teeth bare white and sharp, even in the dark, as if she's cousin to the wolf.

I growl at Cendrillon until she looks down and away.

"It's no strength to name yourself lonely," I scoff. "And the tests help us determine your powers."

"You already saw my power," she said.

"Not strength," I sniff, although calling a flame is no easy thing to manage for some. Not in a time when our magic grows so weak. "Everything is not always about strength. We seek your affinities."

"Look, let me be clear. You do have power, and you even have some skill. But the witch's way is already a lonely and dangerous path, girl. Lonelier still now that every priest from here to Rome makes our craft a crime against God. I will not blame you if you slip back into the shadows and fly home right now."

Cendrillon says nothing, but after a moment I see her shake her head. "No," she says. "I will stay. I...want to stay." She smiles a true smile this time.

I draw out her decision. "If you take the tests and you pass, we learn where you must go to keep your connection to your magic. A water witch must live near the sea or deep, still water or even a raging river. Many witches of the air, of whom there are few, live on the highest peaks."

"And *if* the Stillness accepts you as her own, then you travel along this path with the aid of others at your back. Other women like me.

Me, maybe." I touch my chest. "At least for a time."

"In kindness?" Cendrillon asks, tipping her face up to glance at me with shadowed green eyes.

"I try" I nod, truthfully.

"That's enough."

"So your first task: find me the flower, shaped like a pitcher, that grows in the most secret part of the forest. Fill it from the forest's hidden spring."

"That's it?" she asks.

I nod and find the trunk of a healthy oak on which to lean. My head aches, and a nap would do me much good.

After a moment, Cendrillon ambles off into the forest, making very little noise, and I draw my cloak around me and drift off to sleep.

An hour later I perk up at the sound of branches breaking, most of my aches and pains gone, and the feeling of magic fizzing in the marrow of my bones.

Cendrillon carries the right flower delicately in her left hand, her face dirty again. She's near tears at the fact that it shrivels, becoming more seed than anything else.

"I got lost," she says. "I could hear the water, but I never found it. Does this mean that I...that I..."

I smile. "It's ok, child. The task is two-fold. You found the seed, but water does not wet your walk, as we say. We must keep going—we have four more elements to go."

"Now take the seed and plant it in the earth at your feet."

Cendrillon digs a small hole and lays the shredded flower and the small seed within, covering it up roughly with her dirty hands.

We wait for only a minute before a green vine rises to curl into the air and twine up Cendrillon's leg, wreathing its way to her waist and twining delicately down her arms.

She laughs and strokes the vine as if it were an animal.

"You have the power of the earth, and this next one I already know. Stand still and make your hands into the shape of a bowl," I order, and I call a flame to my palm. I reach out to touch her cupped palms, and in barely a second, flames race up her arms and circle her head in a wreath.

No surprise after my vision. The cinder girl burns bright with green and gold.

"Call the wind to blow out your crown."

Cendrillon squints and pushes her lower lip out, but nothing happens. "I'm trying," she admits.

"Once more. Relax. Take a breath."

We stand quietly, Cendrillon crowned in fire and vines.

I wait to see if the aether will show us the final test, the hidden one, but the fifth element stays silent.

Cendrillon partners to fire and earth, a unique pairing that doesn't match any other witch I know. Powerful, indeed.

I note the place of the moon in the sky and the time of night. This last part will be hardest, as the forest makes her ruling. I go to each of the trees and make a circle around its base. Entering within the circles, I rap sharply on the tree trunks, trying to awaken them.

"Listening is the first lesson, daughter," I say, as it was once said to me long ago. "It's the way women determine the true path forward."

The owl calls again, irritated with my talking, but he acts as harbinger for what comes next. The wind moves. The leaves rustle and gossip, and then the trees come alive.

Cendrillon gasps.

I bow, and as a group, the spirits bow back to me, oak, rowan, Scots pine, dogwood, and yellow beech.

I don't know why the spirits of the trees are female. Maybe it's because they come to women in a form we trust. Wide-hipped, the tree spirits circle the girl and whisper among themselves, the sound of whipping leaves unintelligible to our human tongue. Oak is tall and straight-backed. She purses her green lips and circles Cendrillon with a commanding glare. The rowan turns her beautiful, lined face toward the moon as if soaking light into her berry red skin. Then she grabs Cendrillon's hand and holds her arm out, as if to measure her, running thin branch-like hands along the girl's limbs.

"What's happening?" Cendrillon whispers.

"You're being judged." I answer truthfully. There's no other way between a godmother and her charge, although there's truth and then the whole truth, and I plan to parse my way between the two very carefully, as my mind is not yet made up. "Be still."

Cendrillon straightens.

The Scots pine seems reluctant to come close, but she finally relents and cups the girl's face for a closer look, nodding approvingly after a few moments.

The magic coming off the dogwood spirit intoxicates; her skin looks like mist and smells earthy and clean. The beech shakes and shimmers around both Cendrillon and me, touching the edges of the clearing first. She wears a girdle of shimmering leaves that embellish her yellow breasts and hips, round and happily fat.

The whispering intensifies, as if an argument breaks out. Then finally, each one in turn moves to bow before Cendrillon, disappearing into the earth at her feet. Cendrillon bows back in turn.

When the beech finally disappears, Cendrillon looks at me, pale and withdrawn.

"See what they leave." I make myself stay rooted. It will be no kindness to pretend if this hasn't come out right. The girl, for all her power, is nothing and no one alone, bereft of a community. This is the second wisdom of women, the unspoken one, that can only be learned through the living of it.

Cendrillon drops to her ankles. Her fingers brush along the dirt, and she stands, holding something in her palm.

I stride over to her. "Let me see."

She opens it. There is an acorn, a dogwood blossom, and a rowan berry. Three of the five measured the girl and found her worthy of their gifts. A victory!

"Good," I say. "Very good. You've made a true start of it now."

Cendrillon allows herself a tiny half-bow.

The wind rises, almost imperceptibly at first. There's a low moan, and then a whisper of air, a voice I recognize, a voice far from the sea from whence it came. The hairs on my neck rise with the gooseflesh along my arms. "Beeeeeee-waaaaaaaarrreee."

That's when I hear them. Men. They walk in the wood, slinking through the still dark of early morning. These men hunt, so even when they move soundlessly, the animals feel the killing echo of their feet on the land.

"We should go," I say. I've never seen the trials interrupted. I worry that it's a bad sign, an omen of evil to come.

Cendrillon bundles herself up. I can practically hear her berating herself for washing clean. She wants to be covered in chimney soot again, invisible to all.

Is it the same for the caterpillar when they are born again with wings?

"Let's go," I say. "Now. Before they find us."

We flee.

We move through the undergrowth quickly and quietly. I lead for a while, finding a rising ridge that I hope we may crest and fall down within a more silent valley. Cendrillon follows me for a time and then irritated by my slower pace, circles around me and moves ahead. There's a small copse of Scots pine there and the sound of another fingerling stream meandering nearby.

I stop to listen, covered by a few belladonna bushes. *Deadly, deadly* they whisper. I need no further warning. I push east.

The men lag. I can't hear their steps or voices, but I listen to the animals hide. My belly tightens. How is it that they know the direction we flee?

I grab for Cendrillon but she's still ahead of me. "Stay still," I whisper. I am looking for the edge of the next stream, trying to orient myself so that we may fly away from this threat without being seen.

Whoosh! I hear the sound of leaves and a little scream from the cinder girl. I rush toward the sound, but carefully, carefully as I get close.

The bear pit is nearly eight feet deep and lined with large, wooden spears sharpened to deadly points. Covered with branches and leaves. I pull some of the branches away.

"Stay back," Cendrillon whispers.

This is why the men nip at our heels. They've dug this for a bear, hoping to peel its thick fur and sell it for embellishments on some fine lady's shawl. Instead, they've caught a girl. One of the sharpened wooden spears drives through her side, and another punctures the meat of her thigh.

"We have to get you out," I say. "NOW." I flush with cold and start to sweat. The belladonna's warning plays over in my head, and I think I hear the men's footsteps.

"Leave me," Cendrillon says.

"You cannot hide here," I argue. Gods, to have learned the urge to disappear so well. "Lift your leg."

Cendrillon grunts and tries but lets out a sound that is something of a silent scream. "I can't."

"You must," I argue.

She does it. Luckily, the spear has driven itself into the outside of her leg. If it were her inner thigh she would bleed out in a minute, maybe less.

"I will lift you if you get yourself free of the other stake," I tell her. I pray that the thing hasn't pierced her gut. If so, I will have lost Cendrillon de Boer before she has even had the time to find herself. *It should be me in that hole.*

Two women dead in less than a month.

The wind sounds like the mermaid sobbing.

Enough, I tell myself. *You're not too late. Not yet.*

Cendrillon breathes hard. I hear her tears.

"Let's see if we've caught that right bastard," I hear one of the men say. They start to climb the ridge behind us. They are too close.

I rush to the stream and dip my fingers in burbling water, bringing my cupped palms to my lips. "Obscure," I whisper and breathe over the water, blowing a wall of mist into the air. I fill the cup of my hands again. In five minutes, the fog is so thick that I cannot see two feet in front of my face.

The men shout to each other. "Stay! Hold." They worry about falling into the pit themselves. Good.

I inch my way back to the bear pit, praying I don't fall in myself. At the edge, I see Cendrillon staring up at me wide-eyed.

"You!" she says. She did not expect me to return. "Leave me. With no one here to see, they will kill you too. Or worse." She's pulled herself off the second spear, and I see a patch of blood spreading in the fabric even in the morning's shadows.

"Stop and listen to me." I raise my hands and wave them together, calling the air to gather beneath her. She begins to levitate from the ground. "Stay still."

"I could not move if I wanted to." Judging from the quantity of blood, she should be unconscious by now.

"Listen, foolish girl. If you haven't given up yet, then this is no time to start."

Cendrillon comes slithering up like an ugly snake, wet and oily with blood. I drag a large branch with two split limbs over to her. "Lay across it. I will use the air to float you behind me."

"Here we go a-hunting. We go hunting, by and by." One of the men whistles softly to himself. Otherwise, the woods stand silent. But the men hear us, I think. Their footsteps suddenly sound more careful.

We cross the stream as quietly as we can. Cendrillon does not move at all on my makeshift pallet. I keep hold of the main branch and try to think of what to do next. We need another distraction.

I call fire and twist it toward the pit, barreling it at the wood within the dirt.

"What in the devil?" the man's voice grows louder now, ringing with disbelief, and I turn back to look. "'Tis witchcraft, it is. Something unnatural."

The orange color of flames flickers through the fog. I've managed to set the stakes alight.

"We must keep going. They will start to search in earnest soon. We need to be further away."

"Leave me," she insists again, and I round on her.

"You followed me to this wood, and the spring answered the song of your blood. The elements speak to you. The trees offer you their gifts. So what if the trials were interrupted? There are bigger trials to face right now." The words are pulled from me before I can stop them. "I will not abandon you here."

Cendrillon's face, black with dirt again, turns blank at the words.

I grab her hand and pull her forward. "I will carry you if I have to, and once we get to the edge of the wood we may fly home."

She keeps her hand in mine, and I float the makeshift pallet alongside me.

The men behind us shout to each other. They search freely, now that they are past the pit, trying to find who could've set the fire. Slowly, slowly, they gain on us.

At my side, Cendrillon pants.

"We're very close now," I say, but I panic. I can only feel pins and needles along my spine. And I know I cannot carry the girl through the air in such a state, all the way back to the city.

The men slow. I hear one clearing his throat, and the other lagging and breathing hard. They were not planning a chase.

I turn around and stand at the girl's side. Cendrillon's skin turns cold under my hand. I force myself to breathe in counts of four, in and out. I look at her dirty face. "Are you ok?" I ask.

Cendrillon shakes her head *no*. It's a tiny movement, economical.

If Cendrillon dies, I will break into a thousand pieces, shattering the two that are left from my last failure.

I release her makeshift pallet of branches to the ground as the sound of hoofbeats interrupts the lesser rhythm of my heart.

CHAPTER FIVE

The Acorn Promise

The hoofbeats grow closer and closer. I make my decision in a split second, not asking the girl what she wants.

"Help!" I shout. "Help! We're injured."

Most of the forest's animals have long since hidden or fled from us humans, and no one from Strasbourg would dare ride a horse into this forest without an invitation from the nobleman who owns the piece we travel through, which means whoever gallops toward us must be an outrider, packing supplies.

Most would not care to hear a woman's voice shout as they likely prepare for an aristocratic party to hunt, but I'm counting on whomever it is wanting to shut us up before the nobility arrives.

The hoofbeats slow and then move ever closer to us until the fog breaks and the beast slows, huge, black, and handsome. His sides heave with the run, and I round the front of him to see better who it is I implore.

"Help!"

"What's wrong?" The Margrave Alasdair von Helm leaps down from his mount in a moment's time. I've seen the man before, at a distance. Black-haired, pale, and clean-shaven, he's so handsome and obviously rich he could be a prince. For a minute, Prince Domingo stands before me, summoned from memory.

Then the vision fades. Knee-high leather boots with a soft-turned edge slouch perfectly at Von Helm's knee. His breeches show a lesser black, and his finely made linen shirt opens in a flat collar with short cuffs at the wrist.

Von Helm catches sight of Cendrillon and rushes over to the girl. "What's happened?" he turns back to me.

I stare, shocked that he lifts a finger to help now that he's seen how thin and malnourished the girl is.

Cendrillon pants, her big eyes liquid green. The blood at her side covers the whole front of her dress now. The Margrave takes a knife and runs it along the side seam of the stomacher bodice and the blouse to cut it away. Then he arranges the stomacher to cover her chest, and we both stare at the wound in her side. "We must bind it," he says.

"Wait!" I argue. I search the small clearing for anything that will staunch the blood. I pick a fistful of the right leaves and pack them against the ugly wound.

Alasdair watches. "What can I do?" he asks. "Who is she?"

"No one," Cendrillon says. It's the first time she's spoken.

"She's mine," I say fiercely. *And you cannot have her*, the words stay unspoken. "She can't die." It occurs to me that this is exactly what Mab wants: a damsel in distress. The Margrave willing to play hero.

Alasdair runs back to his saddlebag and pulls out another linen shirt. Using the knife at his side, he tears it to shreds and wraps it tightly around her thin waist. The girl's ribs stick out, and an image flashes in my mind of an animal carcass.

"Her thigh," I say. Despite my misgivings, I lift her skirts so he can see the wound. This one is deeper and uglier. I let him bind it too, wondering how long it will take me to undo his careful work. I hear more hoofbeats and shouting, and I realize that Alasdair escaped his retinue upon hearing my shouts. I let myself like him for one minute before I push him back.

Cendrillon starts to shake. I've seen this tremor before. It's a sign death is near.

"Turn away," I order Alasdair, and he steps back.

I lean down next to the girl and place one hand on the ground and the other on her chest. The magic of the forest swirls up within me. Water, fire, air, earth, and aether, the raw materials of life, suffuse me so much that I fall apart in a thousand ways. I am the droplets of mist that hang in the air. I am the squirrel perched on the nearby branch. I am the dead leaves suffused with the girl's blood too. I am the black dirt that sits beneath it all, waiting to receive.

This last thought draws me back to myself, and after I am myself, I find her. Cendrillon's heart flutters like a new bird, mostly stillborn, and I have no choice. I drive all that life, the life of the forest and the cycles and the bitter wisdom of it all into her chest like a bolt of lightning.

She screams, and I've not been careful enough. Cendrillon glows, and underneath my palm, I feel her skin expelling the bits of wood and cloth that have become dangerously mixed in with her skin and blood.

She's no longer falling apart. Cendrillon comes back together with the magic of winter becoming spring. We're lucky it's the right time. In fall, I might've killed her.

"Ye gods," Alasdair whispers behind me. "You're a witch."

I pull my hand back and stagger away. My sight, so clear before, is now dim. We humans see almost nothing with our eyes.

Alasdair keeps talking, but I can't make sense of what he's saying. I can't understand Cendrillon's response. They stare at each other, the meaty sacks of their bodies so thick and impossibly heavy. I am heavy too. I do not want to wear this meat on me. I am light. I am rain.

Surely, I don't need to return to whatever that body is.

"What have you done, Marina?" a sad voice whispers, warm as the sea on a summer morning. A breeze blows through the clearing, smelling of sand and salt.

Hovering over the bodies down below, the mermaid and I watch as Cendrillon's small, perfect hand raises, holding something inside it. And Alasdair reaches out to take it. What does the cinder girl give him?

No! I want to scream. *Stop!* But I cannot seem to find the thread that leads me fully back to my body. The leaves ripple and gossip around me. The trees shake slightly in the mermaid's wind. Everyone can feel that something momentous happens.

"An acorn," the mermaid whispers.

Cendrillon gives the oak tree's gift away. She gives the seed of something yet to come, and without knowing its meaning, Cendrillon hands her prince, the Margrave, a promise made of magic.

And goddamnit, such promises can never be broken.

A second thundering of hooves pulls me from floating with the air, the mist, the trees. A retinue of servants barrels toward us, angry that they've lost their master.

"You must move her, quickly," Alasdair says to me. The ground around us shows brown and sickly now, and he does not want to be discovered in this barren circle of death with a woman whose dress is half cut off her starving frame and a crone who makes the earth itself die.

The bear hunters draw near at the same time. They shout to each other, as they catch the sound of the riders coming toward us. "Stop! Stop!" They shout. "Danger!" Noblemen's horses are expensive to replace, and the bear pit is deadly.

"You will take her back to wherever she belongs?" Alasdair asks me. He uses the remaining strips of fabric to bind Cendrillon's dress to her body with his strong hands. She's struck dumb by the effort her body made in healing, her face half covered in dirt from the pit, but the other half clean and beautiful. She looks like a saint or goddess, half-shrouded in death.

The belladonna ceases chattering. In fact, the woods stand silent, except for the sound of the approaching retinue.

I shiver and nod.

"You must take my mount, Charlemagne. Get on him."

"Yes," I murmur. I climb on the horse, planning to gallop far enough away that we may finally fly home. Time presses. It's nearly dawn, and we cannot risk being seen over the city streets when I return Cendrillon to the de Boer home.

We cannot risk this man knowing anything more about us.

"I will tell them I was thrown. The horse will find its way home when you're finished with him," Alasdair says. He points to a nearby branch, thin enough to use as a weapon. "Now strike me in the face."

"What?" The boy thinks faster than I do. I'm out of my mind with exhaustion and fear. Healing the girl depletes me so much that I worry I won't be able to ride or fly.

Alasdair puts the branch in my hand. "Now!"

I hit him as hard as I am able.

He flinches but doesn't cry out, not even when red welts appear.

"Once more."

When I finish striking the prince, I climb on the back of his mount. Alasdair whispers something to the huge black and then runs his hand along the animal's shoulders tracing the beautiful curve of its body, finally slapping his mount's hindquarters sharply. The black beast bolts forward, and I pull Cendrillon's still body in my arms, wrapping around her to grab the pommel. Kasimir made me learn to ride his Arabian mares, and the memory sustains me here. I tighten my legs on the barrel-chested beast, kick, and then we are as good as flying.

We return to Strasbourg in two hours. Cendrillon sleeps in my arms while we are on horseback and lolls on me as we fly. She doesn't stir when we arrive back at the de Boer home. The light outside is spreading its fingers across the sky, beckoning the day upward. I knock softly on the back door, saying a prayer to the mother trees, and oh lucky day, the cook opens the door.

"I found a little mouse," I say. I tug Cendrillon through the door. The girl is still near dead on her feet. She can barely talk, although her eyes are open.

Cook stares.

I walk Cendrillon to the warm hearth, noting the smallness of the fire. Cook eats from a meager bowl of gruel, and the bread loaves she's turned out are half-size. Everywhere the miserly nature of the house's mistress is evident.

"You should not be here," Cook says.

"Sister, Cendrillon went to market early and a cart knocked her near senseless."

"And her dress?" Cook asks.

"Caught on the wheel. I had to tear it open to get her free. She'll be nearly useless til she's rested."

Cook frowns, and I can't tell if it's because she's unused to thinking so hard or if she's unhappy the poor girl's still alive.

"Come now," I say, grabbing a loaf and tearing it in half. I put a small piece in Cendrillon's mouth as if she's a bird and silently beg her to chew. "You cannot want the girl to suffer more than she already does. Think of her kind-hearted mother, dead these many years."

"Madame's not awake yet," Cook nods. "You'll have to take her up quietly. My back won't do it. The girl's room is at the top of the third floor."

Cendrillon's room is a closet with a cot. I lay her on the thin bed, tug off her ripped clothing, and find a shift. I pull it over her head, arrange the tableau, and keep the ruined dress in my arms. Leaving the wreckage here only provides an opportunity for punishment.

"Tell Madame that she was trampled at market," I say to Cook, when I'm back in the kitchens. "And the refuse in the streets made her sick. She's burning hot. She should be left alone today."

Cook nods. She's already making a small pot of tea for the girl, which I take as a good sign.

Outside, I say a benediction with the blessing of the oak trees that line the drive. I try not to worry. Surely, she will sleep and rest today, not work.

Suddenly all I remember is the moment Alasdair von Helm galloped into the clearing. Few noblemen would make the choice to save a common girl they did not know.

Cendrillon gave away the forest's first gift, dropping that magical acorn in the palm of her rescuing margrave.

Was it wise? Or dead stupid?

With the tests interrupted, I still have a choice. Will I make the girl my apprentice or not? Perhaps war will pass by the city.

Perhaps the acorn means nothing.

Perhaps Cendrillon will not make it through the night.

CHAPTER SIX

Hounds of War

I'm shaking by the time I walk my way deeper into the city streets. I can't return to Kasimir like this, his servants will talk, but the small cottage I rent in one of the city's poorer neighborhoods stands as I left it, well-stocked and empty. The cupboards hide a full pharmacy of herbs and tinctures. The bedrooms unoccupied and clean.

My head pounds. I barely get my skirt off, but I don't want the fabric to touch me anymore. It's covered in dirt and Cendrillon's blood.

In my mind, I see only the mermaid's small body, halfway transformed, two legs nearly becoming one scaled thing, not quite a tail. Her lips blue with death. They are the same color as Cendrillon's lips as I watch the cinder girl nearly slip away, over and over.

"You're alive, Marina," Amalia's ghost reminds me. "And Cendrillon is too."

Barely.

I get a sip of cool water from a nearby jug and sit, seeing dark spots at the corner of my eyes. Valerian tincture soothes the nerves. I take it and search through my cupboards to find something stronger.

Scotch, the scent holds peat and moss and black rain from the moors of Scotland.

I lift the glass to my lips to forget.

Outside there's a commotion. I'm nowhere near the busy parts of the city, but the sound grows and grows until I cover my ears. Someone releases a pack of hounds. They course, searching for prey. The baying grows loud and mournful, larger than life.

It's so loud. How many dogs could there be?

I go to the door and swing it open wearing only my dressing gown. The canvas of the sky in morning is brushed gray. Across the street, a black shadow darts across stone. My flesh perks at the long howl that follows, then another shadow races forward. Then three. Then more. These dogs are big. They rise high enough to stand nearly to my hip, and they are black, every one.

The cobblestone streets beneath their straining paws are marked red with blood. It pools and splashes at their feet.

I cannot stop watching. They race past my door, and too late, I realize that they are not leaping in joy toward the wide-open woods. These are no nobleman's dogs. These bloodthirsty hounds fly toward the heart of the city itself.

The baying makes my blood run cold. It's an unnatural sound, not of this world. These animals are not of this world. I hear the hounds' slavering breath as if they sat at my feet.

I've heard stories of such things but have never seen them with my own eyes: black shadow beasts, running over the land, unseen by the common eye, but with witch's sight, they terrify.

These are the hounds of war.

I thought we had more time.

Gooseflesh rises on my neck and arms, until eventually the baying stops. My body needs sleep, but now I'm trapped inside a never-ending wakefulness, my mood empty and black as the shadow dogs outside.

I make a fire and try to warm myself with more scotch. I pour a second and a third glass, listening to the wholesome crackle of logs as the air turns cozy, but my hands still freeze and my chest feels as if a weight sits on top of it.

A sharp knock comes on the door.

"Just a minute!" I call, pulling a wrap over my dress, but Kasimir opens the door before I get there.

My lover stands tall in my healer's house, his curly hair unbound and brushing the tops of his broad shoulders. He's too big and out of place in this simple dwelling.

"I didn't have the patience to wait for you, Widow," he says, biting the inside of his cheek, nervous, even though he tries not to show it.

I wave him inside and climb back onto my perch, tucking my feet under me.

"What's wrong?" Kasimir asks, noting my bare legs. He sits beside me and begins to rub my hands and arms, bringing warmth back into my limbs. Then he catches sight of my blood-soaked skirt and stomacher on the nearby floor.

"What happened?"

I shake my head.

Kasimir doesn't demand an answer again. He scoops me into his lap instead. "You should not be here alone, not when you're like this. Come home, and I'll have the servants fill a bath for you." He wraps his arms around me and whispers in my ear.

"I can't. Not tonight." I can't make myself move right now.

"You feel so good," Kasimir whispers to me. His hands are suddenly everywhere. Running up my legs. Stroking my thighs. "I missed you for the months that you were gone."

"What does any of this matter?" I ask, leaning my head back on his strong shoulder. "What does pleasure or pain mean, if we all die?"

Kasimir pulls back to look in my eyes, and his hands still. "What do you mean?"

I can't tell him about what happened in the wood, but the ghost dogs still bay in my mind. "The city's not safe. It's not witches that people should worry about. It's men and their never-ending war."

Kasimir presses his forehead against mine. "You heard that the front advances?" he asks softly.

I nod, although truly I hadn't. The specters tell the truth then.

"There's nothing you can do about it, Marina," he goes on. "You're just one woman, and you cannot save the city. Not alone."

"You're right. We must all do something together or what will happen? We'll lose our livelihoods. Our safety. Security. Our very lives." I stand up and start pacing.

Cendrillon is still alive, I remind myself. She's home in bed right now, asleep and safe, but maybe it's best that we did not complete the tests, if the war's already upon us.

"Come back," Kasimir pats the couch and then holds up his hands in entreaty. "Please. I know better than to argue with you in such a state. If there's that much blood on your clothes, then some fight's already been had. If you want to fight again, Marina, then you must fight. If you want to wait, then you must wait. I want what you want, and I want you back here, by my side.

"There have to be moments of rest too, woman. Come back, please. I've missed you."

I put my hands on my hips and take a step toward him. "I missed you too," I admit.

"Let me make you feel good," he says, grinning. "Surely if the world's going to end, then we should die making love."

He's right. I do want to feel alive. I want to feel anything but this bleak inevitable sadness. I climb onto his lap, and Kasimir burrows his face in my neck. He tugs at my dressing gown and then at the lace underneath, unwrapping my layers until I feel cool air against my naked skin.

He reaches down and licks my nipples, nipping softly.

I pull his face up and kiss him hard.

"Yes, there's my girl," he whispers, centering me on top of him.

I rub myself against him, pulling away only to let him fumble with his breeches. He shoves them down and opens his smalls.

"Now, I don't want to wait," I whisper and slide his cock inside me, feeling myself stretch and tighten around him.

"No need," he says and grabs my hips as I sit in saddle.

"Oh god," I say, riding him. Pleasure comes in waves, pushing away my awareness of anything else.

He cups his hands at my waist, pulling me forward roughly. Then he drives into my center, changing angles to build friction. "Yes, there. Yes. God."

"Fuck, God. Yes," Kasimir urges me forward, letting my pleasure build and build.

I come apart like a bell breaking.

Kasimir pumps once, twice more, and jerks, his body rigid inside mine.

Then we both go quiet.

I laugh and hug him.

And then I slide away and curl on my side and sob until I feel nearly drowned in tears, covered by hurts so old I dare not give them words. This will not be the first battle I've fought and lost. Nor even the third.

Kasimir curls around me. He doesn't like this uncomfortable couch in this small house, but it means something that he's found me here, knowing that the work I do in simple settings is just as important as when I'm Marina Mullenheim, wealthy widow.

After a few more minutes of quiet, my storm clears. I slide my arm back through his. "I must go to the afternoon luncheon tomorrow. I need to tell Mab that the war comes closer. Will you accompany me?"

Kasimir nods and starts to dress. He knows all my masks and the woman behind them.

"I need to sleep first," I say, untangling myself to walk naked toward the kettle that still heats on the fire.

I bring back a clean cloth so that he can mop up our mess. He grabs my hand before I can walk away again. "And after luncheon tomorrow, you'll come home? Our bed's made for two people, instead of that small lumpy terror you sleep on here."

I laugh and haul the steaming water toward the bedroom this time, where I'm determined to clean my own dirt and sex and tears away.

When I am finished, Kasimir's gone. He's left behind a small bowl of strawberries on the table, a parting gift to remind me that sweetness still exists.

Beside it, a pen sits and my small well of ink.

Tomorrow, Kasimir's note promises, as if such a thing were certain.

CHAPTER SEVEN

A Chance Meeting

The wealthy widow Mullenheim makes her way through the best parlors of the city on such a lovely day, including taking lunch at the Duke of Württemberg's residence.

I wear the only good gown I keep at the cottage, a navy wool overlaid by a rich blue stomacher. Around me, the drawing room is full of women wearing dresses much like mine, but I look past their clothes searching for one familiar face.

Finally, I catch sight of Mab's silver-blond mane, her back to me as she talks with none other than the Duke, himself.

"Mab," I call and wave.

It's several more minutes before she makes her way to me, smiling and chirping until she's close enough that I can see how worn she is under the charming veneer.

"Did you see them?" she asks me, without preamble.

"Who?" I ask, pretending not to understand, as we both turn toward the windows to appreciate the morning sunlight.

"Did you know the King of Dutches meets with a representative from Albrecht von Wallenstein today? The Catholic Emperor wants Alsace back in his palm. They're planning an attack, Marina."

I should've known she would be three steps ahead of me. "Kasimir said as much. But surely the Duke didn't tell you all this in the middle of his morning room?"

"After hearing the hounds' ghastly baying, I couldn't sleep all night," Mab replies, not answering my question. "Did you hear them too?" she asks again.

"They ran through the streets near my pied-à-terre. I don't know how any witch could not hear them." I grab a slice of bread sweetened with dried berries from a nearby tray.

"How many?" Mab asks, turning us back toward the room.

I nibble and nod at the ladies as they pass us. I'm not hungry, but even if I were, this gown keeps me from eating much. "You cannot count the number of deaths to come by the number of dogs. That's a myth. No one knows if what's shared will even come to pass. War's not certain. The spirits obey their own whims, as we well know."

"How many?" Mab pinches my arm, tired of repeating herself.

"Too many. More than I could count. The streets were covered in blood."

Mab puts a hand to her forehead in misery. "We've already failed then," she whispers. "Madame de Boer's stepdaughter is not enough to stem the tide of angry young men hacking at the city gates, no matter how talented she might be. What can one witch do? Two? Three? What can any of us do against the rolling tide of war."

I put my bread down and slide my arm through hers, turning us away from the crowd to go to and through where the garden doors stand open. Once outside, I feel as if I can finally breathe.

"We're not done if the forest still stands," I say. It's an old witch saying. "And maybe if the Hearth gathered, we could find some solution. We're more powerful than you think. The new girl brings many gifts, strength among them."

Mab pounces on my words before I have time to regret them. "You met her?"

I pause. I don't want to explain what happened in the forest to Mab or anyone else, but I can't unsee the hounds' paw prints staining the Strasbourg streets red with blood.

I nod. "In the wood."

Mab smiles wide, her eyes alight. "And what did you find?"

I shrug, not wanting to catalogue all of Cendrillon's talents and foibles. The girl should have time to know herself before others claim her for their purposes, even a group with such high purposes as the Hearth. "She bonds to earth and fire. The forest accepts her as its own."

"And was she given any gifts?"

I nod again. "Yes, three. And then we were interrupted." My hands start to shake at the memory, and I slide them into my pockets before Mab can see, telling her the rest quickly.

"This isn't good," Mab smacks her forehead. "The Margrave von Helm isn't going to marry a filthy, starving servant girl, no matter what the bond is between them."

"Surely it's too early to speak of marriage," I say, feeling as if I betray Cendrillon's trust in telling her tale.

Mab taps her lip. "But the second prospect hasn't had such an unfortunate view of the girl yet. He's no Margrave, just a Landgrave, so he would be a step down, but he's in the market for a new wife. The last one died during childbirth." Mab turns me back toward the house, new purpose at hand. "No matter. We must get the girl to the Hearth where she may study. Buy her some new clothes. Teach her to trust us."

"If the girl survives her wounds, her stepmother will still never let her leave the house." I don't want to argue with Mab, but it's no easy thing to take a girl from a family like that. "She has the girl scrubbing chimneys and doing a servant's chores."

"Scandalous. Where's the father? Why don't we ask him?" Mab looks down her nose at me, her sharp gray eyes catching what I don't want to admit.

"You did not bind her, did you, Marina? After all that, you took her to the wood and gave her the tests and then let one small interruption derail our whole plan."

"Interruption," I huff. "I don't know what you mean. We don't have a plan, and I don't..."

Mab pulls away from me and starts to walk back toward the morning room doors.

"I don't want an apprentice," I hiss at her back.

People are starting to stare, and Mab does not want their attention any more than I do. She walks back to me, smiling through clenched teeth and takes my arm in her own, making it seem as if nothing is wrong between us. When we get close enough to the crowd that the sound drowns out our conversation, she whispers near my ear.

"If you took her to the forest, then it's as good as done. You *will* bind the girl, Marina, so that when the time comes, she will do what you say. You know what we face, and you know that we must make sure the forest still stands when all of this is done. That Landgrave owns no small bit of forest floor."

"She's damaged," I answer. "Even if I apprentice her, Cendrillon may never heal. Her magic is strong, but unpredictable, and it will grow worse if she goes to an unhappy household. It's dangerous,

Mab."

Mab pulls away. "Danger's not new, old friend. We face danger on every side."

"I cannot have another death on my hands." Tears scald my eyes. I can feel my face turning red, and for a moment, I see the flash of fish scales in the air. "I won't survive it."

Kasimir slides against my other shoulder and slips his arm through my own. "I think it's time for us to go, Madame Mullenheim," he says smoothly. "Say goodbye to your dear friend and let me escort you home."

"Good afternoon," Mab bows her head and turns her back to me for a final time.

I feel my fury rising to my cheeks. I'm so tired of being pressed into the service of something greater than myself. How can we afford to pay the cost such service exacts?

"Now," he insists, whispering into my ear. "Before you make more of a scene."

"Fine, I do need some fresh air," I snap, and slide away, leaving Madame Mablean and the bastard behind me.

On Strasbourg's streets the next morning, the tradesmen are out, doing their business. Servants hang washing out of windows or in courtyards, while their mistresses shop at the bakery or fishmongers, negotiating for carp caught in the Rhine or bear fur sliced from a beast in the Black Forest.

Past the Cathedral, a great crowd of folk, nearly fifty strong, stands shouting and throwing old food or muck from the streets. I back away from the mob, not wanting trouble, but then catch sight of a girl in their center, young, not more than sixteen with honey blond hair.

My treacherous heart stops beating. Madame de Boer would surely not turn out her own stepdaughter. I fight the crowd to get a better look.

"Witch!" I hear a man close to me yell.

"Sorcerer!" Another woman calls.

"Priest! Priest!" The crowd begins to chant. They want someone to crucify the girl or worse, to tie a bag over her head and stone her to death right here in the afternoon sun.

And still I can't see who's held hostage at the mob's center.

"I'm not a witch!" the girl shouts.

Not her is all I can think at the sound of her voice.

Not Cendrillon. The crowd parts, and I see the girl, pretty enough to cause trouble, her pink gown standing out amid a sea of brown and black clothes.

"I made the tea thinking it would help the little one's cough. I did not think it would hurt her. I . ." She's struck by a large rock on her temple, and the girl falls to the ground.

"Suits her to be knocked out. Now we can't be caught in her spell," a large man, a field laborer from the look of his tanned face and blackened teeth. He's left his cart at the far corner and hovers close enough that he may keep stock of it. "Only the devil would want a woman so fine looking. She's been sucking his cock and taking midnight rides. Probably thought to kill her younger sister before she grew up as pretty."

I want to vomit at the words. So the girl's lost her sister and now the crowds dragged her out of her home to face an even worse injustice. A golden-haired thick-waisted woman weeps at the corner of the mob, trying not to draw attention to herself, the girl's mother, no doubt.

The priest finally comes, a tall, gray-haired man with a sour face. He's thick enough to waddle, but then, the priesthood always eats its fill. The Father moves toward the center of the mob to inspect the girl, who still hasn't awakened.

If she's declared a witch (even though she's not) after she's tortured to confess, then she will be dragged to the edges of the city where a bonfire will be built. Tonight, they will tie her to it and weigh her limbs with stones. The flames will devour her screams until she screams no more. And then the air will smell like burnt flesh and hair for a week.

This man is no Catholic priest, which matters not. Both faiths (Catholics and Lutherans) fight over who can find and kill the most witches in recent years. The names of hundreds of women have come to the godmothers' attention, more than we could ever save, or even train, if we were to find a way to some kind of salvation.

But I want to help. I could cause some kind of distraction. I look around to see if a great sheet of wind might drag the mob's focus away.

"She's dead," the priest shouts, before I can do anything else.

Not her, I remind the sick feeling in my stomach. She's not Cendrillon. She's no one I know, but the refrain offers cold comfort. This scene may be what awaits Cendrillon if no one takes her to train and teaches her how to hide her magic.

Worse, she will be taken alive and tortured to death by the witch hunters and priests.

I can barely breathe as the crowd around me grumbles and disperses, angry that their fun has been taken from them.

"Thank you, Lady of the Woods, Merciful Mother of Us All, that this girl didn't suffer more at the hands of these ignorant people and to you Jesus, brother of all men, lover of the lowest among us." I whisper quietly, and then I'm off, walking away from the crowd.

The church bells ring, telling me it's nearly three in the afternoon now. The clouds part, and I feel a bit of sun on my face. I pass the cheesemonger, the baker, and make myself buy a small pastry from a farmer's cart. Then I stand in the street and eat them, trying to forget the morning, until someone nearly knocks me down.

"You'll be well and truly run over, stupid slattern," the cloth merchant's wife churlishly shouts, but she's right. Down the lane, two beautiful black ponies barrel through, their livery marked by a yellow and blue sash, the colors of Alasdair von Helm, the Margrave himself.

Several people jump to the edge of the street, keeping out of the way of the ponies, and the first rider shouts at them that he would not care to knock down an idiot if they get in the Margrave's path.

Then the Margrave passes, calmly surveying all over which he's master until his eyes fall on me.

Today I wear a navy gown, high-necked, much nicer than the one I wore to the forest. My silver hair is done up in a modest twist, not streaming down like a madwoman, so I tell myself he will never know me. The forest bore almost no light, Cendrillon nearly naked in his arms, and what man would notice anything but the presence of a beautiful woman in his arms?

But then our eyes meet, and the Margrave recognizes me.

"You. There! Madame."

A nobleman on horseback is not hard to escape in the middle of busy Strasbourg streets, so I turn and melt into the crowd behind me before he is even able to halt.

"Stop!" the Margrave calls, but I keep my back to him, knowing that my gown looks like any other. "Stop! Madame, I want to speak to you. We have some business together."

I duck into the next alley, hoping that the crush of the crowd puts him off.

CHAPTER EIGHT

The Stepsisters

I wait, heart pounding, and watch through the crook of a brewer's sign as the Margrave stands merely twenty steps away, searching the face of every person who passes back and forth on their own business.

Finally he decides that I'm gone for good, and Alasdair von Helm climbs back onto his horse and with an angry scowl leaps forward.

Shaken, I change direction, needing to make sure that Cendrillon is where I last left her. The De Boer house is nearly a church bell's walk from the city's center square. I make it in half that time, passing a blacksmith's forge and several other craftsmen. On Cendrillon's street, the houses have space behind the back alley which is where the small house garden and the burn pile that I sifted through two days ago sits.

Hidden I drift through these untidy plots toward the door, listening to Cook hum to herself as she cuts vegetables for a stew.

"Cendri, after you empty the chamber pot, you must bring me milk and cakes," a reed thin voice calls through the window of the upper floor.

I stop to listen.

"No, you must bring me a basin of water. Mama says I'm to wash before we go to dinner at the magistrate's house."

"Yes, Ava. Elisabet, I will help you once I've finished bringing Ava her food," Cendrillon's voice is quieter than I remember. I have to strain to hear it.

"I've changed my mind, milk and cake first. Otherwise, you will stink of urine, and I will want to empty my stomach on you. Then you will have to clean that up as well, stupid *Cendrillon*." Ava uses the diminutive like a weapon.

"If you were smarter, you would've planned it so that we both could be served at the same time, you fool," Elisabet criticizes.

"Yes, of course," Cendrillon says, and in the path below, I cringe. No wonder the girl mistakes herself a mouse. She's daily pecked to death by a pair of carnivorous hens.

I assume from the silence that Cendrillon makes her way to the kitchen below where Cook prepares a plate for the eldest daughter of the house. Through the single window, the platter's a pretty picture of spice cakes topped with icing, candied flowers, and two cups of steaming milk.

My hearing is good enough to pick up Cook giving instructions. "No, your hands are too dirty to touch it there. Come wash. Now carry the tray straight. Here is a sprig of holly to decorate it with. "

Finally, Cendrillon ferries the refreshments back up the stairs. I lean against the main house, still listening to the scene up above unfold.

"I've brought enough for both of you. I will draw the bath in a few minutes, Elisabet," Cendrillon says.

"Ah!" Both women fall upon the food, and for a few moments, the loveliest of sounds, silence.

"That was not sweet enough. Tell Cook to add more sugar next time," Ava complains first.

"Yes," Cendrillon agrees.

"You're staring at my food," Elisabet says. "Are you hungry, Cendri? Would you like a bite?"

There's no answer, only silence.

"Come now, tell us the truth," Ava says, her tone coy.

"I'm not hungry," Cendrillon whispers, but even I catch the longing in her tone.

Do they not feed her? She's a daughter of the household, not a servant. She should eat at an honored place at the table. And after facing near death through stabbing and then me forcing her body to heal, Cendrillon must be hungry.

"Take a bite," Elisabet invites.

"I don't want any," Cendrillon says.

"Just one. It's so sweet. The cake nearly melts in your mouth."

I'm here to learn more about my prospective apprentice's home, so looking from side to side, I check to see that no one putters nearby. Then I whisper to the air and rise above, slowly, slowly, where I peek around the thick brocade of the curtains to see the scene in tableau.

Ava and Elisabet sit on the large bed they share, a feather mattress by the look of it. The bright, white-washed timber frame room could easily hold two and half of Cendrillon's closet, with two windows and a thick well-made rug covering the floor.

Cendrillon stands across the room from her stepsisters, alone. She carries the large ceramic piss pot with both hands, balancing it on her hip.

"I'll tell Mother you ruined my green day gown," Ava threatens. "— If you won't try it."

"*You* ruined your green dress with powder," Cendrillon contradicts.

"Here," Elisabet says and grabs a piece of cake and throws it at the girl.

The cake hits Cendrillon in the chest, the little bit of icing and candied flower sticking to her for a moment before it falls in the urine below, splashing the yellow liquid up on her simple linen shift.

"Enough!" Cendrillon says, dropping the pot on the floor. A wave of urine splashes outward, barely missing the rug. Even by the window, I smell the foul liquid and turn to catch a breath of fresh air.

"Ewwwww," Ava says, screwing up her face. "Clean that up before it gets on the rug."

"I only wanted you to have a taste," Elisabet says. Her face has the horrified look of someone who knows she's gone too far.

"You *should* have a taste," Ava says, her green eyes narrowing. "If you are too foolish to catch such a delicious treat, you should have to taste it now. Otherwise, you've wasted it, and you know what Mother says about waste."

"Never," Cendrillon vows.

I feel a flash of pride. That should put both girls off the attack.

"Go on. Fish it out. Take a bite." Elisabet jeers. She's caught the scent of her sister's cruelty.

Cendrillon holds her hand behind her back, trying to call a flame. There's a spark or two, but nothing more. Where's the powerful witch I saw in the forest?

I draw a breath, trying to decide if there's something I must do. These girls aren't kind, but revealing her magic might make the situation worse.

"Darlings!" A voice trills from below. I tuck myself quickly under one of the roof's dormers. "Oh my sweet girls!"

The voice of Madame de Boer makes me wince, even at a distance.

"Don't move," Ava orders. "We'll let Maman decide this."

The sparks gutter out, and Cendrillon becomes everything of her nickname, small, gray, and drab.

For a moment, I imagine breaking the window and stealing the very breath from the two girls' throats, but I cannot save Cendrillon from the demons who haunt her so easily. Not even magic removes such hidden scars—I remind myself of this fact twice before I calmly peek around to watch the scene unfold once more.

Scurrying away while carrying a chamber pot nearly her size is not an easy task, so Cendrillon stays, as Ava commands. Finally the heavy tread on the stairs comes.

"My darlings," Madame de Boer crows as she walks in through the room, catching sight of the two dark-haired girls. She's a fine-looking woman. Even I can see what Master de Boer appreciates in his second wife. Her waist is still small, her breasts large, and her face pretty in a vapid, elegant sort of way. Today she wears a day dress done in brown brocade and a starched linen ruff that looks uncomfortable. I'm glad that the woman I pretend to be is too poor to wear such a contraption.

"She's hiding over there," Ava sneers.

Madame de Boer turns and sees Cendrillon crouching in the corner. "What are you doing here? Didn't I leave you chores for the day?"

Cendrillon nods.

"Cendrillon stole a bit of my cake, mother," Ava lies, putting her hands on her hips. She glares at Cendrillon from behind her mother.

"Jealous girl," Madame de Boer confirms. "Why must you always want what others have?"

"And I tried to grab it back from her, but something terrible happened." Ava grabs her mother's arm and pouts.

Madame de Boer searches the room for a sign of what Ava hints at but finds nothing amiss. She waits, hanging on her daughter's pause.

"The cake fell into the chamber pot, Maman. Elisabet thinks Cendrillon should have to eat it anyway, since she was trying to take such a silly thing. It would be a good lesson for her, would it not? It would teach her to keep her hands off of our food?"

Madame de Boer weighs her daughter's words. "Come here, girl," she demands of Cendrillon. "And be careful with that thing."

Cendrillon comes over and sets the pot down between them.

"Take it out," Madame de Boer says. "Carefully now."

"No," Cendrillon says, raising her chin and looking her stepmother square in the eye.

Yes! My heart rallies at the girl's courage.

"No?" Madame de Boer says. "You say no to me, the lady of the house? Your own mother? You think I should have to scoop that piece of cake out of the filth?"

Cendrillon does not repeat herself.

Madame de Boer snatches the bit of cake that is left on Elisabet's nearby plate and dashes forward to Cendrillon. She grabs the girl's neck. "If you are so hungry, then you should eat." She smears the cake on Cendrillon's mouth. "Eat girl! Come on now."

Cendrillon's face turns red, and her neck shows splotches of red and purple. The icing smears across her chin, some of the cake too, while the rest drops into the chamber pot with a *plop*.

"You should never waste food," Elisabet pouts, not noticing that her mother has been as wasteful as she herself was.

"You're so careless, Cendrillon. And stupid." Ava brushes her hair and watches herself in a nearby mirror.

"Get out!" Madame de Boer screeches. "Take the piss pot with you and scrub it clean, slattern. Then take every other pot in the house. You'll spend the rest of the day with piss-soaked hands, for your disrespect."

Cendrillon grabs the chamber pot and flees.

In the back of the house, where the chamber pots are emptied and scrubbed with cinders to clean them, Cendrillon finally lets herself cry. She wipes her face clean of the icing and throws the ceramic pot to the ground.

I walk toward her slowly. "Cendrillon. What's wrong?" I take the pot from where it sits and begin the process of scrubbing it. "Something's happened. Let it out, sweet girl," I say. "Those vultures would tear anyone to shreds."

Cendrillon sobs quietly, turning away so I can't watch.

When the crying slows, I sit on a log nearby, keeping an eye on the door to the kitchen. "I'm sorry that happened," I sigh and try to think of what I would say to my own daughter, if she were still alive. "You're such a good girl. You're smart and kind, and you don't deserve their cruelty."

Cendrillon doesn't look up at me. "I'm scared is all. Too scared to show them what I could do." Her blue eyes burn with self-hatred when they finally reach mine.

"Would harming them make the situation better?" I ask, thinking of the girl in the city who died an unjust death today.

Cendrillon closes her eyes against the thought. "No, but it might keep me safer."

Her words echo the thought I just had in the city center. Cendrillon has no one. No one but me, and if she were free from this place then she could start to truly see what kind of magic she's capable of.

"Would you like to be my apprentice?" I ask. "It wouldn't be easy. You have a great deal to learn."

"I already know how to use my magic."

"Yes, but right now, you use your magic the way a child might, instinctively, but without discipline. You have a strong understanding of the elements, yes, and you've been lucky enough to live close to the wood and the blacksmith's forge that your magic stays strong enough, but you know nothing of the first magic, simple spells like bindings and protection charms. And you have very little knowledge of herbs or healing."

I go on. "And worst is the way that your emotions hinder your abilities. Around your sisters, you cannot draw on your own power."

"I can get past it, with more control," Cendrillon says. "I just need to try harder."

"If you believe that control is the solution to your problem, then we have further to travel than I thought, girl."

Cendrillon turns her head away, pretending not to hear me.

"If you start on this path, then you will spend time with me working as a healer. Learning spells to help those in need. Identifying the trees and plants of the wood and knowing their qualities. We will not come to the elements until much later, because you have so much talent there. The focus at that point will be resource management. When you call air, it doesn't come from nothing. Behind that current, a bird is pulled downwind by an absence that was not there mere moments ago. No elements are accessed infinitely, not even aether."

"Infinitely?" Cendrillon repeats.

"Can you cast glamour after glamour? Can you remake the world over and over indefinitely?"

"No," Cendrillon nods in understanding.

"No," I echo. "Aether is the most dangerous element because it draws from the invisible well which feeds us all. And that well depends upon your ability to hold a reservoir, an ability that no one has ever taught you to cultivate.

"Where's your father now?" I ask.

"Papa's a merchant," Cendrillon says. "Always traveling. Never home. His family moved from Sweden to the city, and he's made lots of money here. He enlisted more than a year ago."

"So now he's a soldier, fighting against the Catholics?"

"He still keeps us fed and cared for." Cendrillon repeats the words as though she's heard them a thousand times, the passage in a prayer book oft repeated and never felt.

"Money's not care, Cendrillon, and truth is, you could use a bit more food too." I take stock of her too thin frame.

Cendrillon frowns.

"No matter. We'll wait until he returns to see what he says about you leaving this dreadful house. In the meantime, we'll practice learning the first magic."

"Cendrillon!" Ava's shout interrupts me. "Get back here. There are more chamber pots to clean."

"Just think on it." I stand and prepare to escape through the back alley.

"I will do it. I will be your apprentice," Cendrillon calls to my back.

"Why?" I ask, turning around.

"I'm already hated, both inside and outside my home, for different reasons." Cendrillon follows me, still unwilling to say the word *witch* aloud here. "But the magic chose me."

She pauses. "And…Now I choose it."

I smile. "Then we will walk together for a time," I say, using the traditional phrase. "You as my apprentice, and me as your mistress. It's done."

"Done," she echoes.

"Now come quickly and let us weave your first knot, the one that binds us together." I empty my pockets and find some old thread and luckily two serviceable lengths of green ribbon and one white. "You take one, and I will take the other."

"And the white?"

"That is the Stillness to take / the thread from which the Goddess makes." Simple rhyming words. "Aether weave from my hands / so I may make, and weave, and bend."

I start to weave, instructing Cendrillon how to hold her hands. In a moment, we have a short, braided knot.

"A cunning witch I will become / now our work has bare begun," I say, and Cendrillon repeats. I press the knotted length into her hand. "Now sew this into your pillow before the next new moon sets."

Cendrillon nods, and as she walks away, I have the strangest urge to tell her about my moment with the Margrave on the street, but there's no need. Not now. Not when we've already done so much today.

"Cendrillon!" Madame de Boer shouts. "Now!"

I gesture the girl back toward the house, letting the ribbons slip through my fingers, feeling the invisible threads that bind us draw tight.

CHAPTER NINE

Strasbourg Pyres

We sail a blue-green sea that stretches from each horizon like a swath of expensive fabric stretched across a frame. Our days burn sunny and warm, and at night, the stars twinkle universal secrets to our eyes.

Then a storm falls upon us, Cendrillon and me. The wind whips the gentle ocean into white-capped fury. We rig our sails and try to flee the angry wind, but its wrath is too strong.

"Below deck!" I shout. But the boat is bigger than I first realized, and around us, passengers, (who I also did not see before)—women—crowd fighting to stand amid the wind and the waves.

At the next thunderclap, the ship heaves and most of the women disappear into the water. We few survivors are drenched again and again, until I, too, choke on briny water.

I try to track survivors, catching sight of a lone girl standing on the deck whose delicate features are familiar to me. Beside her sits a coffin. Two coffins. A lump rises in my throat.

"No!" I shout.

The girl climbs in the coffin as a single wave, bigger than all the others rises above us, higher and higher until I cannot even crane to see all of it.

"No!" I shout.

"It's the only way," the girl says, her voice a whisper in my ear.

"Should we dive into the waves?" Cendrillon asks from where she suddenly stands beside me. "Facing the storm might be the only way."

I look back to find the coffin, but it's gone, disappeared into the angry sea. Moments later, I catch a flash of green and gold fish scales and a pair of beckoning hands.

I make my decision. "Jump!"

Cendrillon leaps over the ship's edge, and I follow. The water's so cold I lose feeling in my legs immediately. There's nothing to hold onto in the waves, no purchase.

The mermaid disappears, and I can't find Cendrillon.

My dress grows heavier with every minute. The undertow pulls me, down and down. My lungs burn as I fight to rise back to the top. I cannot breathe with all the smoke.

Water in my lungs.

The water tastes like smoke and burning hair.

I try not to breathe, but the pressure builds and builds.

Finally I wake, gasping for a breath. A familiar scent coats the inside of my nostrils and throat.

"What is it?" Kasimir asks, as he lays by my side. He runs a hand over my spine, cupping the curve of my lower back. The velvet bed curtains rustle with wind that blows in from the open window in the townhouse's second floor.

"Nothing," I shake my head and close my eyes against the knowledge that presses me awake.

The pyres at the edge of the city have been lit, and tonight more witches burn.

After wrapping myself in a heavy gown, with a cape and a fur ruff, I walk beside the river Rhine the next morning, staying far away from where Roland and Sylvie play. The closer I get to the city's borders the worse the stench. Around me, I see signs of newly arrived nobles everywhere, men in livery drinking at the taverns and loitering on the streets.

For a bit of coin and a drink, I learn that two women burned on the pyres last night, but the Stettmeisters aren't done with their scourge. Someone's enlisted the help of a pair of strong men this morning. They bring wood by the cartload outside the city, stacking the long pieces in piles and setting the thicker pieces to the side. These last they will use to drive in the stakes to which the innocents will be lashed.

Another man, older than me, sifts through the leftover ash to find any remaining bone. He will bury it in the fields beyond the city, in unmarked graves, so that the Devil may not find his minions, or so the priests claim.

I make my way closer. "Excuse me, Sirrah," I ask, keeping my hood up and my gaze down. "Why do they stack so much wood, with the bonfires bare burned?"

"Haven't you heard, Madame? The bishop brings in wagonloads of witches today, more than thirty, they say. His priests found them hiding in the town of Schiltigeim, more than they could count, men and women. Even found a few children who've been consorting with Satan, they say." The old sod, still drunk from the smell of him, crosses himself at the words.

The Devil stands behind every one of these fires, every man and woman who suffers persecution, but behind Satan, the land lines around Strasbourg are quietly being redrawn. Kasimir shares with me when the ownership of very valuable property changes hands. This greed is the true work of Satan, but you'd never hear the Catholic nor the Protestant Duke, nor any of their priests admit to such a thing.

"Children!" I cross myself as a good Christian wife would. Everyone knows the church charges for these trials, and the remaining family members are bankrupted by the costs that will be accrued tonight. What many don't know is that the Bishop here wants to extend his faith's holdings into the quaint hamlet to the north of the city. He will annex the town there once he bankrupts its remaining members with these trials.

The common people will mourn and starve because their homes have been taken from them by the men who wrongly accuse their families of wrongdoing.

"Not children?" I repeat myself, trying to keep the panic from my voice.

"If Satan owns 'em, it's better to burn the bodies than let them sow evil among us, Madame. Now go on and let me finish. The priests will be shaving the women soon."

I flinch at his words.

By the time these women are brought in for questioning, their guilt is absolute. If they try to claim they haven't been consorting with Satan, they will be tortured until they do confess. If they do confess, then perhaps the priest will see to break their necks before they are staked into the fires. It's only a rare person who escapes the flames after such a trial.

Very rare.

"Yes sir." I trudge away, ignoring the crowd that gathers to watch.

Two streets down, I slink into the alley to gag, feeling coated with smoke and gristle, but tomorrow it will be worse: thirty more bodies to add to the count.

We must get out of here, me and my apprentice. When the bonfires begin, it sometimes takes weeks for the mob's frenzy to subside.

I don't find Cendrillon when I visit the de Boer estate later that day, not even when I float to the eaves. Finally, I knock on the servant's entrance, sweating and worrying when Cook steps outside to tell me that Cendrillon travels along with her terrible stepsisters to a country estate belonging to one of the surrounding noblemen.

"Is the trip unexpected?" I ask, annoyed that Cendrillon made no mention when we last spoke.

Nearly forty-five, Cook's a large-breasted woman with a mournful face. Today, she wears a brown dress that fits about as well as sackcloth. Next to her, I feel as young and beautiful as a comtesse (Never let it be said that there are no benefits to healing magic). "Mistress got the invitation yesterday. She was in a tizzy all night trying to pick the girls' gowns."

"They left today, right after the fires burned down. Madame didn't want to pass the city's edge before the priests were done. She said it might give the girls nightmares."

That wise assessment is the first thing on which Madame de Boer and I agree, and maybe it's good that the family travels out of town. I'm thankful Cendrillon won't have to listen to the catcalling mob and the screams of the damned tonight.

But then I play Cook's words out in my mind again. "Where do they travel, did you say?"

Cook frowns.

I ask a question that's not my business, so I cluck and nod. "I hope Cendrillon brought something pretty to wear. Maybe she will find a husband? Under all that dirt, I'm certain she's pretty. Not that anyone would know, mind you. The lady keeps her in rags."

"Never fear a man would find her under all that filth. He could never see what was before him anyway," Cook shakes her head companionably, the frizz of her bun making a halo around her head. "Neither though her mother were beautiful. More beautiful than Madame de Boer on her best day." She glances up to see if I'm scandalized by the comment.

I stare at the clouds, pretending to take no notice. *Go on*, I silently urge. Often servants need permission to speak the truth, especially in the kind of household Madame de Boer cultivates.

Cook wrings her work-roughened hands. "No, Mademoiselle's dragged along to the Margrave von Helm's estate only because the girls need a servant. Imagine a daughter of the house treated as a servant! And there's to be a huntin' party tomorrow, or somethin', but Cendrillon will not ride with the ladies, no, even though her father paid for her lessons when she were younger. She's to stay behind as a maid.

"I swear, Madame de Boer humiliates the girl, and her father never notices. No matter. The hateful woman don't understand that the child cares naught for finery or young men, at least not yet."

Margrave von Helm: these are the only words I hear.

Now that she's gotten started, Cook will have the whole conversation herself. "Well, mayhap the hunting party'll be canceled. Them nobles don't like to get wet. And there's rain a' coming, mark my words."

"Aye," I nod. "Good luck to her anyway." I pat Cook on the arm, holding out the basket I bring. "Cendrillon was kind to me at the market. I brought her these pasties as a thank you, but you're welcome to them, now that she's gone travelin'."

Cook stares at me.

I lift the food out to her, and Cook takes it, hesitantly. "Go on now," I encourage her.

Cook stands by the door to the kitchens with the pasties in hand, mute with surprise. "And how does Mademoiselle know you, Madame . . .?"

"Madame de Fleur," I use the name by which I'm known in the south side of the city. "I met the girl on one of her errands, selling my love potions and possets."

"Maybe you should sell her a love potion. That girl needs a bit of magic in her life," Cook says, smiling as she heads back into the kitchens with the gift on her arm.

I hurry along my way. The leaves of the nearby oaks whip in the rising wind—their sound a clarion call to my ears. There are coincidences, and then there's the pull of destiny.

I'm too old not to tell the difference.

CHAPTER TEN

The Star Flower

That night I sleep at the edge of the Black Forest to strengthen my magic. Or rather, I don't sleep and recall every mistake I've ever made during my time as a godmother, starting with the fact that I should've done more to help my mermaid. I should've protected her from the Prince's attention when I first learned of it, knowing that all royals and noblemen can be high-handed in service of their own ambitions and desires.

I will not make the same mistake with Cendrillon.

In the morning, I wash and then after I finish my ablutions, I fashion thirty tiny cairns from stones lifted from the secret stream of the forest and ask the Stillness to bring their souls peace.

Then I wait for the Margrave's hunting party to arrive.

The servant retinue comes first, to prepare the picnic for the gentry at the end of their hunt, and Cendrillon has been included in this group, as Cook said she would be.

I set a glamour, taking on Cook's very features as I head toward the group.

"Cendrillon," I wave. "How can I help?"

Margrave von Helm's people look suspiciously toward me, one comes forward to ask my name, tall and a bit horse faced.

"Charlotte, this is Cook," Cendrillon explains, her face betraying no surprise. "She came late because she had so much work to finish at home and slept on the road last night."

"Feel much'n better this morning," I rub my stomach cheerfully and take a large basket from the hands of the next maid who walks by.

"And Cook, this is Charlotte. She's in charge here."

Charlotte nods, her eyes still narrowed suspiciously.

Cendrillon wears a Dutch blue gown that sets off the color of her eyes, but she twists the aether just a bit so that her honey blond hair appears dull and lifeless, her teeth gapped and crooked. It's very effective. When she smiles at Charlotte again, the woman shrugs and moves away.

Then the Margrave and his party arrive. Alasdair rides the same black stallion. No one else has a horse so fine. They dismount and come to stand and compare their guns as the keeper brings down the dogs. Madame de Boer and her daughters struggle to breathe this rarefied air, staying quiet and talking with the ladies who attend their husband's interests.

I shiver once the dogs come, remembering the hounds of war, but these beasts are small and handsome. A horn blows, and they lope into the woods with such joie de vivre that it makes me smile. Liveried beaters make their way into the forest, keeping the animals focused on their quarry.

The Margrave takes no notice of his servants, not even Cendrillon as I'd feared. He rides near the back, letting his guests go before him. I'd forgotten how tall he is and handsome, his black hair tied back, but I don't think his looks escape Cendrillon's notice.

The hunters quickly disappear from sight.

"*Alouette, gentille alouette, alouette je te plumerai,*" Cendrillon sings as she works, her voice soft and sweet. She whistles a little dipping call.

A pair of sparrows winging toward us suddenly appear as maids. The glamoured birds dart over to the table, picking up a platter of beef and carry it to the table being prepared for after the hunt.

Cendrillon whistles again, and another specter maid darts back to us.

She's enchanting birds to do the work, Christ bedamned. I'm driven to blasphemy and impressed both. The focus it must take to hold those darting and dashing minds together.

Charlotte catches sight of the two women and squints as if trying to remember from where they came.

Cendrillon takes no notice. She keeps working, transferring food from a cart that is newly arrived over to where the hunting party will eat.

The risk she takes is unbelievable, even to me.

I grab a platter of steaming cabbage and follow my apprentice and her false maids. After arranging the platter on the otherwise heaping table, I slide to Cendrillon's right.

"What are you doing?" I hiss at her. "This is dangerous."

Cendrillon rounds on me and smiles. "They always gather round me, the birds."

"What if you lose hold of the spell? What if Madame de Boer comes close and one of these…women lifts in the air or just disappears? What then?"

My voice goes high and loud of its own volition. I take a breath and try to calm myself.

"I won't lose hold," Cendrillon says.

"Unless your stepmother decides to come find you or one of your sisters is mean." I scold. "After today, I will make you swear that there will be no more of this, not until you have better control of your magic."

Cendrillon opens her mouth to argue with me but is interrupted by a scream.

"What's happened?" her face turns as if yanked by a string toward the forest.

"A horse must've broken a leg. Release the birds. Now, when no one's watching."

The two maids disappear.

Still, the screaming goes on and on, two voices now, punctuated by men shouting until suddenly gunshots break the sound.

The forest falls silent again.

"They've finally killed it. We'll find out more when the hunters return."

In a few minutes, the hounds discover their quarry again. They bay and bay, and the women and nobles who are left behind eat, as we servants work together to keep flies from the fruit and wine.

The galloping of hooves draws everyone's attention back to the returned men who gather to drink beer and talk after the Margrave's personal priest comes forward to bless the food.

Alasdair calls the servants over to pray. His green eyes scan the crowd, making sure that everything's in its place. I start breathing again, when they neither stop nor slow as they pass over my apprentice in her pretty blue dress.

We all bow our heads, and I say a true prayer of thanks.

"Bless us oh Lord and this your bread, which we are about to receive. . ." With the benediction made, the servants begin their work again, attending to every guest.

"What was that terrible screaming?" Carrying across the flat field, Madame de Boer's voice grates on the nerves like nettles to the skin, leaving behind a feeling of noxious rash.

"Had to put a pony down. There was a pit. What was it, Margrave?"

"Bear pit. God's teeth. Lady Fortune frowned on us, I'd say," Von Helm speaks after he finishes chewing. He must have all his teeth, to eat so heartily. And he's broad-shouldered, like Kasimir.

"Not just one horse, but two went into the hole before we pulled back. You'll have to fill in the pit. Those dead horses will soon stink," a second man mentions. Portly and round, he doesn't stop chewing to talk. I notice the well-bred ladies turn away so they don't have to watch him eat.

"Please sir, let's not be crude in front of the women," Von Helm directs him. "My apologies." The sisters de Boer, tucked behind their mother, titter at his attention.

"And there was something else, something strange that we saw. The Margrave paid it no mind, but I had to stop to see. There's a circle where nothing grows. A perfect circle, mind you. Wasn't natural. Some evil happened there. . ."

"Not evil," Von Helm says. "You make up stories, Stephan."

"Witchcraft," the priest perks up. "Do you suspect it, my lord?"

Beside me, Cendrillon stiffens.

"No." Von Helm shakes his head.

"Maybe we need a witch hunter?"

"Easy," I soothe the girl, picking up a nearby plate and taking a glass to refill. "Keep on with the work."

Cendrillon turns her back to me.

"Father Elias, that won't be necessary," Von Helm says, his tone more curt.

"We wouldn't want you to be in danger from the Devil and his minions," Madame de Boer says. "A witch can hide in plain sight. I would feel afraid here, with the manor so close to the forest. Or maybe the witch who did it came from afar, from the city?"

I can't help but feel that she puts Cendrillon in harm's way on purpose.

"Tis more likely a bear rubbed the dirt clean, Father Elias," Von Helm says, wiping the thin line of his mouth with a linen cloth.

"If it was a bear, then there's no harm sending for a witchhunter," Father Elias says, warming to the idea. "No one will be found, and you'll know your home is safe."

"Our home *is* safe," Von Helm asserts. His face says that he doesn't like where this conversation has led him.

Neither do I.

"Come now, Margrave," says the man named Stephan, a troublemaker and fool. "That circle was nothing like bear sign. The plants weren't rubbed clean. There was nothing in that soil, not even a seed."

"It's the safest path," Father Elias intones. "I'll report suspicion of black magic and have my fellow ministers come search the circle. Master Feilt is traveling nearby, Margrave. He can bring his tools. We have nothing to hide, so there's nothing to fear."

"Nothing to hide. Hah! There's nothing to see except bare dirt," the Margrave barks, . "Fine, we will let your ministers examine the ground. Now you!" he points directly to Cendrillon, whose head is down. "Bring us more venison." He glowers at the unnamed man who started this conversation. "Let us speak of witchcraft no more."

"Here sir." I act as if I don't understand his order is for Cendrillon and take a plate to the man.

Father Elias ignores his master's command. "We'll have to keep the servants. Anyone who could come under suspicion. I can have the witch hunter here in five days." Father Elias continues.

"We cannot live without our servants for five days," Madame de Boer protests.

"Maybe we will keep everyone at the Manor," Father Elias says. "There are witches in every walk of life who cause such unnatural blights: nobles, merchants, servants…We know not where they lie."

"Father, enough," the Margrave orders and holds out his plate, food uneaten.

Cendrillon goes forward to take the dish, and I see Madame de Boer secretly dart her foot out into the pathway.

Cendrillon stumbles, her glamour faltering under Madame de Boer's evil grin, but the Margrave catches her in his arms, with a full look at her high cheekbones and shining eyes.

Madame de Boer frowns.

Glamour back in place, Cendrillon pulls away as if burned. "Excuse me, my lord." She curtsies again. "I'm too clumsy by half."

"We're all allowed a clumsy moment," the Margrave allows, and is it my imagination or does he hold her shoulders an extra beat?

From his words to the Jewish carpenter's merciful ears. I pray to the

Stillness myself, knowing that that circle's my fault. I should've never healed the girl with a witness.

Despite the priest's words, the merchants and noblemen are sent home from the hunting party, but we servants are kept at Wolfbach Manor for nearly four days waiting for the witch hunter, Meister Feilt, to arrive.

I've heard of Meister Feilt before. He's one of those theologians who follows the dictates of the *Malleus Maleficarum*, or *Hammer of Witches*, published in 1486 by the Catholic clergyman Heinrich Kramer, a text recognized as one of the definitive sources on the nature of witchcraft —a tome I wouldn't use to wipe my backside for fear its filth might rub off on me.

Kasimir, at my request, researched Kramer's origins with several of the older priests in the city. He learned that the man was once denounced and expelled from the town of Innsbruck because of his unnatural fascination with the sexual practices of one of the town's women, Helena Scheuberin. Kramer accused that poor woman of witchcraft too, but the bishop of Innsbruck failed to take up his charge, so Kramer wrote his treatise as an indictment of the man's tolerance.

Those origins are oft forgotten, for Meister Feilt is well-trained in the *Maleficarum*'s logic. Outside of Strasbourg, the Protestant nobility favor the man because of his quick work in breaking his prisoners. Feilt found more than twenty women guilty in the village of Meinen and another ninety, men and women, in Offenberg more recently. Wherever Feilt goes, death follows his path. Margrave von Helm, also a Huguenot, knows this too, which is likely why he protests the man's involvement.

In the meantime, while we wait, black-coated clergy search every rise in the forest and measure the distance between trees, as if such things give any true information about the magic that happened here.

They briefly take an interest in the bear pit. According to the housekeeper, Margrave von Helm sensibly had the pit filled after the hunt, but the priests insist on having it dug out again, just to confirm that there's no evidence of Satan hidden within. The stench was so bad that no one wanted to go near the rotting horseflesh. Now the servants fill it back in again, all the while trying not to gag.

The ministers are skilled at tracking, for they follow Cendrillon and my own flight from the stream to the pit and then beyond to the circle, and landing again at the circle, where Father Elias and his like gather as flies to honey or shit—the latter a more likely comparison, as the circle is excreta of the original presence of magic.

"We must stop this," Cendrillon insists, after all the other servants fall asleep. "It's my fault that circle is there, and now others will pay the price." We've been given a warm room near the kitchens, bigger than the closet Cendrillon sleeps in at home.

"It's best to not even let a trial begin." I know this is true, but I haven't been able to find a way out of the manor. The Margrave's staff watch us constantly, hoping, I think, that outsiders will be killed if there's to be a trial. "Tomorrow, we can slip away when Cook sends us into the forest."

"And what about the others?" Cendrillon asks.

She's right of course. I cannot let these girls burn while Cendrillon and I escape quietly into the night. There must be a way to release all of us at once.

"We won't leave them to suffer. Here..." I whisper the plan quietly, making sure to wake no one.

The next day, once the clergy return to the Manor, we're allowed to go foraging. We don't even have need of a glamour, as the guards they've posted to keep watch doze off to the quiet lull of the wind.

The circle's easy to find because the Margrave lied. No plants grow here. The ground shows a wan brown and pale. And more, when we sit on the dead earth, it gives an eerie, prickling sense: quiet, foreboding, ill.

I place my forehead on the ground, whispering a quiet apology. I should've come earlier, and after checking to make certain the guard still snores, I draw on the breeze, quietly, carefully, to carry me and Cendrillon through the canopy to the secret stream.

The water smells sweet and fresh, its touch so cold it burns my fingers. I drink and think and listen to the quiet. I fill the waterskin and we return to the circle and sit again.

"Stretch your sense into the earth," I tell the girl. "What do you feel?

"Nothing. No movement, no spark."

"Right. The ground here's well and truly dead. I could put my hand nearby and draw the life from another patch of earth, but then the problem isn't eliminated, only transferred. No, to fix this problem we must give, not take away. We must entreat the Stillness, as its magic won't work by force."

I go gather leaves, small hollowed-out nut shells and in a moment, Cendrillon follows. We arrange the objects within the circle in a beautiful star pattern.

"We will use your blood as sacrifice, if you offer it willingly, because you took the power of the earth to heal, and now you may offer some of it back."

Cendrillon nods.

"Now hold your hand above the circle and draw your blade across it. Shallow-like."

I pour water from the holy spring into Cendrillon's palm, listening to her hiss at the cold. "Sprinkle the bloody mixture until every inch of the circle's covered. We will know in the morning if the forest accepts your offering, and perhaps the Margrave's minister will declare it a miracle and leave off his witch hunting."

She sprinkles it in a pretty pattern, and afterward I bind her hand as we walk back to Wolfbach Manor.

That night Cendrillon sleeps heavily, as if some secret guilt's been relieved. I sleep not at all, knowing that what happens next will determine our fate. Near morning, I finally drift off uneasily, finally waking to the sound of men shouting.

The Margrave returns from a ride in the woods. His men spread news through the whole house that the circle no longer lies dull and lifeless. A thin layer of winter grass grows overnight. Flowers bloom too, almost out of season, dainty fairy bells, white petals said to ring the little people home at evening's end.

If that were the end of it, perhaps all would be well, but we did our work too well, for the flowers bloom in the shape of a star, each side straight and well-formed. It's a scab over the wound we'd made so many days ago, and if circumstances were different, I'd be overjoyed.

The forest accepts Cendrillon's sacrifice.

But our attempt to resolve the matter of witchcraft fails, for Father Elias delights in the blossoms too. The shape proves that the work of Satan's been done. I overhear him talking with the Manor's chef who makes his meals. "Meister Feilt arrives tonight. Don't worry, my dear. We'll find the witch who helps Satan play his tricks in the forest."

With those words, we're doomed.

CHAPTER ELEVEN

The Wheel of Fortune

When the witch hunter comes, he separates us immediately, me from Elsebeth, my firstborn, only eight years old. She's blond, as I was as a child, and she loves to sing and talks to anyone who will listen.

But she says nothing now. I tell Elsebeth to pretend that she's deaf or dumb. To act as though the priest speaks a language she doesn't understand. I would make her wholly disappear, if I were able to, but under this much strain, my magic disappears. I'm as ordinary as everyone else.

The trial begins with needles. I bleed when pricked. Everyone does except for one unfortunate woman, Belle. She's led away for torture first.

After that they shave and inspect us. Luckily, I have no moles which mark me as a witch. Nor does Elsebeth.

Trapped with the other men from our village, Loren, my first husband, claims guilt on the first day in the effort to hide me. He hangs, mercifully hangs, before he burns at the stake that night.

They start on the children the second day, to make we women confess more quickly. I hear my daughter screaming but am not allowed to go to her side. The priests who serve the witch hunter offer hourly updates on how many are found guilty. Two burghers are charged. The village priest. Three children, my daughter among them.

Later, I learn that Elsebeth refused to repeat the nasty words they said about me, so they cut out her tongue. And then the priests pulled out her fingernails because she could no longer speak.

I finger my nail beds. They feel whole now, not rough and riptorn as they were for two years after the trial. I shiver against the cold, but it's not cold here, not really. This small, warm chamber reminds me of another similar small, wood-paneled room, with two empty coffins laid on the floor, pine boxes ordered from the gravedigger's son. I pay for for Stefan's and Elsebeth's with shaking hands, as is required, but they are buried empty.

The trials leave no bodies to wash and bless.

"Marina?" Cendrillon asks from behind me. "Are you crying?"

I don't answer. I wipe the hot tears from my face and keep my back to her. I can't speak, not then (more than thirty years ago), not to explain what's happening inside me now.

"Marina?"

I force myself to take long slow breaths. This close to the Black Forest, I feel the Stillness and her long green fingers searching for me, soothing my pain with the knowledge of my magic, a source of solace after so much sadness.

Cendrillon's face turns pale. "Marina! I'm going to go get the housekeeper. You need help."

"I'm here," I finally whisper. "Just give me a minute." I'm here and no longer the stripling woman unable to do anything except watch her daughter be murdered through a curtain of fear. I have grown bigger than my wounds and the scars they left behind, a witch and a godmother charged to keep other women safe. I must be even bigger than my mistakes now.

After a few more quiet minutes, I find the housekeeper and demand that a message be taken to the residence of Kasimir Leiningen-Leiningen, telling everyone who will listen that Cendrillon is his niece, fallen upon hard times. The poor woman is not sure whether or not she should believe me, but she asks the Margrave his advice. Within the hour, she tells me a rider was sent from Wolfbach Manor to the city. The Bastard will be furious with me for being caught unawares, but the Wheel of Fortune is not nearly as kind to those of low birth.

This thing started a farce but will end in flames. I vow to make sure neither myself nor Cendrillon feel their heat. Not again. Not ever again.

If we're not rescued within two days, then I'll kill the witch hunter myself.

The next morning, all eight of us are herded out of the main house and stripped down to our shifts. No servant from the Margrave's own household has been taken, which says much about how the Margrave sees this so-called threat. But Father Elias is in charge here. "We will shave your heads, one at time, if there are no confessions today."

One of the girls start to cry.

"You'll be kept in the doghouse for now, if you aren't thrown outside," he threatens, walking us single file today to the small, meager building. "The Margrave has left you to face God's wrath, and Meister Feilt is the agent of His fury. He will feel no mercy for you, so don't lie. Satan won't protect you here."

Judge and executioner, Meister Feilt towers over us, whipcord thin, with a mean face and black eyebrows that move like evil caterpillars as he speaks. He puts us in a line, and a second priest canes anyone who steps out of formation.

"Do you worship Satan?"

"No sir," we speak in a broken chorus.

"Have you ever met Satan in the forest?"

"No."

"Do you have a familiar?"

"What's that, sir?" One reed thin voice pipes up, and I flinch. It's better not to ask questions here.

A cane shuts the speaker up anyway.

The witch hunter's questions last for hours. Often the same ones. We're not given lunch or even water. The Margrave von Helm comes only once that first day, and his eyes slip over the women in the room as if he tries not to see what is before him, until they come to rest on Cendrillon. He blinks for a moment, and my earlier feelings are reversed. It's funny how fate will often give you a second chance to correct a mistake.

Recognize her. *Please recognize her.*

I pray that Kasimir works some kind of administrative miracle already. Are we to be released?

No, the broad-shouldered Margrave spares not a glance for me. He shakes his head, as if the thing he's seeking can't be found and exits while Meister Feilt is mid-question.

By the time the estate's chapel rings the evening bell, we're all exhausted and marked with welts. They've forgotten to shave our heads though.

Meister Feilt keeps the trial going into the night. He separates us now that we tire, bringing one girl to stand in front of him while he abuses her in front of the rest. Marthe goes first, then Margret, then a third, Cécile. Cécile's yellow hair and pure blue eyes shine, especially in the dirty shed. Cendrillon appears a dull, drab mouse in comparison. She keeps her glamour even now, especially now, as she realizes that Cécile's beauty makes her stand out among us.

Meister Feilt returns to the blond girl for questions. "Did you meet the Devil in the woods?"

"I've not been in the woods since I was a small child," Cécile answers.

"Are you sure? Are you a witch or have you engaged in any witchcraft?" Meister Feilt asks. He pulls her hair suddenly.

"Yes, I mean, no sir. I've not engaged in any witchcraft." Cécile nods, not responding to his abuse, and her collected response only makes him angrier.

"Recite the Lord's Prayer," Meister Feilt demands.

Cécile gets through it, making no mistake.

"The minister says that among all the girls, he believes you to have escaped to the forest to dance with the Devil and practice unspeakable sexual acts. As a witch, did you do these things."

"No sir," Cécile repeats again. Her beautiful skin has turned white and pimply with cold.

"Does she lie?" Meister Feilt pinches Margret, one of the dark-haired girls.

My stomach turns. I doubt Father Elias says any such things. In fact, I suspect the housekeeper's kindness to us before the trial may not be wholly her own. Servants do not often stray from the will of the Master.

"No sir!" Cécile blurts out, shocked.

Meister Feilt slaps Margret hard. Her face marked with a sharp red handprint.

My stomach turns. I rub my forefinger against the stiff fabric of my dress, focusing on the way it slips along my skin. My nail. The cold air on my face.

"Margrave von Helm follows the will of our Prince, who's established procedures to deal with the accusations that have been made here. It is not my place to question the Prince's will. I have only to obey him. And does not God protect the innocent?"

The room is silent.

"Does not God protect the innocent?" Meister Feilt roars.

"Yes sir," Cécile says, and Meister Feilt slaps her too.

She's weeping now, and others join her.

I refuse to cry, goddamnit.

"Douse them," Meister Feilt orders the second priest in attendance, striding out of the building.

The priest gathers up a bucket I had not noticed before and dumps half of its contents over Cécile, Marthe, and Margret. He goes carefully along the row as if watering flowers, filling the bucket between at a long trough. He makes sure to drench each of us to the bone.

I bite back a curse as the clod dumps freezing water on me. He's got rotten teeth, and his impure breath makes me turn my chin.

The girls barely stand, dazed as they are from the cold and lack of food and sleep. My teeth chatter and old bones hurt. I dip into the Stillness to find the closest source of heat, but it's yards away. Not easy to transfer for me under these conditions, not when my best magic is water.

"This way," the priest orders, watching the thin girls with an eye that seems more lustful than pious to me.

He leads us to another outbuilding. The place stands in opposition to our quarters last night. Moldy straw covers a floor that stinks of dog. Fleas jump when Cendrillon sits down, gathering her arms around her, and there's a single bucket of putrid water, from which we're all expected to drink.

"Not another day," I whisper to Cendrillon. "I will not do this another day."

"How can we leave them to die?" she answers.

"How can we stop them from dying? We must escape. Now, before this goes on too long." Outside, the wind moans sadness and death. My mermaid is nowhere to be found, and I thank God for it. "We cannot stop the wind from blowing. We cannot stop the will of men when they are bent on destruction. But we do nothing by going like lambs to the slaughter."

Cendrillon says nothing, and we spend a sleepless night, huddling together and feeling the teeth of the wind biting through the thin wood of the walls.

The next morning we file before Meister Feilt again. There's a fire built nearby and tools on the ground before the witch hunter. I recognize a hot poker when I see one.

I touch my thumb to my forefinger again, a nervous habit. Pulled nails eventually grow back, but no one comes back from the dead. How far will I let the priest go today?

"These are instruments of torture," Meister Feilt says. "Will you confess?"

The room stands quiet.

"Confess and it will be easier for you," he badgers.

Another voice interrupts the witch hunter. "Margrave von Helm," a young footman announces, and then Alasdair von Helm enters the dark room. He blanches at the row of tools before the witch hunter. "Pardon, Meister Feilt, I must call a temporary halt to today's processes."

"The will of God cannot be halted," Meister Feilt parries.

"Just so, but the mercy of God is great. I've just confirmed that one of these girls was left here accidentally by her family relation. She's well born, so she and her chaperone must be given leave to go." Von Helm looks at Cendrillon, and the air charges with something different than hate.

Meister Feilt turns to the girls, speechless for a moment, his jaw working with fury. "No. None are innocent, no matter their birth," he argues, turning back to the Margrave, finding his footing. "They cry false tears, but do not soften your heart, Margrave. These *frauleins* hide something. I smell brimstone in these walls."

"I bow to your great experience, Sir," Von Helm says smoothly. "You may finish your work, once I remove the girl and her woman from the trial."

"No," Meister Feilt shouts. "They are *whores*. Unclean, guilty of consorting with the Devil, of mad, filthy passions. Confess! Confess and you will die before you burn!" He turns back to us, face red and apoplectic, gasping, and I see my moment.

I twist at the air, pulling it away from the witch hunter, so that his momentary gasp is prolonged. He pounds his chest and coughs, stuttering as all wind leaves his body. I keep pulling, loosening, giving just enough that his struggle seems natural.

The Margrave pauses. Father Elias rushes over, taking hold of the evil man's shoulder. "Meister Feilt. What's wrong?" He pounds the smaller man's back.

"It's me. I confess," a small voice says.

CHAPTER TWELVE

Guests and Fish

I whip my head around in terror, searching for who spoke, and my focus on the magic falters. *Not again, no, not again.* I barely keep myself from crying out. We're so close to freedom. Who would be so dumb?

Father Elias' eyes shine, as if this moment could not be made more beautiful. "What did you say, girl?"

Catching a breath, Meister Feilt whispers, choking. "I knew it." Cough. "I knew there was an evil whore among you. Step forward, girl. Admit your nature. You've been consorting with Satan, haven't ye?"

The Margrave looks startled. He frowns, unable to do anything now that the girl's spoken.

"Come now. Tell us your sins."

The child's crowned in blond: Cécile.

The Margrave lets out a breath that I hadn't realized I was holding too. "Surely she's too young," Von Helm's protest breaks the silence into shards.

"Satan steals children to him," Meister Feilt croons.

"Me, sir," another girl speaks, stepping forward, Marthe. "The Devil made me touch myself. He made her touch me too, and it felt so good."

Cécile nods.

No! I want to howl.

"And the rest of you! You joined them in the forest." Meister Feilt cries.

"No sir. 'Twas only us," Cécile nods.

"Such perversion. It's all around us. An easy death for both of you." Meister Feilt turns to us, and below his waist, a tented cassock.

Christ.

The room falls silent. From his angle, the Margrave cannot see what I do.

"You try to lure the rest of us to your evil, filthy ways. To make men lust after you, creatures of lust and perversion yourselves. Don't you? All of you." Meister Feilt walks along our row, lording over us. He stops and stares into my eyes as if he can see into my soul. "And what say you, Madame?"

"I'm just here for my girl." I nod, keeping my head low, angry at how this has turned out. Another minute and the man standing before me would be dead, choked to death.

"No more, Feilt," Margrave von Helm says vehemently. "The rest will be taken back to the house, now that you've found your witches, especially the near noble daughter and her maid." He glances at Cendrillon again before turning to the door. By the set of his jaw, Von Helm's decided that this hunt has gone far enough, and Meister Feilt sees the same. In a city like Offenberg, where the rabble get whipped to a frenzy, the witch hunter pushes and manipulates to bring other victims to the pyre, but here, the Margrave speaks law.

"Go back to the manor house. The rest of you. Immediately," Von Helm says. He catches Minister Elias' arm as he exits the building behind us, speaking quietly. "Break their necks before they burn, Father. I will not listen to screaming as I sleep tonight. No one on the estate will attend."

Meister Feilt curls his lip at the Margrave's words. He won't get the show he wanted, which is likely to send him packing quickly. A witch hunter's fortune grows by theater and malice.

Two girls sentenced to death for lust and enough curiosity to experiment.

Back at the manor house, we eat well and one-by-one wash the sweat and fear away with a small bucket of clean, warm water. I wait at the back of the line, listening to the girls around me moan or cry.

"I did not know such a thing was possible," Cendrillon whispers to me as she dips water from the steaming bucket before us. She's still shaking.

"What?" I ask, now that we're alone, the only two left to wash. My skirt holds a thick layer of dog hair and molding hay, the fabric ruined by the cold-water bath, but I beat the filth away as best as I'm able.

Cendrillon turns away, her fair skin blushing rose, her glamour dropped again. "For two women to do such things?" she finally stutters out. "Why would they want to…" She cannot find the words she needs, and no wonder. Such a topic is unknown to most young women.

"Ah, there are a dozen ways to find pleasure in your body, and nearly double that with another person, man or woman," I answer very quietly. "But let's find another time to talk of such things. We're still not safe here."

"I should never ask such a question." Cendrillon's guilt returns.

"Not unless you want an answer," I say and force a smile I don't feel. I refuse to wear the shame priests dole out like cat o' nine tails. God knows the aristocracy does not adhere to such bullshit. A girl Cendrillon's age (I guess sixteen) often marries by now if she's the first daughter of the house. Madame de Boer maligns tradition, but perhaps, in an unintentional way she's finally done the girl a service; Cendrillon can come to sex more slowly than many women will.

Cendrillon scoots away when I close the door, probably to find more food. Later, she falls asleep on the floor of the warm storeroom along with every woman who washed before me. We've all been shoved in this tiny space for now.

Perversely, my own nerves refuse to release me. I go for tea and listen to the housekeeper vent her ire. Two unfortunate girls die before flames lick the soles of their feet. They knew nothing of Satan. Cécile is the Cook's own niece, a good girl, if a bit wild. And now she dies for what?

Finally, my eyelids droop, even though it must be only dinnertime. I trace the corridor back to the storeroom and find a man silhouetted in shadow.

"My pardon," the Margrave von Helm speaks before I can say anything.

Past him, Cendrillon lolls on her back. In sleep, her glamour falls, and her cheekbones cut a picture of youth and beauty, even as her hair rolls outward in long honey waves.

"She seemed so familiar to me in the doghouse," he says. "But now I'm not sure."

After a bath and a hearty meal, she no longer looks like the begrimed sack of bones he first saw under cover of night.

"Maybe the color of her hair, sir? It's quite common in the city." I gesture back to her, and pull the glamour upward again, dulling her beauty.

He shakes his head, as if confused. "I can't place that face, but I must know her family. Maybe I can send an apology and an invitation along with you for the Bastard?"

"Yes, of course." A servant would never refuse such an invitation, but in this case, there's no need to deliver it. Kasimir would never put my apprentice in even more danger.

"Is it true that she's his niece?"

"Yes, although we never see him. He's a neglectful relation, if you don't mind me saying so." I have never been more happy to disparage my lover. Hopefully this will put von Helm off.

"I'm sure he cares for the girl even if he doesn't often see her. She seems of sweet temperament." The Margrave's manners are impeccable.

"Yes, sir. May I be excused? I'm tired." I yawn and shoulder past as if I'm ready to lie down, although after this exchange I'm wide awake again.

He steps back into the shadows. "Yes, I'm sorry. I was only here to make certain all were fed and warm."

I smell the fires before I sleep, but no screams mar the night.

We do not leave for the city the next day, nor the next. On the third, I ask the housekeeper why we're kept, but she laughs my question away. 'Don't worry,' she assures me. "You're safe. Meister Feilt left the day after the burning. The Margrave merely wants the girl to rest."

The girl.

Maybe Madame Meier tells the servants' version of truth. Madame de Boer's people are not important enough to be returned promptly, so until the Margrave wills one of his men to escort us back to the city, we sleep and linger, growing fat on the wealth of his largesse.

On the fourth day after the trial, I start to feel thankful. Cendrillon gets the food she needs here. Madame de Boer does not offer such lovely repast, neither at the master's table nor in the servant's quarters.

On the sixth day after the trial, the Margrave stumbles accidentally across Cendrillon in the garden, where she helps Madame Meier gather lavender. He asks if she's well or so the housekeeper reports to me later that night with a hushed air of respect. The man can do no wrong on this estate.

The housekeeper assures me he has no ill intentions: Margrave von

Helm inquires due to his concern. Margrave von Helm hates witch hunting. The respected Margrave von Helm believes Father Elias' obsession with the practice to be misguided, a product of his early Catholic training. The longer he is a Huguenot, the further away the practice will recede.

I fight the urge to argue that Protestants burn witches just as well as the Catholics. I have no station here, but I know how quickly the same servants will blame Cendrillon if she falls out of favor as the mermaid did.

The next day's nerves drive me to take Cendrillon into the wood. The estate's chef wants pine nuts for a dish he plans ten days hence. We go to gather, but the instant we are away from listening ears, I lift both of us to the air and travel to the heart of the forest. We trace the hares and squirrels into a warren of briars. We watch the hinds move as one. The spring light softens in the arms of the forest, just as a maiden responds to her lover.

"Why are we here?" Cendrillon complains. She crouches in a borrowed dress, made of serviceable green wool. The color turns her green eyes gold.

"To find the Stillness."

"It's *still* at the estate," Cendrillon argues.

"Do you not feel stretched?" I ask. "You set your glamour every morning, but does your skin itch and do your eyes burn by the end of the day?"

The girl doesn't answer, and I know I'm right.

"Sleep is not enough to replenish your magic fully. The trees and the land will do half the work for you here, if you open yourself to their kinship." She believes the words a platitude instead of practical knowledge. I adjust the hem on my own borrowed gown. "But you cannot hide and make yourself small while doing it. Now take down your glamour."

Cendrillon's cheeks grow more full after nearly a week of eating here. My heart warms at the sight of her smile.

"Now go lean against that tree."

"Which one?"

"The oak."

"Which one is that?" Cendrillon asks.

"Zounds," I curse and point.

The girl dutifully sits.

"Lean against her trunk and listen to her whisper. Put your ear against the ground if you must. Remember she gave you her gift, so she is your sister."

I do the same myself. I lie on my side in the midst of the forest, with my ear tamped against the ground.

Minutes pass.

My legs go numb, but the forest stays quiet today. My mind reminds me of Kasimir, his likely fear and anger at my absence. It asks if we've gotten enough pine nuts, if the servants truly believe us to be witches despite Von Helm's insistence that the hunts are an abomination.

Then all these whispers fall away, and the forest accepts me. I shift to touch the earth with my forehead, instead of my ear, a greeting.

The wild Stillness envelopes me, a green and many-armed thing, towering and feral and full to the brim with life. I become a flea on the back of her skin, a shiver, a tickle.

I align myself to the force that I feel. This is the magic I seek. This is the power that can change the course of a war.

We join spontaneously, in entreaty, a love song. I feel the coursing, tumbling, strength rise through me, and when I sit up, spirits ring the clearing.

"Cendrillon," I whisper.

The girl rouses not. She drinks from the unmade chalice.

"Cendrillon!"

Those green and golden eyes take a moment to focus.

"Sit up."

Cendrillon lifts herself, skin fairly glowing with power and renewal. When she catches sight of the glowing forms who stare at us, she whispers. "What are they?"

"Reveal yourself," I command.

The first comes forward. He's green-skinned, with flowery leaves edging where his neck would be, and lower on his waist, not human but something like it. He approaches Cendrillon first and bows.

"Bow back," I whisper, but she already touches her forehead to the ground.

She stands and reaches out to touch the closest frill.

"No touching!" I say, too late.

She draws back, and a red flush crawls up her fingers and covers her arm. Tears swell at the corner of her eyes, but the girl makes no audible sound, does nothing that could scare him away.

The stinging nettle steps aside when the next spirit reaches her.

Barely humanoid, the rounded form is covered in thick green fringe, that looks soft to the touch. Sphagnum moss thrives in the damp wood of the Black Forest. Any good witch befriends this plant, useful to staunch wounds and heal sores, among other things.

Each comes in turn, a silent procession. The forest's denizens greet my apprentice. This communion is different than that sacrament of bread and wine, symbolizing another, deeper union. Witches do not seek to transcend the earth. We befriend it. We know it.

I stay aware of the Stillness watching us both without eyes. I feel the suit of my own skin and beyond it, the rolling waves and movement of infinite power and wisdom.

A branch cracks, somewhere close, and Cendrillon turns, eyes wide open and afraid.

And suddenly we stand alone. Our feet pound mundane earth again. Cendrillon is she, and I am I. We are separate, afraid of whatever *other* stands outside of our circle of earth.

A stag makes his way slowly toward us, snuffling the ground for fallen berries or twigs, his rack rising above him like a crown of horns. He watches Cendrillon curiously, as if she might move toward him at any moment.

"Now you know many of the herbs we will use in the first magic, not just their use, but their spirits." I check the sky. "It's time to return."

"Yes," she nods.

The wind raises gooseflesh. I borrow its force to carry us closer to the edge of the wood. Then we walk in silence for a time.

"How are your eyes?" I ask.

"They hurt no more."

I try for an explanation and fail, but I know the lesson takes root when I catch Cendrillon saying a prayer of thanks over the basket of pine nuts before they go into the Chef's hand.

We eat with the servants—venison, cold cheese, and warm bread. Cook sits to the side of Cendrillon, holding her arms off the table and off her clothes. She caught a rash in the garden, and the itching bedevils her.

Then we go to bed, the seventh night since Meister Feilt took his leave.

Margrave von Helm returns to watch Cendrillon sleep. He's still as a shadow, but there's a slight, scratching sound that takes more than a few minutes for me to identify.

The man rolls an acorn against the woolen fabric of his trousers, which means if he hasn't already recognized Cendrillon, he soon will.

We must away.

CHAPTER THIRTEEN

Lengthening Shadows

We walk out of the manor the next afternoon, leaving Wolfbach and all its beauty behind.

I want to cry at the sight of a hawk freely climbing over the nearby trees. I want to feel the same air streaming around me. I want to cry because Cendrillon lives where my daughter did not. I live.

Beside me, Cendrillon talks. *Now,* of all times, the blasted girl won't be quiet, and I refuse to stop her unfurling, despite the feeling that rises in my own chest as old memories threaten to drown me.

"The Margrave's home is beautiful, is it not? His servants seem happy. He takes good care of all."

"I saw evidence of that, yes," I reply.

"And he doesn't hate witches. He finds the bonfires disturbing. Madame Meier says his mother was very loving. And he played for days in the forest as a boy. Sometimes they could barely bring him back, he was so wild."

"Where did that wandering boy go?" I ask.

"He's still inside the Margrave somewhere. He must be." Cendrillon answers, not hearing my bitter tone.

"He's dead, girl. Transformed into an entitled aristocrat who feels fine deciding who around him lives and dies."

"Marina!"

"What? I speak the truth. That man was on the verge of recognizing you and what then? You would be blamed for causing the whole witch hunt, and both of us would be burned at the stake. Or extorted for money or sex or worse."

"Marina!" Cendrillon's tone tells me that I've truly shocked her now.

"What do you think will happen when he figures it out—that you and the girl I healed in the wood are one and the same?" I ask her. "To the Margrave, you're a danger—something he has to hide, and men of his station are willing to do only one thing with women they have to hide. Bed them." I try to shock her, saying everything I should've said to the mermaid when she told me of her fascination with the Prince.

Cendrillon walks faster, as if she's trying to get away from the truth. "Enough. He was kind, and he did not have to be."

I can't argue with that, so I change tacks. "He's part of the war. He encourages the fight, along with the Duke, against the Catholic army, and if he follows that urge too far then the forest will be cut down, used for wood to power an army. He orders men like your father to die every day."

"My father's fine," Cendrillon argues. "Even if I no longer wait for him to come back. He may never save me from her. Not like you have." She glances over at me. "Are you taking me back to Madame de Boer?"

I notice she doesn't say *home*. It's a good question. I've been thinking that Madame de Boer's house is not safe for Cendrillon now. Maybe it never was.

"No. Leastways not after we've gathered your things."

Cendrillon nods, looking relieved. "Where are you taking me?"

"To the townhouse I share with Kasimir Leiningen. You're to be my apprentice, so you're my responsibility now."

"Kasimir? The man you told them was my uncle..." She tries the name out on her tongue again. "Kasimir. Is that the man you were kissing in the alley? The man to whom you are not married?"

"I told you twice is married enough, but yes." I relent. "He's my lover."

"Does the Margrave know we go there?"

The question disturbs me. Does Cendrillon really cede ownership of herself so easily?

"No."

She nods as if that's the answer she expected.

"What's the difference between the trees' gifts and the spirits who visited us the other day?" Cendrillon asks, changing the subject as if she finally senses my discomfort.

A good question. I think about it for a few moments, but before I can answer, she returns like a terrier to a mouse hole with more questions about the handsome Margrave. "Why did we have to leave today? He might've already recognized me, and the Margrave kept us from being killed."

"But he allowed two girls, children, to burn. Children who *weren't* witches." I round on Cendrillon, putting my hands on my hips, my anger finally pushing past my grief. She doesn't realize how close we both came to death.

"...But those girls... they were . . . doing something evil," she replies.

"Is healing the Cook's arm evil?" I ask.

"No."

"Is feeling pleasure, instead of pain, evil?"

"The priests say it is so sometimes," Cendrillon replies, more carefully.

"And do they say that to the Count VerClaus for having not just a wife, and several mistresses, but a houseboy who he sodomizes every third Wednesday as well?" I snap. "Or do they ask that his Lordship pay an extra fine, an *indulgence*, and allow him to continue onward fucking everything in sight. You're young, and you've seen so little of the world. Let me ask you this?" I advance toward the girl and step close enough that I can see the yellow flecks in her eyes. "Who's allowed to take their pleasure where they will? And who's tied to the narrow pastures designated them?"

"What's that supposed to mean?" Cendrillon asks, backing up.

"I will make my point more plain. Who burns at the stake?"

"Witches."

"Do they now? Was Cécile a witch?"

Cendrillon shakes her head, her braid unraveling in the rising wind. "Probably not," she admits.

"No, nor Marthe. Nor most maidens who face the fire. Madame Catherine Munchen burned because her land lies near the pastures of the most powerful burgher in Strasbourg. On her death, he bought the land at a price lower than could be believed."

"Not everyone who burns is rich."

"No, nor poor," I amend. "But the poor burn because they are mad or sick, and women burn, all manner, especially those who refuse to do as their husbands, fathers, or priests ask. And the ones who are lucky enough to have land or homes that are of value are even more likely to go to the pyre."

"It's to save our souls," Cendrillon repeats the words so often heard.

"Do you believe that?"

"Do you?"

I won't answer the question for her. Every woman must find a way to see the truth for herself.

We walk in silence for a long while. The sun slowly falls toward the horizon. The wind picks up. My fingers lose feeling, but I save my strength for the flight home. I miss Kasimir.

"What's that sound?" Cendrillon asks.

"What?" The question brings me reluctantly back to the road. Before us, dark, staggering shapes move on the line of the horizon. It takes another heart-pounding moment before the shapes resolve into men, soldiers or at least mercenaries. Cast-offs of one army or another, they litter the countryside, stealing food and supplies wherever they can find them.

"What do we do?" Cendrillon asks.

I check the sky. The shadows lengthen. They might not see us. In another half hour, we could fly away without notice.

Shouts echo from the horizon. We're spotted.

Flames flicker along the rim of Cendrillon's fingers. "Put your flames away, child! And draw your glamour around you. Make your hair appear dark, and I will turn mine blond," I demand, trying to count how many there are.

"So we wait for more to surround us?"

She's right. The men run toward us, and a few hang back, circling behind.

One approaches, his dark hair tied back in a queue. "What are two such lovely women doing traveling alone?" He bears a scar over his right eye, from a blade, judging by the cut.

A good question. Everyone knows it's not safe to travel without protection, and by that, I mean unmarried women may not travel without men.

"The Margrave von Helm left this morning. He led the way for us." I claim tacit connection to the aristocrat. These soldiers won't attack us if they fear retaliation.

"We saw the Margrave this morning. He mentioned nothing of a pair of women following him. Where are you from? Offenberg?"

"Strasbourg," I reply. "We're going home. My husband awaits my return."

Cendrillon still says nothing.

"Is the girl dumb?" The soldier eyes Cendrillon's black hair, dulled by the glamour.

"She doesn't feel safe to speak. She's been through much these last few days."

"Satan stole her tongue. Is she a witch then? We heard there was a burning on the estate. Perhaps they missed one." Another man calls out from behind us, fair-haired and with an unkind laugh.

"Don't joke of such things," the dark-haired man bites out before I can even answer.

"Marthe caused too much trouble anyway," the blond spoke.

"You knew Marthe?" I ask the soldier in front of me.

He nods, face closed.

"I'm sorry for your loss." Cendrillon says, finally speaking.

"Make it up to poor Stefan. Press him against that sweet body and make him feel better." The blond grabs Cendrillon's waist from behind and pulls her against him.

"Release her." I keep my voice quiet and even.

"Or what?"

"Release the woman, Klaus," Stefan calls. He looks around to the five or so men who've gathered around us.

The blond man releases her momentarily.

"It's been a long time since we've had a woman. Two is more than enough for all of us." A third man talks to Stefan. He does not bother to look Cendrillon or me in the face.

"They were taken by the witch hunter for a reason, Stefan. You knew Marthe. Surely you heard the rumor. She serviced two men at one time. Her own father could not keep her from the garden path. If these girls know her..." Klaus hints and threatens us.

"Such bitches sew evil. These women are probably just like her. Friends. We can kill them after. I will dig a shallow pit to bury their bodies. No one will know it was us."

I barely breathe. These men starve, I tell myself, taking stock of their thin faces. They fight like demons against great odds, with no home, sometimes no family to whom they may return. Men like this lose everything in war, especially their humanity.

"No," Cendrillon breathes. "I will not die today." Do I imagine flames on her fingertips again?

I hold my breath.

"The Margrave protects this girl and her family," I lie. I dare not mention Kasimir here. I don't want any thread which they may follow.

"He will find you and hunt you down."

"He will never know what happened," the third man counters.

"Did you not say you spoke with him this morning?" I keep my tone light.

"We did," Stefan agrees.

The sun sinks below the edge of the horizon. The lengthening shadows grow dark. Stefan closes his eyes, and I see his decision is made.

I take Cendrillon's hand in my own, doing what I should've at the first sign of trouble before. "Now," I say and kick upward.

We soar into the sky.

CHAPTER FOURTEEN

The First Proposal

The men shout below us. "Satan's bitches! I told you, Stefan. Shoot them!"

A gunshot tears the quiet afternoon in two.

Never have I done something so rash. Stories will circulate behind us now. If these men travel to the Margrave's property to tell their story, they could identify both of us.

We fly low over the trees, but it takes another two hours before we see the lights of the free city of Strasbourg. Fires surround city walls. We pass above the encampments, looking down below.

"Who are all these men?"

"Troops," I correct.

"Like the men we just met."

"Maybe," I concede. "Or worse. The Margrave arrives tomorrow, but this is why he left with such haste."

"What are they doing here?" Cendrillon asks.

I don't answer, but the truth echoes in my mind anyway.

War.

We land at the far end of the street on which the De Boer house sits and walk in the dark toward the house.

"I don't want to see them," Cendrillon says, stopping at the outer edge of the back garden.

"I can find your things. You don't have to go inside." I remember the notch of her small closet-like room tucked into the top eave of the house. It's been a long few days for both of us, and we've barely managed to escape death and rape, in that order.

Cendrillon nods, saying nothing, but she stops walking, content to watch me go.

I creep quietly toward the dark house. It's early for bed, but perhaps Madame de Boer denies her servants candles at night. Many merchants count their thalers' growth in such small, mean ways.

The kitchen door stands unlocked. I ease my way through, expecting to see Cook at least, but the servants gather in the dining room together, eating and talking loudly.

Madame de Boer must not be home. I straighten my back and listen.

"The Mistress was wrong to do what she did. Sending the girl away like that."

"She protects those gooses of hers as if they are royal hens," another voice speaks, a housemaid perhaps.

A round of laughter circles the table.

So the servants of the De Boer home possess minds of their own and the ability to speak up—at least when the petty tyrant is away.

I creep toward the stairs and make my way up to the top floor, swinging Cendrillon's door open quietly.

The room holds few signs of occupancy, a tiny cot, stripped of any bedclothes. The rest has been cleaned out. All that remains is a basket holding a day dress, barely more than a rag and a child's patched doll. There's no sign of the silk slippers. The bitch erases all signs of Cendrillon's existence. For a moment, I consider burning the house down or at least wiping my own boots on the lady of the house's pillows.

But the first would put ten more people out on the street in the cold with war looming. And the second would ultimately lead to punishment for one of the lot who gather round the table below, and if Madame de Boer's earlier performances prove anything close to truth, then daily life in this cursed house is already hard enough.

I leave the dress and grab the doll.

The servants start a round of *Il est des nôtres* as I hurry back down the stairs. I turn the last corner and come face to face with Johann, the big brute who threw me out of the house on our first acquaintance. He blinks, trying to decide if I'm truly there.

"Who are you?" he finally asks.

"No one," I answer.

"I've seen you before. Hey! I've seen you before!" He grabs me by the arm.

"Good heavens." The man's strength cuts off my circulation, and fear prickles in my armpits and at my gut. So I jerk and manage to break free in his surprise.

I search for something with which to bash him. The others continue to sing. They don't hear us yet, but if I can't stop him from shouting, they will.

I pick up a heating brick from the nearby shelf and wait for him to come closer. When he grabs at my hand again, I lift my skirts with one hand and kick him between the legs.

He bends low, catching himself and gasping. "*You bitch*. What are you doing here? The girl's dead."

Is Madame de Boer so sure of herself? The bare room above shouts yes. But despite my desire to howl the truth, I keep quiet; it serves my purposes to let the lie stay. "And you did nothing to prevent it," I say, bringing the brick down on his lowered head.

Johann drops with a satisfying clump to the floor.

"What was that sound?" The singing finally stops.

I go still. If I'm discovered, I cannot use magic to flee. If anyone should reach out to the Margrave von Helm and tell the truth of our earlier escape, a whole pack of witch hunters follow our trail.

"Johann?" A voice calls. Maybe the housekeeper?

"He's never had a head for vodka. Probably drunk. Like us," Cook whispers, loud enough that even I hear her, and the room erupts in laughter.

I pat Johann's shoulder. I would drink myself into a stupor too, if I had to put up with Madame de Boer's bullshit.

"We should check on him."

But no one does.

I wait ten minutes, long enough for conversation to return. And Cook proposes another song.

Outside again, the cold night air welcomes me. I don't hurry, trying to decide how to explain to Cendrillon that her things have disappeared.

Psssstttt. A whisper surges toward me.

"Cendrillon, is that you?"

A glimmering flame answers me.

I make my way toward the burn pile.

"Look," she says and, snapping her fingers, lights a small, dried evergreen branch. The flame catches and then roars to life, illuminating the ash that lies below.

"My coat," she says dully, using the branch to shove the half-burnt pieces to one side. "My dressing gown, given to me by my mother. I have nothing beautiful left."

I open my mouth and close it again. She cries. In the bare light of the flame, her braided hair falls across small, sloped shoulders, and her clear face, no longer knife blade thin, reddens.

"Be glad that all your ties to this house turn to ash, child. Now let's go before we're discovered." I offer no condolences, as I can barely contain my own sadness and fury.

"I don't believe witches burn because the priests and noblemen save our souls." Cendrillon stares into the fire. "But why? Why does anyone do such horrible things? It's so evil."

I take a breath. "That's a much more difficult question to answer." There are big evils and small evils, as our day reveals. Sometimes the small cuts hurt worst.

"Why did he allow them to die?" Cendrillon doesn't name the more personal pains. *Why does my stepmother hate me? Why does my father betray me with his absence?*

I hug her, unable to stop myself, and Cendrillon's tears mix with my own. We cry for Cécile and Marthe. We cry for Cendrillon and the hateful acts done to her. I cry for my mermaid and finally for my own daughter, Elsebeth.

And for the soldiers still on the trail, raping and pillaging their way across the countryside.

I cry for all the unvanquished evil that still walks the earth.

"You could've been killed. Marina, you must leave word of your plans, especially when they're so unhinged, and you must include me in the knowledge of any so-called family I've unexpectedly inherited," Kasimir says for the twentieth time. "I didn't know what to do when I got that letter. If I should rush to your side or stay away."

Kasimir and I lie side-by-side, not sleeping, in the four-post bed. The fabric curtains block out any light, but even so, I put my hands over my eyes, their weight comforting.

"I only wrote to you because I was desperate." Exhaustion tugs the edges of my awareness, dulling my thoughts.

"You will tell me your plans next time before you leave, and you will not leave the city without sending word of where you will be."

It's late, so I say the words he wants to hear. "Of course. Now, can you please speak more quietly? I don't want Cendrillon to hear us."

My apprentice sleeps only one room away, on a bed bigger than she's ever been offered. I could've taken her to my small house at the outskirts of the city, but the girl's safer here. Kasimir's title affords both of us great protection, and in our free city, he aligns himself with neither the Huguenots nor the Catholics, a fact which makes me love him all the more.

"You could've been killed."

Kasimir only repeats himself when he's very upset.

"And yet here I am. Alive. Aren't you glad of it?"

He ignores the barb, staying silent so long that I start to fall asleep.

"How many dead?" The question wakes me up.

"Two girls from the nearby village."

"The reason?"

He doesn't mean witchcraft.

"They…experimented with each other. One girl seems to have been the village flirt. I came close to killing the witch hunter, but then I was interrupted by the girls' confession. Wolfbach's village priest heard it, as did Von Helm. One death can be an accident. Three will bring the more witch hunters down on the manor and town."

"I need more information to be part of any plans. And if you had murdered him, what if that hadn't worked?"

"But I didn't murder him. And now I'm home with my new apprentice, and we are safe. At least for a time. It will be remembered as an adventure." I try to be flippant, even though I don't feel it. "Isn't that why you love me? For my adventurousness?" I try to tease and roll onto my side to grip Kasimir tightly as a burr.

"That is only one reason, and not the best." But Kasimir's voice softens, and lengthwise against me, his body already responds. We kiss, and then we grow quiet for a long time, touching.

I still. For a moment, I return to the field, to the soldiers and their intended rape.

Kasimir stops, aware of my changing mood, but I can't bring myself to talk.

"We met a band of soldiers on our way back," I finally whisper.

He holds my face, as if to feel the emotion that lies just underneath my skin. "You escaped them unharmed?"

I'm glad of the dark now, for my face heats. "We fled," I concede. "By air."

"In daylight!"

"No choice," I answer. "But hopefully they will not go back to the Margrave's house and ask more questions."

Kasimir pulls the covers tight around me and tucks me against his chest. "And if they do, I will swear that you were here for the whole day."

"They will not recognize the Widow Mullenheim anyway, but I'm happy you're home. Truthfully, I didn't expect to find you here. I thought you were in Wurzburg another week."

Kasimir sighs and pulls back a bit. "They burn bodies faster than women can birth them there and beyond. The Prince Bishopric's thirst for so-called justice defies all logic. He hangs everyone. Nineteen priests. Children. And so many women."

"So you flee back to the city because of new trials, just like me."

There's a silence that stretches so long my eyelids droop again. "I couldn't stomach any more of it," Kasimir finally says. "Soldiers out for a fight, the screaming that goes late into the night. The roads are dangerous. I think you should stay home for a while."

There's something else, something he doesn't want to say.

"And?…" I wheedle and break free of our cocoon to climb astride him, hoping the movement will wake me up.

Kasimir runs an arm up my thigh to my waist. "Marry me, Marina. Let me cloak you in safety and keep you happy and well fed." He reaches up to kiss me.

"A third husband is unseemly," I demur, taking a moment to kiss him back. "And no one's safe from the trials, especially not me, especially not now. What if those soldiers make their way to Strasbourg? What would happen to you if I'm accused?"

"Convention is the best defense against charges of witchcraft, as you well know. Just being unmarried makes you more of a suspect. Let me take you to fêtes and parade you in front of jealous men, and then I will take you home and make love to you knowing that you belong to me." He drapes his large hand just over my heart.

I cover Kasimir's hand with my own. "I'm already yours."

"But not legally," he says. Kasimir holds a lawyer's mind.

"Exactly," I say. *Which is why I do not owe you the explanations you demand.*

This second part I don't say aloud.

I've heard the argument Kasimir makes before. Mab made it just as convincingly when she introduced me to my second husband, Georges Mullenheim. The thought of Georges conjures dark hair and bright eyes. My second husband was a sweet man, and he offered protection to Roland and myself, a gift that meant more to me than he could know. Georges grew up in Strasbourg, and as a Stettmeister, he owned the full power that a wealthy and well-connected family brings.

But death finds us all. After Georges died (consumption), I promised myself never to marry again. Kasimir knows this. I can no longer bear children, and my work grows ever more dangerous. I will not bring a husband into such risk, preferring to face it alone.

"Don't ask it of me." I plop down on the mattress beside him, my voice sharp, the mood gone. "I won't endanger you, as I did Georges. I could not bear for you to die too."

"You already bring me into it. I've inherited a new niece, whom you've brought home to live with me. And otherwise, I will ask whatever I want of the woman who freely uses my name but will not offer me her loyalty in turn." Kasimir tickles me, to dispel my sour mood, until I laugh and scream. He covers my mouth to quiet me and then flips me onto my stomach and presses his length against me.

"Loyalty is not all you want from me," I tease, and he bites at my neck sending a pricking sense of cold down my spine.

"Love," he whispers in my ear as I roll back on my side. "And I could stand a bit more peace. Quiet." He covers me and pushes inside, staying still for more than a minute while he kisses my cheeks and forehead and earlobes.

It's me who finally urges him into a rhythm. We move together slowly, every touch tender, reaching the pinnacle at the same moment.

After, Kasimir cleans away the traces of our lovemaking from my thighs, and I fall asleep in his arms, a niggling question burrowing into my mind like an insidious worm.

Why does he ask for my hand in marriage now when he knows I'm against it?

CHAPTER FIFTEEN

Fox and Geese

It's been months since I've seen Madame Zell, but the woman instantly commands my attention, or rather her dress does, a yellow patterned silk with wide sleeves that drape gracefully to her wrist and a small, manageable bustle. Even Cendrillon's eyes, normally hooded, widen at the contrasting white lace that edges the neckline.

An astute businesswoman, Madame Zell acts as a walking advertisement for her own good taste. I would frequent her shop even if she were not the most notorious air witch in the city.

We retire to my dressing room, where Cendrillon releases her honey blond hair and undresses to a simple cotton shift. "Magnifique!" Madame Zell exclaims, clapping her hands in appreciation. The girl's natural beauty shines. Cendrillon stands on slender well-shaped legs. Her finely molded collarbone gives a sense of delicacy above strong shoulders, well-shaped from doing work.

"Yes. Proceed," I dictate and act bored, although I feel anything but. I love a new dress, and although she struggles to hide it, keeping her face turned down and eyes shuttered, Cendrillon can't stop herself from running a hand over the closest pile of fabric, a delicate white silk appropriate for nightgowns and fine underthings.

After poking and prodding the girl for another hour, Madame Zell declares Cendrillon measured. She flies forth the fabrics using her magic and gives us time to *ooh* and *aah* our way through her inventory. After deliberating, we decide on a deep blue silk, shot with silver thread, and another silk in hunter green. Cendrillon will wear these gowns for formal occasions, not while working or traveling. For most days, we pick a dark wine-colored wool, almost scandalous in its softness, and one more in green and blue each. Two browns round out her wardrobe—a drab brown dress makes it possible for almost any woman to move through the city unnoticed.

Madame Zell knows me well enough not to ask why such a lovely girl, being fitted for fine things, also needs to have a few sturdy and poor clothes.

We keep secrets together, my modiste and I. After all, this woman's shop fronts the Hearth. She's well accustomed to hiding truth in plain sight.

Next, we turn to the trimmings. The white silk returns, and we order two chemises and a single whalebone corset. Cendrillon needs a cape fashioned from the same blue and hunter green silks lined with fur for balls and dances and a cloak that will be done in a hearty brown lined linen, again for purposes of anonymity.

After the morning's work, we tire. Madame Zell begs off, happy to be about the creation of a new wardrobe, and lunch comes before us, a plate of salted pork and fine cheese, with olives from Italy gifted by my late second husband's far-flung friends. Cendrillon eats with her trademark gusto, but I make a mental note to employ a tutor. The girl can't continue to eat like a wild animal and move freely through the most expensive parlors that Strasbourg offers.

And then I encourage a bath. New habits of cleanliness need reinforcing. Cendrillon takes my hint and departs, planning to relax for the remainder of the day. I don't think the girl's been invited to indolence before, based on her quiet joy at my proposal. My own bedchamber cleverly keeps a large basin close to the fire, and I wash with warm, scented water too.

At nearly half past eight, the servants ring us to dinner. Kasimir sits at the head of the table, to my right as is our custom. Cendrillon emerges from the afternoon a different woman. Her hair hangs in beautiful ringlets, and someone, Kasimir's housekeeper most likely, modified one of my old dresses, a greenish gray, the color of winter's growth. Maybe Madame Zell sent something she could alter quickly, realizing the girl couldn't wear servant's clothing while she resides at such an illustrious address, not without drawing comments from our staff.

"Mademoiselle," Kasimir bows. He does his best not to stare, but he follows the custom, pulling her chair out so that Cendrillon may comfortably sit at the dining table.

"Sir," Cendrillon replies. "Thank you for allowing me to stay in your home."

"I welcome Marina's charge as my own daughter," Kasimir says.

The words turn my eyes wet. I blink back the tears I had not known lay hidden there.

Do Cendrillon's eyes also sparkle more than they should?

"What's for supper?" Kasimir asks the butler.

"Roast beef and asparagus. Potatoes. Pheasant. And your favorite, sir, blanc mange."

Kasimir nods his pleasure and whispers to Cendrillon. "I hear your stomach growling."

"We ate hours ago," she whispers back conspiratorially. "I'm starving."

"Marina did tell me you love a good meal."

I want to kick Kasimir under the table. He betrays me to gain her confidence.

"Above all else," Cendrillon replies honestly.

"Well, let us begin," he announces, just as steaming platters make their way to the table.

Cendrillon eats more carefully tonight. She's traveled so far, so quickly. A mere fortnight has passed between discovering her filthy, disheveled form climbing the chimney and the young miss who sits down to dine tonight.

"A surprise," Kasimir announces once we finish. He nods to one of the men waiting on us, and the servant brings forward a letter I hadn't noticed laying on the sideboard.

"An invitation?" I ask, taking note of the lovely cream paper and the gold filigreed edges.

"To Gertrude von Zorn's house party, a mere week hence," Kasimir answers.

A lovely surprise! Gertrude is not a witch, nor a godmother, but I enjoy her company, nonetheless. Her party offers a lovely opportunity to have Cendrillon practice social graces, if only we were not trying to remain unnoticed.

"Decline the invitation," I direct, seeing Cendrillon's face fall.

"I've never been allowed to attend a party before," Cendrillon says.

"Maybe we can go for a just a short time," Kasimir cajoles.

"Not a good idea. There are people we do not want to see. It's better to stay home and…" I trail off as Cendrillon breaks in.

"Please, Marina! May we?"

I tap impatiently against the table foot, until Kasimir covers my hand with his own.

"It may not be such a bad idea, *amour*. Cendrillon's next move is important. Now that you've put her in my care, we must announce her place in the household. For her protection, if nothing else. And to make your story stick." He doesn't say more, but I understand. If those soldiers do arrive in Strasbourg talking about flying witches, it will be much harder to lodge a claim against the Bastard's niece.

"Fine," I grumble, routed by the partnership between the two.

For a few minutes, we eat quietly.

"And what is your role in the coming war, Monsieur?" Cendrillon asks my paramour, after dessert is served.

"You may call me Kasimir, my dear. After all, we're to be family. Now tell me. What do you mean?" Kasimir volleys the question with another question, setting his spoonful of uneaten custard aside.

"The footmen in the hall said the battlefront comes to Strasbourg. They said you and the Duke of Württemberg met with the city's Stettmeisters to decide our future. Will you draft soldiers to protect the borders or will you and the guard travel back to Wurzburg where the fighting grows thick?"

My face flushes with heat. *What is this?*

"You hear much," Kasimir smiles, but behind the smile, irritation hides.

"They all say you're on your way back to battle. Maybe within the week. And that you were nearly killed on the road home."

"Only a skirmish, no real danger. My men speak out of turn." This time his tone makes it clear that there's nothing more to say on the matter.

"There is fighting in Wurzburg?"

"On the way," Cendrillon corrects, turning back to Kasimir. "Right?"

Is this why the man tries to marry me? He wants to widow me again? I stand, and Kasimir instantly stands too.

"Tonight we sleep at my son's home," I say to Cendrillon. If I stay, we argue, and I need not argue with any man who is not my husband.

"Your son?" Cendrillon's tone fails to conceal her surprise.

"Tell Kasimir how much you enjoyed our stay here."

"It's wonderful!" Cendrillon babbles happily. "I love the tall ceilings and the paintings. And the hot water. Madame de Boer, my stepmother, she had nothing so fine."

"Most people don't," I comment and make my way toward the bedchamber where I may pack.

"Marina! You have spent the last fortnight in danger," Kasimir calls, but I pretend not to have heard him, and Cendrillon, sensing my need for escape, clasps his hand and pulls him further toward the viewing hall.

"Do you have any children's books, Monsieur? I would like to learn to read."

"Probably not." He pauses. "I can send for something."

"No, but is there something suitable you could read to me after dinner?"

And the two proceed away, leaving me to climb the stairs and nurse my hypocrite's heart alone.

I wake the next morning to the sound of Cendrillon and Sylvie laughing. It takes some time before a maid helps me wash and dress but when I descend the stairs, I see the two girls play Fox and Geese.

"Good morning, Shatzi," I call.

"Good morning, Grandmere," Sylvie sings back. She plays the geese, ostensibly the easier part to take.

"Good morning," Cendrillon nods, more gracefully and then, jumping her red piece over one of Sylvie's whites, she says, "Got you."

The simple game of strategy is a contest between one fox and thirteen geese. Players move pieces to any vacant adjacent spot on the board, but only the fox may jump another piece, as Cendrillon does.

The object of the game is for the geese to capture the fox by surrounding him so he cannot move.

The fox must try to remove as many geese as possible or at least enough of them so that they cannot sustain his capture.

"Hhhhmmmm," Sylvie says. Both girls stare at the board in concentration, and I'm reminded of how young Cendrillon truly is.

"*Maman*," Roland nods as he walks into the room. He works for one of the city's lawyers, no longer an apprentice, now one of the firm's main men.

"Why are you still home?" I take the plate piled high with sausage and egg that the serving girl offers to me and watch Sylvie move her geese safely away from the fox on the board.

"I wanted to make sure nothing was wrong," Roland says.

I feel a pang of regret. My decision to flee Kasimir's home in the middle of the night appears ill-thought and rude now.

"Nothing at all is wrong," I smile and put my plate aside. "I wanted you to meet Cendrillon, my new helper. She's a distant niece to Kasimir and new to the city."

Cendrillon looks at me, her eyes widening only a fraction.

Roland notices the gesture and understands that I lie. His brows draw together. "Of course, we too support Cendrillon. Don't we, Sylvie?" he says.

"Only if I beat her. She is a wolf in fox clothing." Sylvie nods, making another move, and suddenly Cendrillon's red fox is surrounded by white circles.

"You're good at this game," Cendrillon grins. Her golden hair frames her heart-shaped face, and in the morning light, her green eyes shine clear and untroubled.

"She's too good. She needs to remember what it's like to lose." I slide down to the floor beside Sylvie and take up the red piece. "Now let us play again, child. Cendrillon, I will show you how to take several geese at once. So her numbers don't overwhelm you next time."

Both girls scoot closer, and Roland waves a quick goodbye. He obviously decides more questions can wait, thank God.

I stare at the board and quell my unease. I may be outnumbered, yes, but I can still move across the board with much freedom.

"What is more valuable than thaler?" Cendrillon asks me the next day as we walk along the Rhine. "My father used to say that gold—or silver in this case—rules all. I understand him more now, I think." Mention of her absent pater takes me by surprise. I glance sideways, trying to read meaning behind Cendrillon's expression, but her brow stays smooth and unlined.

"Information," I breathe. "Be very careful when someone withholds information from you, especially when gold or property exchanges hands."

Cendrillon stops walking. "So that's why you got angry. Is it not up to him to decide what to share? Most men tell their wives nothing at all about their business."

The girl's mind moves quickly, I'll give her that.

"Which is why I am not married. After all, what is marriage except a merger of assets, eh?" I say, in a mocking tone. Every woman hears this phrase repeated from birth, so as to assuage the sting of being sold off to the highest bidder.

"What can women own?" Cendrillon asks. "I mean, unless they are widows, such as yourself." She incorporates an understanding of this new facet of my character well, the widow of Stettmeister Mullenheim. Such alacrity gives hope. Cendrillon still constructs a new image of herself after all. Today she wears her face unmasked, her hair coiffed and primped. No glamour at all.

"Why their vaginas of course."

She gasps. And covers her plump pink lips with a newly manicured hand.

"Most men want unlimited access to a vagina, especially the vagina of their choice."

"Blasphemy." Cendrillon turns red and grabs my hand to hurry me along to a little bench twenty steps hence. "Don't speak so loudly."

I whisper this time. "We just saw two women die for touching one another. Why is love between such women something worth burning to death for? I mean, not for the participants; pleasure is self-explanatory. But for the witch hunters and priests."

"It's a sin." Cendrillon's eyes stay wild.

"Maybe. Maybe not. No—there," I point. Kasimir awaits us, at the end of path, just as he promised.

"Ownership," I respond. "In this case, the word carries both legal and emotional meaning. If women are property to be bought and sold, then men must own even their pleasure."

We climb up into the carriage. Kasimir sits to the right, wearing breeches and a nicely made linen shirt with full cuffs. His doublet reveals a pattern of blue that entwines both the shade of Cendrillon's day dress and my own navy, a subtle but clear nod of support to us both.

The carriage takes us to the correct address. Kasimir says nothing of import, sensing my continued anger, but he puts his hand on the small of my back. I move closer into the circle of his arm as we enter, the touch signifying agreement. Cendrillon's entry into the world of wealth takes precedence over all else.

Lady Gertrude's husband serves as a stettmeister on the governing council of Strasbourg. He is also a good friend to the Margrave von Helm, a connection neither Kasimir nor I miss, but despite my uneasiness, the Lady's support means more than the possibility of seeing Von Helm again so soon.

I peek over at Cendrillon, enjoying the confidence of her straight back and easy posture.

Not even the Margrave von Helm will recognize such a beauty as the same girl ragged and torn on the dog house floor. If her connection to Kasimir is not pointed out, I think we will escape this first engagement unnoticed..

A servant announces our entry. Gertrude's day parlor shines in the afternoon sun. The wood paneled room holds blue irises and other gifts from friends, celebrating the success of a recent party, and of course a number of the city's wealthiest young women and men.

"Welcome Marina Mullenheim and Kasimir Leiningen, bastard brother to Johann Kasimir, Count of Leiningen-Leiningen."

"And who is this vision?" Gertrude asks, in one glance taking in Cendrillon's fashionable ensemble and beautiful face.

I pause and smile fondly at my apprentice. We decide together that the name her stepmother calls her should not be the first thing her new friends hear, and Elina, the name given to Cendrillon by her mother, is derived from that great beauty, Helen of Troy, meaning torch. In this way, out of ashes, a new fire is born.

"A young friend, Elina Lerner," I try out the name for the first time. The Lerner's are a smaller branch of Kasimir's common family.

"It's wonderful to see such familial support," the Frau von Zorn says. Her words signify that she understands the intent of our visit. "I'm excited to introduce you to the young men and women of our fair city, Elina."

Newly named, Elina bows her head demurely and keeps her green eyes averted.

We circulate through the several rooms of Lady Gertrude's salon. Kasimir instantly finds a circle of stettmeisters and nobles discussing politics, and I pull my apprentice toward a lovely chaise lounge where we sit together and talk.

An hour later, a ringing sound interrupts the festivities as a handsome young man steps forward on the heels of his father, Gertrude's husband, Stettmeister Zorn. "We're excited to announce the engagement of our families," Zorn says. "Friedrich von Zorn asks Anna Wurmser for her hand, and the lady accepts."

Applause.

Anna appears suddenly, dark-haired and fresh-faced, a young man grasping her small hand tightly, as if to make sure she doesn't flee. Another elder steps forward, pushed by his matronly, grey-haired wife, perhaps Anna's father and mother. "We offer a townhouse in the west borough of the city as a small gesture of happiness at the union," he says, naming a coveted address to the crowd.

A toast celebrates the newly minted couple.

Kasimir speaks at my elbow. "They receive much more than that, by my estimate. The girl expressed frustration at the union, but rumor holds a babe's on the way. It doesn't matter that the babe isn't Friedrich's, poor lad. The Papas' Zorn and Wurmser care not. Together, they own all the buildings leased by the weavers and leather merchants to the east of the Rhine. The merger is a coup."

"Property," I whisper to Cendrillon, who is subtly paying attention to our private conversation. "Assets."

"Don't stoke the girl's dissatisfaction, Marina." Kasimir disapproves. "You've been twice married, and have children of your own. Elina needs no one's leave to take joy in the natural order of things."

"Do not spout such drivel at me. Many of these people live most unnaturally, as you well know."

"Yes," Kasimir waves me down. "Mergers are not the stuff of romance, but when a man and woman lie together, most of the time a child emerges nine months later. That *is* nature, even you would agree."

I open my mouth to argue, but Elina turns, and all color drains from her face.

"What is it?"

"I must leave. Now!" Elina slumps against me, looking around for somewhere to hide.

"What's wrong?" I ask, searching the crowd for what could've set off her instinct to flee.

Madame de Boer should not be here, but she moves through the crowd, just the same. Today, the sharp-faced woman wears a pus-colored yellow. Thankfully, she does not catch sight of us, passing onward into the next parlor.

"She's gone," I whisper. "And you have nothing to fear. We will be here to protect you…"

I'm interrupted again by a feminine squeal.

"*Aiiiyeee.* Is that? . . . It is! . What are you doing here? Maman said that you were dead."

Of course, her daughters follow. The youngest, Ava, catches sight of Elina, her mouth hanging open like a gutted fish.

"What are you doing here, *Cendrillon*? You do not belong here." Elisabet hisses.

I don't correct her because I do not want a scene, and now, no one listens to her unimportant chatter.

"Neither do you," Elina says. "Sitting squarely among the merchants as you do."

"How dare you?" Elisabet draws back, her face flushing pink.

Kasimir appears as if from nowhere and steps in front of Elina, towering over Elisabet. "I beg your pardon, *ma chérie*. The woman you address attends by invitation from the Alderman's wife herself. Elina Lerner is a distant relation of myself, through her mother, and newly named as the charge of Widow Mullenheim."

"Are you the one who's bought her such fine clothes?" Ava asks, a note of envy to her voice. She notices that the blue wool Elina wears is finer than her own gown.

"You've made yourself into a whore then?" Elisabet spits out.

"You will not talk to her like that any longer." It's time to teach the girl how to fight back.

I bind Elisabet into stillness.

Her eyes go round. She can't move. She can't even speak. "Not another unkind word," I quietly warn.

Ava's eyebrows nearly touch her hairline.

"Your sister swallowed something unpleasant," I speak slowly. "Greed leads directly to this kind of ill fortune. Ava, you must learn her lesson without the unnecessary pain."

Elisabet's face darkens, and Ava takes a step backward.

"Otherwise, you will both be eating piss-soaked bread and begging in the streets. Or worse." The reference to urine doesn't escape either girl.

"Help!" I shout, and both girls jump. "The girl chokes! Help her!" I release the air in Elisabet's throat, and she falls to the carpet, gasping and flopping like a beheaded chicken. The crush of people closest to us finally notices what happens.

Gertrude von Zorn rushes toward us. "My dear, are you all right? Get a glass of water," she calls to a passing servant.

"She's fine. She choked on a bit of gingerbread," I say, patting the girl on the shoulder. "Don't eat so quickly next time, *ma chérie*. It's bad manners."

"Come. We must find your mother. Maybe those corset strings pull too tightly." Kasimir pulls Elisabet to her feet at Gertrude's behest and ushers her into the next room.

"Wait, I have a message for your dear mother," I call genially to Ava, who prepares to follow her sister. "Please pass on to her that

Stettmeister Mullenheim's widow bids her household well and is sad that we won't have any more communication this spring. None."

I pat Ava's shoulder kindly and lean closer to speak more quietly.

"I bear you no ill will, child. You've done nothing wrong besides being cruel, and how you could learn to act differently under your mother's tutelage? Listen well when I tell you: Elina deserves kindness, just as you and your sister do, despite being born to your harpy of a mother."

Ava stares at Elina, as if trying to make certain we see the same person. "But she's nearly an orphan. Worth nothing. No connections. No prospects."

"Surely, you see that's not true," I correct, gesturing out to the room. "One day, Elina Lerner may bring you opportunities you could have never imagined."

"I *am* no one. No one you know. Not anymore," Elina says scornfully, but her eyes prick with tears and her face turns bright red.

"You're the apple of my eye, darling." I try to take Elina's hand, but Kasimir pulls my arm from the opposite direction. I turn toward him.

"I need a word," he demands, pulling me away from the girls. He leans down to whisper in my ear. "The Stettmeisters say that Johann von Werth leads his troops to the Black Forest in an effort to draw Württemberg into battle. The Catholics want the city, but they don't think they can take it. Not yet."

My heart spasms. "What?!"

"They plan to burn it to the ground, starting tonight."

The room presses too loudly on my senses. I can't see past the crush of bodies.

They will destroy everything. The beautiful trees, all the animals, and going deeper, the magic that churns beneath.

"Just a moment." I turn back to Ava, in time to watch her disappear through the crowd.

"Elina?" I grasp for my apprentice's hand and find air. "Kasimir. Find her!"

CHAPTER SIXTEEN

The Dogwood Blossom

"Call the carriage," he says. "I will find her."

I nod and slowly make my way through the crush. Outside, the Zorn footman points to where Kasimir's carriage already arrives. He helps me into the conveyance, with the support of a strong arm.

Elina sits inside, her beautiful face red and tear stained.

"My dear!" I take her hand in my lap, so glad I can barely speak. "Kasimir still searches for you inside."

"I'm sorry I ran away," she says, lower lip trembling. "But I saw him, and I didn't know what to do."

"Who?" I ask. "Kasimir? Why would you run from him?"

"I saw the Margrave, but I could not face him. Not like this." She gestures to her tear-stained face.

"You have nothing to be sorry for, sweet girl," I rub her upper arm, where the corset doesn't restrict feeling. "Those toads behaved terribly. I'm nearly in tears myself."

"I could never do what you did, in a room full of so many people. I'm not so brave."

"You are, and you will be. I saw you in that bear pit, and I saw the flames on your fingertips with those soldiers. You're braver than you think, and you know when it's time to act. Trust yourself."

There's a sharp shout outside the carriage, and we take the opportunity to pull back the curtain.

Kasimir stands at the house's entryway talking to another man, tall and well formed. I can't make out the second man's face, but my gut identifies him immediately.

"It's him," Elina confirms. "I knew he would follow me, Marina. I felt it."

"You have a bond," I admit out loud, unwilling to say anything more.

Kasimir refuses Von Helm. His stance turns wide and defiant. He's magnificent in those calfskin breeches.

Then my lover strides toward our carriage, leaving the Margrave behind him.

Von Helm stays at the top of the stairs, eyes trained on our departure, the stance of a hunter catching sight of his prey. He wants to follow our flight, but stays still for now.

Fast enough, the horses canter forward and then we're on our way home.

The instant we walk through the entrance, I instruct the servants to help Elina to bed. I send along a cup of hot brandy to help the girl relax and sleep. She deserves to forget her stepsisters' abominable behavior.

Then I send a small note to Mab, telling her that the forest faces attack. We must call the coven together.

I creep onto my balcony, checking the horizon as if I could see the forest alight at this distance. But I can't, of course.

"I want to go with you." Elina's voice interrupts my thoughts. "I heard Kasimir, and I know that you're going to the wood. I want to be brave."

She knows that I'm leaving nearly before I say it to myself, so I don't argue. It's time that she start to take her place by my side. "It will be dangerous, but we can gather information to bring back to the Hearth. We may be able to stop them."

"Then we will stop them together. Please let me go."

I nod. "Get your cloak.

In the air, fur-lined cloaks protect us from the cold, and with the moon still not risen, we move as shadows.

Eventually the horizon turns orange, and the smell of woodsmoke rises in the air. We avoid the fire which spans nearly ten klafters, taking its measure, and instead fly south and a little west, skirting the war camps that line the northern edge of the forest, and finally land to catch our breath and listen for the first time without wind rushing past our ears.

Leaving Elina deeper in the wood, I skulk close enough to hear the men who camp there drink and sing and, in some cases, fuck. (Whores make easy coin off an encroaching army, if by easy one means plentiful but very, very dangerous work.)

Then we slip past the few soldiers who keep watch over the steadily burning trees and make our way deeper into the forest until we find the stream.

Once we stand beside moving water, I cut a small branch from a nearby hazel tree. There, we anchor ourselves at two different points in the stream's wending, facing one another.

"Tonight we call upon the first and second magics. And as the soldiers use fire against us, we match them with the enemy of fire."

"Water?" Elina asks.

I nod and draw a bag of salt out of my pocket and draw a circle around us, stepping inside once I am back at the water's edge. "That's right, and a bit of air. Now lean down and scoop up water in both of your hands, making a bowl."

Elina ties her skirt up and wades out into the stream, dipping her hands in once she is ready.

"It's cold," she hisses.

"Yes, that's good. Now come toward me, face me."

Using the hazel branch, I sweep air over the water in Elina's palms, whispering a rhyme to fix the spell.

"That fire which burns in the forest tonight /
Belongs to men with ill-gotten might /
May air and water combine to rain /
That the forest may heal and be peaceful again. /
Mark this spell for a fortnight or more /
Routing the threat from the Black Forest floor."

Trails of fog shoot from Elina's hands upward into the sky. As they rise above the tops of the trees, white clouds lengthen and grow.

Soon the moon and stars are covered.

I smile. "See how the clouds are shaped like the scales of a fish, a good sign, but it's not enough. Gather more water."

Elina fills her cupped palms again.

I repeat the spell, the air growing colder.

Soon a steady rain begins to fall.

I smile at the angry shouts I hear from the forest's edge.

"Marina, why must we take care of the woods?" Elina asks. "Why does the forest herself not make it rain?"

"Maybe *we* are the way the forest herself makes it rain. Maybe we are the forest's arms and ears and eyes. Maybe we are its legs. Just as

Stillness is the source of our power."

I myself know not the truth.

The old stories tell of women who walk on water, who sing entire ships to their death, who are able to bind men to their will with a single word, and a few exist who may still work such magic, Violante among them. But I have never seen such things.

"There are tales of witches who slide between worlds, between times, or who transform themselves into beasts or monsters, depending upon the needs of the moment, but these abilities exist no more."

"Why?" Elina asks.

"Because there's so little wildness left, almost none anymore. This is all we have."

Elina places her hand on the bark of a nearby willow tree and whispers, "I see now why this place is so important."

Elina and I bow our heads and say a prayer of thanks for the Stillness and the Leap. We walk the circle of salt twice, before sweeping what is left away.

The rain already destroys most of it anyway.

As we take to the sky and head for home, we briefly linger to observe the building rain drench the soldiers' fires. The men will not sleep comfortably this night.

Two weeks later, we return to the forest–Elina, Amondine, a water witch from the Hearth, and me. Our leather boots squelch in the damp earth. The forest stands quiet, weighed down by its near constant watering. And still the soldiers gather at the edge of the wood, looking even more haggard and damp than the last time.

Our rain spell falters. Tonight, the stars peer down at us, a sign that the power we unleashed no longer looms.

"We cannot set the spell again, Marina" Amondine says, her dark hair and black cloak make it hard to find her in the faint light. She flows forward, checking the boggy, gross mud. "We're causing an imbalance."

"An imbalance is better than the alternative," I argue.

"There must be another way," Elina speaks from my side.

"What?" Amondine snaps, throwing her long braid over her shoulder.

I gather my cloak around me and we silently make our way to the heart of the forest, winding around the swollen path of the stream.

Amondine is not wrong. The unnatural rain wreaks havoc.

My head clears, and my heart reaches out to the magic's Stillness.

What more can I do to keep you safe?

This deep in the wood I cannot hear the soldiers. I hear nothing. Nothing, except.... A small tinkling sound, like bells around a feminine ankle. My eyes stay closed, too afraid to scare whatever it is away, but when the sound stretches and turns alien, I peek.

A woman strides into the clearing. Not the mermaid's spirit that I expected—this woman's form shines, as if she is made of stars, but the light is dense. The pressure in the clearing increases. Long hair tumbles past her shoulders, light-brown, one side bound in ribbon and braided over her ear. She carries a bow so large I would fall forward under its weight and a quiver of arrows strapped on her back. Her dress, white and glowing, falls to the top of her knee, no further, so that she may move freely through the wood.

Who is she?

"My Lady." I bow before her, this figure who radiates a light and power that does not burn, only illuminates. I keep Amondine and Elina behind me, but in the corner of my vision I see both witches go down on one knee too.

Before me, the Huntress takes my arm and brings me to standing. Her touch feels like frost on my skin.

"Why are you here?" I ask.

The Huntress, turns her ear, as if listening for something beyond. A crashing sound interrupts the silence, branches breaking and a loud snuffing that I recognize immediately. And then a bear breaks through the underbrush and stands, taller than any bear should be, the height of two men. He stands at the right shoulder of the Huntress. His haunches glimmer with the same shine she wears.

I cower. His fangs drip with something, maybe blood and lather, but Huntress directs my sight past the bear to where a road opens up like a black mouth in the midst of the forest.

"You want me to take this path?" I ask, knowing instinctively that it was not there before.

A howl interrupts the question. And then a second.

Wolves invade. They stride to their mistress's left side, eight, no ten, more than I can count. Their fangs show grayish white in the half dark.

A second road appears, a fork at my feet.

"A choice," Amondine whispers behind me.

"Which way should we go, goddess?" I look between the two roads and again at the Huntress, taking in her shining brow and her sly smile, fierce and full of knowledge.

Dark-haired Amondine takes a step backward. "Be careful, Marina. The Huntress is not known for her kindness. We should return to the Council to talk this choice over."

The bear goes down on all fours, snuffing and raking a claw across the ground. He moves slowly, chewing for a moment on a stick.

Maybe the motion tells me something. Maybe Amondine's words are wise. We should not rush forward in the face of danger. Maybe we must move slowly and carefully as brother bear.

"Maybe you are not the one." The Huntress raises her chin and looks past my eyes.

Somehow, I know that if I do not make my choice, then this moment slips away, never to come again. Then the choice may be made by another.

Another sound, so quiet I almost do not hear it, leaves shifting under the weight of an anxious body.

"Elina!" I whisper, keeping my anger at bay. "Stay behind me. Now!"

"Mistress," Elina comes to my elbow, eyes downcast. She gazes up at the Huntress, as if the Lady hangs the stars herself, and without warning, flings herself past me prostrate at the goddess' feet. "Please help us. The army tries to burn down the wood, but we would keep this place safe at all costs. For you. For the trees. For the magic within its border. Show us how."

I stop breathing. *Now is when she chooses to be brave?*

The Huntress strokes the ear of the closest wolf with her glowing fingers before urging it forward.

The wolf approaches Elina carefully, sniffing the top of her head. He butts playfully against her skull, and when she lifts her face in awe, he licks her tears and paws at her feet.

She wraps her arm around his neck.

"Elina," Amondine hisses. "He's no puppy. Stay back, foolish girl."

It's a sign. I speak from some unknown part of myself. "The wolf. I choose the way of the wolf."

"Marina," Amondine warns. "I will have to tell Mab of this."

"What do you offer the pack, witch?" the Huntress asks. "Your ghosts offer me nothing. They smell of old fish and ash."

So she can see the mermaid and past her, to the graves I've left behind. I pause, considering.

"I have something," Elina nods, speaking before I'm able. She holds something out in her hand.

"What's this?" the Huntress asks, plucking the white thing from her palm.

I make out the edges of a flower. It's a dogwood blossom, the second gift of the forest.

"Hmmm," the Huntress says. "The dogwood is cousin to the wolf. Fierce. Loyal. Protective. Yes, this might do. It will bind you tightly. It will demand much. Will you do what it asks, child?" The Huntress crushes the blossom in her fingers, and when she releases the remnants back to the forest, the pieces fall in a shimmer of glowing dust.

"Yes," Elina nods, not looking up at the goddess again. She doesn't hesitate even one moment before giving herself over.

Don't let her go alone, I hear the mermaid's voice against my inner ear. Amalia is here then, witnessing this moment. *The seas are stormy tonight.*

The Huntress looks at me, as if she too hears the words.

"Me too!" I cry. "I am the girl's pack."

"I will allow you both to hunt as my wolves tonight." The Huntress nods, after a careful inspection.

I bow down at the Huntress's feet.

"And me?" Amondine asks.

"Your fear holds you back, but I will still put your cowardly heart to use. Go warn the others of the danger. Tell the witches to keep this sanctuary safe, as they are sworn to do." The Huntress frowns. "Out of my sight. Now. Away."

Amondine turns to pick her way through the woods and flies into the night.

"We're ready. Do it now." Elina turns her face up, eyes glowing with a remnant of the Huntress's light. "Before we're too late."

The alpha wolf nudges her at the words and waits as Elina presses her face into his neck. Already, her form changes, torso elongating, legs shortening.

Changeling magic.

I bend down, and my apprentice comes to me as a wolf, licking my palm. She nips my neck hard enough to hurt and growls.

"This can't be so. Such magic no longer exists." It is a moment before I realize I spoke aloud.

Elina bites me again, and a pain starts in my gut, exploding outward. My bones stretch and bend. I rip out of the human body I've known my whole life.

Gasping, I put my head between my paws. The forest sends me a thousand signals through my nose. Clean water. The path of a doe and her fawn. The magic of the Huntress, her will like a rein over my fury.

I am of the pack. We are one.

I smell them almost immediately. The men sleep so close, huddling against a cold wind that starts to blow. They believe themselves safe outside the arms of the forest.

They are not. Together we sprint down the road to the left of the Huntress. Elina leads, spurred by the alpha. Her choice creates a new future for our pack.

For a moment, I remember Amondine and the godmothers, the women to whom I belong and who I protect in this fight. My pack. I remember all the witches burned, the poor, the mad, the wealthy and titled, and I want nothing so much as blood on my teeth.

Then the clouds break, and the moon urges us onward, her shape the memory of a glimmering bow in the sky. We find the war camps in minutes. They lay in the bracken beyond the protected arms of the trees.

The pack moves silently. Elina rips the throat of the first soldier without warning, and I take the second before he screams. The alpha's gray fur looks almost blue in the firelight. He tackles the closest tent. Elina slips behind him, moving with fury and power.

I follow, blood tasting sweet in my mouth.

My wolf ears hear screams and curses differently. Words are unintelligible. Pitch and tone take on new meaning. I register only fear and fury in the men beyond.

The pack attacks like an arrow, shooting deep into the camp. A musket takes down one, then two of my brothers. I feel their deaths as if they are my own. We are a pack. We move together. The rear guard closes in from the flanks. They drive stragglers into the central part of camp where we can kill with ease.

After a fortnight of rain, the ground turns to mud in my paws. My nose makes the sound of fear manifest: shit, piss, and two-legged animal becoming meat. Muskets click, their match cords too soggy to ignite their powder.

A dying soldier lies nearby, gurgling, his throat gone, his face a mess of blood and torn muscle. I break his neck and move onward. I am not hungry, although my wolf mind registers that I will eat well tonight.

We claw and bite our way through a hundred men.

Many of us do not survive but my keen ears register hundreds more soldiers running off into the night, the smell of their fear trailing them. I keep Elina's scent close, as the Huntress instructed, attacking nearby, so that I am always aware of her movements.

Hours pass, or so I realize when the sky begins to lighten. My coat is wet with blood and rain. The sounds of fear quiet. I see less well in the light and fight the impulse to run back to the forest.

Elina still hunts.

I follow her deeper into the tents. This is where the generals and noblemen sleep, if sleep were to be had. These spaces lie empty, and my wolf brain registers only that the prey who once were here fled. My human mind finds a word, *cowards*, but the wolf in me understands. Fleeing keeps these men alive. We don't need to kill every man, just break their pack.

Someone tracks us. I hear him behind, moving silently. I whistle to Elina. *Retreat.* I try to drive her left, but she ignores me, chasing a woman who hides twenty feet away within a swiftly built privy.

"I see you," the man whispers. I circle away, watching him as he approaches Elina.

The man carries a stick.

Not a stick, the human part of me whispers. *A gun.*

I stand behind him now.

He lifts the stick to his shoulder, his hands fumbling with the powder and blowing on his match cord till it's red hot.

How does she not hear him? This is no young, smooth hunter. His gut hangs over his breeches and stained coat. My wolf brain tries to make sense of the symbols sewn on its shoulder but cannot.

The woman inside the privy notices what is happening. "No!" She screams. "I'm in here. Stop. Don't shoot." And she bolts out of the door toward the closest tent.

The sun breaks over nearby treetops, glancing out of the clouds.

Elina snarls and leaps at the woman's back, at the same time that the musket bangs.

The sound deafens. I hear nothing afterward, but I can smell the tang of gunpowder, like poison in the air. Elina drops mid-leap, and the human part of my mind screams, "NO!" just as the sun hits me. Suddenly everything hurts all at once. My bones stretch and collapse. My teeth shrink. I taste iron so strong it makes me wretch.

"Elina!" I shout, with my human tongue.

She pants on the ground, her right haunch leaking blood.

Is this the danger that the Huntress foretold? I stole this girl back from death once, but I'll not be offered the same chance twice.

My legs feel cold. My breasts. I stand naked, and behind me, the hunter stares.

"You there. Witch!" he shouts. "Witch!" Who is this man wearing Swedish colors in the middle of the Catholic camp?

No one comes to his aid.

A scout? Trying to figure out what has Von Werth's men on the run.

I turn my back on the man, listening to him fumble with his gun. Stripping the dead woman of her skirt, I pull a sodden shirt from a nearby line, keeping Elina as wolf in my line of sight. Maybe I can carry the beast into the heart of the forest. Maybe the stream will heal her.

I will not repeat my earlier mistake and steal life back from the earth. I waver. And the sun still rises.

Elina transforms the instant the sun touches her fur, and the hunter stumbles forward.

"It can't be. This must be a vision, sent to torture me. Cendrillon?" He says. The man's voice sounds softer this time. "Is that you, child?"

"Papa?" Elina lifts her head, something of the wolf still in her eyes. Her thigh bleeds freely.

"Why? How?"

I back away and dive into the nearest tent. Of all the soldiers, in all of Christendom, we've stumbled across the girl's absent father.

"How did this happen?" he asks. "Why are you here?"

Silence follows. I rip a sheet from the closest cot and then find a uniform in the closet, French, judging by the coat of arms on the shoulder, but the wool will warm the girl's bare skin.

I hear the sound of more powder being poured and the draw of the musket ramrod.

"Stop!" I shout and race back out the opening. Monsieur de Boer's arms shake as he draws the gun to his shoulder to shoot.

"No, Papa!" Elina still naked, tries to stand. "It's me. Your *Elina*. I am trying to protect the forest. That's all."

"You're the image of your mother," Monsieur de Boer coughs out. "And you're stained, just like her. Evil, like her. What you've done to these men is monstrous…"

I throw the sheet over Monsieur de Boer's head and face.

Elina's Papa beats the air from inside, trying to get free. His musket drops, and I kick it away.

The gunshot cracks so loud that I step backward, looking around to try to find its cause.

Elina's father drops, blood spreading across the sheet like ink on an unwritten page.

"NO!" Elina shouts. She still can't properly stand, so I fling the woolen greatcoat over her and pull her up.

"We must leave him here. Lean on me." We huddle our way behind a nearby tent, me still trying to find who made the killing shot.

Through the tents, a single soldier watches us flee. He makes the sign of the cross, a soldier of the Holy Roman Empire then, a sign that there's at least one survivor.

Elina sags onto me. Putting both arms out, I call the wind to carry us from the tents to the tree line and into the forest beyond. Once there, I wrap my arms around her cold, shivering form and keep us low. The shouts of the dying mar the landscape, but no one notices our retreat.

We find our cloaks on the forest path and rise in the half light of morning, Elina barely able to make the air obey her.

Keeping to the shadows, dark shapes cover the horizon as we angle back to the city, moving through the thin tree lines and against the shadows of farms and cottages. Below us, the Catholics flee toward open ground. Their panic takes them out of the forest's arms, but drives them toward the city.

What have we done?

CHAPTER SEVENTEEN

Of Trees and Rings

"Heal me," Elina demands. She lies on the thick brocade coverlet on her bed, stripped down again. It doesn't escape me that she's more comfortable naked since becoming a wolf.

How much about you did the Huntress change? I wonder.

"No," I argue. "I break the rules only when it's necessary. You won't die from the gunshot unless there's fever. Furthermore, we're back home, not in the forest, and I cannot draw life from the rugs and bedroom furniture."

"But it hurts," Elina whines and touches the bullet hole that still bleeds.

"And it will hurt yet more before I dig out the ball. Lie back now."

Outside, the sun cracks the morning open.

"Aaaaaaahhhhh!" She falls on the bed, panting, not much in pain because the opium does its job. Elina's pupils turn pinprick small, and her eyes stay unfocused as the minutes pass.

After another twenty minutes, the ball sits on the bloody sheet, and I still stand above Elina, holding a bottle of jenever with which to wash the wound. Elina grows quieter the longer the operation drags on, so I talk. I talk incessantly, trying to prevent the conversation from turning toward the topic I want, at all costs, to avoid.

But eventually I become engrossed in stitching her flesh back together and fall silent.

"My father died."

I nod. "Yes. As a soldier in the Swedish army, death was a possible outcome of employment."

"He almost killed me. *Me*, his own daughter." Her voice holds a kind of washed-out wonder.

"He's gone, mon coeur, and good riddance. He abandoned you long before today." The words escape me before I can stifle them.

"You didn't like him?" she asks.

"I didn't know him, God rest his soul. But I don't like that he left you to the likes of Madame de Boer and her ill-mannered daughters."

I tug the needle too sharply to cut the thread, and Elina winces. "Ow."

"Sorry." I focus on the task at hand. "Almost done."

"She was a witch, my maman."

The girl doesn't talk enough about her mother. "Do you remember her as such?" I ask.

"Yes. No. I don't know. Papa . . . seemed to think so."

"Often the talent traces a family tree, but sometimes a witch just appears as if conjured in a line where no magic existed before. Both are possible. Perhaps he just sought an excuse," I offer.

"To kill me?" She asks, matter-of-fact. "I doubt it. Papa told me once that he married Madame de Boer because she was exactly what she seemed to be."

"A bitch," I reply, trying not to jab the girl again.

"Marina," Elina scolds, but then stops herself. "No, you're right. She *is* terrible." She tries to roll, but her right arm suddenly seems to not work properly.

"Stay still."

Elina needs to cry, to scream, to come to pieces in my arms. Between the gunshot wound and the betrayal, I'm not sure what's worse. But the opium ensures she feels everything at a distance. The drug deadens the pain of the body and soul.

I probe the wound gently.

There's a knock on the door.

"We require no service," I call. "Elina is not well, and I take care of her." I slide a coverlet over the girl's half-naked form in case my enraged housekeeper bullies her way into the room with mulled wine and a posset of herbs.

"Marina, we need to talk," Kasimir calls through the door.

"Now?" I ask, annoyed. Hours have passed. It's late morning, judging by the light trickling past the thick curtains, and I still haven't gotten to sleep.

"Now," he confirms.

On the bed, Elina stays quiet. She drifts at the edge of unconsciousness.

I wash the wound with alcohol one more time, pull the bloody sheet out from under her, and half drag the girl fully under the covers, making sure Elina's head stays high enough that if she vomits, she will not choke.

"Coming!" I call and head to the door, swinging it open a foot's length.

"Really, Marina? I'm barred from a room in my own house?" Kasimir raises an eyebrow at me.

I step halfway through the door. "She's had enough opium to down a horse. I will not exploit her in a vulnerable moment."

"Go sit with the girl." Kasimir calls to a maid who must be near the bottom of the stairs.

Once I appoint the girl to her position and entreat her to watch carefully over her charge, I make my way back to my lover and take a closer look. Kasimir's unbound hair puffs out in a unkempt cloud. The lines at his eyes make dark grooves. He looks as exhausted as I feel.

"You spent the night carousing?"

"Gathering information," he corrects. "Your Margrave found me after you left. The insufferable man gave me an earful about how lax I am in my abilities as a chaperone. He was angry that little Elina was on his estate and being treated so poorly by Madame de Boer. Nearly shouted at me that she could've died."

"He insists that I hire another companion to watch over her. The man finds your supervision ill-advised, and after listening to all you've been up to, I nearly agree."

I frown.

Kasimir goes on. "He asked me to set up a meeting with you, *Madame Mullenheim you*, because he does not know that the two women are one and the same. He wants a formal introduction, insists on something proper. What if he recognizes you from the forest?"

"Deny the request," I turn to go back inside Elina's room.

"Yes, I thought that's what you'd want, so I told him that I'd sent the girl out of the city to a maiden aunt to rest and recuperate and that a meeting was impossible right now. I mentioned that I'm not offering a dowry for the daughter of a far distant cousin whom I barely know, even if my known lover, the Widow Mullenheim, sponsors the girl. Which only made me look like more of an ass."

I put my hands on my hips and wipe my hair back from my

forehead with still bloody hands. "That's not good. Now word will get around that the girl is penniless and her introductions in the city will not go as well."

"I'm not done. All my putting him off did nothing. He sends this." Kasimir hands me a blue satin box. There is a stamped signet upon the fabric that I instantly recognize.

"Oh no." I feel less tired by the second.

"Yes, exactly." Kasimir nods.

"You did not put him off at all."

"I tried, Marina, but the Margrave's intrigued by your apprentice. He sends this in apology for the literal trial she endured."

I can't catch my breath. The girl's father lies dead not even a day's length. Elina is lying on the bed with a bullet wound, and now: the gold band holds a single emerald framed by a pair of sparkling diamonds. Delicate and whimsical, such a piece suits a young lady perfectly.

"Beautiful." Kasimir approves.

I hold the ring up to the candlelight, watching it sparkle. "Every woman loses her mind over jewels as lovely as this . . . this . . . bribe, especially one who's been too poor to have enough to eat. No. It's too quick."

I slide the satin box into the pocket of my skirts.

"Marina," Kasimir warns.

"Don't use that tone with me," I snap. "I'm not a child, to be chided so. The girl is drugged right now anyway."

"You agreed to take Elina from her family because she's canny as a fox. She deserves to find her own destiny. You would want the same."

He's right, and I hate it that he's right. "Call a second maid up and have her check on Elina and her nurse every thirty minutes. I overdid the opium paste, and I want at least two pairs of eyes on her until tomorrow. Her wounds will hurt more then."

I head toward the stairs.

"And where do you go? You must sleep sometime."

I take the first stair before turning to call back. "The Catholics run toward us, not away."

Kasimir nods. "I heard as much, and Von Werth has not even arrived. The troops burning the forest are an opening salvo to draw the Duke into battle. How did your work there fare?"

"Later. I need to talk to Mab." I hurry down to the bottom landing.

Kasimir watches me, calling down. "You should mention to her one final thing, my love. The Duke and his circle are filling their coffers for battle. Württemberg encourages his friend, the Margrave von Helm, to marry straightaway to one of the city's brightest and best. They want gold and now. That might be more than enough to take your apprentice out of the running."

"Elina has no gold. You said as much."

"Yes, she resides out of the city with my maiden aunt, so there's no need to offer her a beautiful ring. And you go to Mab to talk of trees, of course. Not rings?" Kasimir asks after me.

I do not answer him.

The Hearth stands empty and dark as banked coals. Only a few witches wander through its main hall, and nary a one whom I know. I climb the stairs, knowing that Amondine will have made her report.

I consider what I can add; the old gods walk among us again. And myths may be proven true. News both more and less than I hoped to bring, for the forest may be safe now, but our attack barely stems the rising Catholic tide. And the message seems clear: the Holy Roman Empire kills everything alive to earn victory. They take resources from the backs of common laborers, food from the mouths of babes, and winter fast approaches.

Perhaps the Duke of Württemberg and Von Helm must fight back, anything to draw away the attention of the Duke of Lorraine and General von Werth.

At the top of the stairs, I don't knock, swinging the door open to find Mab sitting at her desk, drinking a cup of hot tea, a small, white-haired woman who looks like nothing so much as an ordinary grandmother.

"Marina!" she stands, back straight, drawing an air of strength around herself. "I expected you hours earlier."

"I got here as soon as I could."

"What's happened?" she asks, catching sight of my hands, not fully clean of Elina's blood.

"The girl was shot. I came straight here after seeing to her wound," I confess. I quickly corroborate Amondine's report of the Huntress and start with the story of our transformation.

"I knew something strange was going on?" Mab says, when I'm done. "But why does the goddess show herself now? And will she come again? A battle does not win a war."

"I don't know." I answer truthfully. "I made a silent prayer to the

Stillness, asking how I could help the wood, and then she was there."

"You've done so many times before?" she asks. "I've made prayers to one such as she and have never seen such a thing."

I nod. "No one has. Not in a hundred years or more. Could it be because of Elina? Could the girl have some power we do not" I ask the question we're both thinking.

A map spreads across Mab's desk. I see mountains and dark green triangles that mark the woods of Alsace. Someone's steady hand draws and redraws boundaries that shrink until the wild all but disappears, except for the Black Forest, and shapes move on the map too. Symbols that must mean something to Mab. The longer I look, the more I see.

"What is this?" I ask, trying to get a better glimpse. I've never seen such magic before. This must be how Mab knows so much.

"A gift," Mab says. "And yes, I'd guess it to be two hundred years old, if a day."

"So old," I breathe, wanting to touch the thing.

"It tells me only tragedy. The soldiers are gone, but they leave destruction behind." She taps a broad brown swath, marking where the soldiers left only mud and stumps behind. "The forest's magic is much weaker than it once was, even from my childhood. Soon it, and we, will be no more."

"The Stillness exists everywhere and nowhere," I contradict, reciting the words as they were first spoken to me.

"And the Leap is magic made manifest. The love of the wolf for the hare. The love of the bear for honey. The love of the trees for the earth, water, and air. From that love springs the five elements, the last is…"

"Aether, the most like its mother, the Stillness, which bears her hidden likeness," we say together.

"But what to do when the elements no longer have a home?" Mab asks, her voice so quiet I barely hear her. "I never liked the trees as you do, Marina but what will happen when they are all felled. What will the witches become?"

"This is why we keep the Hearth hidden," I breathe. "And the wild places untouched. So that we protect what others forget."

"It's my life's work to keep the witches and other women safe," Mab says. "Remember that, when I tell you what I know next."

"Württemberg plans to attack the Catholic army. He won't wait for Von Werth. He drafted as many men as possible from the city and will drive them down south toward the forest. He expects a rout, but when

Von Werth and his Catholics hide within the trees, the Duke will burn the forest down."

I answer. "Well, I've shaken Von Werth from the trees for now, but to no benefit. His men ride toward the city. Maybe bankruptcy will help us. Kasimir says your Duke needs money to keep up a fight."

"Yes, he's trying to force the unmarried nobles to marry."

The map could not show her that, I don't think. How does Mab get her information so quickly? I almost ask, but she interrupts my thought.

"I've found a bargain we should not refuse. The Landgrave Wiltstern is ready to marry again, and he's heard that Kasimir's niece is a great beauty. He's willing to take the girl without a dowry and settle a large sum to the war effort. As I mentioned, he owns a small portion of the forest. He swears to keep it safe. The Duke gets the funds that he needs, and Elina will be near the forest. Her magic will only grow stronger there."

"It's a good solution, Marina, for all of us."

I shake my head. "No. Elina is in no condition to be engaged. It will be a couple weeks before she can even walk without pain. The girl's father just tried to kill her. She needs time."

Mab raises an eyebrow at my speech. "We can announce the engagement now and plan a party in several weeks. Thaler can cross palms now, when it's needed."

"No, Mab. There's something else," I pause. I had resolved not to mention the ring, but I need to slow the spider's scheming. I pull the blue satin box out of my pocket and set it on the map.

"What is that?" she asks.

"I didn't have a choice, or at least I thought not. I had to do something, so I tied the girl to Kasimir when it looked like we might not get out of the trial, thinking the mention of nobility might slow the witch hunter's willingness to burn children. A slim chance, but I was grasping at nothing. Now that we're back, the Margrave von Helm sends an apology to my apprentice, named niece to Kasimir Leiningen-Leiningen. Obviously, he's taken with the girl. That's no simple 'I'm sorry.'"

Mab opens the case and draws a breath, staring at its sparkle and shine. "Did he recognize her from the forest?" she asks.

"Not yet." I don't have time to tell the full story now. "But any day, he will put the two together. I think the truth already lies at the edge of his mind."

Mab snaps the case shut. "Then we stick with the plan. Von Helm is a good match, but it's too risky, him knowing the truth of who and what Elina is."

My head starts to pound. It's been too long since I slept. "She's not ready for marriage, Mab. She's barely been out of the house. Never allowed to play or dance or meet any man."

"Most women are married by her age." Mab waves my words away.

"Most women have never been shot through with a musket ball," I counter. "Elina's life will never be that of most women. She deserves to decide her own fate."

"Let her make the choice then. Give her the ring and tell her of the Margrave's offer and see which way she goes. Von Helm owns more of the forest than the Landgrave, and he can afford to put money into the Duke's coffers, if he chooses."

I take my leave, refusing to argue. I want nothing but the best for my apprentice. I will have to buy some time.

It's past noon when Kasimir's manservant lets me back into the house; I climb the stairs immediately to Elina's chamber and knock on the door.

"Come in," a soft voice says.

The room is dark inside, the curtains drawn. A single candle burns on the nearby table.

"Close the door!" Elina commands. She crawls to sitting, her face flushed. "Quickly now. The light hurts my eyes."

I pull up a chair beside the bed.

"I'm so cold, Marina. And the bullet wound pulses with pain. I can scarce breathe."

"What has she had to eat?" I ask the maid, Bernice.

"Nothing, madame. She says she's not hungry. I forced her to drink water. I added two blankets. But it didn't seem to help. Nothing seems to help."

Bernice wrinkles her brows as she looks at Elina and pats the coverlet kindly. She's a sweet girl, just a bit older than my apprentice, so she doesn't recognize the signs of opium withdrawal.

"Fever?" I ask.

Elina ignores us both as we talk. Her fingers gather the coverlet and worry the raised brocade on its surface. Occasionally, she scratches her right arm, which rests unnaturally still. It's the only part of her that doesn't fidget.

"No Madame. I am worried, but so far, she's safe."

"We will check the bandage again tonight, but you may go to bed, my dear. I'll stay with Elina."

"Are you sure, Madame?" Bernice asks.

"Yes."

Bernice excuses herself.

"My father never loved me," Elina says, as the door shuts closed. "Not after my mother died."

I turn back, surprised. Tears track her dirty cheeks. With her honey blonde hair still curled by sweat and a bit of dirt or blood, Elina looks like the orphan she now is.

"You don't know that, and the sadness you feel is not totally your own. The drug drags your spirits low."

"Is that why I feel so wrong? Why my arm won't lift? Do you think the Huntress did this to me? That she's unhappy with me?"

"I think the Huntress cares not for any of us," I answer. "Not really. Not in the way we care for one another. It's more likely from the battle. Did you hurt your paw fighting? When you were a wolf?"

"No," Elina shakes her head. "I felt so good as a wolf, Marina. Free to follow my instincts. Free to run. Free to bite. To kill."

I let that statement alone.

"Let me inspect it." I draw Elina's arm carefully from the gown.

"Ow, zounds, it burns right here," she says, and barely touches her shoulder. "And here." At the elbow.

I run my hands along, looking for any wounds or scratches, but the skin is unmarked, not swollen or hot. Then I feel more deeply for the bones underneath, carefully, as Elina whimpers. Everything appears to be in place.

"Let's wait until tomorrow morning," I say, stumped. "I will inspect it again in the daylight then, when I can see more than feel."

"I can't sleep," Elina says. "I hurt too much."

"I know. It's the drug. It's wearing off. I can give you a bit more. But tomorrow you will feel worse."

"No. It's no worse than living with my stepmother. I just wish…" She starts to cry again.

"What?"

"My mother's silk slippers. I hid them under the floorboard in my room. I forgot to tell you when you got my things. I have nothing else left of her. I don't even want the doll my father got me. Not now." She drifts off into silence.

I can think of no reason to go back to the de Boer home until I remember that Madame de Boer doesn't know that her husband lies dead a hundred miles south. The army rarely reports to families quickly, if at all.

I could make a call on the morrow and give her the news, secretly collect the slippers, and return by afternoon.

"Sing to me, Marina. Make me forget how I feel." Elina turns her face toward me, weeping again.

I slip onto the bed beside her and gather the girl in my arms, careful of her shoulder and elbow. She's still so thin, barely a maiden. What can Mab be thinking, to sell her off before Elina even has time to recover? Will a bit of forest even be enough to protect our magic?

Maybe the sea witch had the right of it. Maybe we witches are meant to die just as the mermaids do. I'm so sick of fighting the fate of the world.

Elina leans into the hollow of my shoulder, and I stroke her matted hair back from her face and sing a song my mother sang to me.

"Mes amis que reste-t-il" *My friends, what's left? What's left for the kind-hearted Dauphin?*

CHAPTER EIGHTEEN

Bound by Love

I stumble to my own bed at nearly eight o'clock that night and sleep until the early morning, when I wake to Kasimir's fingers curled around the soft part of my stomach, the hard length of him against my back. I twist and sigh and seek the necessary before climbing back in bed to savor his warmth.

"*Bonjour, mon petite chou,*" he whispers in my ear.

"Bonjour," I whisper back.

"Did she sleep?" Kasimir asks, kissing my neck and tugging me so close that our two bodies become one tangled mass of bone and muscle, hardness and soft skin.

"At six bells this morning, briefly, and even then not well. We sponged her with alcohol though and changed the sheets again. I left her listening to Bernice sing. I hope the poor girl got a chance to sleep. We should get her a new dress and give her time off to visit her mother, for all this work."

Past the brocaded shadow and fringe of the curtains, the sun shines on a new day. The floor and walls of the room lay crisscrossed by bars of shadow and light. In the shadow on my dresser sits the blue satin box, untouched.

I huff and push against Kasimir.

"Hmmmm." I feel rather than see his smile. He kneads my shoulders and back, squeezing and rolling everywhere that aches. "I think it's time to give you a bit of pleasure for every drop of pain."

"I'm too tired," It's true, but already I feel a pulse of heat between my legs.

"Then let me do all the work," Kasimir whispers, rolling me onto my back. He kisses my mouth and then along my neck.

"There," I say, letting the pleasure tighten into pinpoint pricks as he kneads and kisses and licks. "Yes."

Kasimir runs his hands along the seam of my legs and then back up to cup my waist.

I try to pull him on top of me, but he resists, kissing downward to the soft places on my stomach and then lower.

I send a long breath out, as little shocks play outward from my core. Slowly, slowly, my fatigue falls away as excitement breathes new life into my bruised body. He whispers occasionally against my thighs, and kisses and licks, until finally I cry out in pleasure.

"Up," I say, tugging him over me so we can move together in rhythm. It is not long before he urges me into another peak of pleasure. The next moment, he meets me. Then we are both trying to stay quiet in the morning stillness.

Afterward, I nod and tug him back up and arms around me, where he bites my neck, making me shiver. "I could sleep if I were still for more than a few moments, but I should check on Elina." I move toward the edge of the bed.

"In a moment…" Kasimir runs his fingers lightly along the inside of my arm and around my shoulder and neck. "Just wait a moment here with me." Twined together as two trees, I fall back asleep.

It's nearly the afternoon when I wake again, to the sound of someone moving around the room. Kasimir is up and dressed, rifling through items on the nearby dresser, with the look of a man who's been doing errands.

I sit up, stressed that it's so late. "How's Elina? Does her wound need to be dressed again. Is there fever?"

Kasimir comes over to sit on the bed. "Relax. She's been seen to. And still no fever. Not yet. Now tell me, since you could not last night, how fares the forest?"

"Elina and I emptied the camp, but I do not think that's the last of their forces."

"I've heard nothing about two witches," Kasimir teases. "The scouts send rumors of wolves the size of two men."

"Women. Two women," I correct.

Kasimir's face carefully goes blank and a little pale. "No. How?"

"Magic, darling. What do you think I do when I'm away?"

"I didn't know your power extended to *this*. So that's where Elina's bullet wound came from? Were you injured too?" Kasimir pulls back further to look me over. He checks my arms and torso, letting his clever hands linger in my soft places. "It was truly you?"

"We had help," I admit. "You would not believe me if I told you." I push mention of the Huntress away because she doesn't belong here, tucked into a soft bed in the heart of one of the most civilized cities in Europe.

Kasimir still chews on the information. "Those men had lives, Marina. Children. *Wives.*"

"And if the forest burns to the ground, then those children will have no food. No shelter. I know you can't understand, Kasimir, but try to see it from my perspective." I sit up and frown.

"No. You've done nothing good, in killing those men. As you said, if anything you push the front closer to the city. If the troops can't stay there, where will they go?"

"Ah!" I rise and pull on a clean linen shift from my drawer. "I tried watering them out of the weeds, and that didn't work. At this point, I don't know what will work. It's been more than twenty years and still your noblemen fight. Over what? Ideas. And power. But no chick crawls back into the egg. Will it take another hundred years for them to admit that Catholics die as well as Huguenots. And witches bleed the same red as both."

"Was this your plan all along? What does Mab say?" Kasimir asks, trading places with me as he lies back on the bed and watches me dress.

"It was not," I admit. "She says that we cannot count on the goddess to save us. She knew nearly as much as you and more. She has an offer of marriage for Elina's hand from the Landgrave Wiltstern. As if the girl is ready to marry! We argued, and I told her of the ring. She said to leave the decision to Elina then."

Kasimir raises an eyebrow. "Well, if both of us believe that to be the right choice?"

"False hope is no hope. I know who the girl will choose, if given the choice, but when Von Helm figures out that the nearly dead ragamuffin, the pretty servant Cendrillon from the witch hunt, and Elina Lerner are all one and the same, he will change his mind. Worse, if he knows of her true power, then he'll send Elina to the witch hunter himself."

"He may never make the connection," Kasimir confides. "I would never know all you are up to, if you didn't tell me. Now I'm not sure I want to know more."

I let that last statement alone, even though a part of me howls to touch it. "Elina is injured. She deserves a space between living in a home in which she's treated as less than a servant, owned by the lady of the house, and belonging to the man whom she marries. There's no going back to the freedom you have when you belong only to yourself."

Outside our bedchamber, I'd be burned alive for such a thought.

"So is that what's between us? Is that why you keep me at arm's length even when I am buried deep inside you?" Kasimir asks, his tone deceptively calm. "Your freedom?"

I can't answer him, suddenly struck with a clawing feeling in my throat. I walk toward the window and try to breathe. I did not mean to say so much out loud.

"*Everyone* is bound to something or someone, Marina. No one knows that better than me, brown-skinned in a city of white men, half-brother to a nobleman, respected but not noble myself. My world is ruled by the aristocracy, whom I must serve if I even want a place at the table. Only my leash sits much tighter than yours." His words are laced with anger and pride.

Turning away from the blinding light, I finally focus on Kasimir's features, the broad cheeks he inherited from his Moorish mother, his full, sensual mouth, and the hard line of his jaw.

"So I choose to tie myself to those I love and who love me in return. And I put my somewhat considerable influence toward keeping those safe who would not otherwise be safe. And cannot marriage be that? Can marriage not be a shared journey? With both parties seeking to be bound only by love?"

I hear the word *bound*, as if it echoes through the room.

Kasimir waits.

A knock on the door stops me from answering.

"Yes?" I call, clearing my throat.

"Can I come in?" Elina's voice sounds tired, even through the wood, and almost certain of rejection.

Kasimir rubs his hands over his face and takes a deep breath. "We're not done with this conversation." Then he straightens and pulls his linen shirt back into place. He nods when he's ready.

"Entrée!" I call.

Cendrillon opens the door carefully, using her right arm and cradling her left against her belly. She wears the soft blue woolen dress but no ruff and no collar. The dress is more shapeless without a corset. I'm not sure how she manages to move her hip.

"No fever then?" I try to joke, but she's in such obvious pain that the statement falls flat. "Come lie on the covers, near Kasimir. It hurts just to watch you move."

Kasimir plumps the pillows beside him and pats the coverlet.

I help the girl to our bed, ignoring all rules of propriety. Elina is family now.

Pack the wolf in my head growls.

"I'm sorry about your wound," Kasimir puts in helpfully. Once Elina settles, he reaches close and pulls her into a careful side hug. "Marina told me you were cavorting in the forest. Terrorizing men," he teases.

"I can still taste their blood," Cendrillon replies quietly, tears tracking her quiet, devastated face. The bleakness that the opium left behind still burns in her eyes.

To his credit, Kasimir keeps his arm around the girl. "Many men kill from anger or pleasure at having power over another. But there's no sin in defending a person—or place—that's unable to defend itself. Animals live by a different code. Simpler. More pure."

He whispers into her hair. "Do not let your heart hang heavy, *Cendrillon*. Remember your new name. Elina Lerner, you are a torch. You are a warrior."

Elina cries harder and leans into Kasimir's shoulder.

When her sobs slow, Kasimir reaches to the bedside table and hands her a small, embroidered handkerchief with which to wipe her eyes.

I let out a breath I didn't know I was holding. In moments, my lover turns the girl's guilt and fear into something she's able to bear. I walk to my dresser and pretend to apply oil to my face and hands, wiping away my tears.

"Now, let me look at that arm," I say, once the tears pass, and bustle over to feel along its length. "Did Bernice check it again?"

"Yes. She inspected me." Elina frowns. "She found nothing."

Under my fingers, the bones feel right. They sit correctly in the sockets. Nothing appears out of place.

"It hurts though?"

"It burns," Elina says.

"Here?" I touch her shoulder joint.

She nods.

"And here?" At the elbow.

I stretch my witch's awareness toward her body, but I sense nothing so much as tightness. The life force stops there or is bound up, I can't tell which. Maybe the Huntress did leave behind a secret wound?

No, it doesn't make sense.

Maybe the change, from woman to wolf and back again, triggered some kind of sprain?

"Let's bind it up so you don't have to hold the arm in place." I move over to my wardrobe and pull out a long silk scarf, dyed a light blue. I bind the arm into a sling and tie it off in an elegant knot at the back of her neck.

The light continues to shift. It no longer shines on the bed, catching the edge of my dresser. A ray of sunshine highlights the items that lay there.

"What is that?" Elina behind me.

"What?" I pretend not to know what she asks.

"That box. The blue one."

Kasimir covers his smile. I glare at him, but he shrugs, eyes crinkling, as if to say *I had nothing to do with this.*

"What?!" Elina cries out, noticing his gesture.

"Funny you should ask." I walk over to the dresser and pick up the box. In my fingers, it's warm, almost hot to the touch. I turn back to Elina, watching her face, now more relaxed, tucked as she is against Kasimir's shoulder. "It's a gift. For you."

"From you?" Elina sits up straighter, pulling away from Kasimir and tucking the handkerchief in her pocket.

I want to lie to her. If Kasimir were not here, I might. I can almost feel the strands of fate weaving me into this moment, with this decision to make. But my sins are already too numerous to count.

I sigh. "No," I shake my head. "It's a gift from the Margrave von Helm."

Elina's mouth breaks into a full smile. Her green eyes, before dull from pain, sparkle and begin to shine. "He sent something for me."

"Something very special," I nod. I put the box into her hands.

She opens it slowly, pulling the ribbons away and lifting the lid as if she is afraid to see what is inside.

"A ring!" Her face reflects the brilliance of the gems. "But this is not a gift for a servant."

"No," Kasimir says. "It's a gift for a lady. A lady whom you admire."

Elina slides the ring over her finger, and I swear the band fits her small, delicate hand perfectly.

"It's too fine for me," she says.

"It suits you perfectly."

"There's a note," Elina says, pulling at a slip of paper I hadn't noticed. The thin stock unravels from below the ring's setting

"Le cœur a ses raisons que la raison ne connaît pas."

"The heart has its reasons, of which reason knows nothing," Kasimir reads over her shoulder. "I am sorry, Mademoiselle, for all your suffering. I know not the reason, but I hope you heal from it."

Elina sighs, and there's a world of motion in the sound.

I roll my eyes. "Yes, yes, it's beautiful. But you must focus on your knotwork today, my girl, rather than fanciful gifts. Even if you feel poorly, you must master the smaller spells of our trade. We should review moon summonings too, as that came into play in the forest."

"Yes, Mistress." Elina says dutifully, but her eyes don't leave the ring.

CHAPTER NINETEEN

The Widow

Another day passes before I can make my way to the de Boer household. On the street, I walk near a pair of Venetian priests, dressed in black cassocks despite the sun, and a group of merchants recently arrived from Bavaria, road weary and travel-worn. A few shops down, a regiment of soldiers, fresh from some skirmish, lounges outside a tavern, drinking beer and heckling passers-by. One of them wears his dark-hair back in a queue and has a familiar scar over his right eye, Stefan, from the countryside.

I turn away, but before I can bolt, the soldier somehow notices me. "Hey! Madame!" I hear the man call behind me. "You're familiar to me. Where are you from?" I ignore the call and pray that he won't put my face to the scene in the field, the near rape, and most importantly, our escape by flight.

He follows. *Christ's wounds.*

I take the next left and slip into a chandler's shop, watching as Stefan and now Klaus, the same blond from before, search the street outside. Once they return in the direction from whence they came, I exit the shop, one pair of beeswax candles richer, and turn south, keeping the hood of my cloak up until the city grows quieter.

Finally the de Boer house rises before me, its white and half-timbered exterior looking like nothing so much as iced gingerbread, disarmingly sweet. I make my way to the front door, not the servants entrance, and the wooden slab opens before I even have a chance to knock.

"We aren't taking visitors today." Cook answers the door, belying any sort of propriety. She wrings her hands, not looking at me and wearing something more sackcloth than dress. "Madame de Boer's not well, and the rest of us are busy."

Does she answer doors because Elina is no longer here to do it?

"She'd better be well enough to see me. I have news of her husband. You may tell her that the Widow Mullenheim is here." I barge my way past Cook's bent back, nervous that she will recognize me. I've worn a lovely blue merino today with a silk stomacher embroidered in doves, and a mildly starched lace ruff, so that the servants here understand me to be a woman of consequence. I alter the aether a bit, so that I look more beautiful than I truly am.

"And what news do you bring?" Cook asks, hands on her wide hips, searching my face, her tone respectful to a stranger.

"None for your ears. I will tell your Mistress of your impertinence though." I swing through the room with my wide skirts, heading back toward the kitchen now, with no further need to dissemble. "Shouldn't you offer me something to drink? Beer? A small glass of wine?"

Cook follows. "I've naught to offer you, Madame. Mistress can't stand the smell of food these days. We're serving cold meats and fruit for dinner tonight."

"Is she sick or pregnant?" I ask, waving away a meager crabapple Cook weakly brandishes in my direction.

"Don't see how the second 'twere possible. The Master's been gone for months now." The words escape Cook before she thinks better of them, and taken aback, I wonder how subtle the woman is. Does Cook hint that Madame takes lovers? Or does she truly mean that the woman can't be pregnant?

"What of her daughters? Where are those sweet girls?" I ask, avoiding the topic of lovers entirely. After meeting the late Monsieur de Boer, I can understand why Madame might stray to another, more caring bed, and I don't want to know anything that may make me like the damn woman more.

"Ava and Elisabet?" Cook's tone conveys all that it needs to. "Those two eat bonbons and talk of nothing more than eligible men in the city. Elisabet is of the age to marry, and Ava too, if the rules are stretched a bit, as they might be when war threatens. Both girls desperately want to be out from under their mother's thumb."

"I wanted the same at their age," I admit, trying to ignore the word war, as it echoes in my ears. I close my eyes against the memory of men falling to their feet, throats torn out and bloody.

"Normally Madame squires them around the city meeting young men, but recently, the lady's health declines. She pays no attention to those girls, even when they are behaving badly." This last part Cook whispers and looks to the hallway to make sure no other servants linger nearby.

"What do you mean?" I lean closer, playing the part of a gossiping lady.

"They whisper among themselves as if they are sharing secrets all the time. Then Ava asked me for foxglove seed, not something I ordinarily gather from the market, and soon after the request, Madame's health began to decline." Cook's wringing her hands again and watching the door and hallway nervously. She worries enough to tell a stranger, mostly because she doesn't know what to do if her suspicions are correct.

This situation plays out across Alsace a thousand times. A family member falls sick, or the crops fail, and without explanation, servants or neighbors begin to suspect that witchcraft is at play.

"I will talk to the girls," I promise. "As soon as Madame and I finish our tête-à-tête. I will make certain those girls make no more mischief in the house."

"Thanks be to God," Cook intones and crosses herself. "It's hard for the girls without a good father in the house. And Monsieur has been gone so long. He left soon after the wedding, and well, he mourns Cendrillon–his first daughter's–mother. She was so different than Madame de Boer."

"I have not met this girl," I lie.

"She were kind. Too kind for this world. But if Monsieur de Boer were here, he would set them girls right. After all, he did so well with Cendrillon."

I say nothing, not wanting to remind the woman that I have no power to exert over the daughters de Boer. That really I have no right to be here at all.

"Is Madame de Boer abed. Is there something I may bring the lady to settle her stomach?" I ask. I pat my pockets and pull out a candy cane I bought earlier at the bakery, intending to bring the sweet home to my apprentice. "Perhaps this? It's a new confection, made from mint and sugar."

"If a bit of sweet helps to settle Madame, I'll buy a hundred more," Cook puts in bluntly. "I'll send you up to bring her cheer. Wait while I make some mulled wine. 'Tis past time for Madame to be out of bed."

I feel a thread of unease. Madame de Boer must be ill if the order of the house falls apart so easily. But I nod and ask Cook to pour a small glass of beer to quench my thirst. Inspired by having a guest, Cook lights a fire under the hearth, and soon the room is filled with the aroma of ginger, cardamom, and grains of heaven.

A half hour later, tray in hand, I climb the stairs, noting the smudged, small windows that line the stairwell. From the outside, the building looks in good repair, but here, the walls show grimy with woodsmoke and cobwebs. I draw a nearby curtain back and release a cloud of dust.

"Blech," I cough, keeping the drink free of dirt, and follow the directions Cook gave me to Madame's bedchamber, right of Cendrillon's closet on the next floor.

At the door, I knock twice, awaiting a response, but when there is none, I walk through anyway.

The de Boer bedroom is big enough for two families, with enough light coming through the windows to read by. At the far wall, a four-post bed, and tucked inside, the woman whom I seek.

Madame's sallow face lays against her linen pillowcase, white and peaked. This is not a mere stomach upset. The lady may be struck with influenza or worse, plague. I fall back and search my pockets for a handkerchief, wrapping it around my mouth before I enter the room.

"Madame," I call, keeping my tone light. "It is Madame Mullenheim, a friend of your husband's. I've come to visit you with news of your beloved stepdaughter, and Cook sent me upstairs with your daily posset to rouse you from your illness."

Madame de Boer's dull eyes turn to take me in, and in seconds, I see to my surprise that she recognizes me. "You're here to gloat," she says and takes in my clothes. "And dressed much nicer than before."

"Non, Madame," I take the woman's hand. I can't help myself. I'm about to tell the Mistress de Boer that she's without a husband. Hopefully Elina's father saw fit to bequeath the house and its grounds to his second wife, otherwise all three women and the servants besides will be out on the street. "But I do have a bit of bad news."

"You can tell me nothing more terrible than what I already know. My chest is wracked with heat, and I cannot breathe properly. While I'm sick, my daughters languish, as I'm unable to do the work that a good mother must do in finding them husbands." Madame de Boer turns her face away from me to cough. She wears a muslin nightgown with a fraying robe wrapped tightly at her waist.

"And are you not curious about Cendrillon?" I cannot help but goad.

"Don't you mean *Elina Lerner*? My daughters told me what you said at the party. I don't know how she's done it, but be careful before she betrays you too. That girl is a stray dog. No child of mine, and I don't concern myself with her whereabouts."

"Elina Lerner is the true daughter of Monsieur de Boer," I insist, moving to firmer ground. Madame de Boer may be sick, but if she insists on being a selfish bitch, then I'll respond in kind.

I take in the broad, well-appointed room, nothing so fine as Kasimir's townhouse but big, spacious, and well decorated. The curtains hang lined with gray cloth. A dress lies, unworn, on a nearby chaise in a similar shade of gray, and Madame de Boer's red face looks strained and tight, her eyes swollen.

"You know," I say simply, realizing the truth. "You know that your husband lies dead."

"That beautiful, generous man is gone, and without him, I am nothing." Madame de Boer covers her face with her hands and weeps openly. "I felt it the instant he was gone."

My jaw drops. I did not know Madame had the capacity to love so much within her small, clenched heart.

I pat the woman's arm, and stare at the ceiling while she cries. It's two times too many that I've listened to women mourn the loss of a man so ill-equipped to be a father and husband. What did Monsieur de Boer do besides make money?

But I suppose some men don't even do that.

"Here," I say, moving away from the bed. "I've brought you something up from Cook. She swears that it will help you heal." I bring the mug of warm, mulled wine to Madame's elbow.

Madame de Boer struggles to sitting and takes the earthenware cup between her hands. She sips quietly, tears still running down her face.

"How did you find out?" I ask.

"A soldier, conscripted into the same army came to tell me. My love died in a camp outside of the Black Forest, shot by one of Johann von Werth's men. He was buried in a mass grave there."

This last brings a fresh round of tears.

"It is wonderful that they let you know where he's buried." I amend. "But what I want to know is how did a Strasbourg merchant come to be fighting for Sweden?"

"He was born in a village outside of Halmstaad. Always dreamed of returning home," Madame de Boer says. Perhaps the posset does some good, because she sips again and turns toward me, her eyes finally curious and sly. "How did *you* know he died?"

I stick as close to the truth as I am able. "Kasimir, half-brother to Count Leiningen-Leiningen fights alongside the Duke of Württemberg. He saw a list of dead from the battle and recognized the surname, de Boer."

"And how?" she asks, but I cut her off.

"Kasimir, my beau, knows of my devotion to Elina. His late mother and I were good friends. After learning of your family's ill fortune, he adopts her into his family. She will never return here. After the treatment she received at your hands, he forbids it."

Madame de Boer flings herself back on her pillow. "Your *beau*," she repeats, doubtfully. "A near noble adopts that. . .that. . ."

"Darling girl," I fill in the empty space. "My husband, Stettmeister Mullenheim, died more than five years ago. Enough time has passed to consider a new love. And Kasimir knows what the girl's adoption means to me, and to Elina. With her father dead, there's no one else to care for her."

I let that barb sink in. "Monsieur sponsors her entry into Strasbourg's finest circles. Through him, Elina is sure to land a powerful husband."

Madame de Boer's chin moves up and down as she gulps in air. She looks at me, measuring my fine clothes. "Maybe you don't know," she finally says. "The girl's mother was a witch."

"Don't start making up stories," I scold and bare my teeth to let Madame know I mean it. "The girl's squarely under Monsieur Kasimir's protection. I just came to tell you about your husband's death to be kind."

"At the age of seven, that little monster could command the broom to sweep and light a fire in the hearth by snapping her fingers. She kept my Elisabet and Ava tame. She coaxes vegetables to grow, in the heart of winter! And now you steal her from me. The house is filthy. My girls openly revolt. It will take five servants to replace her! And now . . . this?"

"Surely, you jest. You were prepared to let her die an unjust death, so just continue to act as though she's dead to you." At least that last part is partly true. "It won't be that hard."

"You expect me to stand by while that girl rises even as my *petites étoiles* falter. She's a witch, and witches, if not kept in their place, should burn. I will report her to the new Stettmeister." Madame scoots forward and swings her feet to the side of the bed.

"I will warn Kasimir and his close circle about your penchant for lying. Grief truly makes fools of us all."

"You bitch," she shouts, standing.

"Madame, you're not at all retiring as Cook said," I scold, smiling and pretending goodwill. "You must stay in bed and recover. Your daughters need you."

I'm satisfied that whatever ails Madame, she'll survive, if only because she's mean-spirited enough to do so. And I've done my duty in making certain she knows of her husband's fate. I predict that in a week, the merchant's widow will be sashaying around the house ordering her servants to meet her every demand, and Cook will curse my name.

"Don't presume to tell me how to master my own house," Madame de Boer glowers, looking a bit like the sallow harpy I remember. She sits back down, as if surprised that she'd gotten out of bed.

"Drink more wine. There's a peppermint stick on the saucer. It may settle your bilious stomach. Now I will say goodbye to Elisabet and Ava. I'm sure they remember me from the Widow's salon."

Madame de Boer lays back down and turns toward the far side of the room, giving me her shoulder.

So the girls did not tell their mother everything. "Perhaps Kasimir knows men who might be good matches for your girls." I dangle the opportunity before her like another peppermint stick. "I would like to see Elina's half-sisters settled."

Madame de Boer doesn't answer, but I'm sure that such a possibility buys her silence, at least for a time.

CHAPTER TWENTY

A Dangerous Spell

I creep into Elina's closet next, finding her slippers under the floorboard as she said. Tucking them deep inside the pocket of my cloak, I head for the third room. The stepsisters' door stands wide open. The young women are nowhere to be found.

I steal inside, immediately seeing why Madame de Boer misses Elina. Her daughters fling clothes about the space with no care for their keeping. Unfinished plates of fruit gather flies. A small hoop of needlepoint lies on its side unfinished, and a basket of yarn spills across the carpet.

Near the cooling fireplace, I spy a small book I don't recognize and beside it what at first appears to be a very dirty doll.

The girls are too old for such toys, so I go to inspect and learn which of the two hoydens is so sentimental that she keeps the soft things of childhood close.

Upon inspection, a thread of panic curls into my stomach.

The little figure is sewn of linen and, judging by the pretty scent, stuffed with walnut shells and lavender. She wears a dress made from the harsh woolen fabric many servants wear. Most of her hair is sewn from handspun yellow thread, but I notice amidst the thread, actual human hair is woven. And the figure's face and arms have been marked by cinders.

Someone makes a poppet of Elina.

I pick up the doll carefully but drop it immediately. "Ow!"

A bead of red blossoms on my finger.

I touch the poppet more gingerly this time and find pins crudely lodged in the doll's shoulders and elbows.

For a moment, I cannot breathe. I hear only the crackling sound of the fire in the hearth dying.

A little flame leaps from the fireplace onto a nearby rug, and a thin stream of smoke rises.

Should I let the whole lot of vipers burn?

I weigh the possibility a long moment before stamping out flames.

The outdoor hall echoes with sound. Both girls climb the stairs, giggling to themselves. I slip the poppet into my pocket, careful to turn the pins sideways and prop myself up on the edge of the bed.

Ava flings the door open, her dark hair wildly swinging, but she makes a full stop once she catches sight of me.

"How did you get here?"

Elisabet follows behind her. "Get out!" As the eldest, she feels entitled to lead, but she stays near the door, probably remembering the last time we met.

"I brought a posset and peppermint sticks to your mother. She needs care. As you know, she isn't well."

The girls pause, considering why I might do something so kind.

"You care nothing for our mother. Why are you really here?" This again from Elisabet. Her pretty face mottles with anger.

"I need not answer your questions," I respond. "As I have questions of my own. Your mother's lethargy, her confusion, are symptoms of foxglove poisoning, an herb which Ava asked Cook to buy last week. You've been stupid, both of you. Playing at witchcraft. Do you know how dangerous such a thing is? And not just to your mother, but to yourselves?"

Elisabet turns toward Ava, her brow drawn. "What is she talking about?"

"She lies," Ava says, flinging herself on the nearby bed, but her cheeks look more flushed than before. "Don't trust anything she says."

"You told me that you were bringing mother medicine." Elisabet said. "You told me the tea would help her to feel better."

"I wasn't trying to poison her. I wanted her to rest. Elisabet, it would be better if we could attend events together, without Maman. You know it would. She's so demanding. And now she cries all the time. She's no use to us."

"But witchcraft," Elisabet says the word with pure hatred.

"No," Ava says, her face flushing red. "Herbs I gathered from Cook."

The insinuation is so subtle. *Not my fault,* Ava's words hint. Cook is behind all this.

I know which girl made the poppet now.

"I'm sure Ava didn't know the harm she caused. And I've instructed Cook not to get any foreign herbs or plants from the market for the time being. And now that Ava knows, the problem stops. Right, Ava?"

Ava nods.

"I must be on my way." I stand. "But I will return in a week's time to check on all of you. Ava, will you help me down to the kitchens?"

Elisabet's eyes turn to slits, but she doesn't fight the request. I see in the pinch around her mouth—she's afraid of me. Good. I will take what I can get.

Ava edges her way toward the fireplace, putting the yarn back into its basket and the needlepoint inside too. If I didn't know what she was looking for, I would see nothing more than what she intends, a young woman tidying her room.

Her movements become more panicked, as she doesn't find the poppet.

Outside in the stairwell, I grab Madame de Boer's youngest daughter by the arm and march her to the bottom of the stairs. Cook bustles over to me but turns bodily away when she realizes who I have in tow.

"Excuse us, please," I call, propelling Ava through the kitchen and out the servants' door. "The young Mademoiselle and I have something to discuss."

Outside, Ava jerks away and shouts, "Release me at once, you crazy bitch."

"If you shout nasty words at me again, I will take this poppet up to your mother and tell her the extent of the *witchcraft* her daughter attempts. Or maybe I will skip Madame de Boer and walk down to the Cathedral to report a suspected witch to the priest on duty there."

Ava opens her mouth and then closes it again. "I will tell him you are a witch too."

"Oh will you now? Well, I'm protected by a nobleman's name. Are you? No. Now, not another word until we're much further from the house. To the burn pile."

Ava turns without a word and heads in the direction I ask.

Once there, she turns and squats, using a stick to dig at the damp soil. I try not to notice how the sun turns her face into that of a child.

"Do you have any mastery over the elements, girl?" I keep my voice gruff.

"What's that mean?"

The answer brings me relief. The girls don't understand Elina's power, even if their mother does.

I grab a nearby log, cut to the right length, and drop a few more twigs on top of it. "Light it," I order.

The girl frowns in confusion. "I brought nothing to strike a flame. That's Johann's job."

"Well then, if you can't do that, show me your other powers," I coax. "Can you raise the wind? Can you summon rain?"

"I can't do any of those things. I don't have any powers," Ava admits, chewing on her nail and rocking back on her haunches. "And I've not met Satan yet, though I tried to summon him." She whispers this last.

"Oh ho. Do not tell me any of this! I don't want to hear it. I'm not your priest, here to take your confession, girl."

"What is so special about her?" Ava asks, her cracked voice betraying the depth of emotion. She puts her hands on her waist. "Maman hates Cendrillon. We all hate Cendrillon. And then you took her from us, so Maman should be happy, but she cries all day. She cried even more when she learned that Cendrillon was at Madame Zorn's salon, wearing dresses finer than any we own."

"Child." I make my voice kind. "Your mother doesn't mourn your half-sister, though she should, and she knows that you are special too. Don't worry. You will make your own way."

"I know I am special," Ava sneers, her pretty mouth twisting. "Half-sister! Hah! No blood binds us. Maman always said Cendrillon was not worth the leather of our shoes. I made her kiss my shoes once, just to remind her of how worthless she was. Return her, you old bitch. Return her, or I will make her regret that she tries to rise above her station."

I can barely keep myself from stealing the air from Ava's chest and watching her gasp a last breath. *She's a child,* I remind myself. Children *learn* to hate. They're not born with hatred in their hearts.

"This may surprise you, Ava, but every person, even women, even poor women, are children of God. In the Wheel of Fortune, some are born into a lowly station, and they serve the powerful or maybe the not so powerful. But regardless of their station, every person deserves to be treated with kindness."

I pause. "Elina is not one of those women born on the sad side of

Fortune's circle. Elina was born wealthier than you, and to a family where she was loved and spoiled."

"And then the Wheel turned. Her family fell upon misfortune. Her mother died. Her father remarried and stayed home less and less. And your mother arrived, in the middle of Elina's story, and as you might imagine, everything changed, even her name. Elina, who was once given her every desire, became a servant in her own home, known only as Cendrillon, little ash."

"God rewards those he loves most," Ava spit out. "He punishes those who fail him."

"Is that why you needed the poppet?" I ask, catching her eye. "To fulfill God's will? Isn't witchcraft the work of the Devil?"

Ava's face turns red, and she swings to stare at the house, giving me her back, just as her mother did a few moments ago.

"Witchcraft may or may not be the Devil's work. I've never met Satan, and I'm not a priest to declare it such." I must be careful here, very careful. My words are tantamount to witchcraft themselves. "But making a poppet of Elina *is* evil. And Ava, your stepfather died on the battlefield at the Black Forest, and your mother can barely get out of bed because she mourns him. Or maybe she just understands what happens to a woman with no husband and no income in the city." I pause, driven by a need to be truthful. "I think she truly loved him though."

"I don't believe you. She hasn't told us that. She would tell us," Ava cries. Her eyes fill with tears.

"Now you will be given the same chance Elina was given: will you rise above the terrible thing that has happened to your family and be kind and gracious to those around you? Or will you heap pain and sorrow onto the circle of those closest to you?"

I snap my fingers and push the girl back toward me.

"And Ava, one other thing." I swing the carrot in front of her, after driving her with the stick. "The Wheel of Fortune turns for us all. One day, Elina Lerner may be the person who can best help you rise. Remember that, my dear."

Elisabet shouts to us from the door, "Ava, Maman says it's time for you to come inside. Cook made lunch."

Elisabet's finally found the backbone to rescue her sister from a stranger's caprice, as she should've done a half hour ago.

I wave and wait for both girls to disappear inside the house, and then I turn home, poppet still hidden in my pocket.

* * *

Back at the townhouse, I draw the curtains and bar the bedroom door, so that we won't be interrupted.

"I've found the cause of your pain. It's not the Huntress who cursed you. Nothing so challenging as that. Just a spiteful girl." I carefully pull the poppet and pins out of my cloak pocket.

Elina stares at the doll in fear.

"I do not want to touch it." She sits up in bed, wearing a fresh linen nightgown and smelling of rosewater and lavender. Bernice must have brushed her hair, which hangs unbound and clean.

"You don't have to touch it. I will do the work, but you must watch me unravel its power. This provides too good an opportunity to learn." I soothe and walk over to the dresser, searching for the white, black, and pale blue ribbons with which we must work. I also pull out a small bag of salt, a green-topped pin, and a pair of scissors.

"Dirty magic," Elina opines, scooting forward carefully, so she doesn't move her aching arms too much. "I can feel the pain radiating outward from the doll to me. If I close my eyes, I see threads binding us." She turns away. "I don't like being in the same room with it."

"Poppets can be used for healing or love, just as knots may be," I scold. "And you are far too young a witch to have so many prejudices. Better to see each branch of magic as a tool to use when the time is right."

But I prefer elemental magic too.

"Why would Ava do such a thing? I hate her. I really, truly hate her." Elina rages, clenching and unclenching the bed cover in her hands.

"She feels lost. Her mother mourns her dead husband and seems to forget even her own daughters."

"She misses me waiting on her hand and foot. She wants to have someone to toy with. Someone to hurt."

The statement is too close to the truth for me to answer comfortably. I bring out a silver tray on which I will work and lay it at the foot of the bed.

"Watch." I command. First, I set the poppet down carefully in the middle of the tray. I wrap the ribbons around where the poppet's heart would be, speaking these words aloud. "By silken threads, I do bind." I braid the three strands of ribbon carefully together until they represent a foot's length. Then I wrap the threads around the poppet's mid-section, tucking the end into a snag in the sewing, so that the end resides inside the doll.

"Why don't you just take the needles out?" Elina asks.

"Questions after."

Now I lean down and kiss the doll. "With a kiss, this spell doth end." And then I take the salt in my fingers and carefully rub it all over the doll.

Elina breathes a deep sigh of relief and surges closer. "The pain. It's less. Already!"

I hold up a finger.

Using the scissors, I carefully open the doll up at the seams, pulling out all the stuffing and cutting the fabric with which it was made into small strips. When the poppet is fully pulled apart, the hair taken off the head, I separate Elina's hair from the rest. Then I feed each piece slowly into the flames.

There is a nasty smell that rises in the room, as the fabric and hair burns, and Elina covers her nose.

I feel sick to my stomach.

It is a while before either of us speaks.

Finally everything burns to ash. I fish out the needles. "Breaking your connection to the doll annuls the needles' power totally. We don't want there to be any affinity lingering between you and the dismembered poppet."

Elina nods.

"Move your shoulders and arms for me again."

Elina swings them wildly, jumping out of bed and rushing over to hug me. "They're perfect. Just as they were before."

I hug the girl back. One wrong thing turns right, and I feel something deep within me release. Then I recall my earlier conversation. "Madame de Boer knows of your powers."

"Did she realize you share the same?" Elina asks, sitting back on the bed.

"She suspects," I cock my head, thinking. "But she won't make an accusation, not yet. She may need of Kasimir's resources, now that she's a widow, and the Widow de Boer understands all too well how important friends among the aristocracy may be."

"So I'm safe," Elina breathes.

"You'll no longer be cleaning chimneys for your stepmother, no."

My answer is careful, but Elina doesn't notice. She launches herself at me again, hugging me so long and hard, that I almost don't notice the tremors.

I pat her back and rub in circles. "Don't cry, love. There's no need."

She raises her head and wipes at the corner of her eyes with her nightgown. "Can we go to the park? We can walk along the river and find something good to eat from the market." She throws the curtains open again, her ring reflecting rainbows in the room.

"Bernice!" I call.

The girl comes in, staring open-mouthed at Elina's sudden transformation.

"I have a message to send to Madame de Boer," I say.

"Yes," Bernice waits patiently.

"Please tell her to stay free of any beverages not made by Cook's own hand. And that Madame Mullenheim will come to check her progress ten days hence." I don't think Ava capable of matricide, but it's better to be cautious in such affairs. She plays with power she does not understand, and Madame de Boer would try the patience of a saint. The foxglove, the poppet, these are not choices of an innocent girl.

"I'm never going back there. This is my home now," Elina sings. "With you and Kasimir. Home. HOME!"

Bernice shakes her head, smiling at the other girl's smile. "Petit a petit, l'oiseau fait son nid" *Little by little, the bird makes its nest.*

Once Bernice dresses Elina in the blue wool, same as my own dress, with a stomacher of cream linen and a lace ruff, Elina drags me into the city's sunlight. The streets teem with soldiers, and so my heart never stops stuttering, knowing that Stefan and Klaus ride among them still able to recognize me despite my careful disguise.

CHAPTER TWENTY-ONE

Dreams and Visions

That night I do not sleep. I cannot not rely on a charm hidden under the bed to keep Elina safe, as I did with my mermaid. If the knowledge of roving soldiers were not enough, the Margrave's ring pushes me past all comfort into terror.

I could seek a meeting and tell the Margrave the truth about Elina, but wisdom gained second-hand is scarcely valued. No, I must make Alasdair von Helm piece together the truth himself. After all, I know now that although Württemberg loves to watch witches burn, the Margrave does not share this same impulse. He's more likely to flee than fight once he learns the truth.

After all, what man wants a witch for a wife?

According to Kasimir, the Margrave von Helm stays with the Duke of Württemberg while he resides in town. According to Mab and her increasingly secret knowledge, Alasdair von Helm sleeps on the second floor in the westernmost part of the Duke's residence, where he keeps his own hours and counsel without interruption. I toy with the idea of trying to work a spell on site, but it's not necessary.

Some magics are subtle, while others act as direct as poison in the veins. Aether, the element of illusion, may be the most subtle of magics, but it's well-suited to weave into dreams. After all, dreams are where many of us hide our secret desires.

Once I am sure Kasimir is asleep, I skirt the city's shadows to my healer's cottage, where it's quiet and I can act unobserved. Outside my door, the moon holds only half full, but it grows, which serves my purposes well. I set a bowl of spring water on the doorstep, watching with my witch's sight until the water glows with trapped moonlight. Then I bring the bowl back into the house and lock the door, so that no one interrupts me.

I cover the window and, once all my tools are out, set salt around the table in a sacred circle.

Once I've secured the space, I set a brazier on the table and light a fire there, crumbling dried mugwort and chamomile into the flames and wafting the smoke in the four directions.

Not letting the smoke dissipate, I burn strips of the linen shirt that the Margrave bound around Cendrillon's side. Burning the man's clothing makes sure that the vision I send goes straight to the Margrave's mind. Careful not to douse the flame, I drip a few drops of moonlight into the fire, knowing that moonlight amplifies whatever message is sent.

Around me, the cabin fills with smoke and steam, the stuff of dreams. First, I call forth an image of Elina lying on the floor in the forest, her face covered in dirt and her side and leg bleeding freely. Then again, in the doghouse, scared of all that she sees. The smoke alternates between her two faces until they merge, becoming one and the same. I chant as the smoke moves and reforms.

"Dream of child in rags and ash/
sticky with blood, she faced a death/
You aided on the forest floor/
and then inside the doghouse door/
See these two faces, the honey blond hair/
The lips and nose and mouth so fair/
bind these two and see the same/
woman in both and then again/
in the girl you chase and follow/
Through morning room and noble borough/
These three are the same/
in body and name/
The truth hidden there/
See it now clear.

Elina's smile comes into focus, the rest of her framed in wisps of white. She smiles as if she looks up at someone, swinging her bell-shaped skirts I realize that this is what my apprentice looks like to Alasdair von Helm, eyes shy and sweet, mouth curving in invitation. Elina reaches her arm up to twine around the neck of her lover, as the Margrave's mind takes hold of the dream.

"Not yet," I whisper and wave my hands to beat the magic back into submission.

"This woman you seek to find /
more than the fantasy of your mind /
Carries magics of her own /
fire and earth and blood and bone /
The wind and water answer to her /
and so shall you, if you stir /
A witch she is, a witch she'll be /
The truth, obscured /
Now you…

"Seeeeeee." I whisper this last word and let it sink into the silence.

All at once I am no longer here and now. I travel with the smoke into the Margrave's dream, where Elina twirls and twirls, like a girl dancing. I twist the magic until her skirt becomes the circle of flowers from the forest, a sure sign of witchcraft. Then I'm in the dream, a full-figured woman with a frown and fear writ large across her features. I'm on the ground, healing my apprentice of her wounds, and Elina glows, suddenly whole. She floats up into the air, healed.

I pull her back down and rearrange the scene until she is sleeping peacefully on the floor of the storeroom at Wolfbach Lodge, Von Helm's own house. But the walls turn rough as bark and leaves rustle around us again. Kasimir rushes into the clearing and bows down beside Elina. He brushes her hair back from her face. Alasdair strides into the dream as well, but this time when Kasimir protests his place, Von Helm sweeps my lover aside. Kasimir disappears as if he were never there.

Elina holds something out to the Margrave. It's just the two of them now. She holds the acorn out, and I see my chance, coaxing a tendril which weaves its way up Elina's arm, blooming and becoming not a tree but something just as green and vibrant. Soon, she's wreathed in vine and flame, and crowned in flowers. I can feel Von Helm lean into this vision. He feels drawn to my apprentice's power.

"Who are you?" he asks, and in his gaze, her features become softer. She is a maiden, ready to meet her mate.

"No, she's nothing so simple," I say, waking myself up from the dream a bit. I growl and twist my fingers until the forest floor is full of wolves, who bow before Cendrillon just as the Margrave does. "See her fire. See her strength."

Von Helm stands and begins to back away. Finally, the fool is afraid.

"What are you?" he asks, as I coax the magic to transform Elina into one of the wolves. "A witch. A goddess?"

Elina's features blur back to something more than human, perfect, as Von Helm wrests control of the dream from me.

"Ye gods, enough. Just see the truth. That's all I ask." I pour the rest of the moonlight over the flame until it's snuffed out. It takes a few more seconds for the dream to recede, long enough for me to watch the shadows writhe and contort into shapes I don't recognize. I am not sure I accomplished what I meant to do.

"It will have to be enough," I console myself and sleep on my simple bed, alone.

We head the next morning to church. Kasimir insists that we formally introduce Elina Lerner to the city, and there's nowhere more staid than among the pews.

The Cathedral de Notre Dame de Strasbourg rises above all the other buildings in the city, indeed above anywhere else in all of Christendom. Construction began on the chapel in the eleventh century, reportedly on the site of a Roman temple, but the building burned down before it was truly underway.

The spire looks down at us now, a testament to the architects who began building again a hundred years later. They still aren't done. Stacks of slate and stone sit on the west side of the building, waiting to be used.

My witch's blood sings whenever I get too close to the chapel, as it does now, a sign that the predecessors of my people claimed this spot as a holy site long before Christ's followers ruled the land.

Even Caesar mentions the Druids briefly, in his own notes, or so Kasimir tells me, and Mab confirms that her godmother told her the same, passing the story from mouth to heart over a thousand years or more.

Kasimir, a converted Huguenot, occasionally attends services as his brother or the Duke require, but as an unmarried widow, thankfully, I'm not required or even invited to accompany him, as I would be as his wife.

Another reason the prospect of a third marriage chafes.

Passing through the crowd which throngs the entrance, I glimpse hundreds of biblical scenes, carved in miniature, many depicting torture or suffering. Spearlike ornaments menace as we pass through the arch. Their message clear: be afraid here.

In minutes, I sit among the middle pews, wearing one of my best dresses, a French silk from Paris, because Elina demands it, and Kasimir approves.

They finagle to put Elina on the marriage mart. Church, after all, is the best place for a respectable young woman to meet her future husband.

"Kasimir, Kasimir, we're so lucky to have you join us," the Duchess of Valois-Anjou gushes from the pew before me. The woman's wearing a wig and a ruff that sticks out nearly twelve inches from her skinny neck.

Kasimir bows his head over the proffered hand. In this light, his brown skin shows dusky and handsome. "You've met the widow Mullenheim?" Kasimir asks, gesturing back toward me.

The Duchess nods.

We don't sit together, my lover and me. Not here. Such things are not done, not even by the aristocracy. The wealthiest in the city attend mass or have family ties like Kasimir that allow them to sit in the coveted spots, rather than out in the churchyard with the unwashed masses.

I bow my head at his acknowledgment and keep my eyes trained to the ground, as does Elina beside me.

"And beside the lovely widow, my new ward, a cousin from further south, Elina Lerner of the Leiningen-Leiningen family."

Elina raises her head, at the sound of her new name, her gold-streaked hair arranged in a demure chignon. She smiles shyly.

"The Stettmeister's Widow will be christened as Elina's godmother next week," Kasimir continues. "As my ward's original sponsor died."

The Duchess nods and bows her head as the boys' chorus begins to sing, and the Bishop begins mass.

Margrave von Helm sits several rows before us, up and to the right, his seat marking him as a favorite of the city's powerful council. Kasimir's words cannot travel the distance, but the Margrave turns anyway, as if something tugs at his attention.

Her head bowed, Elina doesn't see his careful study, and after a moment, the Margrave resumes listening to the liturgy. He has no choice. To keep watching the girl will draw too much attention.

All the men kneel. The women stay on our pews, heads bowed. We cannot move freely in our gowns.

To my right, Elina murmurs along as best as she's able.

"Who is that?" I hear a quiet whisper in my ear.

"What?" I keep my voice low and turn my face toward Elina's eyes.

She looks upward to a nearby stained-glass window where a demon sits, drawn in red glass, chained and surrounded by tormented faces.

"These devils, they're everywhere," Cendrillon whispers, and I inspect the colorful scenes as I haven't in some time, noticing not for the first time the misshapen, horned faces who occupy so many panels.

I take Elina's hand to comfort her.

"And they move. Especially him."

For one moment, my vision twists and tilts as Satan leers at me from above. No, not Satan. The longer I look the demon's face stretches and lengthens, his horns break and twist until they become antlers. Something wild pants against my neck, pressing down on both of us.

"That's no devil," I say and shake my head, as if trying to break free of some influences. "It's a much older god."

"Who then?" Cendrillon asks.

"The Horned One."

Cendrillon bows her head, breathing fast and hard.

"Peace, child," I hold her hand and bow my head as if in prayer, casting outward with my witches' sight, but I see nothing.

In another minute, the pressure eases, and the rest of mass proceeds as planned. The old gods make no more appearances, and the Margrave doesn't deign to notice my apprentice again. He seems scared off from even the sight of her, and no one asks from where the ring on her right hand comes.

Perhaps the aether's vision makes the Margrave reconsider his position. Often the truth acts as a better curative than any lie.

CHAPTER TWENTY-TWO

Haunted

The invitation comes the next night, swathed in gold-leafed paper and cleverly stamped with a stork, the city's symbol of fertility and luck.

Elina unwraps the letter and hands it to Kasimir to read the contents aloud.

"The Duke of Württemberg invites the city's daughters to an Equinox masque to be held in two weeks' time at his residence in the city. Every daughter of marrying age will be welcomed, regardless of rank."

The young page who delivers the message tells us the rest. Unsubtle, the Duke plans to build the coffers of the city's wealthy by encouraging new alliances. He knows several noblemen or near noblemen who are ready to marry. Yes, the Margrave is mentioned, but in the same breath Kasimir. I even hear mention of Landgrave Wiltstern's need for a new wife.

"I know the woman I want to marry," Kasimir says, taking my hand. He's nettled that the Duke didn't include him in fore-knowledge of the party, and that his name is being bandied about without his consent. "And I'm not interested in another."

The page pales.

"He sends the message the Duke gave, love," I chide, softly. "It's a tale the Duke wants his man to tell. The stuff from which dreams (and fortunes) are forged."

Kasimir's skin stays the same warm brown, but I see his anger is still there.

"Tell the Duke to take his blasted invitation and…"

"Please may we go?" Elina asks, turning to me. "I've never been to such a party. I would like to dance—I've been practicing."

I pause, thinking about the Margrave's dream and his marked disinterest in Elina at the church service. I don't want to endanger the work that my magic did, but perhaps another chance for him to snub the girl will drive the lesson home. "Are you even able to dance? Does your hip not pain you?" I ask.

"Have these gone out to every household in the city?" Kasimir asks, still irritated.

"Most everyone who matters," the page nods.

Over the next several days, his words prove true. Nearly everyone in the blasted city is invited. Most of the city's poorest daughters won't come, of course, but some ambitious families scrape together their resources and search for a serviceable dress because the masque represents an opportunity not to be missed, the marriage mart being the primary exchange in which daughters are bought and sold.

I hate commerce.

Privately, once Kasimir cools down, he shares that the Stettmeisters welcome the distraction that the masque provides. Von Werth's army gathers force, and the Duke's party and high-handed invitations quicken the hearts of the rabble, so that people will dance and fuck their way to the very eve of war.

"I'm not beautiful enough to keep the Margrave's attention," Elina says to me. "He didn't even notice me at mass." The Huguenots no longer use that word, but I don't correct her. It's the first time she's brought up the snub, so I scarce breathe, willing her to say more.

"My waist is thin, and my shoulders too broad. I look like a man." She turns from side to side, staring at herself in my mirror.

"The Margrave's already seen you without your clothes on," I point out, needle in my mouth, as I sew a button back onto one of my most serviceable dresses. "He certainly did not mistake you for a man."

She blushes, as if I say something unseemly, and holds out the hand on which the Margrave's gift sits. "No, I suppose not, but you don't have to speak so boldly."

"Gods," I roll my eyes. "You must grow far more comfortable discussing nakedness to ever enjoy being married to a man."

"Surely no one speaks so much of being naked. And what if I never marry? I thought I would not, but now I do not know what I want." Elina replies, sliding her hand in and out of her pocket and staring at something in her palm.

"What is that?" I snap, hurrying over.

"Nothing important."

"Show me."

She opens her hand to show me the tiny red rowan berry, the third gift of the forest.

"Why do you carry such a thing out in the open? It's too powerful. And so small. What if you lose it?"

Elina pinches the seed in between her first and second fingers, holding the thing up to the light. "What is it good for?"

"Only you may discover what the forest's gifts give," I say irritably, fighting the memory of the acorn in the Margrave's palm. "Now put that thing away, in this." I offer her a satin pouch from my top dresser drawer.

She slips the seed inside and tucks it back in her pocket.

"Now what's this about a curse?"

"The first time I met the Margrave, I was speared to death in the woods. The second nearly burned at the stake. What's next? Am I to be hanged?" Elina ticks off her fingers, keeping the satin bag with the rowan berry inside her other palm.

"Two times does not a pattern make."

"You are right. I'm sure you are right." Then she turns a critical eye to the mirror again. "May we call the modiste, Marina? I need a costume for the masque."

I oblige, sending a footman to make the appointment, but the answer comes back that evening. Madame Zell can meet us two weeks hence—after the masque.

"I have nothing fine enough to wear," Elina protests. "Every girl in the city plans her outfit, and I will arrive wearing my sensible navy silk."

"Stop fretting," Kasimir says that evening when Elina expresses the same fear for the hundredth time. He sips wine and smiles at his charge. "I think the man already loves you."

"How can he love her?" I ask, before I can stop myself, my volume rising with my frustration. "He knows nothing of her, not really. He likely does not even remember her."

That is not true. With the dogwood blossom, they were bound, a familiar voice whispers. It's the first time I've heard my mermaid since the forest, and her voice sounds more distant than before.

"That's not true," Elina argues, echoing the mermaid, making her message louder. "He did ask me about myself, at Wolfbach Manor, and he sought me out again at Madame Zorn's party."

Before I can argue, Kasimir clears his throat. "Make a game of it, Marina. A wager. Elina may go to the masque as whomever she pleases. Disguise herself as she likes. The Margrave's work will be to find her."

"Find me?" Elina asks.

"I could find Marina in any room, no matter what she's wearing. There's something that ties me to her. Something not unlike magic."

I feel the love bond between us at Kasimir's words, surprised by its strength.

"What is it, if not property or assets?" Elina asks. She turns to me. "Do you feel the same bond?"

Kasimir laughs and turns to me. "What would you say?" he asks. "I know you like my property and assets, Marina." He waggles his brow at the words suggestively. "But is there something else that lies between us?"

I ignore his impudent question. I still haven't recovered from thinking that he was nearly killed, and if the battle comes to Strasbourg, I know Kasimir will be out in the thick of it.

"What if the invitations are marked? Then he will know her immediately. It will be his task to find Elina in the crowd."

Kasimir nods, understanding my question immediately. "I'll exchange our invitation with one from another family, and we can plan for her to arrive with a bevy of girls. Don't worry, my love. We will make this a test of the Margrave's mettle."

I don't want to get the girl's hopes up, especially knowing that my magic may have dispelled his illusions. "I'm not a part of this daydreaming and cosseting. The masque will be a chance for Elina to dance and meet young men. The Margrave doesn't even figure into the picture for me."

Elina crows and claps her hands. "So we're going! But we have no costumes. I would not even know who to be."

I wave Elina's concern away. "I will sew something for both of us, since Madame Zell cannot oblige." There's more than enough time to alter one of my old gowns, and I have a pile of costumes from years of balls and soirees. "Enough now. Let us put our focus toward more important topics."

"What's more important than the masque; it's the biggest event of the year?" Elina teases. Her golden hair is gathered in a silver net that catches the light as she cocks her head.

I make a rude sound. "Have you so quickly forgotten the life that most of Strasbourg leads? Have you forgotten the true work of a witch, apprentice?"

Elina casts her face down at my scolding. "You're right. Of course you are. I just have never been to such a party. I'm worried I won't know how to act, and the Margrave did not even notice me at church."

"Most men are only able to focus on what's in front of them. Maybe he can't forget what happened on his estate and wishes to let it go. Maybe he needs to make a bundle of money from whomever he marries. In any case, don't worry. There will be other men."

"You heard that the Landgrave also seeks a wife. Mab has said he's open to offering for you." I lamely finish.

"Marina," Kasimir entreats. "As you said, we will see who Elina finds for herself. Isn't that what you wish? For her to make her own choices?"

He has me there. "Dresses and costumes! Is that all either of you can talk about? No, she goes with me to the other side of the city in the morning. We have work to do there."

You cannot hide the girl from her fate, no more than you could save me from mine," the mermaid whispers, and it's not my imagination—she sounds as if she speaks to me from far away.

Morning sun erases any memory of my mermaid. I plan to take Elina outside, but then I can't find the girl. She's not in her bedroom or mine, or the library, which is her favorite haunt of late.

I finally find her in the small growing room that sits off the back of the house, surrounded by mustard greens and leeks that Kasimir's chef cultivates for the kitchen. Elina wears an old apron over her dress and stands before a mound of dirt and a copper container nearly the size of a beer barrel.

"What are you doing?"

"Planting the rowan berry." Elina fills the copper form, pouring trowel after trowel of dirt until the container is full to the lip. Then she holds up the small red seed before burying it.

"Why?"

"I woke with the thought and decided to follow its urging." She grabs a nearby watering urn and drenches the empty earth.

I wait til she's done, chattering about costume ideas, and in another hour we're on the city streets, enjoying sun and blue skies. Elina and I both dress in our drab browns, hair tied back, and today, I alter my face and ask Elina to put her own glamour in place.

"A cunning woman works mainly with the first kind of magic. Today we will focus on simple spells for healing," I lecture Elina as we open my small home. It's clean and well-stocked as I pay to have it kept. No sign of the recent midnight ritual.

A small rowan bundle hung in the window signals to the neighborhood that I'm open for visits, but no thaler exchanges palms here. My goal is to serve those who need it most.

The first person to visit is Madame Berthel, the ragpicker's wife. I take in the woman's swollen face and know she's with child again. Her husband needs only look her way for a babe to fill her belly.

But I wait for the poor woman to tell her need to Elina.

"Are you La Guerisseuse's apprentice?" Madame Berthel asks, the title she calls me means healer. She's short, only fifteen hands high, with most of her teeth gone. Her once bright features worn from birthing and feeding the seven children her husband has already given her.

"Oui," Elina replies.

"And can you help me as well?"

I busy myself in the corner, pulling out crockery and checking to see that nothing important molders.

"I hope so," Elina says, her voice soft.

"Have you ever known a man?"

"Of course. My father." Elina says, and then pauses, realizing what is being asked of her. "Um. No, I haven't." Her face turns pink at the words.

"I carry a traveler I cannot tend to, girl. And La Guerisseuse has helped me rid myself of one I cannot serve before. Can you do the same?"

Elina turns back to me with wide eyes.

"My girl knows that a mixture of pennyroyal and rue will serve your purpose, especially so soon." I say smoothly, pulling a small cloth bag from the back of the cupboard. "Come back if there are complications."

"I will, Madame." The woman leaves without another word.

And we hear another knock on the door.

This time a fisherman approaches. He's hooked his palm fishing the canal, and the wound festers. This cut requires herbs, not magic, so I make a wash of vinegar for him to use and dispense precious myrrh for the infection.

The gentleman goes on his way.

When we are alone again, Elina turns to me. "So this is the day-to-day work that you do?" she asks.

"Most of the world's problems are simple," I tell her. "They don't require more serious magics. They only ask that we understand the plants and animals of the forest and the properties that promote healing."

As if to prove me right, we see a flood of minor complaints and ailments throughout the day. Monsieur Dubois' arthritis ails him. Monsieur Gilles' left ear won't stop ringing.

Madame Ritter suffers from a swollen and hot breast. Her babe cries so loudly that Elina swears under her breath, but a hot cloth applied over a half hour and a sharp massage brings milk back to the nipple. Mother and baby leave happy and with full bellies. (I am happy to share a bit of the cheese and bread I brought for our lunch.)

I dispense another dose or three of pennyroyal and rue to a run of gray-haired women whose backs bend under the burdens of child-bearing and unending work. Elina watches these exchanges with wide eyes, her mind beginning to calculate what marriage truly means.

And I am reminded that the best teaching is often be done without words.

We see two more men. The first limps through the door, his young face drawn with pain. The poor boy suffers from a bullet wound to his thigh, which never healed properly. After inspecting the drawn, angry flesh, I offer a poultice and make the young man promise to walk the length of the canal several times a day, with stretches at night for him to do by the fire.

And finally Monsieur Schlumberger menaces, old codger with nary a job nor a home.

"La Guerisseuse, my gut hurts." He holds his stomach and whines.

I've heard this complaint a thousand times. "It's the spirits you drink, Monsieur. Stop them. But not all at once," I direct. That may lead to the old man's death.

"Spirits, I say. Good idea. Do you have any brandy? Or vodka? It 'twill make me feel better. Or you, young miss. So pretty. So kind." He wanders near Elina, trying to grab her arm and back her toward the table.

"I keep no spirits here. No. Do not touch her. Out. Out!" I threaten to batter the man with my broom, and the old rooster takes flight.

"May we go home now?" Elina asks. Monsieur Schlumberger

frightens her. And the day's work is hard and somewhat boring.

"Not yet." My witch's sense tingles, as the Stillness speaks without words. I look to the empty door expecting to see someone there. "Do you feel that?" I ask.

Elina frowns, as if trying to sense something just out of her reach. She shakes her head no soundlessly.

"We wait."

When the sun sinks closer to the lip of the horizon, and the sounds of the city begin to turn to the street's children being called in for their last meager meal, I hear a quiet knock.

"Come in, come in," Elina calls.

Another woman crosses the entryway, this one young and clean, with all her teeth, and hair that matches the nut brown of her dress.

"Would you like a cup of tea?" I offer.

The girl shakes her head no and keeps her gaze at the floor.

"Why have you come to visit us?" Elina asks.

"No reason." The girl shakes her head again. "I should not have come. I should go." She stands between the table and the hearth like a cornered animal, eyes darting back to the door.

I nudge Elina behind me and take a seat at the hearth in the closest chair. "Come, sit for a moment. We have a hot cup of mint tea and a bit of buttered bread." I nod to Elina to prepare the food and bustle away, leaving the girl alone.

After a couple of minutes, she darts to the chair and sits, gulping air as if she goes to her death.

"Here." Elina offers her a steaming mug and a plate with bread warmed over the fire.

She sips but doesn't touch the food.

"Be still, girl," I comfort. "Eat something. What's your name?"

"Colette. Colette Murner." She takes another drink, still perched on the edge of the seat as if ready to take flight. "They said you helped many of us in the city. More women than we could count."

"I have, Colette. I've helped others, and I will help you. Now what is it that you've come to share?"

The room falls silent.

I wait.

"The Devil spoke to me," the girl finally whispers, tears rising to her eyes. "The Devil spoke to me, and now I'm damned, La Guerisseuse. They will burn me at the stake. And then no one will be left to take care of my little sister."

"Ssssshhhh." I take the girl's hand. "I doubt very much that the Devil wants much from a sweet girl like you. But tell me, what did the Devil say?"

"They're coming," she whispers. "He told me to flee the city, because they're coming."

"And do you see visions, as well as hear voices?" I ask. Maybe the girl sees the future. Such a power is enough to terrify even the most prepared witch.

My question seems to free her tongue. Colette shakes her head, her brown hair falling away from her eyes. "No. I hear one voice. Noises. A bowl broke, my father's favorite."

"And do you always hear the Devil in the same place?" I ask. It's a stupid question, but I don't yet understand what we face. Sometimes bad questions lead to better ones.

Colette shakes her head. "I heard him in church." She opens her mouth to speak, staring at the door again as if she might bolt. "In church. I must be damned." She shakes her head and tears come again.

Elina makes a strangled sound, and I catch her eye, shaking my head *no* softly. Whatever happened to her at the cathedral is not the same thing, I'm sure of it.

Colette puts the mug down on the table and stares between Elina and me, noticing something passes between us. "Something's wrong with me, isn't there. What is it?" she asks, her voice rising in alarm.

"Nothing," I say. "There's nothing wrong with you." I take her other hand in my own and through the contact, I let my senses reach out to her, scanning. "Are you well?"

"Well enough to work most days. I have to now." Colette taps her foot against the chair.

I let her go and lean back, mentally ticking off the possibilities. She's not ill. She doesn't see the future. But something's wrong. She isn't eating. The girl weighs almost nothing. And she can barely sit still. She's afraid.

"Once I could offer her healing water," I hear the mermaid whisper to me. She's back with no warning. "No more. When I became human, I gave all that up, and now I'm less than human. I forget myself, Marina. Soon I will be nothing more than a breeze."

"Did you hear that?" Elina asks, looking spooked.

"I hear nothing." Dead women don't speak, I remind myself and shake off my awareness of the mermaid's ghost.

The front door slams, and we all look up, startled.

"That's me," Colette says. "That happens most days. Doors closing. Bowls breaking."

Dead women—or men—don't speak.

Unless they do. Unless they have something to say. My mermaid follows me because there's something she wants. Not vengeance. Not anymore. She's a spirit of the air; she could go anywhere, but she still comes back to me.

I start to pull herbs from the shelves.

"You said you're the only one left to watch your sister." I grab a handful of rowan branches and bind them with a white ribbon. Then I start to briskly sweep any dirt out the door.

I prepare the space.

"My mother's been gone since my sister was born, but my father died only a few months ago." The girl goes quiet, unable to keep talking.

"In battle," I confirm, straightening.

Colette nods. "We needed the thaler. It was his first battle. Shot straight through the gut."

"Do you have something of his?" I ask.

She reaches into the pocket of her dress and draws out a small piece of wool. "From his favorite hat," she says.

"Keep that, for now." I search the cupboards for a small bag of salt.

"Here," I shove it into Elina's hand. "Line the windows and doorway. Then draw a circle around the three of us." I pull out a bundle of dried sage and light a twig in the fire. "Stand." I tell Colette and light the sage, letting the smoke cover her and then me in turn.

"Is it a demon?" Elina whispers when we three stand inside the circle.

"Nothing so sinister. A ghost. A guardian. I believe it's Colette's father. Now let us all take hands."

I breathe into the Stillness, giving Elina time to acclimate before opening myself. Through my witch's sight, the room appears shadowed and worn. I briefly catch sight of the apprentice bond between Elina and me. My eyes travel near the windows, the table. And in the far corner, I see something that shimmers like blue and gold fish scales.

"Is that him?" Elina asks, looking in the same direction.

Amalia is still here.

"No, she belongs to me, or me to her. We are looking for someone who is here for Colette," I say aloud, hoping the mermaid understands me. "May this circle be blessed. May we be protected from all evil and any who would do us harm." We release our hands.

I feel a tug from my left side and turn to catch sight of a man-shaped darkness. The ghost's features are worn through, almost indistinct in the soft light of the fire.

"Put the wool on the floor between us."

Colette reluctantly puts the piece of wool on the floor.

"Is there anything you want to say to your father?" I ask softly. "He's here now, with us."

The mermaid floats closer, watching the other ghost with curiosity.

Elina looks at her and at me but doesn't ask any more questions.

"Papa," Colette begins. "I miss you. I need you to be here. Now." She cries for a few minutes. "Marguerite and I love you. We will be good girls. I will work hard."

I rub Colette's back in a slow circle, as tears come again. "It's good to say something to release your father's spirit. He stays here because of your grief. Even his words to you in church—they were a warning. He wants to protect you, even from the grave. He's a good man. He loves you very much."

"I do love her. And little Marguerite." The ghost's voice comes as nearly a whisper. He grows clearer with the words. Now we can see the outline of a strong jaw, his hair hanging over the collar of his soldier's uniform.

"Papa, I know you love us," Colette says. "And we'll work together. We'll be fine without you." The words are flat though. I can feel the fear in them.

The ghost looks at me. "My aunt. Tell the girls to go to my aunt in Villion. She will take care of them."

"Your father wants you to know that you can find a home with your aunt."

"Marguerite, the little one is named after my sister," he nods.

"Your aunt Marguerite," Elina repeats. "In Villion."

Colette nods, tears surfacing again.

"Monsieur Murner, you've done what you needed to do." I say to the ghost. "I'll make sure your children find their family. You may go forward in your journey."

The ghost floats easily through the circle and draws closer to the wool.

"What's happening?" Colette asks.

The ghost reaches out to stroke his daughter's cheek.

"He *is* here," Colette breathes. "I can feel him. I can feel how much he loves me."

Elina cries, tears silently streaming down her cheeks.

"You're free." I whisper, and there's a sudden flash of light.

Monsieur Murner is gone.

Only my own ghost remains, bound to me, and whatever our shared fate will be.

CHAPTER TWENTY-THREE

The Rowan's Gift

The next package arrives in the early evening, beautifully wrapped in linen, with nary a love note to be found. So mysterious. So lovely. The Margrave displays a kind of discreet extravagance I admire. So I send the gift up to Elina, thinking that my magic must not have worked. The vision does not deter the man. I am nearly ready to give up anyway.

A scream erupts through the house.

I race up the stairs, worried that the Margrave oversteps, that somehow he's triggered a memory from the witch trial or worse, the bear pit, but I should've known better.

Elina sits huddled on her bed, the box shoved to the floor. She weeps and tugs at her unbound hair.

"What's wrong?" I ask. "What happened?"

She gestures to the unwrapped gift.

A dress, or rather, a sackcloth of rags sits in a disorganized lump. The garment smells of urine and worse. The rest of the linen is smeared with shit and ashes.

"A stupid prank," I say, gathering the pile up. "It must be your stepsisters, those horrid girls. I will beat them black and blue this time."

"There's more," Elina says. "Can you read it?"

A bit of yellowed paper sits within the stinking mess. I read aloud from the spidery script. "Three witches burned this week. I know where another lives."

"They threaten me," she says.

I nod. "Yes. They struggle without you. Madame de Boer has been in her bed for two weeks. After your father's death, they don't know what to do."

"And how do you know this?" Elina asks me, straightening and drying her eyes on the sheets.

"I saw them, when I found the poppet."

"Why?!"

"I needed to tell Madame that her husband was dead."

"Why?!" This time she almost shouts.

"It's no easy thing to lose a husband, Elina. Often a woman loses her livelihood. In some cases, her safety."

"So you care more for them than you do for me. Do you not remember what she did to me? How cruel they were?" Her face flushes red.

"I remember." I keep my voice calm.

Elina fights back tears. "I'm not safe. Not even here with you and Kasimir. I will never be safe. Not as long as they live."

"You mustn't think that way, *ma fille*. Now that you are with us, Kasimir and I will do everything we can to protect you."

A knock on the door interrupts me.

"Are we expecting company?" Elina asks.

"No, and I'm sure it's no one important. Kasimir is out to dinner. Pay the noise no mind." I sit on the bed and move closer to give her a hug.

Elina stays stiff in my arms.

A knock on the bedroom door stops me from saying anything more.

"Yes," I call, irritated.

Bernice opens the door gently. "Madame, there's a man here to see you."

I keep my hand on Elina's shoulder. "Tell him I'm busy."

"He says it's very important, Madame. He must talk to the Master or the Lady of the House."

"Very well," I sigh and stand. "I'll be right back."

She nods, face still red and tearstained.

I take the stairs quickly, still annoyed at being interrupted and almost slide into the young man who stands by the door wringing his leather gloves.

"Monsieur," I nod.

"Madame." He stands straight-backed, hair tied at the nape of his neck. "I've been sent by Stettmeister Vallon to tell you there are several sick children one neighborhood over, Ma'am. We aren't sure they will make it."

"Oh no," I take a step back. "Is it plague? Should we stay indoors?"

"Non, Madame. I'm sorry to ask, but there have been reports of strange characters in the neighborhood. People coming and going late in the night. And the children are very sick."

He pauses. "Someone saw a black cat."

I begin to understand the warning being delivered. "A black cat?"

"It was on the street outside your house."

"The Stettmeister thinks the illness not natural?" I ask.

"No, Madame. I don't know, Madame." The youth has the decency to bow his head

"Someone believes that a witch causes the trouble."

He nods reluctantly.

"The occupants of our home have been accused?" I ask, feeling my heart pick up the pace and trying to keep the same terror I saw in Elina's eyes from my own.

That package arrived not thirty minutes ago. Maybe it did not come from the stepsisters after all.

Not an empty threat, someone wants me to know.

Maybe the soldiers found a way to follow us home? Or maybe it is a coincidence.

"No," the young man shrugs. "But the Stettmeisters want the Bastard to know. He's not home. You will tell him?"

"I will tell him," I nod and promise, as a good wife would. "But Monsieur, I promise you that this house is free from any kind of Satanic influence. We keep no cats here, other than a calico to eat our mice. You may ask the Chef or any of the servants."

He nods but does not ask to speak to our staff, a good sign that this is only a warning.

"And I myself will bring the children soup and make sure their parents are soothed. Why I went through my own troubles with Kasimir's niece. She was very unwell for a time. Very unwell. Again, you may ask the servants if you want to know more."

A stray thought comes—Roland and Sylvie, and I'm thankful they live far from us here, in a different part of the city.

"Thank you, Madame." The young man smiles apologetically. I can see in the slope of his shoulders that he's glad to go. He did his duty.

The threat is delivered.

* * *

Michaelmas arrives near the autumnal equinox. The book of Revelation, not oft heard in the church's halls, tells how the strongest of angels, Michael, cast Satan and his demons back to hell. So on Michaelmas morning, church bells ring to celebrate the victory of light over darkness.

Such stories rouse the rabble. Sensible families lock their daughters away on Michaelmas after dark arrives, making sure that if witch fury rises in a crowd, innocent women or children will not be burned.

But Kasimir escorts Elina to evening mass despite my protests. I take the opportunity to finish secretly what sewing I have left on Elina's costume. After several late nights, I've successfully altered a well-loved white silk gown with a cream and navy overdress to fit Elina's thin frame. Tonight, I finish the final stitching on the bodice and adjust the neckline, making it scandalously low. The lace ruff for this gown won't cover the girl's beautiful neck and small décolletage. It wings backward to accentuate her high cheekbones and luminous eyes instead. The movement of the fabric echoes in the wings which will complete her costume. In candlelight, the gown's fabric nearly glows, the detail adorned as it is with gold thread.

When I'm done, I rummage through the few things I brought from the de Boer estate and manage to find Elina's mother's shoes, their delicate spun silk so thin as to be sheer. And I bring out a golden domino mask and the pair of white and gold angel's wings used for another Michaelmas party long ago. My little costume box accommodates a doe mask, a sorceress cloak, and even a pair of rabbit's ears, but for my apprentice, an avenging angel seems the right choice. Now Elina's costume for her first masque is complete.

The sound of the door nudges me from my work, and I shriek and run back toward the further reaches of the house, skidding my way into the small planting bench, arms full of fabric, and stop.

Gooseflesh rises on my arms.

The girl's instincts prove true. Elina plants her rowan seed. And from it, a full-grown tree stands.

"Marina," Elina calls. "Where are you? Mistress?!"

I don't make a sound, but one of the servants betrays me because in another moment, Elina and Kasimir stand beside me, mouths gaping at the branches that rise just above our heads, making a symmetrical arbor under which we're sheltered, emitting, at least in the relative darkness of the room, a soft, glowing light.

First we meet a goddess in the forest and then Satan becomes the

Lord of the Forest in the midst of church. Now this.

"It's a sign," I say.

"Is it…" Kasimir asks an unfinished question.

"The Tree of Life: the rowan."

"What does it mean?" Elina asks. Her fear shows in her big eyes and trembling hand. No one has told her that such things are possible.

"That we're meant to show courage, to offer protection, and in turn be protected." I say the words on instinct, but as if my words summoned the sound, knocking begins outside.

We turn toward the front of the house as one. My ears begin to buzz, as soon as I hear shouting. The evening's mischief rises, and the bad feeling I had earlier bears fruit.

"Keep her upstairs," I shout to Kasimir—I'm already throwing the gown and everything else in my arms to the floor and rushing toward the front rooms. "Or here."

I run toward the kitchen, calling orders. "Do not answer. Let no one inside. They seek to murder or maim, but if we give them no answer, they will pass."

"Should we douse the candles too, Madame?" Bernice asks as I rush by her. Bless her and the rest of our servants that no one asks why I, not the master of the house, shout orders.

"No. Do nothing. Say nothing. Make it seem as if the house is empty of its master."

The mob pounds against our door.

"Witch. Witch! Satan rides her." And "Bring your bitch out, Bastard. She's brought sickness to children. She will bring death to you too."

Kasimir walks in behind me, quietly listening.

"When we burn her, she will scream for mercy. Satan's tears. She's been letting him fuck her on the nights you aren't home. Whore." There is the sound of something smashing, not inside the townhouse, but outside. I try to gauge where the mob's attentions fall.

Elina creeps forward from the shadowed hallway.

"Back," I hiss. "Do not listen to this filth! Bernice, get her out of here!"

Bernice tries to pull Elina back in the direction that she came, but my apprentice ignores her. In a quick battle of wills, Elina wins, pulling away to stand on her own. Bernice makes a helpless gesture at me.

"Come here," Kasimir commands quietly, not to Elina as I first think, but to me. I ignore him.

He turns me bodily into his chest, closing his hands over my ears.

For a moment, I can't feel anything except pressure, and the slow and steady pulse of his heart.

The shouting outside dulls to a murmur.

I take one deep breath, and then another.

We stand together like that for a long time. The low rushing sounds slowing and finally stopping as the mob moves on searching for someone else to burn.

"We're not safe here," I say, my voice muffled to my own ears. "That's the second time they've come. Someone's talking about us. We should escape the city, and flee to Paris."

"Strasbourg is our home, and we will not be forced from it," Kasimir whispers, finally releasing my ears. "I will find the rumor's start."

Your home, the words lie on the tip of my tongue, unsaid. *I'm happy anywhere there are wild woods.* A wedge left unused.

"Are they gone?" Elina's voice wakes me from my thoughts. She shakes like a leaf caught in an unexpected storm.

Kasimir draws her close, and we step apart to make room for my apprentice to slip between us. She pauses but finally lets her shoulder rest against Kasimir's, still shaking.

He leans his forehead beside hers, cheek to cheek keeping his hand on my back. The touch roots me into our makeshift family. "We're safe."

"No, we're not." Elina shakes her head and tries to pull away.

"For this moment, we are," I correct, my arm keeping her with us. "Sometimes that is all you can ask."

"It's not enough," Elina argues.

I hear the unshed tears in her voice. It is time and past time for me to accept the promise Elina laid down in the forest. Maybe I have been like the girl in my shop, seeing all the pieces but not comprehending the whole.

Maybe the answer to every problem we face has been laid before me.

"Come now," I take Elina's hand and pull her back into the house, back toward the hothouse where her dress lies on the floor before the blessed tree. "I made something for you."

I make Kasimir cover her eyes until I can hold up the dress before her.

"What is this?" Her voice sounds full of emotion again, when he uncovers her sight.

"They're for you. For tomorrow. So that you may shine like the beautiful gem you are." I shake the dress, and Elina pulls it into her arms, exclaiming over the colors. When she finds the silk slippers, her eyes fill with tears.

"Your mother will be there with you the whole time," I assure her. "Celebrating the beauty you've become at your first ball."

Elina throws her arms around my neck. "This is too much. It's perfect. It's…"

Kasimir comes forward to lightly rub her back. "Sssshhhhh. Peace now. It is all for love of you," he whispers.

At that, we both cry.

Finally, Elina raises her head and looks at me, taking in the last part of her costume. "Wings?"

"You are a gift from the heavens," I smile and jest. "Or a fairy child, perhaps."

"If so, then you are my fairy godmother," she hugs me fiercely.

I laugh.

"And the silver buried here? Is this a trick?" Elina asks. "Another gift."

"I gave you no silver, only gold."

"No, look at the tree." Elina says, wonder in her voice.

I look over. The rowan tree still glows, shedding soft light on the room.

I will have to keep the servants out of this room. We do not need rumors of glowing trees that grow up overnight, not while revelers are out hunting witches. Such a thing of beauty is an easy topic for gossip.

Kasimir lets out a low whistle. "Marina, look to the base of the tree."

Elina already crouches before it, her dress carefully laid to the side. Her hand covers something in the dirt, grabbing it, and I watch as she pulls a silver handle and whatever it is lengthens until a moment later, she stands in the room, sword in hand.

"Magic," Kasimir whispers. He bows his head and makes the sign of the cross, betraying his Catholic childhood.

Don't do that, I want to say, but I can't talk yet. This mystery is too big even for me.

"Such a thing cannot grow from a seed. And it should not fit," Elina says. She asks me. "How could this fit inside that?"

She's right. The huge copper pot that holds the tree's roots is two thirds as deep as the blade's length.

"I did nothing of this," I confess. "I don't know from where the weapon came."

Elina stares at me with wide eyes. She finally whispers, "All I could think, when they stood outside shouting at us, was that I needed a weapon. I needed something with which I could kill them all."

The tree's light grows dim now that the sword is in Elina's hand.

"This is not the magic of the wood." It is the first thing that comes to mind, and I say it without thinking. "Nor practical magic. This is magic of the third kind."

Elina's brows draw together. "Have I done something wrong?"

"Peace. My words don't tarnish the gift." I reach my witch's sense out toward the blade and feel death. This weapon carries terrible magic within it.

"How could this happen?" Elina asks me. Her face seems still and solemn as a saint's. All thought of pretty dresses forgotten.

I shrug. "The third magic is beyond our knowing. You can practice magic for a thousand years, if a witch could live that long, and not understand everything about it."

I go on. "You needed a weapon, and here a weapon is offered you. That kind of pure conjuring is something about which we understand very little."

Elina nods, as if it is the simplest thing in the world.

I don't let my feeling of dread show on my face. No mother wishes for her child to go to war, and that is where the weapon points. For what use is a sword, except in battle?

Kasimir moves to light candles, as the tree now stands nearly dark. "You must carry the sword tomorrow night," he says. His hushed tone tells me that a part of him still bows his head before Elina.

"To a party?" she asks.

"I feel better sending you into the lion's den armed," I admit, thinking on Kasimir's words. My lover is smarter than I am in so many ways. "In the dark, some men will feel free to take license. If you have a weapon, you may protect yourself."

"What if the Margrave doesn't want fury coming home to him? Women are to offer respite from battle, not a reminder of it. What if he's not impressed with me?" Elina frets, but I see in her eyes that she loves the sword. And she does not let the blade go until she retires for the night.

Maybe the wolf inside my girl is not so easily tamed after all.

CHAPTER TWENTY-FOUR

A Love Spell

The day of the masque arrives, and Strasbourg buzzes with excitement. Children run errands and yell to each other happily in the street. The paper reports that more than four hundred of the city's daughters attend the evening's gala, and if rumor holds true, those who are too poor plan smaller masques across the city besides.

Everyone plans to spend the evening dancing and making love as light perfectly balances the coming darkness, for that is what winter is —a sweep of dark cold that will last for more months than I care to count. Christian stories aside, the equinox begs the lie the priests tell us, for light does not always vanquish its foe. Balance is a momentary condition in nature.

Still, it's hard to feel anything but anticipation when the air in the city holds a glimmer of gold. City streets appear washed and clean. Even beggars take a few spare moments to scrub clean.

I run my errands early, seeking news of any more witch burnings. Finding none, I send a note to Mab that Elina attends the masque tonight.

When I return, my apprentice still sleeps. She wakes near eleven, when Bernice prepares a bath with rose petals and amber. Like many aristocratic daughters, she leaves the bath to begin her toilette at noon.

Bernice dries Elina's hair slowly and then curls it, so that the straight honey blond waves turn out lovely curls which will later be pulled back and coiffed under the top ribbon of her golden mask.

Elina doesn't eat the rest of the day, whether by excitement or design. She fasts and drinks a little water, eats a handful of berries. We play dice in the bedroom and talk of nothing of consequence. By the time evening comes, her stomach, already tiny, spans no more than two handbreadths across.

And then it's time to dress. I help Elina into the white silk bodice and stomacher first, laying them over her silk shift and tying the cream sleeves on carefully. When we pull the skirt over at least three under layers, I attaching it with stiff thread that later will be carefully ripped back out. Once the ensemble is complete, Elina pulls on her wings. I loop and sew the bands that fix them to her shoulder blades, adding a wind charm in the shape of a feather bound to onyx inside each wing, to hold them aloft for a few hours.

Kasimir arrives, already costumed in a stylized wolf mask and gray and black doublet.

My lover *oohs* and *aahs* over Elina's dress and wings, the doting father. He's brought a pair of diamond earrings from his brother's wife and watches with pride as the girl glows putting them on.

And then there's just enough time for a spell of transference. We put the sword and a small bag of marbles on opposite ends of a set of silver scales. I cover both objects in smoke and sand, saying a few words of blessing as I weave a ribbon between the two, and then their properties merge and shift, redistributing the weight.

Now Elina may carry the sword all night, hanging to the side of her skirts, and it weighs nothing more than a handful of small stones.

By this time, I dress. If Kasimir is a wolf, then I may be named a shepherdess. My gown glows a lovely pink, the color of which no real shepherdess has ever worn, and I carry a crook by which I may watch over my sheep.

Metaphors abound.

We ride to the Duke's party in an open-air carriage. Elina's wings are too big otherwise, and as we travel, we watch the city transformed by night. The line at the Duke's residence stretches back several streets, but like all the revelers, we point and stare at the many costumes as we slowly make our way to the entrance of the party.

"He will never find me among this many people," Elina murmurs.

I pat the girl's hand.

"Think of who else you might meet this night. You never know what fate has in store."

I feel her smile more than see it, Elina's mouth almost hidden by the domino.

Finally, we make it to the entrance and are announced. Inside, the

Duke of Württemberg stands near the tall arched entrance to the ballroom. Ungainly, he wears a short beard to hide his weak chin and clothes of a finer weave than almost anyone around him. Kasimir and Elina bow before me, my apprentice's wings rising regally above her straight spine. I hear murmurs as the crowd marvels at her costume.

Nearly a hundred people mill around on the dance floor and beyond. The musicians tune their instruments as a dance ends.

A man comes forward to bow before Kasimir and I. "May I ask the angel to dance?" He dresses as a knight, with an impressive shirt of chainmail over his breeches and tall black boots. This knight's helmet is a suggestion, made of stiff silver paper that covers only his forehead and cheeks.

Kasimir turns to Elina in question, and my girl nods.

The knight takes the angel's hand and pulls her toward the dance floor, the crowd parting from the sheer size of Elina's wings.

"Is it him?" I ask Kasimir. The evening's purpose may be harder than I first anticipate, with so many faces covered.

"No," he turns and takes my hand, and we walk around the dance floor, watching the two lines of men and women float forward and away from one another in a simple rigaudon.

When the music changes again, Kasimir pulls me onto the floor for a bourrée, and then we return to the sides of the large room to chat with various Stettmeisters and noblemen.

The revelers follow this same rhythm, moving between dance and drink to breathlessly whisper at one another over the music from the sidelines. The Duke's servants circle the room with silver trays on which there are crystal flutes of white wine and other harder liquors.

Without meaning to, Elina takes center stage. With her wings impossibly aloft, I never lose sight of my apprentice, and I don't think she leaves the dance floor once during the first half of the night. Her hair shines in the candlelight, curls drooping gracefully over her shoulders, and the white of her dress makes her seem a star in comparison with the dim colors that surround her.

Kasimir and I watch the hours turn.

I finally spot the Margrave at nearly midnight. He stands by the entrance, talking with Württemberg and surveying the room as only a man born to the silver spoon can. His black hair is tied back tonight, and of course, he wears the mask of a sly fox, red and brown, its wooden carving handsome and clever.

The rest of his costume echoes the fox pageantry: a long, sleek coat of red brown. His breeches, a darker brown, tight and tucked within a pair of tall boots. Searching, it takes only a few scant minutes before he catches sight of his prey.

Elina.

A new dance starts. Von Helm does not approach her directly. He asks the girl most immediately to her left to dance and the music begins again.

The Margrave circles Elina in this way for some time, as if he fights some inner gravity.

When he briefly ducks off the dance floor in the next round, I corner him.

"You seem smitten, Margrave." I bow my head and look up, so I see the moment when he realizes who I am.

"My dreams are true then," he breathes, without preamble, looking out onto the floor again.

I say nothing.

"I'm meant to marry for coin, but there may as well be no one else here tonight," he says under his breath. Turning to me, he asks, "Am I under her spell or yours?"

"You know what she is then?" I answer his question with a question, holding my breath. "Who she is?"

He nods. "The girl I helped you hold together in that clearing. The very same one who escaped Meister Feilt. I'd say I know as much as any man might. She comes to me in my dreams, as a wolf and a maiden and a forest queen."

The music and laughter press against my senses, making it hard to focus.

"Is it magic that makes me feel this way? As if I cannot breathe? As if I cannot stay away?"

"The two of you worked this spell together, I think, as all lovers do. The acorn helped though, of course it has. I would undo it if I could. I tried, but the time has passed for such things."

Kasimir appears at my side. He nods to the Margrave and leans into my ear, his breath panting through the snout of the wolf mask. "Marina, this is what Elina wants. For saints' sake, she wears his ring."

I yield to my lover's wisdom, stepping out of the Margrave's path.

On the dance floor, Elina takes the hand of one of Stettmeister Vellin's handsome sons, unaware that Von Helm strides toward her, intent on interrupting. There's not even an exchange before the city's favorite son scurries away and then she stares up into the Margrave's eyes.

The musicians begin their next song, a *pavana matthei,* the most romantic of dances allowed for a couple.

The lovers clasp hands.

All the room watches.

Von Helm takes Elina into his arms, and though other couples twirl around them, it's as if they dance alone. Elina's silk slippers occasionally peek out from beneath her swirling skirts. The sight keeps her mother in my heart. I wish she could've seen how beautiful her brave daughter becomes.

Kasimir whispers in my ear. "They're wonderful together, are they not?"

I can't argue. There's something here that feels meant to be. Everyone else senses the magic of the moment, and we all become a part of their story.

The pair turns and twirls, and the air around them shifts and sparkles. Elina's happy and unguarded face shows a faint glow.

"Elina." I say aloud. I bring my hands up and try to break the spell she's unconsciously weaving, walking to the edge of the dance floor. I send a whisper of wind to carry my words only to her. "Elina, remember where you are. Remember *who* you are."

People around me murmur. A few of them notice that the couple is somehow brighter, illuminated with a light all their own.

The lovers' eyes stay locked on one another. For these few moments, they live in their own world, apart from prejudice and hatred, unaware of the whispers that start to rise.

Kasimir strides onto the dance floor. He calls something to the musicians, something to make them stop playing, rudely interrupting the twirling bodies.

And still the lovers don't awaken. The room might burst into flames, and still they would stare into each other's eyes.

Flame. *Fire.* I smell smoke. Something is burning.

I turn toward the scent. A great gray wall billows through the room's far arches, covering the musicians first.

"Fire!" Someone yells. "The ballroom's on fire."

Women start to scream.

This is how their love begins. That's the first thought I have, as the orderly ballroom falls apart.

Men yank women off the dance floor. The musicians grab at sheaves of precious paper and leather cases, packing instruments quickly away.

A mob forms near the room's entrance. The space echoes with shouts and crying.

"Everyone, calm down," someone calls, most likely the Duke of Württemberg's steward, but I can barely hear whatever he says next. Servants help those who cannot help themselves toward the doors, but the line backs up. They begin to slowly shuffle the most needy away from the common entrance. And visibility decreases as more and more smoke drifts into the ballroom.

With the musicians quiet and trying to scramble from the fray along with the guests, I realize that their noise covers other sounds. A musket shot echoes from the nearby street.

More screaming from a large man in a powdered wig, to whom I finally shout. "Be quiet!" But it does nothing to help. People turn foolish the more afraid they get.

Kasimir stays close to my shoulder as I fight to go deeper into the ballroom.

"Where are they?" I scan above the crowd for Elina's wings or a glint of sword in the smoke. Or even a scant brush of red brown from the Margrave's mask.

"I've lost sight of them," he replies. "They were in the center of the dance floor, and I didn't get a good sense of the direction they fled."

I creep toward the closest corner, thinking that if I map the room from its edges, I will most certainly find the missing pair. "Did you expect this?"

"The fire? I know nothing about it. Maybe the Catholics decided that such debauchery close to a feast day is to be punished? Or maybe a mob turned angry when they were denied entry. This *is* the most sought after party of the season, Marina."

I keep my head down, trying to see through the vaporous smoke. "You think that's all this is? A group of angry citizens?"

"I don't know." Kasimir keeps his hand firmly on my elbow, but there's a catch to his voice that I don't recognize. "Marina, stop for a second. Look."

I feel a rush of cold air and hide behind a nearby colonnade. Someone finally opens the outer doors and windows to clear the room. Using my hands and a few whispered words, I make the air sweep the dance floor and push back toward the entrance.

"Again," Kasimir whispers. "I thought I saw something."

I make sure no one is watching before I work the spell again. For a moment, we see a pair of white wings rise into the too thick air.

"There." Kasimir crows. He pulls me onto the dance floor, where we stumble blind for a few moments before we find them.

Von Helm lays on the polished marble, his fox mask off to the side, his face too white and still.

"He won't wake up," Elina cries, face tear-stained as she kneels over him. She's cast her golden mask on the floor, and her hands flutter above his chest like a pair of restless birds. "Why won't he wake up?"

"Let me take a look." It's not easy to get down on my knees in such thick skirts, but I finally manage it.

The Margrave's chest doesn't look to be moving.

"I can't get closer," I say in frustration. My stomacher is too stiff for me to lean. Next time I go to a costume ball I will pretend to be a man so that I may move more easily.

Elina looks up at Kasimir. He's already on his knees on the other side of the nobleman, checking the Margrave's breathing by leaning his ear to the man's mouth

"Someone threw a candlestick. It caught him in the temple. He's too heavy for me to move."

"Fools," Kasimir curses. "Don't worry. He still breathes. He just needs a minute to come back to himself. And the smoke isn't helping."

I hear a second round of musket fire.

"What is that?" Elina asks me.

"Idiot men out to cause trouble."

"Because of a party? Or is it the army? Alasdair said Von Werth's men are on their way—"

She's interrupted by another punch of musket fire.

I cannot stop myself from echoing her use of Von Helm's first name.

"Alasdair?" I force myself to keep talking. "Said an army? Could they be here?"

Kasimir knows I'm talking to him. "It's possible. Maybe they attack at night to surprise the city?"

I feel my chest closing. "We're not ready. We should not be here, dressed like this." The smoke in my lungs makes it hard to get a full breath.

"Marina, we can't tell what's happening until we're out of this smoke. I must find the Duke. I need more information." He pleads.

"We don't have time. He needs to get clean air." I don't like the unsteady rise and fall of the nobleman's chest. "We'll take him the other way."

I've never been to the Duke's house before, but if it's like every other nobleman's home, there's a back entrance which the servants use to escape the smoke-fogged ballroom now.

Kasimir lifts Von Helm onto his shoulders and begins to carry him toward the far hallway, away from the rampaging crowd.

I grab Elina's hand. She pulls me to standing, and we follow. We pass through a great hall with statues and black paintings of weak-chinned noblemen.

Once we make it to the kitchens, we're safe enough that Kasimir pauses and leans Von Helm against a nearby wall, heaving. It's hard work to carry a limp body so far.

"I'll take it from here." I see no more servants and using my hands, I gather a pallet of air on which we may float Von Helm outside.

Kasimir leads, looking to make sure that we are alone at every turn, but it seems all the servants have emptied out. The smell of smoke hangs heavy even here.

Elina frets. She touches Alasdair's face and shoulders as if they know one another intimately. I have to stop myself from cautioning her, in case anyone should see.

Elina writes her own love story now, and I finally admit to myself that this is not even its beginning.

"I owe him my life," Elina says to me, as if she can hear me thinking. "He cannot die before I repay my debt."

"I do not think a debt is all that binds the two of you," Kasimir says. "It looks like love."

Elina's face turns pink.

Kasimir smiles and pats my apprentice's back.

Something catches on my witch's sense, flickering and dancing. I try to focus on it and can't. The thing is too far away.

I bear down on the awareness.

Fire.

Not here. I hear the animals scream.

The Black Forest burns.

I turn back to Kasimir. "You must carry him." I put the Margrave back down onto the floor and gesture to a nearby cart that is normally used to collect vegetables from the market.

Kasimir brings it over, and with Elina's help, we load Von Helm into it.

"So this is where I leave you." I grab a servant's cloak from where it hangs nearby and turn back to my family. "I will meet you both at home in the morning."

"What? No. Why?" Elina's face turns stricken. She takes a step toward me and then looks back at the unconscious man.

Kasimir takes another slow look at me but says nothing. I know he thinks of every way it's dangerous for me to move through the city alone.

There's no way he can sense the wild woods burning, but staring into his eyes, I feel as though he knows. Somehow Kasimir knows that everything I hold dear is threatened all at once.

More musket shots. Kasimir pulls us to the ground.

"I have to go. The Hearth must meet. Now. The men of the city cause mayhem tonight, and maybe we can quiet them before the battle fully arrives." I pause, trying to still my heart. "And beyond, the forest burns."

"You can feel that, even here?" Elina asks.

I nod. "The Stillness speaks to those who would listen. I must go to the Hearth."

"What can I do?" Kasimir asks.

"Keep Von Helm safe," I answer. "Take him home, so that the lovebirds may finish their dance and kiss. Then we will hear wedding bells and the whole city will tell the tale of your remarkable love, darling."

"No," Elina says.

"No? Alasdair will think you have no interest," I tease. I force myself to keep my tone light.

"I'm coming with you."

"*No, you're not.* What will the Margrave von Helm think when he awakes to find his lady love gone?" I frown and put on my most stern face. This is a burden I will not allow the girl to take on. Not yet.

"*You* are my mistress. I don't obey a husband, not yet. I'm your apprentice, Marina. I will follow you to the Hearth."

Elina turns back to look at Kasimir with a question in her eyes.

"Go," Kasimir says in answer. "If he cannot love you like this, it's better to find out now."

I hear the unspoken assent as if he whispers it in my ear. *Kasimir knows me as I am and loves me for it.*

As if in answer to my thoughts, my love gathers me into his arms and whispers in my ear. "Be careful. I think the fighting draws close faster than we imagined, and the streets are not safe."

I nod into Kasimir's hair, feeling the way his hands press warmth into my bones.

Then with Elina's hand in mine, we flee into the night.

CHAPTER TWENTY-FIVE

The Last Trial

The bells of the Strasbourg Cathedral ring on feast days and the sabbath. The autumnal equinox marks neither of these, but I've taken care to find a hidden pathway into the church for when we might need to alert the witches of imminent danger.

Two short rings and a long. Elina helps me pull the rope in pattern three times before the priests sleeping nearby make their way to us, shouting and calling their dogs.

Unfound, we slip back out onto the city streets and make our way toward the Hearth, stopping in an alley once I notice that my apprentice limps.

"What's the problem?" I ask. "Did you sprain something?"

"No. One of my slippers fell off in the ballroom. I didn't want to slow us down."

I frown and start opening up doors in the modest side street nearby, finally stealing a sturdy pair of boots and helping Elina into them. Then together we take off her wings. They will draw attention, good and bad, and just now we need stealth.

The Stettmeisters have runners out and gendarmes, who patrol everywhere, trying to ensure that revelers return home from the Duke's party, and other, smaller parties. Soldiers sing drunkenly, holding hands and calling out to passersby, and I thank the Huntress when I see no one I recognize.

Elina and I manage to hide from the worst of the catcalls and slink through more side streets to the Hearth. We aren't the only ones. On a night such as this one, women stride carefully even in pairs, cloaked and daggered against the night.

Inland from the canal, we climb toward the modiste's shop, a large, dark timber frame building with peach plaster walls, well-made but indistinguishable from the shops on either side of it.

Past the false front, we find the large room beyond the modiste's storefront filled with tables overladen with the fruits of the harvest. Women of every kind drink wine at the table and laugh, skin dark and light making a rich tapestry of color in the candlelight. There's a table of Jewess', witches who normally don't join except on high holidays, and the city's few Moorish witches wear only white tonight, with ritual a meaning known only to them. Together, we're a menagerie of misfits and miscreants, forgotten or merely hidden from the eyes beyond those that would watch us and judge.

Even before our arrival, food already begins to be cleared away. After all, the Cathedral bells can be heard all over the city.

Mab approaches us as we enter. "Your dress is beautiful," she compliments my apprentice. "But who are you meant to be, child?"

"The angel Michael, the avenger," Elina smiles cautiously, her eyes darting to me for some kind of cue. "But I shed my wings on the way here."

Mab laughs as if my apprentice jests. She directs the girl to get a glass of wine.

"Did she meet the Margrave?" Mab asks, taking my arm. "Were they seen by all? Is the fait *acommpli*?"

I ignore Mab for a moment, feeling angry that even now she schemes to sell my apprentice to the highest bidder. Then I remember how the lovers looked tonight. "Yes," I nod. "The Duke's party performed its purpose. I imagine Elina's engagement will not be the only one made tonight."

We hear the boom at the same moment, louder this time—too close to be invaders, which means that the Stettmeisters fire cannons in answer to Von Werth's army's approach.

Half the women in the room scream.

"The battlefront come to Strasbourg. Stay calm," I shout. I feel flames flicker through the leaves and branches a hundred leagues south. "The Black Forest burns tonight too. We must do something now, Mab. Not later."

The witches around us are starting to watch. By her pursed lips, Mab does not want me to say such things aloud.

"*Now*," I whisper again more quietly.

Mab doesn't answer, and I can tell she's angry.

I call out the orders, without asking if I may. "Ladies, put away the food. We gather in council."

A dozen witches move to clear the tables, and several more begin to sweep and clean the ceremonial space.

I wave Elina over to me, feeling stupid in my pink dress, the color saccharine against tonight's bitter end. We climb the stairs together, holding hands, letting the others follow.

Two stories above the street, there's a large open space hidden between the two-pointed chimney of the building, away from the street side and canal. At this time of night, the air feels cool and calming against my flushed skin.

More witches trail us, climbing the stairs in pairs and threes, nearly thirty-five strong, far fewer than in years past. They settle on the outer edges of the gathering space, not wanting to get any closer than they must.

No one but Mab knows of my colossal failure with the sea witch, I remind myself. And no one knows of the mermaid's suicide. They keep their distance out of fear of my power and age.

"What happens now?" Elina asks, at my arm.

I shake my head and don't answer.

The godmothers whisper as the space slowly fills.

"Sister, step forward. Who calls this meeting and why?" Mab finally arrives, a queen, back unbent, long white hair spooling down her shoulders. She resents my behavior downstairs and feels forced into this meeting. And she's frightened. We both know that we have so little chance at success now.

"I do." I step forward and raise my voice. If it's a show she wants, I will deliver. "Marina Mullenheim."

"And why do you interrupt our celebration, Marina?" Mab can't keep the irritation from her voice. "Winter comes soon enough."

Tonight is the night for which she's been waiting. Elina and the Margrave declare their love publicly, and in the morning, we will negotiate to bend their engagement to our cause. Mab planned for the powerful men of the city to offer us a reprieve from their unending intrusion into the woods, and now all of her machinations and manipulations may literally be going up in smoke.

"It's not winter, but war that we should be afraid of. The Black Forest burns, and Von Werth's army is nearly here."

"You can't sense that, not at this distance," Amondine, the water witch, interrupts.

She's too young to know that there are a handful of witches who feel the life of the forest so far away. I'm one.

"If Marina claims the wood is attacked, it's true," Mab finally confirms. "It is as Marina says."

The whispering crowd grows louder.

"What can we do about it?" someone calls out. "You've already stopped the army once, Marina, and it did nothing."

"Let them come." A woman calls from the back of the room. "Our stores are full. What does this fight have to do with us?"

It's too dark to identify the voice calling the question, but whoever it is, I hate her. I hate every small-minded woman in the whole city who believes that they will remain whole while everyone around them suffers.

Suddenly I'm so sick of arguing. I'm even more sick of hiding. "This is the question we're always asked, and we always answer the same way. It's not our problem; we do not have enough power to turn the tide, but now these stupid men bring the battlefield here."

Surely self-interest motivates. I go on. "If we do nothing, then we will die. Or starve to death—if there's a siege. Your family. Your children perhaps."

"And if we don't protect the forest, then our power will weaken." Elina steps forward beside me.

Mab turns to the girl. "What do you know of this, girl?"

"Only what Marina has taught me," Elina admits. "But Marina showed me that the Stillness speaks. Maybe not with words, but *we* have words. What we don't have is time."

She no longer wears her wings, but it's not hard to imagine Elina as an angel again.

The crowd hides another round of naysayers. "No."

"We will be fine."

"You take for granted the power that the Black Forest feeds within us," I shout a warning. "Without it, our magic may be no more."

"We cannot leave the city on the eve of war," a witch shouts from the crowd, Catherine, a fire witch, her red hair nearly throwing sparks.

"Protecting both the city and the wood is too much," Mab agrees. "Maybe we could do one, if we used all of us, but both. There's no way."

"But Mab, we must do both." I pause, not sure what else to say.

"This was avoidable. If only you had convinced the sea witch to sink the ships, we would not be here. This is your fault!" Mab argues, her white skin turning a dusky rose. She has decided to make our disagreement public.

"What is this?" someone asks, her words soft and flowing, Amondine probably.

Mab speaks to the crowd. "Marina visited Violante Aramburu. She was supposed to persuade the sea witch to sink the Spanish Fleet. To end the war. But she failed. She failed, and now we may all die." Mab raises her bitter voice, whipping the crowd.

"Violante would never have agreed," I answer, shouting. "She cares nothing for us here in Strasbourg, so far away from the sea."

"Cowards! You're all waiting for Marina to save you." Elina draws her sword and shakes it at the night. The blade catches moonlight, and everyone turns silent. Elina looks to me, her face white as a saint's and goes to her knees. "Well, I will go to the forest to fight. Send me tonight."

Mab pulls at Elina's arm. "Don't be stupid, girl. Go home to your lover and beg him to marry you. We will stay within the city walls and let the men kill each other beyond. The Margrave may ransom a part of the forest in treaty, if he wins, if you ask it of him as his love. And then the woods will grow back, if it is the will of the Goddess."

"Yes!" I hear a few voices crowd. They're scared.

She gives up so easily—Mab—in this crucible.

I realize suddenly that I have fought every battle she asked of me, yet she herself is unwilling to go to war.

"I don't want to whisper and simper," Elina says. "I want to fight." She raises the sword she grew from a rowan tree again, a miracle of unknown proportions.

Mab frowns. "Why do you carry a weapon among your sisters, girl? Don't you know the ability to offer death is no way to measure power?"

Another witch from the crowd jeers. "Women do not fight on the battlefield, where there's no victory to be found. There, the Reaper triumphs over us all."

"I will protect what is of value with whatever means I have," Elina says valiantly, refusing to be shamed. "Will you do the same?" She turns to the crowd.

"Aye. Aye." A few witches call back, emboldened by her brave words.

"They want to help." Elina turns back to Mab. "*We* want to help."

"And how can we stop a battle from starting. We do not have the magic for this."

"We must try," Elina argues. "We must try something."

"Think how few witches remain." Mab chastises me. "We may lose even more."

I have lost so much. My daughter. My first husband. The mermaid. And all because I said nothing. Did too little. Let the world's ways lead me to despair.

"All of the most beautiful creatures surrender to death," I reply, and the hair on the back of my neck rises as I recognize the sea witch's words in my own. I correct myself. "All creatures surrender to death."

Did Violante know that this is what we would face?

The air stirs as I speak. Amalia's voice comes to me from far away. "I remember those words. I remember! That is what the sea witch said to me. She made me feel trapped like a spider in a web."

I have felt the same thing—too many times.

Trapped.

In a web.

A web! "How many of you can work the air?" I turn to the other godmothers.

More than a dozen hands rise.

"We can weave a web around the city. It will take something big to anchor the spell, though, something alive."

"The river?" Elina grabs my arm. "Let me go with you. I can help."

"The river has too much movement. Marina, if she were practicing magic longer, your apprentice would know that. Come now," Mab warns me quietly, catching my arm. "Your apprentice is barely a witch. She does not count among our numbers. Every other woman here risks discovery without her vow of silence."

"Mab's right" I turn to Elina. "The women here will not welcome you to battle if you can later identify them to be burned. You must be a godmother to go further than this, Elina."

I did not mean to offer this path so soon. I meant to give my apprentice time to make love, have children, and then be called to the work.

"Then make me one," Elina says, leaving no time to argue. "Make me a godmother now so that I might help, and so that the rest of you know my silence is assured." At this last, she nearly shouts.

The witches speak up at her words.

"She's too young."

"Nay. She knows nothing."

"She will turn us in." The witches of the Hearth have much to fear these last few years.

"You don't know what this means," I argue with Elina too. "Your life will no longer be your own. Even in marriage, you must cast aside your husband's wishes and put your fellow witches first."

"You said I would know when to act, and I do. Trust me, Marina. I spent too many years without a family, with magic as my only companion," Elina says. "And I have never felt as alive as when I stand in the forest. If I'm truly to have a home, then the woods are the only place I belong."

"No," Mab says. "We've never taken one so young. The arrogance of youth is folly. Marina, this will not do."

Mab pretends concern for my apprentice, but she thinks of Alasdair von Helm. Her plan falls apart before it is even woven into the fabric of the world.

"Who are you to forbid me anything?" Elina demands.

"Give me your hand," I grasp my apprentice's arm and pull her to standing. "Godmothers, gather round. We will let the magic decide."

My apprentice's last and final trial begins.

Someone takes a bit of chalk and draws a circle around us.

The godmothers stand silent, each having been through this before. The air on the roof turns heavy and thick.

"She's too young to make up her own mind." Mab digs again. "We typically wait til a woman has born her first child."

"I'm seventeen," Elina calls out. "Old enough to marry and bear children, though I haven't yet, and I'm old enough to choose this too."

The crowd falls silent.

"There's an exception to every rule," I contradict. "Mab served the godmothers for nearly four decades, with nary a babe to show for it. We must give the girl her chance, even if it is not in the season of our planning. Now, let's begin."

I nod to the four women who gather at the cardinal points of the circle, each of them witches at the height of their power. I stand at the east and speak first to get the ritual underway. "I am Earth."

"Air," Amelie, a well-known godmother, nearly as old as Mab and me, speaks for the north. I feel the flutter of wind around us, as her elemental gift shows.

"Fire." Catherine, the fire witch, steps forward to take the south's position. As she speaks, a ring of flames flares above her brow.

"Water," Amondine, speaks for the west. The air thickens with the heaviness of rain.

Around us, the circle begins to glow.

"And I, aether," Mab says, from the center, where she stands on the other side of my apprentice. "For what is real is given and received in the Stillness."

Elina's face glimmers in the soft moonlight. She clutches the sword and goes motionless.

Time slips slowly by. I don't know if it is two or ten minutes before she whispers to me. "Now what?"

I worry too. What if the magic doesn't respond? What if she's judged too young? But all I can say is what was said to me so long ago.

"Sssshhh. We wait."

At my words, the air itself starts to spark, little tendrils of light dance around us. Catherine nods in approval at her element's appearance. Slowly, very slowly, the sparks dance and move until they form the outline of a stag, crown rising above his proud muzzle in thirteen points, a beast made from fire and light.

I can't help but think of my vision in the church, and it's as if I summon the very image because in front of me the stag shifts, takes on a different form, four legs becoming two, a man wearing a crown of horns.

In all the godmother ceremonies over which I have presided, I have never seen such a vision. The gifts of trees and animals are most often bestowed: the wisdom of the owl, the keen discernment of the hawk. Very rarely, one of us is visited by the spirit world, but never before by a god. And yet, the king of the forest stands before us.

"The Horned One," someone whispers, echoing my thoughts.

The hair on the back of my neck prickles. This is how legends are made, and I don't like it. Legends are filled with heroism and death, and Elina is too young for either.

The Horned One goes down on one knee before the girl, and Elina, acting on instinct, bows back to the forest's king, holding the hilt of her sword for support.

"Bring out the needle," I whisper, and Mab suddenly stands between Elina and her king.

Mab reaches into the empty air, and from the fingertips on her left hand, there emerges a shining, silvery thread. In her right hand, she holds a needle made only from moonlight. After a moment, she threads the thing.

"Bind them."

Mab starts by looping the thread from the highest antler she may reach, working backward to catch the King's form in the thread's hold and then circling it back to capture Elina.

She moves back and forth weaving the two together. Every time she drives the needle of light through a portion of Elina's body, her shoulder, her thigh, the girl sucks in a breath. Mab's needle pierces something more than flesh.

The ceremony is meant to be painful. Such pain foretells the truth of the journey to come.

The Horned One stands and stomps his foot, displaying the barest show of impatience. He tugs backward, as if to get distance from Elina, and she is pulled forward, off balance, dragging her weapon with her.

"Done," Mab says, and ties off the string.

"Now a godmother and a witch, Elina, you are bound to the gift offered and in turn cast your magic to the service of the Stillness and the Leap, to the benefit of your sisters, the elements, and your mothers, the trees, and finally to us, the witches with whom you are forever family."

"I do," Elina murmurs, after Amondine instructs her what to say. "I will protect the forest. I will serve my sisters, every one. And I will forever be bound to the secret magic of the Horned One." Keeping hold on the sword with her right hand, she flings her left arm around the god's neck. The binding grows tighter, the string glowing as it sinks into the skin of the king and the girl.

Elina and the Horned One disappear.

For a moment, there's only silence.

"Where is she?" Mab asks. She turns to me, her eyes wild. "Where did they go?"

"Wherever they were called." I keep my voice calm, reminding myself that the Stillness will not harm my apprentice without good reason, and Elina aligns herself to our cause by her own choice.

Nothing about tonight goes the way I hoped, and a part of me wonders if somehow, I've done something worse than marry the girl off to the highest bidder.

Mab's words echo my own thoughts. "You've done something. You've hidden her from us. Where is she?"

Amelie slides a foot through the circle and says the holy words that were mine to speak. "I break the circle that the spell may continue on."

Everyone starts talking at once.

"Did you see the stag become Him?"

"The god was here tonight."

Mab gripes at me. "We should never have let her bring a weapon into the circle. Maybe that is why she was taken? Maybe we've offended the god."

"Mab, I've never seen the Horned One. And His presence here tonight is a miracle to my eyes. Peace." Amondine's voice flows with the ease of water over rocks, her blue-black hair catching the barest hint of light. "This is a magic deeper than we know."

I nod, my throat full of appreciation at her unexpected support.

"No two gifts are the same, but she's strongest in fire and earth. I count Elina among my own," Catherine speaks to the circle. "And I never abandon my own."

"Aye. She's one of ours." I don't recognize the voice, but I see a few sparks light in the crowd.

"Fire balances water," Amondine says, and Catherine smiles in response. It's an old saying, taking me back to the memory of my own godmother ceremony.

"A water witch of no small power," Mab christened me.

I'm probably not the only person remembering that moment, when the Stillness brought me something never seen before in this age, a vision thought to signify the return of magic itself.

A mermaid, her scales beautiful and shining with magic, and when we were bound, Amalia sang a song of such longing that I never forgot it, not through all the long years until I finally heard her sing it in Spain.

What a lie that moment of beauty was!

Amalia surrendered her voice for a dream of love, and nothing came of it but death.

I try to keep Elina from the same fate, or worse, but she and the Margrave rush headlong toward each other, even knowing the challenges they face. Why would they choose such a thing?

Where is Kasimir tonight? Already strapping on his armor? This marriage, this adventure he speaks of is nothing like love. It can't be.

I've thought these same thoughts a thousand times. I don't know what to do. I don't know how to save so many. I don't know how to save myself.

Mab's sharp voice slices through my thoughts. "The sword is a thing belonging to men, an ancient object of power. It doesn't belong here."

Catherine throws more sparks. "What's your quarrel with the girl, Mab? The god chose her. Are we meant to argue?"

I nod in agreement. "The forest first offered gifts from the oak, the dogwood, and the rowan, not a bad showing for one come to magic so late. "

"Now the girl's gone, and we gain nothing," Mab says. She raises her voice. "If we weave a web and protect the city, then we leave the sacred forest to burn."

"She's angry with herself, because she believed the girl's marriage was the answer to the rising tide of war," Amalia's quiet voice whispers in my mind. "She can see no other way, because she has not walked the road of death, not like you have."

"How would you know where she has walked?" I ask. Tears creep to the edge of my eyes.

"The spirits of the air blow here and there, learning whatever must be known," the mermaid explains.

"Then tell me what do. How to right this wrong," I ask Amalia. "So that I don't lose the forest, the way I lost you."

"Stop whining when there's important work to be done. Loss is like a bell ringing in the silence. It wakes you up, though many prefer to stay asleep." Amalia's form takes shape before me as she speaks, becoming a cloud of black hair and glistening blue-green scales. "It breaks apart what is bound."

The words strike a chord. I do not want to be broken again. I want to weave this world together. To bind what has been broken.

We have been looking at the battlefront and the forest as separate problems, but they are part and parcel of the one challenge we witches face. What if we do not split our resources and ourselves but instead bring the problems together. Bind them.

Binding spells are very difficult in the best of circumstances but binding the Black Forest to Strasbourg—impossible.

But already, I start to think of how to do it. Elina had the right of it; we must find an anchor, but it would need to be a piece of the forest, something alive. A bit of dried wood or a handful of earth would not work the kind of powerful magic that we need.

The rowan tree.

"I have an idea," I turn and grab Mab's arm. I gesture the four witches closer, fire, water, earth, and air. "We can bind the two places together *before* we craft the protection spell. Then the one web will cover both the city and the woods. We can drive the men to fight—and die—between."

Amondine pursed her lips. "Do you think it would hold for both?"

"Yes," I nod. "If we have the right anchor."

"And what would that be?" Mab scoffs. "There is nothing so strong here."

"Elina's third gift grew into a rowan tree. It stands nearly ten feet tall in Kasimir's solarium, a tree of the Black Forest inside the city gates. If we can bury mirrors facing one another and put more scraps from the forest at the edge of the city walls, we can imbue the power of place into the spell."

"I could weave the air between them," Amelie says, thoughtfully.

Catherine jumps in. "We would need the tree to stand at the edge of the city, the eastern gate, facing the forest."

"It won't work," Mab says, pulling me away from my excitement. The stars above seem to dim at her words. "It will never work. Everyone go home. Marina, you stay. We must find the girl. We may still be able to sign those marriage papers tonight."

I ignore my mistress. I climb on a nearby ledge, my pink dress dirty from the city's streets. "We must work fast," I call, interrupting the witches as they shuffle and conjecture. "We must try. I need five women to help me gather materials to begin the spell. The rest of you, we will meet at the eastern gate before the sun rises. Come now. You and you. You two," I tug at Catherine and Amondine. "Follow me home. And everyone, be careful of robbers."

To my surprise, the godmothers scatter and obey.

CHAPTER TWENTY-SIX

The Holy Tree

Protection spells work best when cast by moonlight. I lead the witches through the still raucous streets to Kasimir's townhouse, checking to see if my mermaid hovers nearby, but the air hangs quiet now.

She's disappeared again.

At the townhouse, someone leaves a cart in the alley. It takes three of us to drag and lift the tree in the air, floating it out of the solarium to the cart. We take off slowly through the streets, one of us still bolstering the integrity of the contraption with magic. The other two carry the rest of our supplies.

At the edge of the city, we meet our sisters, who are already hard at work. Boughs from the Black Forest have been bound on the upper right and left corners of the west and northern gates, and a line of salt and blood is drawn across the upper wall. We see the city's eastern gate, where Amelie sweeps the ground sending the dust of travel away.

When we stop, I see a handful of witches keeping watch from the shadows. Most I cannot name, but Amondine and Catherine begin to whisper instructions. Soon the air above this part of the city wall holds two witches quietly tying more boughs and spilling salt.

Amelie herself takes the mirror to the highest part of the wall and stakes it, making sure it is positioned so that when the sun rises, its rays will strike the surface. By then, another witch will have planted a mirror at the forest's edge too, so that each one reflects the other.

After that, I keep my eye on the little watch house to our right, but so far no one comes out to demand answers. Or even notices the whispering sounds of movement as several witches follow my instructions, digging up a circle of cobblestones from the street so that the tree may sit directly on top of the earth.

"Amondine," I gesture, and the water witch steps forward, bringing a large urn from the cart. She pours water from the secret spring over the packed earth slowly, muttering a few words of blessing.

"Quiet," I caution, as Christine, a stout healer from the poorer part of the city starts to wheel the tree toward me with Amelie's help. "This way. A little more to the left."

Together, Amelie, Catherine, and I use strips of air to lift the tree outside of its barrel and shift it to the circle of packed and damp earth newly cut into the middle of the cobblestone street. The gates of the city stand not ten strides beyond.

"Right here!" I encourage. The only other sounds are scuffling and the creeping of the wheels as a younger godmother, rolls the cart away.

I worry that the spell will not take, but almost immediately, the rowan tree grows bigger. Now the branches stand nearly twenty feet high. They no longer glow golden, but in the dim moonlight of the morning, I see a silver tarnish.

"Who goes there?" Finally a guard awakens, a large man with a bulbous, red nose. He interrupts our concentration. "What are you women doing up so early? And HEY! What's happening with that tree? Get it out of here. You cannot place such a thing in the road!"

The rowan's branches shuffle in the wind, and the roots already sink into the ground as if they were planted there many years ago. "I had a dream. Saint Odile sent me to the gates, and it's here, just as I saw. A true miracle." I shuffle my feet to and fro as if I can't contain myself. "A rowan tree at the gates, grown up nearly overnight, a miracle of Saint Odile. You must protect it, sir? I saw you in my dream too."

"Wot's this?" The guard scratches his belly and stares as if he doesn't understand me. There are sounds around us as early-rising merchants begin to stir.

"In my dream, the saint insisted that if I came to the gates this morning I would find a holy tree. It's a symbol of our city's strength in battle."

"Your name?" he asks.

"Do you need a name to witness the same miracle I see? Such a thing is only possible by God's grace." I sound crazy, even to my own ears, but hopefully my words keep him from thinking. "A whole tree grown up overnight."

"See here. This tree must come down!" The guard argues. "Haven't you heard that tomorrow we see war, and the city's men must go through these very gates. We can't have a tree blocking their way."

"The fighting won't be so quick. Not here surely," Christine cowers, her fear not totally feigned.

"So Saint Odile said." I look at the guard more closely as he makes his way around the tree again, limping slightly. "She told me about your knee, Sir. You must take a handful of the tree's leaves. Boil them and drink the tea each night before bed. It will help your bones."

The guard doesn't answer. He stares up at the leaves for a time. Then he goes down on his good knee, shakily, and crosses himself before it.

"It's a miracle, Madame," he nods in affirmation. "I will tell everyone of it. What was your name?"

"I must tell you again, I'm no one. My name's not important. Tell your masters that Saint Odile blesses the city. Ladies, come now. We must go to church to pray."

Catherine steps forward and motions the other women away.

In another moment, the man's face turns red purple. His eyes widen as he claws his neck. In another beat, he collapses in a heap on the ground.

"*Mon Dieu*, Catherine, did you kill him." Amelie whispers behind me in shock.

I swear too. "Christ's wounds, get the air back in him. We don't want murder on our hands."

At my shoulder, Catherine rolls her eyes. "He's fine. In ten minutes, we'll be gone, and he will only remember the miracle. Now start the next part of the spell. We must move quickly. If Amondine buried the mirror in the right place, the city and forest meet, and the two become one. We must cover them both."

"Ladies," I whisper and call our small group together. "Lift your arms and pull the wind toward us. We must draw the aether in long strips." I move my hands in a complicated pattern and swing my palms upward, sending long strings of magic billowing above us. To my witch's sight, they glow like thick strips of golden fabric flung across the top of a frame.

"I'm to cross yours, so that the magic covers us like thatching?" Amelie and Christine confer before nodding. They turn and begin weaving the air with their hands. Their weaving looks different than mine, the long strands showing cool blue. Together, above the city, I begin to see a covering that looks not unlike a giant tent, bigger than any made with fabric and needle.

"How does it work?" a witch I don't recognize asks from where she stands by my elbow.

"As long as the city doors stay closed, no harm will come to those of us who stay inside."

Her eyebrows climb as if she doesn't believe me. "And when they open?"

"The longer they stay open, the weaker the spell will grow."

"So we must make the spell strong to stay for as long as we are able," Catherine interrupts.

I pass her a bag of gunpowder and sheets of linen from the cart and send the other witch along with her. I make more pouches of powder with long trailing strips of fabric, passing them out to witches in pairs. "Place these on different corners throughout the city. Light them, but make sure the fuse is so long that you have time to escape before the guards see you. Light two. Then two more after that. And then two more. That should distract as long as we we need."

"Mischief and mayhem," Catherine nods, taking two more pouches than she needs. "My favorite."

At those words, we witches melt into the night.

Kasimir still lies sleeping by the time I return at nearly half past five. He snores, and I don't bother to kick off my dirty shoes, slinging back the linen sheets and grabbing him at the shoulder.

"They cannot open the eastern gate."

"What?" His groggy, sleep-addled brain makes no sense. "Where's Elina?"

I love my man that this is his first question.

"She's gone." I stand and pace the room. "But I will find her as soon as I've taken care of the city." I turn back to him. "Listen. They cannot open the eastern gate. The soldiers will marshal soon. I heard gunpowder going off throughout the city. Tonight or tomorrow, the fighting draws close, but we must keep everyone inside."

"They should not be here for four days at least," Kasimir breathes. He starts to understand.

"They're much closer, I tell you!" I try and fail to keep the anger from my voice. "And the godmothers wove a spell over the city, but it only works if everyone stays inside."

"But Von Werth will think us cowards." Kasimir's voice takes on a deeper tone, and he sits up, not bothering to cover himself. "The Stettmeisters' guards are sworn to protect the city, as am I."

"If you care to protect the city, then you will do as I ask." I pace again, the oak floorboards cool under my bruised feet.

"Marina, no." It is not a word that often falls between us, but the tone Kasimir uses brooks no misunderstanding.

As if to punctuate our conversation, we hear the distant sound of another of Catherine's small pouches being set off.

"They're here." Kasimir stands, naked, his cock waving like a weathervane.

Bernice knocks gently. Kasimir covers up as she brings in a porcelain basin of steaming water and then leaves.

"I told you!" I climb to the far side of the bed to grab the chamber pot and crouch over it.

Kasimir pulls aside a curtain and surveys the street.

"You will see nothing from there."

I stand, finished, and begin to wash. For a moment, we are as reflections in a mirror, not touching, separated by something as thin as glass, Kasimir putting his clothes on in reverse of me disrobing.

"I must go to the Duke and see what the Stettmeisters decide. After last night, they will both have gathered their men."

"Make it take longer. If you must take the men out, go through the west entrance. I don't think that will disrupt the weaving as much."

"It will add hours to their march."

"Yes, but the city will be safer."

"Enough!" Kasimir never raises his voice to me. "Magic can do much, but it cannot stop a musket ball, Marina!"

"Don't you dare talk to me in that imperious tone about something which you don't understand."

A small cough interrupts us. Bernice is back. Both Kasimir and I, him wearing smalls and me stripped down to my underskirt and chemise, turn toward the bedroom door.

"There's a man here, waiting for Mademoiselle. What should I tell him?" Bernice asks, keeping her eyes to the ground.

"Where's Elina again?" Kasimir turns to me.

"I believe she's gone to the forest, although I don't know for sure."

"With whom?" Kasimir asks. He must not have heard me the first time, for his eyes darken when my answer does not immediately come. "You did not let her go alone?"

"I did not *let* her do anything," I spit back. "She's her own woman as am I, but she has the best company I'm able to offer her."

"What's that mean? You're being too careful with your words. Don't speak to me in riddles and half-truths. Come Marina, one moment she's nearly our daughter, the next she's able to make her own decisions, just not about the husband she wants?"

Kasimir advances on me, taking me by the shoulders and staring into my eyes.

Another cough interrupts us.

"Unhand me, sirrah," I say, with all my dignity, and step back from Kasimir. "The truth is, she went of her own volition, and I could do nothing about it."

Kasimir's face turns dark red. He opens his mouth, about to retort.

"The man below says he will not leave until he conveys Mademoiselle Elina to Margrave von Helm."

Bernice's voice climbs up in this last part. She does not like being between us in such a mood.

"Then you may tell him that because of Marina, he may be staying a while."

I ignore Kasimir's hard tone. "Just go to your Duke, Bastard. Let me take care of the Margrave's man. I'm comfortable dealing with any number of imperious requests from arrogant males."

I move to the dresser and begin pulling the hideous pink gown on again.

"Let me help," Bernice scurries over to me and takes one look at my skirts before going to the chifforobe and pulling a serviceable gray wool out of its doors. With her help, I step into the softer, clean skirt.

"Marina," Kasimir says, and I know by his tone of voice that my strategist now tries a different tack. "The men *must* defend the city. There's no way to keep them inside, but I will do my best. I will entreat the Stettmeisters and the Duke, if I see him."

I stare daggers at my love. "Don't lie to me."

I sweep past him wearing a simple gown, no ruff, almost indecent, but if the Margrave's man arrives so early as to be rude, then I but return the favor.

Kasimir follows me, saying nothing else, and at the bottom of the stairs we part ways without a by-your-leave, him to his Duke and me to the Margrave's lackey.

CHAPTER TWENTY-SEVEN

The Margrave's Man

The man standing in my entryway looks tired, so I guess that he hasn't slept yet either.

"Monsieur," I nod my head as we pass into the drawing room, and when I pause near the street side window, he immediately begins.

"My master, the Margrave insists that the Lady Elina Kasimir Leiningen-Leiningen be escorted to his Strasbourg home immediately. He wants to personally thank her and you for her heroism yesterday evening at the masque of the Duke of Württemberg."

I nod, keeping my face composed. "Elina did guard the Margrave when the crowds rioted, but the Bastard delivered his Grace home. So why does your Master not seek this rescuer?"

The Margrave's man's face says he agrees with my logic, but he cannot openly contradict his master.

Looking at Bernice, who hovers nearby, he lowers his voice and takes a step closer.

"The Margrave wishes to propose to Mademoiselle. He planned to do so last night, but their meeting was cut unexpectedly short, and now he *insists* that they finish the conversation. He instructed me to bring her and her family so that they be protected in the coming siege."

I don't react to this disclosure, and I can tell that my behavior surprises him. But my next words are even more of a surprise. "Well, you must tell the Margrave that the young Mademoiselle is not home."

The Margrave's man squeaks in answer. "Not home?"

I don't dignify the question with a response.

He hesitates, unsure what to do. The man's surprised that I do not tell him that he must speak with Kasimir instead. He knows, as do I, that this is the traditional way of things. What aristocratic girl is given leave to choose her own husband, after all?

"In that case, is it possible that I speak with the Bastard Kasimir?" He comes to the point reluctantly.

"Also not here," I respond, checking the dirt under my nails, and looking through my lashes at the man.

"In that unlikely case, I was given very specific instructions to wait." The Margrave's man starts to sweat.

"You will wait for several days, I think. Bernice, please get this young man a cushion and some food. He looks as though he hasn't had time to eat or rest since yesterday's evening meal was taken, and we do not want him to collapse. Now what is your name, sir?"

"Pierre, and forgive me, Madame," the man stutters, his face turning red, but I like Pierre all the more when he stammers out his next question. "Elina Kasimir Leiningen-Leiningen was at the party of the Duke of Württemberg a mere…eight hours ago?"

"Yes," I nod. Exhaustion begins to hit me, and I sway a bit on my feet. "Toast!" I call back to the kitchens and take a seat on a nearby settee. "Send in toast and eggs. That should be a start."

"No need, Madame," the Margrave's man protests. "I do not see how the girl could've gone far."

I'm now truly impressed with Pierre's determination to do his master's bidding. Noticing the bag that he carries, I gesture to it.

"What do you bring? More gifts?"

Pierre turns and pulls something from the leather bag. It's Elina's mother's shoe, the white silk a bit more tarnished from all the evening's dancing!

I try to take the shoe from his hand. "Oh dear, I did not think we would recover this beauty. Thank you for returning it, Pierre."

He snatches the shoe back, hiding it within his bag once more. "I'm afraid I am not able to return the item to you, Madame. The Margrave von Helm demands that I only try it on his lady love."

"Why how stupid!" I exclaim, before I can stop the words flying from my mouth. "Many women share the same size foot, as do many men."

Pierre's face reddens. "Yes, Madame, but Margrave von Helm claims that the beautifully turned ankles of his lady love are like none other."

"What drivel," I snort.

Bernice arrives with two full breakfast plates. Ah. Our Cook contrives to lure me into eating through a demonstration of manners.

"That was fast. Sit, Pierre, and let us discuss your master's stupidity at length." I take the first plate from Bernice and set it on a nearby table.

The Margrave's man, seeing that I am about to take my repast, cannot refuse, and for a few moments, the room fills with the sound of two exhausted people eating.

After I sit back and use the napkin Bernice so kindly left to wipe the grease from my mouth, I gamble that truth is the best path forward between the Margrave's man and me.

"You may try that shoe on every woman in all of Strasbourg, but the Margrave von Helm will not find his lady love. She's gone, Pierre, away from the city. My goddaughter disappears on urgent business."

"What kind of urgent business does a young Mademoiselle…"

"I'm afraid I can't answer that question." I stand. "And now if you will excuse me, I make my way to my bed, having also not had the chance to sleep yet. You may sleep too. You will not be interrupted here."

Pierre stands, clears his throat, and bows.

When I am at the door, he speaks again.

"My master is determined to marry the girl," Pierre says softly.

Another distant boom punctuates his words. I do not know if it is the city guards or another of our distractions.

"Württemberg goes to fight Von Werth's men, the Bastard at his side, either today or tomorrow, and I daresay, the Margrave von Helm will be called to his side too. Or they will stay here and cower. We will be lucky if the city is not under siege by nightfall, Pierre. Distract your master from his silly preoccupation with this news."

Pierre nods but only says, "Once I bring your charge to him, I plan to do just that."

I disappear upstairs, held up by a dull sense of unease and Bernice's clucking attention.

I sleep for a mere three hours. Bernice's cousin, Jacques, is a soldier in the Stettmeisters' free army, and from his mother, we learn that the city's elders ignore the miracle of the rowan tree and march their men through the eastern gate by noon.

The people of the city turn mad. I make my way to that same gate weaving through women rushing home with as much food as they can buy from the market. Children play and squabble in hushed tones, begging from anyone who passes. Men bark at one another in the street. I see two fistfights before I am able to get to the gate.

Above me, the protection spell shows fibers of aether and air picked clean or broken. A split starts at the eastern gate and like a run in expensive silk traces an opening outward across the tenting top of the city.

Still, no number of guards is able to move the tree which grows even bigger than before. The priests stand around it, arguing over whether it is witchcraft, or not but no one suggests cutting it. Everyone agrees on the miracle of its growth, and so our spell holds.

I see at least five women pray before it, leaving ribbons tied on its lowest branches.

But the battle draws closer. Occasionally, I hear a cannon shot in the distance. Reports come back that two hundred of Strasbourg's men die in those first few hours and a thousand more Swedes.

According to the soldiers' fearful murmurs, munitions already run low. The Duke awaits a shipment from Sweden, and he thought the battle another week or two off. His miscalculation may cost a thousand lives.

By the time the sun sets, I am nearly overwrought with nerves. I don't know where Kasimir is. I catch two men sharing that two miles away the battle-weary soldiers lay down on the field's edges, setting tents and lighting fires. I stay put in a nearby cafe, barely able to sit still. At dark, the gates to the city close again, but I can still do nothing to fix the spell. Too many people still circle the tree, touching it and praying.

We do our work too well.

Other witches arrive. I catch sight of Catherine and Amondine, and once we talk through what must be done under cover of darkness, I hurry home instead of staying.

I need to eat but cannot.

I lay on the bed where we sleep and make love. Every time I close my eyes, I see Kasimir wearing black breeches, the Duke's symbol tied around his arm. In my heart, I know he's ridden to the battlefield in protection of the city he loves so well.

He does not come home that night.

By morning, a soldier appears to let our house know that Württemberg arrives back within the city's walls. He seems not to know that Kasimir is missing. He reports to me only after I insist: the fighting grows more intense. Württemberg means to bend the Stettmeisters' ears, emphasizing the danger to our free city if we do not send more men.

Whatever the Duke says works though. A decree comes down mid-afternoon that every able-bodied man must report at the eastern gate to be given a weapon and rations before being sent outside our walls.

The spell's strength dwindles further, and where's my love?

I count the hours that second day, finally deciding what I must do near night's fall. There's only one place where the Forest God would take my apprentice, and Kasimir, wherever he is, will be furious if I do not return Elina to our home.

No matter that a battlefield lies outside the city walls. Everyone I love faces danger, and I know what I must do.

I will find my love and rescue my apprentice.

Or find my apprentice and rescue my love.

I can't wait any longer. I escape the city tonight.

CHAPTER TWENTY-EIGHT

One Pleasure, A Thousand Pains

The Duke of Württemberg's residence does not look quite so fine this evening, with servants scurrying in and out of every entrance. I try to follow the path to the front gates, but I'm blocked by a long line of women, or girls rather, about Elina's age, chaperoned by a rabid pack of mothers and aunts.

The line stretches back from the front entrance of Württemberg's manor onto the cobblestone streets, and although it feels rude, I stop one of the most talkative *Mesdames* to ask what is happening.

"You haven't heard? Margrave von Helm searches all of Strasbourg for his hidden *amour*. The woman fled his grasp after they shared a single dance, and now he vows to marry her."

"Where did you hear this?" I ask.

"His footman, Pierre, has visited all the best households in the city. He has her slipper! And he's asking that each girl who claims to be the Margrave's lady love try it on. It's ridiculous, I know, but..."

"So if he goes from door to door, why is there a line here?"

"He hasn't found the girl yet, and no one wants to be left out. We come to him now, instead."

The woman flushes pink. Her daughter, a short girl with delicious zaftig, keeps an ear tuned to our conversation.

"Are you the Margrave's love?" I gamely ask her.

"Not at all," her mother responds for her, grinning as if we conspire together. "But perhaps Von Helm doesn't remember what his true love looks like. The lighting in the ballroom plays tricks with the mind. And my Françoise is a true catch."

I nod and smile back at a game well-played and elbow my way past the long line into the front entryway, cursing the Margrave's man for his persistence.

"I must speak with the Duke." I demand of the closest footman. I repeat the same thing to each servant sent to me in turn until finally I stand before the Duke's housekeeper.

"You'll have to wait, Madame." The woman, tall and thin-cheeked, with a severe jawline nods me backward from whence I came. "There is a war outside our gates, and the Duke is taking no appointments today."

"I need to find the Bastard Kasimir, who fights on the battlefield as one of the Duke's own men, so please let the Duke know that the widow of Stettmeister Mullenheim demands to speak to him. Now." My voice drops with the command.

The housekeeper looks down her nose at me. "Fine, Madame. I will tell the Duke himself. And when he instructs me to throw you out of the house, I will do it. Gladly!"

She strides down the hall. I wait until I see her turn at the farthest corridor before sprinting as quietly as I'm able after her.

Madame Housekeeper climbs a flight of stairs, passing a rather handsome library before knocking politely on a closed mahogany door.

"Enter," a man calls from within.

Madame disappears inside the room. I wait until she comes out again, closing the door smartly behind her. Giving her another couple of minutes to disappear toward the first floor of the house, I wait.

Then, without knocking, I fling the heavy thing wide open.

Mab, her long white hair braided back, turns toward me where she stands by the window.

"You!" I goggle, speechless. "Here?"

"Marina, I'm glad you've decided to join us," Mab says, her raised eyebrows the only sign that my appearance surprises her. She moves closer to the Duke, who leans against his desk, a fat man with wispy shoulder-length hair.

"I'm here to find the Bastard." I retort. "And to tell your Grace that you make a mistake sending more men into battle. If you keep the city's forces inside, no one else need die."

The Duke turns to Mab. "Is this true?"

"Of course not. Her plan is sure to fail. Which is why I am here, on my hands and knees begging for you to pressure the Landgrave to marry the chit now, on paper, before Von Helm returns to claim her."

"What?!"

"The Landgrave's property extends deep into the Black Forest," the Duke says, tapping his fingers on the top of his desk. "Lady Mablean insists that she has your paramour's ear, and that in exchange for a portion of the forest…" the Duke gestures to a piece of paper I had not noticed before. "…Elina Leiningen-Leiningen's marriage to the Landgrave Wiltstern can be quickly finalized now, with none present."

"Mab!" I say, shocked. "You trade my goddaughter like horseflesh."

"Very expensive horseflesh," the Duke says and laughs loudly at his own joke.

"NO," I put in firmly.

"Marina, Von Helm will never sell his portion of the wild woods. He told the Duke as much on the evening of the masque. It has belonged to his family for centuries, and he refuses to part with it, even for love."

"No," I repeat.

"No?" The Duke echoes me, as if he has never heard the word. He runs his fingers along his mustache and truly looks at me for the first time.

"So you are the witch the Bastard Kasimir is so enamored with?"

I flinch at being named so openly. Württemberg bears responsibility for murdering thousands of witches throughout Rhineland.

"Do you slander me, Your Grace?" I ask, my face flushing.

"And Kasimir's goddaughter is a part of this too? Is she a witch as well? Did she slip Alasdair a love potion? Is that why the man pursues such a poor little rabbit?" The Duke shifts his bulk uncomfortably. He strokes his beard and eyes my figure. "I myself prefer older women, a bit more seasoned."

Mab frowns.

"Where is he?" I blurt out, unwilling to be distracted.

"Do not answer her? What will you trade for that information, Marina?" Mab asks, walking closer to me.

"Are you *with* him?" I ask Mab, finally taking in the comfortable fit of her skirts and the stomacher only loosely tied. I've never seen her braid so messy.

The Duke takes her hand and covers it with his own, pulling her back into his orbit. "She is mine."

I frown. "Everything is a resource to be expended on your behalf, isn't it? Even your woman is to be owned. And for what? Sex. Money.

No. Power. On the street, they say that you lost nearly a thousand men yesterday, mostly Swedes. And you're likely to lose a thousand more today. Soon the ground itself will bleed at the sound of your name."

The Duke releases Mab's hand to rub his rib absently, as if pained. "None of us escape this battle unscathed," he says.

I gather the meaning of his words from watching the action. "An injury. So that's why you returned. And did my love return with you?"

The Duke sighs. "Christ, you're tiresome. No. The man wanted to keep fighting. He believes he has something to protect, I suppose, having never been married. I've been married twice. You learn a bit about the nature of women in the marital bed. How untrustworthy you all are, even the best among you." He smiles fondly at Mab with these last words.

I waste too much time with this fool. Kasimir could lie on the battlefield right now. I raise my hand to draw the air from his lungs.

Nothing happens.

I call a flame to my palm. I do not care if I have to burn a hole through the Duke's chest.

The flame flickers weakly and then is doused.

"The protection spell over the city," Mab whispers. "It's too much."

She's right. Where the Stillness lies full and bright, I feel only the absence of a power I've known my whole life.

"It's bleeding the forest's magic dry," she says.

I can't believe the secrets she speaks in front of this man. She gives all of us away with her words, and she says them so casually that the betrayal must not be new.

I square off to Mab, when suddenly my power returns. The Duke's face flushes red and then purple.

"Mab, your Duke chokes. Perhaps he bit off more than he could chew. You should help him," I say, speaking slowly to let the seconds pass.

"Stop it!" Mab flutters her hands and pulls against the hold on air that I have, but I'm stronger than her.

I realize that I've always been stronger than her.

Württemberg's eyes bulge as he tries to draw in a breath. "Help me. Mab, help," he wheezes.

I nod sweetly. "Duke, you look unwell. Lady Mablean, untie his cravat!"

"Marina!" Mab argues, doing as I say. "You're ruining our chances to own a swath of the forest. If the Margrave ever finds out the truth about Elina, he will disown her."

"He already knows the truth, Mab, and he loves her still." I retreat until I find the door handle in the palm behind my back, releasing my hold on the air. "Not as a negotiation."

The Duke draws breath, clutching his throat. He coughs.

"Now listen to me, you fat fool, and I will tell you how to survive the battle in exchange for the Bastard's exact location."

Württemberg coughs again and rubs his chest, eyeing me with more care. "Do not offer me a foul spell, witch. Your kind knows nothing of battle. I want none of your lies."

"Is that what she told you?" I nod toward Mab. "How well do you trust the witch you keep by your side? Did you know that *my kind* can oft see the future? I can tell you yours now, if you like."

I have come to my end. The war may claim me. Or the fire. But if I make it to the other side of this, I will never again lie in chains waiting for a priest to come shave my head.

"You will die today if you not heed me, that much I know. But if you leave me and my kind be and follow my teaching, then you will live to fight many more battles." I dangle the possibility of escape before him.

The Duke's eyes narrow. "You speak in riddles, bitch. Tell me clearly what you mean."

Mab purses her lips, but she doesn't say anything.

"Kasimir's location first," I demand.

The Duke rubs a hand along his jaw, watching me. Finally he turns and inks out a quick map on a piece of nearly ruined parchment from his desk. "Kasimir's probably dead by now. He was in the thickest part of the fighting."

Mab comes forward to grab my hand. "Let us sign the marriage papers for Elina before you go. You know she will forget Von Helm in time, and we can sleep knowing the forest is safe."

"Never," I vow. I go forward and pluck the map from the Duke's hand, expecting him to call the guards any moment, but Württemberg stays silent.

"I've seen the spell above the city, Your Grace. If your soldiers stop trampling in and out of the eastern gate, it will hold." With the door handle in my palm, I pray that it is so. "But you must not leave."

"My people will think me a coward."

"Your people will know you are a survivor," I say. "They will respect that you have done whatever it takes to keep the city strong."

Mab turns away from me, walking back toward the window. We both know that she's ruined. The Hearth will never let her lead gain, not after learning the truth of her alliance.

I wave the map in the air, and make a little bow. "Remember my words, Duke. Do not leave the city walls. Do not cross the river to the battlefield again. Instruct the remaining men from afar. If the Stettmeisters keep the gate to the city closed, you will stay protected, and in fact, the city will survive too. Mark my words."

The coward nods, rubbing his wound again.

I back out the door slowly and then run.

On the lower floor, I turn left toward the line of mademoiselles, rather than right toward the front entrance.

Each girl waits for a few moments until her name is called, and then she and her mother or aunt step through a pair of tall arched doors into an elegantly appointed sitting room.

I peek through the opening on the next summons, apologizing to the women who I cut off in line, and slip inside.

Pierre, the Margrave's man, stands at the far end of the room near a brocaded chair, holding Madame de Boer's shoe with all the ridiculous solemnity of a chambermaid helping a queen to her toilette.

I recognize the girl who sits on the chair and the woman who hovers beside her, large-breasted, wearing a nauseous peacock green stomacher over a dark green skirt.

Elisabet de Boer watches as Pierre sits on a low stool before her and unlaces her boot.

The Margrave's man tries to slide the slipper on her foot.

The delicate silk strains and stops halfway over the girl's fat arch.

"Mademoiselle, I regret that this is not a fit," Pierre says, in his quiet, close-mouthed fashion. "Your foot is too big."

"Pull harder," Elisabet orders. The girl's dark hair is braided in a crown, and the style gives her a regal air she otherwise would not have.

"I cannot damage the slipper," Pierre insists.

"I will do it," and Elisabet reaches down with both hands to yank the thing upward, but Pierre stops her with a gentle hand.

"No."

"Let Ava try," Madame de Boer interrupts, giving Elisabet a raised eyebrow. "Darling, sweet poppet, we cannot help it that this *servant* does not recognize how to properly dress a lady."

"Stupid man," Elisabet huffs. She waits as Pierre returns her own boot to her foot and then kicks upward, pushing the man off balance so that he falls backward.

"Darling," Madame de Boer scolds, but from her tone, Pierre and I can both tell that the woman silently cheers on her daughter's ill behavior.

"My turn," Ava crows and scoots onto the chair as soon as her sister stands. She holds her foot outward, nearly kicking the Margrave's man in the face. "Take it off."

Pierre flinches and scoots his stool back. "Oui, Mademoiselle."

He takes off Ava's boot and slides the slipper up Ava's foot easily, but the thin lace hangs off of her foot. After another moment, the slipper falls by itself to the floor.

"Not a fit, I think," Pierre says.

"Definitely not." I move toward the three women, raising my voice so that all may hear me.

When Madame de Boer catches sight of my face, I wave and smile so that she sees my teeth.

"But our daughters must try to make the best match they can." I keep my tone light as meringue.

Ava stands without allowing Pierre to put her shoe back on her foot. "What are you doing here?" She turns back to look at Madame de Boer frowning. "What is she doing here, Maman?"

"I don't know. I had no idea the Margrave kept such low company," Madame de Boer sniffs.

"I might ask the same of you," I reply, but look toward Pierre.

Ava slides her shoe back on, hopping on one foot. She spits at me as I draw close, missing, and the gob flies onto the Duke's perfectly polished floor.

Pierre stands and speaks stiffly to Madame de Boer. "Your daughters are not a match. You're free to go, Madame, you and both of your ill-mannered daughters." His tone makes clear that the seeming request is an order. "We have many more mademoiselles to inspect."

"Well, I never expected to be treated so unkindly," Madame de Boer says.

"Is there a problem?" The Duke's housekeeper leans through the doors, summoned by the slow-moving line.

"This man does not know the treasure he passes by," Madame de Boer seethes, as the woman and her ducks waddle away.

"Pierre," I turn back to the Margrave's man once the room clears.

"This search is folly. I told you the girl is not here."

Pierre gestures to a footman at the door to hold the line outside. He wipes sweat from his brow and smiles at me.

"Ah, Widow Mullenheim. I must thank you again for the delicious breakfast with which you provided me yesterday morning."

I nod in answer.

"When the Margrave returns, I must prove to him that I've done everything I could to find the woman he loves."

"Even if he asks for an impossible task?"

"Dans les faucons, les chiens, les armes et l'amour, pour un plaisir mille peines," Pierre returns to me and shrugs the philosophic shrug of a Frenchman.

In hawks, hounds, war, and love, for one pleasure a thousand pains.

I could not agree more.

I slip out of the southern gate, in a crack between two houses and use the swiftly moving air to fly across the canal. Despite the depleted and shifting magic, Annabella will do her best to close the fissure I've made behind me.

Beyond the city, the battlefield stinks of death. Men fight, moving the front line closer to the city. I skirt the edges of their ranks, keeping my cloak up, and luckily no one notices me. Further afield, where the battle started, the ground runs red with blood, and flies cover bodies and bite horses, dead and alive.

I search the area the Duke marked first, empty now that the fighting draws closer to the city. Hundreds lay on the field. The sounds of pain and suffering fill my ears, but I stumble through their littered forms anyway.

"Help me, mother," a nearby soldier says, barely more than a boy. Intestines spill out like foul sausage from the wound in his gut. "Help me."

"I'm here, my sweet boy," I promise. I lean down and brush his blond hair away from his forehead before drawing my knife across his throat.

He convulses, and the air thickens with the smell of piss. Then he's gone.

A soldier nearby watches. "Come to me next," he croaks. When I get closer, I see that one of his legs has been crushed. "Help me. Bring me a sweet death."

The words lay me bare. I'm no surgeon. I can't saw the leg from his body, and in good conscience I cannot kill a man who would otherwise survive. I move one and look for Kasimir. He's not here. So I summon sleep, taking care to siphon my magic slowly and leave the poor man for a field doctor to find.

Another calls out. I bow instead to the body before me. Someone slit the soldier's throat. Blood covers his chest, and even as I watch, the spirit passes from his body. I close his eyes before the vultures pick them out and whisper a blessing for safe passage.

"An angel," someone nearby breathes. "The angel of death. Come to me next."

Maybe the prayer makes meaning of this mess because I spend hours offering death to those who would otherwise suffer. I use nearly no magic, not wanting to pull from the power that the spell over the city needs.

Around me, soldiers carrying munitions mistake me for a grave digger or a robber. They don't waste time on either. I keep my black cloak on and carry a tall walking stick, in case anyone tries to hurt me, and I search every face for Kasimir.

By the time the sun sets, I'm covered in blood and smell like piss and shit myself. I've looked into hundreds of faces for my love and not found him. Under the slowly darkening sky, gunshots and cannons stop firing. The battle ceases for another day.

Campfires burn close to the banks of the river Ile, too close for my liking. Most of the tents pitched bear the markings of the Duke of Lorraine or Von Werth.

The Catholics route Württemberg. If the Duke's forces fight again tomorrow, there may be no more Huguenots left.

Suddenly I can't breathe. The stench overwhelms me. I lean over, gagging, and empty my stomach near a stiffening corpse.

"Here. I'm here," a voice calls, familiar, and I whirl around to see the man who speaks. He lays twenty feet hence, facedown, black clothes muddy and torn.

Black clothes. And the Duke's symbol on his arm.

I've found him!

I rush to Kasimir's side and try to roll him over. A bullet hole in his back leaks. The back of his uniform is soaked with blood. His breath bubbles with the sound of a collapsing lung.

"Kasimir!" I tug hard to get him on his back, hearing his heart pump once, twice, more slowly a third and final time.

I can't see through my tears.

"Goddamnit!" Finally, I turn him over, the empty face staring up at me is foreign.

This body is not Kasimir.

Not him.

None of these men are him.

I have come all this way and found nothing. I've spent too much time here and with nothing to show.

I close another corpse's eyes. "Where are you, my love?"

But no one, not even the wind, answers me.

I will find Elina instead.

CHAPTER TWENTY-NINE

The Forest Cave

I find blackened stumps and ash for a league's depth into the forest. The burning went much further this time, which is probably why the spell in the city falters. The soldiers appear to have moved on though, leaving only smoke and wreckage behind.

"Elina! Cendrillon!" I shout all the names my apprentice may answer to until my voice turns hoarse but no one answers.

The moon wanes tonight, not a good sign, as we seek to gather strength and protection, but I ignore the pang of worry and keep walking and shouting. "Elina! Where are you?"

It's too much, to lose both my apprentice and Kasimir in the same stroke.

"Elina!" My voice croaks.

Finally, exhausted by the day's death and failures, I find a small cove of moss and lay down to sleep under my stinking cloak.

I wake hours later, disoriented. The clearing fills with a thin, watery light that distorts more than it clarifies. Only the silver backs of the trees are visible tonight. I listen to the Stillness and make my pounding heart slow.

Patience.

Magic floods my veins.

The crack of a branch sounds like a gunshot, but I refuse to release my calm. I wait until I hear the leaves shuffle and the snort of a large beast.

The Horned One stands before me, two-legged, wearing the head of the stag, and I know that if I were to count the points his rack would match that from Elina's vision.

He's naked from the chest down, and that is how I know I'm not dreaming, because his big cock stands straight up as if he were all rutting beast and not half man.

I'm too old for *sensibilities*. I brush the leaves and sticks from my clothing and stare as some part of me notes that every story, every tale holds a bit of truth, for if the Devil is this, if the Horned One is *he*, then the priests' insistence of his power, his virility, his utter commitment to instinct and sex and life is more true than any person imagines.

The Horned One *is* the forest, and in him, the forest is unbearably, violently, riotously, alive.

Suddenly the air in the clearing feels thin, almost too thin to breathe, and I drag a loud inhale to bring more of it into my lungs.

The Horned One still does not speak. Maybe he cannot?

"Where is she?"

"The girl bound and buried the sword," he says simply. "So that our forest may stay protected. It's an older magic than the simple spell you and your sisters weave."

Do I hear a faint approval of Elina underneath his words? "What do you mean *bound and buried*?"

My witch's sense notices that around us the animals stop moving. Some edge away. None in the wood choose to interrupt my audience with the forest's king.

"You're a rather puny witch," the Horned One observes. And the pressure in the clearing becomes *more*. I feel all of my age until I can barely stay standing.

"Why can't I find Elina?" I ask again, forcing myself to demand an answer.

"The wyrm trapped her when she willingly took that gift, witch. I've brought her here to make its cost less."

"The sword? What wyrm?" I ask.

The Forest God shakes his head, as if to knock away an irritating fly. "The sword's magic demands death in repayment for victory. Someone must die. There must be a sacrifice." The Horned One huffs, as if in frustration.

"Who?" I ask. "Who must die?" I feel as though I stare down at him from outside my body.

The Horned One chuffs and paws the ground with anger. "Even gods are not immune to the laws of magic. Do you hear me? The girl offered herself."

And suddenly I no longer care that I speak to a god. "No."

"It is not yours to decide," the Horned One says.

I argue. "*It is mine as much as anyone else's.* Elina is my apprentice, not yours. She does not belong to the wyrm who you say brought her here. And no, there will be no sacrifice. No more maidens taken into the wood to die. If we need to protect the wild with magical swords, in the way of men, so be it, but I will not surrender the most talented witch to be born in Alsace in decades to be a *virgin sacrifice* on your altar."

"Not my altar." The Horned One turns his head as if listening to a sound I cannot hear. He snuffs the air and strides toward a nearby oak, whose width spans more than double the length of both his arms, and runs his antlers against it, cutting the bark, snorting like a beast.

I begin to laugh. I bend over with the power of it, and as my ears work fine, I hear well how mad I sound.

"Take me to her," I command, readying myself to fight a god if he refuses.

The Horned One lifts himself away from the tree trunk and turns toward me. "This way," he says and turns to walk deeper into the forest, in the direction from whence I came.

"I've been that way," I call, swiftly taking up the path.

"No," he says.

I look around us, seeking the ash trees and the small stand of poplar through which I earlier passed, but it is as the Horned One says. The forest around me grows only graceful willow and cherry trees. Large ferns cover the ground. I've not been here before.

Ever.

I don't recognize the path we take. Mist drifts on either side of us, and at some point, I reach out to touch its twining tendrils.

"Stay on the path," the Horned One warns, without looking back.

My hand drops back to my side.

The Horned One slows as the trail slopes right and then left until suddenly a black mouth yawns before us. He stops.

"What is this place?" I ask. The air coming from the mouth of the cave feels warm and smells faintly of sulfur.

"A very ancient burrow, known by more than one name to more than one people."

He stands near the entrance, watching my face, and paws the ground near the opening.

"What happens from this point forward is unknown even to me," he warns. "You tread an ancient path but forge a new purpose. I've paid my debt to the one who hides within, and I will have no more part in this. I cannot aid you, but I offer no harm either. Your journey is your own, witch."

He pauses. "But I prefer to keep the girl, since we are bound. Save her, and I will offer you a boon."

I nod. "I will not lose her. I cannot." I promise myself and Amalia.

"This is where I leave you," the god says.

I take a breath and summon flame. Then I step into the darkness.

The flame flickering in my palm illuminates a large chamber, nearly twenty paces long. Nothing much lies within it, except for rocks and sticks and odd bits of fur and plants, the remains of some kind of den.

"Are you sure Elina is in here?" I call back, but the Horned One no longer stands outside. He's gone.

I take a breath and walk deeper into the darkness, the light of my flame dimming as the magic struggles to find its hold underground.

At the back of the cavern, a small opening exists, large enough for a person to walk through.

I gaze into that crevice, not wanting to go alone, but after a moment, I decide to pass through. If the Horned One wanted me to die, there are easier ways to kill me. I must either trust the god of the wild wood or accept failure.

And I will not fail. Elina lies somewhere within the borders of the forest, and I must find her.

After a few steps, I grow more used to the darkness that envelops me. I see only a few steps in front of me, and past that, I walk blind. My breath escapes me, and I try not to think about what will happen if I get lost beneath the earth.

Then the path before me diverges, and I must choose which direction to take.

Why didn't the Horned One tell me more? But I think and smell the stale air and in the end, listen to my own inner prompting to go left.

Time's hard to measure underground. When my breath grows short, I stop for a few minutes, and then I press on again. After another passage of time, the darkness before me feels bigger somehow.

"Elina!" I shout and hold up the flame before me.

The path widens into another chamber.

My light bounces off of a table, with one chair, pulled slightly out, as if once occupied. And beyond it, a catafalque made of stone.

Elina.

The girl lies on the stone bed still as a knight's corpse, her white and navy skirts spread around her. She holds the sword's hilt with both hands, the blade dividing her face into two halves. Even in the flickering light, her cheeks look lightly flushed. Her hair falls down around her shoulders in golden brown ringlets.

"Elina," I whisper. I gently place my hand on her shoulder and shake. Her skin feels warm to the touch, not cold and stiff as a corpse might. "Wake up."

She doesn't respond, not to my words or my touch.

I inspect her more closely, looking to make sure that there isn't some sign of a wound or of poison on her skin. I check her stomacher and ruff. I slide my hand inside the pockets of her skirt and pull out a small knot, woven in pink and red ribbons It binds fabric that I recognize, a bit of Kasimir's favorite handkerchief and a curl of fine silver hair taken from my brush.

A love knot.

"You stupid girl," I say. She learns my lessons too well. Elina's connived to make a spell that binds Kasimir and me together. The handiwork is lovely, the edges of the knot tight and strong. Is this why his absence cuts me so deeply? "How dare you?"

But it does no good to question a sleeping apprentice on the ethics of cunning magic, so I slide the knot in the inner pocket of my cloak and grab the sword's handle, trying to slip the weapon from her grasp.

The pommel comes up easily, but beneath it, Elina's skin turns an alarming shade of white, then gray as if she were long dead.

I release the sword and watch the effects reverse. She appears as if sleeping once again.

The flame in my hand flickers for a moment, and I smell a thick smell at once familiar and strange.

"Who's there?" I hold up my flame, but the light only illuminates an empty portion of darkness past the stone bed.

"If you wish for the girl to die immediately, then take the sword from her hands," A voice rises out of the darkness, old and creaking with disuse.

I say nothing but walk forward, looking for the owner of the voice.

"But perhaps that is the point? Once the witch accepted the burden, victory's assured. Her death must mean nothing to you compared to the safety of your forest."

Anger rises in my chest, but I'm stopped from replying as the smell grows reptilian and cloying.

The darkness before me twists. Light reflects off a thousand surfaces, scales, and my mind struggles to understand what I see.

A dragon, black and so large that it *is* the darkness. The beast snakes its neck outward to meet me, turning sideways, so that I may stare into an eye the size of my own head.

I can't breathe.

My flame grows, the closer the beast draws, as if it breathes magic. Around us, the walls of the cave shimmer with crystalline beauty and gold.

"What do you mean, she's accepted the burden?" I finally gasp.

"The blade promises victory to those who know its secret," the dragon replies, its voice echoing off the walls. "It's there in the thing's nature, the double-sided blade: loss is the only way to gain. Death the only path to victory. It's a nasty bit of magic. Made by and for men. A bauble from another age."

"My apprentice surely did not know the blade's true nature when she accepted it," I say angrily.

"No, but she cast her need widely, and I thought to answer it. She wanted to deal death to her enemies, but I offered her much more: the chance for victory on a larger stage. When she came here and learned the blade's true cost, it did not deter her. She wanted those who pursued you to die."

I remember the mob outside of Kasimir's house just before the sword appeared. "You tricked her!"

The dragon's head retreats back into the shadows, and I struggle to make out the shape of its massive body. It's easier to see the walls of the cave, solid gold, and the glow of crystal at its feet. "Peace. What need do I have for such a sword? None. Hold your tongue, witch. Your apprentice will be a hero. Your forest needed someone willing to offer something of value on its behalf. A death for a life. The girl said all she had was herself, but the Forest God could not bear to lose her straightaway. He bargained for more time. So she sits there. Not aging. Trapped between the now and then.

"Maybe it's a mercy then, to take the blade. Then you do not draw out her death." The creature laughs, the terrifying sound of knives scraping together. A foreleg steps forward, closer to the light, revealing five claws long and sharp as steel blades.

"Is all of this hoard yours?" I ask, sweeping my arm wide.

"The treasures of the earth belong to no one," the dragon answers, its voice soft and deadly.

"So I'm to believe that you hide here, staying underground, surrounded by crystals and gold by *accident*?"

"It doesn't matter what you believe. My duty is to guard this place from the grasping hands of men–women too–just as it's the Forest God's job to protect what grows above."

"And Elina?"

"A beautiful maiden, to be sure. I did not know the Horned One had chosen such a beauty until he brought her here."

"He traded her to protect the wood." I said.

"Pah! The god's bond to the girl had not been made when I offered her the sword. The forest's safety was not secure. I only wanted to stop men from digging and crawling. There are days when the veil thins. When it does not take a god to tread the path to my lair," The dragon scorns. "The Horned One insisted on leaving the girl here once she made her decision. He demanded I slow the magic's pace."

I retreat, circling the catafalque on which Elina lies. The dragon slithers forward, nimble despite its size, and curls a single claw protectively near the base of the platform.

"She makes a lovely spark." The dragon croons, using the mermaid's word for Elina.

"If you revealed yourself to the world out there, the world above, then there would be no need for this war. The forest could continue undisturbed." I cover Elina's hand with my own, refusing to abandon her to the beast's grasp. "And they would all know that magic is real. That the world they fight to control is much, much bigger and more wild than any imagine."

"Pah!" The dragon scoffs again. A small puff of smoke escapes out of a mouth full of needle-sharp teeth. "And what then? Your dreams dissipate like clouds. You believe your armies would cease fighting, witch? No. They would join together and turn on me. They would hunt my kind. They would dig into the earth to find the treasures that I and others like me hide."

I cough when the smoke hits my lungs.

The dragon snarls. "Humans make use of every bit of knowledge, every scale, every treasure to further their own selfish ends. No, I will not involve myself in human affairs. I do not exist to make meaning on your tiny stage. It will be another thousand, no, two thousand years, before your kind realize that they bear no more importance than the rabbit or deer."

I hold my tongue, for have I not thought the same thing countless times over the last fifty years of my life? And if I lived half the span of the creature before me, I would only be more firm in my belief.

"But Elina?" I ask again, my voice softening. I look down and brush the hair back from her face and feel my heart convulse in my chest. "How long does she have?"

The dragon turns its head up, as if listening to something beyond the sounds of the cave. "If I so choose, I might keep the girl here for a hundred years or more. I may let the god look upon her from time to time. For what is out there for her but suffering and grief? Above ground, she would age, lose her beauty, and her strength. She will break on the wheel of the world in so few years, just as you have, just as all humans do. But here, she remains young and beautiful until she passes." There was bitterness in the words, and a longing. Both claws held the catafalque now, as if to pull Elina back to him.

I fight the urge to flee. It's a dragon's nature to hoard beautiful things, and like the men above, this beast sees Elina as something to own.

"Elina's place is not here with you, stuck between living and dying. Her path is up there, in the midst of the war, and yes, it involves pain, the loss of beauty, of suffering, and even death. But not like this."

"You answer your own question then," the dragon slithers backward into the darkness. "Separate her from the sword, if you may find a way, and the wild wood will be no more."

I cannot bear to hear the truth in those words. For a moment, tears surface, and I cover my face, turning away from the dragon.

A voice whispers to me from the Stillness, familiar, heartbroken itself. "Do not make the mistake I did." The mermaid's ghost, a spirit of the air, speaks in my mind. "Do not abandon yourself to your grief."

The dragon casts its head from side to side, as if it hears the mermaid speak. Its neck snakes out again, to dangle above me like a great weight, even as its eyes search the corners of the room.

"For now the city is safe and bound to the forest. But you are not released, Marina. Look at me. See how I tried to get free of what was to be. That way does not work." The mermaid's voice is so quiet now that I can barely hear her.

"This cannot be the only way to protect the forest," I turn back to argue with the dragon. "I want to know how to release Elina from the sword's grasp, so that she may be free."

I hear a tap, tap, tap, as the blades of his right claw strike the golden wall.

I press. "You say that you exist only to guard, not to hoard, and to keep safe the world's treasure. Then let the girl decide where her place is. Do not keep her trapped here as this…whatever this is. Do you not yourself long to fly? Long to search the skies?"

I had not noticed how Elina's face drains of color. In her hands, the sword gleams brighter than when I first entered the chamber. Its grasp on my apprentice tightens.

"Let us share a riddle," the dragon finally says, slithering forward again and circling its head low so that its neck wraps around the base of where Elina sleeps. "Let it be a test of your mettle, and if your heart proves bold enough, I will sever the sword's hold over the girl. And you may take her back."

"Do not trust him," the mermaid's ghost warns.

"One riddle," I agree, my chest rising with hope. Perhaps Elina will survive. Perhaps we will escape this hidden cave.

"If you have me, then you want to share me. If you share me, then you don't have me," the dragon intones.

I wrack my brain, saying nothing.

"Help me," I quest outward wordlessly, but the mermaid says nothing. So I stay silent, turning the words over in my mind.

The air in the room heats.

"Make your guess!" the dragon calls. "It's time."

I make this journey so far. Alone. On my own.

And now there is nothing more I can do.

I've failed. I lost my mermaid, Amalia

If I lose Elina, then I will be alone again. I will have no one to teach. No one with whom I may walk this lonely path.

That's it.

I will be alone.

Alone.

"Loneliness," I say. "The answer is loneliness, for if you have me, then you want to share me. If you share me, then you don't have me."

"NO!" The dragon roars. "The answer is a secret. A secret!"

"Both are true," I protest.

"There can only be one answer, witch." The air heats again.

"You're not as wise as you should be if you believe that, beast."

"*I am your secret,*" the mermaid's ghost whispers, suddenly by my side. "Now you may know the truth because you answered the riddle well. You are right. There isn't one way to freedom. Quick. Grab the sword and drive it into the dragon's heart. The price must be paid, the life taken, but the magic cares not by whom."

I hesitate.

"Who whispers and sneaks in my cave? Who threatens me?" the beast roars.

"NOW!" Amalia demands.

I take the sword from Elina's hand and with all of my strength, I swing it wildly into the dark.

She turns even more pale. I can see the life draining from within her.

"Aaiiiyyyeeee," I scream, swinging the heavy thing around.

"No!" the dragon thunders. "Keep back." The cave itself trembles as the wyrm tries to pull itself away from my reach.

I strike again, but the illusive darkness of the dragon's hide slips away from my grasp.

"Do not touch me with that blade!" the dragon warns.

I ignore the warning. And lunge forward hacking at the air, once, twice, then the blade strikes true. I drive the steel up and under the foreleg of the dragon, toward the center of its chest.

The blade slides in nearly to the hilt before it stops cold, held fast by the scales, a stream of green ichor flowing from the wound.

The beast screams.

"What have you done?" it roars. The dragon whips its neck down to look at the wound. "I'm the last of my kind. When I die, there will be no more. Do you know what that is like?"

I release the blade, which slowly slides out of the wound. More ichor flows, coating the floor. "Yes," I say, slipping, unable to stand. I can't believe I have done such a terrible thing. "Yes, I do."

To my left, color floods back into Elina's face, and she sits up. "Marina? Is the forest safe? How am I alive? If I'm not dead, I must've failed." She frowns.

There's a loud whooshing sound. The air in the cave turns so hot that the skin on my face and chest pulses.

"Get down! Zounds." I pull Elina off the pedestal and nearly drag her toward the crack in the wall from which we came.

Elina turns to see the dragon's head following us, needle sharp teeth dripping with venom.

A song fills the cavern, a song I thought to never hear again after discovering her broken body at the sacred fountain. Amalia's stolen voice rises, at once a prayer and a lament.

The dragon takes a deep breath.

Elina slows.

"Faster," I shout, not letting her turn back, but my voice breaks the mermaid's spell. "He will roast us."

Flames cover both of us with a rushing sound, and then the pain grows and grows until it touches every inch of my skin. My hair goes up like a torch. I scream until I feel my voice falter. My clothes light and burn away. My skin crackles, the fat underneath bubbling. I feel my eyebrows peel off and open my mouth to scream again.

But my mouth won't work. My throat fills with smoke or maybe all that is left of it is smoke. The skin on my arms already black and charred.

Beside me, Elina stands at the heart of a bonfire. She's an outline of shadow, white bone relief against blue flame.

That is what I must look like, I realize, not breathing, not screaming, only pulsing unending pain.

Death. This is the death that awaits me, to be consumed by fire, not at the stake, as I thought, but by the dragon's flame.

"I will save you, just as I should've once saved myself," the mermaid whispers, her tone urgent. Her voice sounds very far away. I try to turn toward it, but there is nothing of me to move.

I hover above two piles of bones on the floor, ashes falling like snow. Looking at them, I realize that one pile is me and the other is Elina.

I watch the dragon calmly pick its teeth with a claw half the size of a hangman's blade. It bites at the wound where ichor still flows freely.

"It's too late for saving," I think back at the mermaid, staring at the piles. "Just look at us."

I feel a weight so heavy that it threatens to drag me down further into the earth. And just then, I become aware of a thin thread connecting me, my awareness, to the pile of ash and bone. "What is this?"

"You must not let go of that thread, Marina. Keep hold of yourself. A great deal can be done just by willing it to be so." The mermaid hovers nearby, fully formed now. I see strands of hair out of place, and scales sparkling as if light strikes them through water.

The mermaid swims over to the piles on the floor. She stares at them for a moment and then looks up at the cavern's crystal ceiling, beckoning once, twice, with her finger.

I see water condense and begin to drip, slowly at first, and then more and more until there is a steady stream of water flowing from the crystals to our remains.

"I offer my last gift to you."

The piles on the cavern floor do something. They grow and reshape. The bones begin to be covered with striations of red flesh and muscle.

The water flows from the ceiling more freely.

"No," Elina says beside me. "How is that possible?"

I jerk in surprise and turn to see her ghost-self floating, hair tied back, her face as dirty as it was when I found her.

This is how Elina sees herself, I realize.

The dragon picks at its scales, throwing the sword across the cavern floor until it bangs against the catafalque. He bites again at the wound, as if it pains him.

"I was so foolish. I gave up, but I will not let you do it, Marina, because you are not *done*." The mermaid seizes me, not with a hand, but I feel something uncomfortable, like I am a butterfly being squeezed back into a caterpillar's shape.

"No," I argue. I tighten as if I have a body, but when I do that, all I feel is pain. A pain greater than I've ever known. "I don't want to go back. It's too hard."

"Yes," the mermaid agrees. "Life is awful." She seizes Elina too.

Elina's body begins to twitch, the reforming skin red and cracked and bubbled. The healing water drips slow, and where it touches, the muscle grows, the bubbles of fat smoothing out until here and there are patches of smooth white skin. Her hair begins to regrow.

Still I fight the mermaid.

"No. I'm dead. The godmothers will call my spirit if they need me."

"Not everything you do needs to be for someone else," the mermaid says. Her voice becomes very quiet at the end. I can barely hear her. I look around for her, but I can see nothing through my damaged eyes. "You may choose to live for yourself. You may choose love."

Then I'm back in this hideous body. The skin on my back bubbles with every movement. My forearms are charred and oozing. I can't move, not yet, or see, so I lie beside Elina and wait for the water to finish its miracle.

Eventually my mortal ears begin to register a rustling sound that echoes through the cavern.

"Come," I croak to the wyrm, still blind. "Come be healed of your pain here."

By the sound of it, I judge that the dragon slips forward and brings its breast to lie beside me. I hear the healing water fall across it, as steam billows into the room.

"The sword's demand for sacrifice was paid twice. Now we're all three free." My voice sounds rusty.

The wyrm slips deeper into the cave without another word.

Eventually my sight returns. Still unable to move, I stare above us at a glowing shape that ever so slowly fades until there is nothing left, and the healing spring turns dry.

"Goodbye," I whisper to the mermaid, a spirit of the air no more.

Amalia doesn't answer me. She's too busy becoming something more beautiful.

CHAPTER THIRTY

Mirror Images

Elina and I emerge above ground, where the Horned One stands sentry at the cave's mouth.

When Elina stumbles, still pink and scarred from the fire's touch, the Forest God comes over to cradle her in his arms and snuff her neck.

I strain but can't hear the murmured words that pass between the two.

"The spell holds?" I ask. My voice creaks as if never used, and in a sense, it hasn't been.

I have a new voice.

A new life, and I will be goddamned if I offer it on the witches' altar again. I have given enough to keep the city safe and the forest still alive.

The Horned One nods. "In the morning, the last soldiers marched from the forest's borders toward the killing field. I smell their blood and rot even here."

I sniff the air experimentally, but smell nothing, and flex my hands, newly raw and remade. "Come, Elina. We have to get back to the city." I take off on the trail.

The Horned One stays by Elina's side, as if tied there. She strides side-by-side with Him a few paces behind me, saying nothing.

When the undergrowth thins, and the forest's edge is in sight, Elina nods downward, pointing at a single pane of light.

We scrabble toward the mirror that was left here at the start of the binding spell. In its surface, the carnage increases fivefold since I picked my way through carrion birds and dead bodies.

"So many," Elina whispers, peering at the battlefield's reflection. "I did not know when I took the sword that so many would die. I wanted only to protect what I love."

"This war is waged with or without your help and not for the sake of love. And if you had kept the sword, you would have died," I argue.

"I died anyway."

"No, you became something new. We both did," I clarify. "But then maybe that is all death is… a passage to something new."

The wind rustles in the trees as if in agreement. A hawk circles the sky.

Elina turns away when we see the man closest to us in the reflection convulse and spew blood as a sword drives through his chest. "The battlefield lies between us and the city then? Must we pass through that?"

I nod. "The mirror only reflects what the ground outside the city sees," I say. "I don't know what else we will find."

"And the mirror there?" Elina asks.

"Reflects these peaceful trees." I tremble, thinking about the carnage we might find. Even in the small, gilt frame, I can tell that the Duke's men fell in greater numbers than his enemies. Kasimir could be one of those men.

"I don't feel ready," she says, unconsciously reaching for the Horned One. He comes to stand near her shoulder, not touching, but more close than is proper. "To go back. What if the fighting has made its way into the city walls?"

"Then we will fight beside our sisters. If the battle goes so far, then they need us *now*," I pester her, ignoring the god's hulking presence. "We must go home."

"Home. The Margrave," Elina repeats, as if she only now remembers the man with whom she is nearly engaged. "The Margrave expects me back."

I nod.

Beside her, the Horned One paws the ground once more, and lopes off toward the forest. Then with a flash of light, he is gone.

Elina stands quiet, watching. "Will I ever see him again?" she asks.

"He is a god. Who can answer that question for sure? But you are bound to him. And him to you. The magic may make you meet again."

I pray my words are true.

"It's time to go home."

Elina takes my hand, and we fly toward the city.

The field of death stinks to the upper reaches of air. Above, it's even easier to see the belt of war that cuts the countryside.

Elina and I turn north and east over the battlefield at Willstätt, but as we draw closer to Strasbourg, I see that the woven protection charm hangs intact, only fraying at the edges. Below us, the town stands several leagues past Strasbourg's edges, nearly burned to the ground. A few brave souls poke through the wreckage, but otherwise we see only more dead bodies and carrion birds.

And in front of us, the Willstätt bridge collapses, and the water crowds with soldiers hopelessly searching for fallen comrades. It's hard to know the full cost of the battle, but I would wager there are nearly two thousand dead outside the city.

The Catholic Emperor prevails in this battle, but I feel as if the witches win. The forest still stands and so does the city. Success!

Only one question pounds in my heart. I am too cowardly to speak it aloud.

What of my love?

We land in Strasbourg proper, taking care to make sure no one notices two women landing onto the winding side street from the air, walking the last several miles to the city's eastern gate, despite our exhaustion.

Soldiers gather inside, city gendarmes, but no one opens the gate yet. Just inside, Elina's tree grows nearly thirty hands tall. No one takes any special notice of the thing now. Swarmed as it is with bodies, it becomes a part of the surroundings, a miracle turned commonplace. In another hundred years, I imagine children will gather under its branches to play marbles and pick pockets.

The godmothers still keep watch. Amondine drinks beer at a nearby cafe. When she catches sight of me and Elina, the water witch flows forward. "The forest still stands?" she asks. Of course she can't see the reflection in the mirror, as it is affixed to the top of the city walls.

Elina nods and glances at me, as if unable to explain what passed within the cavern.

"The mirror stays up. Von Werth's men joined the nearby battle, leaving the forest intact, barely a league burned before the men moved on from it. There's nothing more to be done for now."

I give no mention of the sword or the Forest God or the dragon in the cave. "And how fares Strasbourg?"

"The Duke of Lorraine writes the Stettmeisters to request that they open the city to Catholic forces, but they refuse. The Stettmeisters insist that Strasbourg will remain free of allegiance. We lost very few men, almost none in comparison with the Swedes. But I've heard they burned Willstätt to the ground. The Duke of Württemberg survives, as does the Rheingrave Otto and Margrave von Helm." Amondine glances sideways at Elina at that, but my apprentice makes no motion that the news matters to her.

The Stettmeisters declare a holiday tomorrow now that the fighting is over. The church bells have been ringing every hour on the hour. They will open the gates tomorrow or the day after, and take every able-bodied man they can to burn or bury the bodies."

As if to punctuate her words, the Cathedral's bells peal.

Elina pulls at my hand, and I wave Amondine away. We will begin to unweave the spell in the morning, after I've had some sleep.

First, I must find Kasimir.

We do not even make it to the townhouse before the Margrave's liveried man stops us on the street. "Elina Leiningen?" Pierre says. He looks like he still hasn't slept since the night of the Duke's masque. Dark circles form under the footman's eyes, and his hands hold a tremor that they didn't have before.

"Yes?" Elina looks at me in confusion. She still wears the white and navy gown she left the city in, dirty and leaf encrusted. The mermaid's healing water works all sorts of miracles, it seems.

Even so, she looks like she's come back from a journey of many months, not two days. The hem of her gown hangs thick with mud and leaves, and the girl's skin shows more inflamed than it otherwise might.

"Margrave von Helm entrusted me to bring you to him when you returned from your recent travels." The man doesn't even pause. "He remembers your evening together fondly, and kindly requests your presence for further…conversation."

Elina looks at me as if the man sprouted wings and proclaimed he could fly.

Pierre misreads her confusion.

"Your godmother may accompany us," he says.

I notice the curricle that waits not twenty feet outside the door of our home. "This is ridiculous," I wave him away. "Elina has not even had time to rest."

"Please. PLEASE, Madame," Pierre pleads. "The Margrave returned from the battlefield today, incensed that we've been unable to find his beloved."

"Beloved," Elina repeats faintly. Her cheeks color at the word.

I cannot stop myself from thinking of the Forest God and the way Elina looked in his arms, but it is not my place to mention such things now.

"He regrets that he was unmanned at the Duke's masque," Pierre whispers. "He wishes to prove his ardor."

"Mon Dieu," I curse. "The man was struck in the head with a stone. Is all of this wounded pride?"

"Marina," Elina entreats softly. "It was a very lovely dance." Her arms wrap around herself for a moment, as if she remembers the way Alasdair held her.

"It's your decision, your destiny," I nod to the girl. After what she's lost and won, Elina earns the right to choose who she wants to wed and when.

"I would like to visit the Margrave, but at the moment, I'm not fit for traveling," she begins.

"May I…" Pierre trails off, unsure of how to ask the question, but I anticipate.

"Go ahead," I nod. "If it makes you feel more comfortable giving the girl a few hours to make herself presentable."

The Margrave's man runs to the carriage, drawing out a leather bag. He pulls from within it the silk slipper, drooping, stained, and more worn than when we last saw it.

"That slipper has been tried on every eligible daughter's foot in the whole of this city," I explain to Elina. "Your *beloved* is a determined man."

"What have you done with my shoe?" Elina scolds Pierre. "That silk slipper belonged to my mother. It's very precious to me, spun as thin as glass. The poor thing barely survived an evening of dancing. Why would you put it to such use?"

Even as she speaks, the light in the street changes, becoming golden with the sun's edge. Elina leans against my shoulder, trembling and worn and allows the Margrave's man to go down on one knee before her. She lifts the hem of her gown, barely showing her delicate ankle, still pink from being newly made in the dragon's lair.

Pierre slides the silk slipper on Elina's foot easily, and despite its worn appearance, the thing fits like a well-made glove.

"It *is* you. I found you! Mademoiselle, forgive me. The Margrave will buy you a new pair, five new pairs, if you would be willing to accompany me back to his residence in the city."

"How many women fit the slipper?" I ask. "Tell us true."

Pierre's face turns red all the way up to the crown of his bald head. "Only Mademoiselle."

"How many?" I ask again. "Do not tell us pretty tales, Pierre."

"42," Pierre finally stammers. "But none as beautiful as, you Mademoiselle."

"And I'll wager there were none who fit it who also reside at the residence of the Bastard Kasimir, where you somehow still lurk, despite the war outside our gates."

"I must change," Elina insists, shooting me a sharp glance. "I will accompany you to the Margrave's home within the hour."

A generous frame of time, given that she's newly reborn.

Pierre nods but stays close as we knock on the entryway. Kasimir's footman swings the door wide, shouting back into the house when he sees both of us. "They're home! The ladies are finally home."

I hear a whoop and a loud squeal from Bernice as she hurries down the stairwell.

"Kasimir?" I ask, stepping over the entryway. "Where is he?" I scan the stairwell and the hallway past, looking for his broad shoulders.

"The Master returned last night, asking the same question about you," the footmen answers.

"He returned. He returned! Wait! Where is he now?" I can't stop myself from yelling. "Kasimir. Kasimir! Is he injured?" I turn back to ask them why my lover's booming voice doesn't call down to me.

The footman winces at my tone. "Monsieur Kasimir left an hour ago. Said he needed to stop the pyres from being lit. Said you would never forgive him, Madame. It's too soon to burn more witches, I say. There's been too much death already."

"I argued with Monsieur," Bernice said, giving the footman an angry look. "I knew Madame would want him to stay here where you could put eyes on him. He's not had a scratch, Madame. Monsieur fought bravely but managed to get back into the city before the Duke's forces were routed. Said the coward stayed inside the walls even as his men fought."

"Kasimir should've acted the coward," I say tartly. Tears run down my face. It's too much. I've not only been given a new life, but a new love too.

The footman opens his mouth to argue, as does Pierre, but both stay silent at the look on my face.

"Does Kasimir usually try to stop the fires?" Elina turns to ask me. She nearly sways on her feet, and I feel the same pull of exhaustion.

"Not usually," Bernice answers for me. "But he said you knew the women who were on trial."

By this time, the street outside turns nearly dark. The pyres will be built by now. We don't have much time.

"Knew them how?" I ask, a pang of terror in my chest.

"I didn't recognize the names," Bernice declares. "Not from among all your many friends. Two girls nearly her age, I think." She nods her head at Elina. "Oh, I'm so glad to see you home!" she exclaims, throwing her arms around my apprentice.

"Two?" Elina and I speak as one.

"Girls that Mademoiselle Elina knows. Monsieur said they were like family to her."

Madame de Boer's daughters aren't witches, just ill-tempered and mean, but women have been hanged for less. Much, much less.

We both turn around and start to run.

CHAPTER THIRTY-ONE

My Heart's Choice

"Mademoiselle," Pierre shouts from behind us.

I hear a horse galloping, the rhythm flooding my senses as the curricle pulls alongside Elina and me.

"I can get you there faster," Pierre says.

"Yes!" I climb inside and pull Elina alongside me. "Fly, Pierre. As fast as you are able."

I'm not sure if the horses understand my urging or if Elina whispers to them in their own tongue, knowing her affinity for beasts, but our speed increases.

The smell of burning hair and flesh rises on the wind.

Pierre stops the curricle at the edges of a jeering crowd. We slip through their mean ranks. Faces turn to take the two women in, their cheeks dirty and thin. Wafts of thick, greasy smoke break up their ranks.

I shove through the crowd, so angry that I forget my exhaustion. Elina's hand in mine, we approach the pyres.

"Ava! Elisabet!" Elina shouts. "NO!"

They hang dead by the time we arrive. Neither girl recognizable. Their bodies are nothing more than black char and grisly, stinking smoke.

"Ava!" Elina screams again, her voice twisting in pain.

It was not so long ago that she saw her father die, and now her sisters swing dead before her.

Murdered.

But now is not the time to grieve. I wrap my arms around Elina and push her away, not looking anyone in the eye.

"Who's that!" Someone shrieks nearby. "Who calls for my dear girls?" A sallow-faced woman makes her way to us, thin face puffy with grief.

"Madame!" Elina pulls out of my arms and rushes to Madame de Boer. "What happened?"

The woman slaps Elina across the face. "They burn for witchcraft," she screams. "My darling girls. You taught them this. It is all your fault."

"What here?" A man speaks nearby. There's a commotion behind us. He pushes forward to show himself. Stefan, the soldier from the field. "You!" he says. He grabs my upper arm so tightly that I gasp in pain.

"I don't care what Cook says. It is your fault. You are a witch. A witch."

The blond soldier stands behind him, Klaus. He smiles, murder in his eyes. "These are the witches who flew away from us." He shouts to the crowd. "The woman speaks the truth. These are witches too. Let us burn them."

Stefan reaches for Elina, but she dances away. "These men aren't soldiers. They are rapists! Murderers," Elina screams.

Klaus tries to grab her and misses. "We only wanted a bit of fun. We didn't know you were Satan's whores." He spits in Elina's face.

"Stop it!" I scream and try to jerk away but Stefan's grip is too tight. I can't break free. "Stay away from her!"

"Unhand Madame," a deeper voice speaks behind us, and I turn to find Kasimir dressed in black, wearing the armband of a Duke's soldier, his curly hair bound back in a soldier's queue.

I leap toward my love's arms, but Stefan holds me fast.

"You bitch," Madame de Boer shouts like a yapping dog at Klaus' heels. "Get the priest. These two taught my daughters the dark arts. They brought Satan himself into my house." Tears stream down her angry face.

"Kasimir, get this man off of me," I beg. I speak to the crowd. "We did nothing of the kind. We had nothing to do with her daughters' stupidity."

Kasimir's brown face blanches. "Marina," he warns. "Say nothing more."

The crowd closes in around us, jostling forward.

"Witch!"

"Burn them!"

I fight to breathe, knowing that the witch hunter will ask me about every visit. Every word I shared with Ava and Elisabet. That's if he pauses before declaring my guilt. *If* the mob doesn't take us now.

"You must flee," I tell Elina. I scan the crowd and catch sight of a white-faced Pierre nearby, gesturing him close. I twist away from my captor as much as I am able, shouting "Take her. Now. Drive her to the Margrave's door. Do not wait another moment. He will protect her."

"They're all witches. Her too." Klaus grabs Madame de Boer and pulls a knife from his hip.

"No!" She shouts and tries to shout again, but the blond soldier's hand draws across her throat so quickly and then blood falls in a sheet.

Madame de Boer gurgles. Her green dress turns black with blood. The blond soldier releases her body to the cobblestone street.

Kasimir shoves Klaus away. "Stop it. You are not a priest. Murderer!" He kicks Stefan, and I am dragged backward in the soldier's hard grip. "Release Madame Mullenheim now. She's no part of this. You will be forced to answer to the Margrave von Helm and the Duke for your crime."

My captor cuffs my arm like a chain. I feel blood settle under the skin in a bruise. A part of me already reviews the many women I watched die in the fires. I escaped the dragon only to be brought before the crowd. My mind goes to the moment Kasimir and I met. Elina's dirty face washed clean in the forest. The mermaid's ghost as she passed into the light.

What will I become next?

There's a scurrying sound and more shouting from farther away.

That will be the priest, I think. The fees will be exorbitant, because I'm well known in the city. They will seize my properties and levy them from Roland.

Sylvie will have nothing.

Surely the Margrave will protect her. Or Kasimir.

"Go," I order Kasimir. "Take Elina. Find the Margrave. It's too late for me."

"Release her!" Kasimir shouts, his words echoing my own. I see his large brown hand drawing a knife from his own boot. Behind me, I hear the sounds of a carriage and turning, I catch sight of Pierre, who stands and draws a musket from the seat beside him. He loads the thing clumsily.

The crowd parts.

The gunshot echoes off nearby walls and buildings, so loud that at first I can hear nothing but the ringing of my newly made ears.

Stefan's hold on me loosens, and I look up into his slack-jawed face, watching blood blossom through his coat like a poisonous flower. People scream, I think, because I stare at open mouths. I hear nothing after that gunshot so close. Smoke obscures my vision and I wave my hands, using magic to move it away.

The next gun shot takes two more with it. Past Stefan, Kasimir's down too, falling back, blood soaking the shoulder of his uniform.

I race to his side, determined to protect him until a doctor comes. No matter my fate, but if I'm to die again, I will die as I was born: a witch.

Beside me, Elina stands taller. She puts both hands out and screams. Darkness streams from her fingers. Black clouds, not there before, scud across the sky. She pushes everyone away from us in a wave of wind, flinging bodies against food carts and shops and passersby.

Klaus shouts again. "Whore! Satan's bride!"

I weave a glamour faster than I can think. I make everyone see only me. All the magic Elina works, as the clouds bridge the sky and block out the sun, belongs to me in their eyes.

"Unnatural," the woman closest to me hisses, before the darkness envelops her and she falls to the ground.

Around us, men and women cross themselves and flee or fall as the darkness hits them. In moments, the square clears.

The girl has done it.

I grab Kasimir and twisting air, I push him toward the carriage.

"Elina!" I shout. I make my way through the darkness with my love, stepping over the bodies of the fallen, not sure why I can see so clearly. "Elina!" The darkness ends at the end of the next block. And Pierre is there, with the curricle and the horses. I slide Kasimir into the carriage as Elina runs up to us.

"Get in. All of you. Go directly to Von Helm's. Stop nowhere else."

"No," Kasimir says. "I won't leave you." He's afraid to die; I see it in his eyes.

"They need to dig the ball out, you stupid man. You must stay alive though, so that we may be married." I kiss him.

"Marry?" he asks stupidly.

Elina's love knot burned to ash in the dragon's fire, so I know that the clutching, straining pain in my heart is not magic. I wrap my arms around him before pushing him backward. "As soon as we are able. It is time for me to leave the Hearth's work behind."

"Pierre, make sure that Kasimir's seen to as soon as you arrive. The ball must be drawn out, and his shoulder bound. Then as long as we can keep the infection at bay, he will survive."

"And me?" Elina asks.

"You must accompany him to make sure it is done right. Go to your Margrave. I will meet you both there."

I kiss Kasimir on the lips again, wipe his brow, and bid Pierre drive as fast as he's able. My time grows short. The priests will seek Kasimir's townhouse and pound the doors down searching for the witch who turned day to night.

We must be gone before they do.

So I must move quickly. I have two goodbyes to make if I'm to leave this place, my home, forever.

Keeping my hood up, I take the side streets through the city until I reach Roland's. Taking care to make sure no one follows me; I knock on the timber door once and open it before anyone has time to answer. Luckily, my son stands inside, pulling on his coat.

"You're here!" I cry and throw my arms around Roland. I kiss his stubbled cheeks. "My love. My sweet boy. Where's Sylvie? I must say goodbye now."

Roland frowns, as if he senses the import of my words. "Goodbye?" is all he says aloud, echoing me. "Now?"

"I cannot stay here," I say. "I'm discovered." Tears rise when I speak the word aloud. "I must leave Strasbourg."

My home no longer.

"Don't worry. I wasn't followed."

Roland pushes his shoulder length hair back, pulling away, and I see the same fear I saw in his face as a boy, the fear of being left behind.

I reach up to take his face in my hands and brush the dark hair back from his forehead. "Don't worry, my boy. I'll be back." I lie. I cannot be sure of it. But I hope. I hope to see my family again.

Roland shakes his head and pulls away, turning his back to me, his voice thick with grief. "No, Maman, if it's not safe for you, then it's not safe for us. You must know that."

I had not thought of this, but he and Sylvie have my name, the name of my second husband. They live a modest life, well enough off in Strasbourg, but if the witch hunters come for Elina, surely they will also seek the blood of my body.

He's right—they aren't safe.

Sylvie wanders down the stairs at that moment, wearing a linen dress and dragging along one of the poppets I sewed for her. She hums a tune I've not heard before and snaps the fingers on one of her hands.

My witch's sight catches on the movement, seeing something immaterial and twisting. It's not sparks, nothing so simple. Sylvie twists and winds her fingers, as if holding threads and I squint, trying to see with my witch's sight what she pulls at. Something moves and twists again, but I can't see what she grabs.

Une souris verte/ Je l'attrape par la queue /Je la montre a ces messieurs, she sings.

It's a children's song, "A Green Mouse." I've heard a thousand times, but this time the hairs raise on the back of my neck.

A little mouse is trapped by her tail/ The men say dip it in water/ dip it in oil/ and it will become a snail.

The pitch of Sylvie's voice twines off key.

"What are you singing about, my love?" I walk over to her and crouch down to pet her blond hair, which falls in ringlets around her face.

"I don't want to drown," she says, looking up and catching my eye. "Like the girl in the well. And I do not want to be burned alive either, not like you, Mimi. Or Cendrillon."

"Elina," I correct her. "She goes by Elina now. And what do you mean?" I ask, keeping my voice light.

"A little mouse trapped in a cave," she sings. "I'm not a mouse, but I may be trapped too, just like her. Just like you."

Chills rise on my neck. "Sylvie," I look my granddaughter in the eye. "What are you saying, ma cherie?"

I feel the tendrils of her magic brushing against me.

"Tell Mimi. Tell me now." I grab the arm that doesn't hold her poppet.

"A mouse and a dragon / fighting with swords"

Roland comes up behind me. "Let go. You're scaring her," he says quietly.

He's right. Sylvie still hums, but unshed tears shine in her eyes. She doesn't pull away though.

"Oh love, sing on. I love your music," I say. I release her arm, hug her, and wipe her eyes. "I never tire of hearing you sing." Sylvie keeps humming, but she doesn't speak again. She pretends to put her poppet to sleep on the stair.

Roland and I step into the kitchen.

"She's a witch too," he says, the look on his face stricken. It's not a question.

"It's too early to tell for sure," I answer. The weird tuning of Sylvie's voice plays through my mind.

"She's done that before. Turn strange. Sing a song I should know, but it's not right. It's different."

"My wise son, you see what I did not," I answer, deciding suddenly. "She'll never be safe here. Not now. You must come with us, Kasimir and me."

"Where are we going, Mimi?" Sylvie's voice pipes up from the other room, as if she heard our whispering.

I don't know the answer. Paris, my first choice, will never do, not with my granddaughter showing such powerful magic so early. We must choose a different path than the one I had thought.

"North, toward where I was born," I say, deciding as I speak. "We will go toward the sea."

"Where the hills rise like waves, and the river where you will rest is?" Sylvie asks me.

"Pack your bags. Don't answer your door." There's nothing I can do now to help her with her gifts. That will have to wait for another day. I take Roland's hand. "We meet at the city's western gate before the ninth bell. We will have horses, but pack light. We need to go far in these first few days."

My son nods, his brow smooth. Roland's face no longer fearful but determined.

"Till then, Maman," he says, grasping my hand in his own, and kissing both my cheeks.

I'm gone before he can say *au revoir*.

It takes nearly another hour to slowly make my way across the city. I enter through the Duke's kitchen this time, disguising myself as a servant. I bring a basket of apples and insist that the Margrave's young fiancée see my wares. No one understands how I know the woman is here, and I grumble and fight. I'm good at making such a fuss.

As do all unreasonable women, I persist.

"Bring your husband-to-be," I demand so that all can hear when Elina arrives.

The servants bustle to obey her order. They already treat her as their mistress, a good sign.

"Madame Mullenheim," Alasdair von Helm bows politely and kisses my hand, showing the good manners not to remark on the dirt my cloak shows or the way I smell.

"Did you take care of Kasimir?" I ask. "Is he well?"

"The musket ball's gone. We've cleaned the wound as best as we're able. Now we need to wait."

"I cannot," I argue.

"Is there going to be another miraculous recovery?" he asks, smiling fondly over my head at Elina.

"It won't work. Not here." I don't explain further that that kind of magic doesn't work amid marble floors and Grecian columns. "But bring him. We have almost no time. And let me tell you what else we require."

It takes another hour, but someone in the Duke's house has fine clothes that I borrow. I wear mulberry red silk skirts covered in raised gold whorls and a matching stomacher. My white lace collar lies flat, instead of a thick, starched ruff. The fabric feels fine and thick, its weight comforting on my frame.

Kasimir stands an inch shorter than the Margrave, but at our request, he borrows a fine black doublet and hose, with a thick woolen coat to wear on the road.

"And one more thing," I say, and Alasdair nods, offering me a conspiring smile.

"Are you sure you want to do this?" Kasimir whispers in my ear. He's stiff, from the gunshot wound, but standing, a good sign. We walk side-by-side on a path that winds through the Duke's magnificent gardens, seeking a hidden bower of late blooming roses.

"Here," Elina says, helping Kasimir to the right spot. The Margrave von Helm stands between us. Elina holds my hand for a moment and hugs me, tears in her eyes, before stepping behind me.

"Now, I should ask, do you wish to marry each other?" The Margrave asks, his face serious. "Both of you."

Kasimir nods and takes my hand in his larger ones. He looks into my eyes but speaks from somewhere deep inside his own heart. "Yes, I desire to marry you, Marina Mullenheim. May all I have be yours, my body, my heart, my honor."

Behind me, Elina sighs like a lovesick girl.

I pause. I vowed to never marry again, but that Marina died in the cave under the earth. She fulfilled her vow. This Marina is new. She must marry not for protection, as she did the first time. Nor to hide her people behind the cloak of power, as she did with the Stettmeister Mullenheim.

Do I wish to marry again?

I close my eyes and reach into the Stillness, feeling the pulse of the earth beneath me, and the trees and flowers around us. *Yes, yes, yes,* they say, echoing the pulse of my own heart.

I recall the mermaid's final words to me. I have lived and died by my vows, and now I need not serve anyone's desires but my own.

I make my heart's choice.

"Yes, I consent to marry you, Kasimir Leiningen-Leiningen. All that I am is yours, my heart, my body, my honor." I echo Kasimir. "May we be bound in earth, in air, in water, or fire. And may the aether itself recognize our love."

The air glimmers at my words, and we are both wreathed in light. The Stillness signals its pleasure.

"The rings," the Margrave intones, unsure what to do with the magical blessing. He searches for Elina. She steps forward and puts a small pouch in each of our hands.

After I put a simple gold band on his finger, Kasimir slides mine on me, the metal shaped like a blueberry branch, twined round my finger.

"A kiss!" Elina demands, laughing. "A kiss!"

We need no urging. Kasimir leans his forehead against mine and kisses me softly, as if we have never done this before. In a moment, his need deepens and with his good arm, he presses me close enough that not even a feather could slide between us.

"Stop. We will embarrass them," I whisper, after he's stolen my breath away.

"A few more things must be done." The Margrave von Helm leads us back to the house, where a solicitor waits. We both sign the papers to gift Elina the townhouse, our accounts, everything that will be left behind us. By this time, Kasimir can barely move, with his shoulder bound, but he stands until the papers are signed. The witch hunter's tithe will take none of what we own, because it is not ours to lose any longer. Elina will be protected by the Kasimir Leiningen family, even in our prolonged absence, regardless of her husband's wealth. And Roland remains his father's heir.

Elina holds my hand throughout this last part. She cries and pulls me close after the ink dries. "You're leaving, aren't you?"

I nod.

My smart apprentice anticipates my need. "I've made sure they prepared a case with traveling clothes for both you and Kasimir. You may not want to wear your wedding clothes as you ride."

I smile.

Elina's face turns thoughtful. "Alasdair, we must smuggle them out, but not too far. Kasimir needs to rest tonight."

"I've arranged for a carriage to take you to the first inn past the city walls. And horses for the morrow."

I turn to look at the man who is practically my son-in-law. "Horses for us, Roland, and Sylvie. So four good horses, which you will not have returned." I shrug and frown. "I'm sorry. I would not ask if it were not necessary."

"As you wish," Alasdair von Helm nods, keeping Elina tucked into his arm. "I'll have them buy two more mares from the Duke, and have additional stores packed and sent after you, to arrive at the inn by morning. Of course. I will do anything for the woman who kept my love alive."

At his words, Elina sparkles more brightly than the gemstone she wears on her elegant finger.

And Alasdair proves both generous and smart. The Margrave doesn't need an infamous godmother standing trials in Strasbourg, reminding everyone of what magic his fiancée may be capable of working.

He writes a fairytale in which I play only a minor role.

A mistreated girl.

A fated dance.

A silk slipper.

Even now, I hear the servants whispering to one another. These people know nothing of mermaids and gods and dragons. The Margrave sews his false story from a thousand small truths, obscuring my apprentice's true bravery. And I flee, allowing it. Such is the work of a godmother, a witch hiding in plain sight.

Still, Elina loves her crafty fox. I see the truth in the way her eyes follow him through every room and past the walls into the future they build beyond the here and now. The acorn binds the two together, as the love knot did for me and Kasimir, but Elina chooses to answer its call. Magic cannot exist without its maker.

I know not how my apprentice will twist her wolf heart to make it fit the manicured halls of the aristocracy, only that it is her choice to do so, and who knows what may grow from such a choice?

Beautiful things are often born from the smallest germs of wonder and mercy.

My love for Elina grows from one such seed.

My new life with Kasimir, a pale green shoot wholly unexpected, now grows from another.

THE END

About the Author

Coranna Adams is a fantasy and romance author based out of Asheville, North Carolina. A student of the Odyssey Writers Workshop, her work has appeared in the *Great Smokies Journal* and *WNC Woman*, among other publications. She is the co-creator of the podcast, *Best Practices in Education,* and a graduate of Warren Wilson College.

If you enjoyed *Cinderwild*, please leave a review or rating on Amazon and/or Goodreads. Reviews and personal recommendations are an important way for self-published authors to be successful.

Find the next book in the *Maiden, Mother, Crone* series out on Amazon or in bookstores and libraries in Summer 2024. Keep reading for Chapter One of *Sylvie, Let Down Your Hair*.

Ask a witch to explain what magic is, and you will never get the same answer twice. She may say magic is earth, air, fire, and water, a tepid answer, but true. Another will tell you that magic is aether, the invisible element which makes up the Stillness and the Leap, or instead the movement between all the elements, or even a beckoning between woman and the wild.

I myself cannot explain it, not truly.

I can bind a stone to a feather and transfer the properties of each to the other.

I can call a flame or the rain.

I can bind the wind.

But ye gods, I cannot perform the most basic magic every woman works. I cannot make a baby.

I count this failure by the cycle of the moon. I've been married to Alasdair von Helm a little more than eight years, so ninety-six times I've failed so far.

This summer I will count past one hundred.

I see the trees of the Black Forest from my bedroom window here at Wolfbach Manor, which I'm not allowed to open at this time of year because of the chill. Servants keep my fire burning. They bring wine when I call. They clean the chimneys, or their children will, once the weather turns warm. It's the work I did as a child too, the work I did before I became my godmother's apprentice and then a witch in my own right. I still bear the scars on my forearms and legs from climbing the chimney in my stepmother's house.

There are more tasks I'm kept from doing as the Margrave's wife: putting new thatching on the doghouse floors; taking the sheets to the Lodge springhouse to pound clean; scouring the gardens for more greens; sending the men to hunt; finding meat for the table myself.

We do not talk about my failure to produce a child and heir, my husband and I. Sitting down to dinner, we talk about the weather, or news from Strasbourg. Tonight, which may be any night, I pass Alasdair the soup tureen and think of the moon—as we eat perfectly roasted quail, a soft loaf of bread, three kinds of cheese, and a soup made of spring peas.

So many months the moon has grown fat and full above me, a reminder of my body's betrayal.

"What color gown will you wear on Thursday?" Alasdair asks me. A distraction. My husband, the Margrave von Helm, sits across from me, so handsome he steals my breath. He wears a linen shirt, beautifully woven, under a doublet of black velvet sewn through with silver thread, and although he sits, I imagine his tight black breeches and knee high boots beneath the table.

For a moment, I imagine standing from my chair and walking over to him, asking him to unlace my stomacher and dropping my skirts to the floor. I imagine laying across the table and offering myself to my husband as the meal for the evening.

"Pink for the St. Valentine's feast?" Alasdair prompts me when I don't answer.

I stay silent, for if I have to speak, I will scream, and then what will the footmen think?

"We will go to mass in the chapel," Alasdair says again. "Father Elias asked me to invite the servants to attend. They will like that." He smiles.

I twist, my back itching at how tightly I'm laced. It is as if Marceline thinks I'm getting fat. Or maybe she hopes to convince me that my stomach grows when we both know it does not. I bled for seven days and stopped only a night ago.

"Must we attend?" I finally ask, sensing disapproval from Jürgen, the footman who stands closest to me, ready to take my plate when I am finished. I take a few more sips of soup from the correct spoon and then nod my head. Klaus, Jürgen's partner, eagerly steps forward to whisk the remaining half bowl away.

There was a time in my life when I would've devoured everything on my plate with my fingers and licked it clean afterward. A time when I would've left nothing behind. I stab at the squab on my plate and tear a strip of meat off, chewing it savagely before looking up to find Alasdair watching me with a question in his eyes.

"I will wear red," I decide, not answering what passes silently between us.

Am I all right?

Yes. No. I don't know. "In honor of the saints who died."

No black for the children I haven't born. Nor sensible brown wool in memory of the servant I once was. Certainly not pink, the color of chubby skin a mother kisses. How I want to celebrate birth, not death! I want the soft milk smell of a baby in my arms. I want to grow full and round as the blasted moon in her glory, but my body cares not for my desire.

So red.

Red for all that is wild and free.

Red because Father Elias won't like so much color in Wolfbach Chapel. He prefers to see me in soft blues or greens, with a ruff that covers the rise of my breasts.

Alasdair talks to fill my silence. "The Roman church honors three saints on St. Valentine's Feast. According to Father Elias, it was not legal to wed in Rome during Christ's time, his followers continued to perform marriages in secret, so that love may go on. He feels that we should still celebrate the love that God has for us, even if we no longer pray to the saints."

My husband is a Huegenot.

"Not permitted to wed? Is that true?" I ask. "What did people do?"

Maybe I'm just being churlish. Everyone celebrates Valentine's feast, regardless of the way the martyrs died. Here near the Black Forest, away from Strasbourg or any other city, the land remembers older rituals, formed in the time before Christ, even if its people do not.

Alasdair nods his head at me, as if he knows I'm thinking traitorous thoughts. "Would you like to go into the library after dinner, my love?" he asks.

I don't read well, of course, but Alasdair does. And the library does hold a few books that I love to hear him read again and again.

"Did I get a letter from Marina?" I ask, a question to answer his question. I miss my godmother just as much as I did the first first months she was gone. More, because now that we've moved from Strasbourg to the forest, I have no other wise women to consult on my failure. I don't understand why my body won't perform the most basic task it was built to do. Again, I wonder at what the dragon's fire took from me in that cave. It is no small thing to die and be brought back to life by a mermaid's sacred water.

Marina would have an answer. And if she did not, she would find one. My godmother's wisdom is deep and practiced in a way my own is not.

Alasdair glances over at Jürgen, who shakes his head no. He answers, "No, my love. But Paris is more than a week's ride away. I would expect a letter later this month or next, in March. After the snows ends."

So more than forty days hence. Christ's wounds, does time truly pass so slow here.

"I'm done," I put my napkin on the edge of my plate, making sure I've finished all the food I took. That means that the remaining feast will be laid for the servants or saved to be remade in a different meal tomorrow, so I'm sure that nothing of use is wasted. "I would like to hear you read when you're done." I smile, but inside, I feel nothing. I am barren earth. Soil where nothing, not even weeds grow.

Alasdair smiles back and nods. My answer pleases him. "Thank you, Jürgen, Klaus. Dinner was excellent. Please let Chef Garnier know that we appreciate his incredible work." He puts his napkin across his still full plate and nods.

Jürgen bows his head.

Alasdair stands, and I appreciate his tight breeches as he walks before me to the library.

My maid, Marceline, and I turn toward to the lavatory, where she holds my skirts up while I relieve myself. We aren't always this formal in the house, black velvet and heavy silk skirts. Just on Sundays. Then we return to the library where Alasdair sits, looking exactly like the Margrave he is. His black shoulder-length hair falls away from his broad shoulders. He smiles at me and says something, but I don't hear it. His straight wide teeth and broad mouth make me want to kiss him.

I walk to the window instead. Outside, it's already dark. The sky shows the soft twinkling of stars. Despite the protesting noises behind me, I open the door and walk outside into the cold, closing the warmth behind me away.

The shock of cold turns my skin taut instantly. I feel my nipples tighten, and wrap my arms around myself to keep warm. Without the light of the house, the sky becomes a tapestry of light and shadow. The pregnant moon steals my breath from me.

I search the field and brush below, stretching my witch's sight in a seeing that extends not from my eyes but from my mind and heart.

Nothing.

My powers feel useless. Every day I let myself be pushed from meal to meal inside this pile of rock and plaster, room to room, as if I am a child. Even the maid who cleans my chambers has more freedom at Wolfbach Lodge than I do.

The silence chafes. I'm restless. I feel the forest's green

tentacles reaching into the deepest parts of me, but our shared magic lies fallow, a static connection. Even the forest sleeps tonight.

If the Stillness takes note of my frustrations, She doesn't answer them.

I should go back inside.

But I don't. I stay, leaning against the low railing on the edge of the balcony, turned away from the light and heat. A gust of wind raises the hair from my head and rifles it with impudence.

Why do no animals move? Why does Brother Owl not punctuate the night?

Something prickles my senses just outside of my line of sight.

I hear the chuffing sound before I even see the stag, and although the cold burns against my skin, I stop moving my hands along my arms to make heat.

Is it him?

The Forest God has not visited me since we were sewn together by the invisible needle. Occasionally I sense him while I walk one of the trails, but I have not seen nor touched him since Marina saved me inside the dragon's cave.

I push my musings away. I am so sick of longing for something more. No longer who I once was, and who I am now feels like marble sculpture of myself. Stiff. Cold. An image of a moment frozen in time. A downtrodden girl plucked from ignominy and ashes by her powerful husband.

Looking backward, I see that Alasdair's head is bent down, reading from the Bible.

Perhaps I served the only purpose for which the god needed me, when I took the cursed sword and prepared myself for death. Perhaps he's angry that Marina, my godmother and mentor, rescued me from the sword and drove it into the dragon's breast. Whatever the reason, the Forest God leaves me to my marital bliss, as he should.

I hold my palm out and call a bit of flame, just enough to hold up as I look outward onto the field again. If a servant sees me, no matter. They know what I am, even though Alasdair pretends differently. They call me Lady of the Wood behind his back.

I can barely make out the stag's shape, four legs (not the two I'd hoped), but he's a big thing, his fur heavy against the press of cold, his chest dark brown struck through with white. He turns his head toward me, and I count the points, ten, no, eleven. This is no young buck.

"What have you come to tell me?" I whisper.

The stag raises his head, a mirror of my own watching. The smell of him drifts toward me. My senses still burn bright from my time transformed as a wolf. Food. Water. Sex. I smell all of these with an intensity that almost no human feels.

The stag ruts. He's come this close to the manor to look for a mate.

"She's around here somewhere," I murmur. "Just have a bit of patience. Go north. Turn toward the copse of birch trees." Several hinds like to come and nibble at the soft grasses that grow near the edge of the trees there. I see their shadows against the scrub when the moon is full, as it almost is now.

There's a click behind me as the door opens, and I extinguish the flame in my palm.

The stag races soundlessly away, barely visible movement on a black canvas.

"Asche, you must be cold. Come back inside," Alasdair says. He throws a fur over my shoulders. He must've held it by the fire, for its softness burns my skin. My husband turns me toward him.

"I like the cold," I say, but even I can hear how childish I sound. "Thank you." It does feel good. I put my mouth up to my husband's and we kiss for a few moments. The heat around me ignites a flame within. I pull Alasdair's doublet wide and slide my fingers up under his shirt, stroking the taut muscles of his stomach.

"Feck your hands are cold," he says in my ear, pulling back away from me. "And stop baiting me, woman. Your monthly course just stopped, and the doctor says you must rest so your humors will balance."

"I'm not tired." But I allow myself to be led back inside the library, where the heat feels cloying. I still smell dinner from the next room.

Dead meat, a voice inside my head speaks, the wolf I once was. I remember the taste of blood in my mouth, hunting the battlefield with Marina. Blood red is the dress I will wear in the chapel on Thursday.

My husband chucks a finger under my chin. "Listen to me read, love. I will tell you a story…"

I nod obediently and take a seat on the silk brocaded couch, but a part of me follows the stag into the darkness, toward paths Alasdair never walks.

Acknowledgments

I am so thankful to the team of writers and readers who made this book possible. First, thank you to my husband, Eruch (www.eruchadams.com). My love, you are my fellow creative adventurer, my first reader, the best idea man out there, and you have a knack for knowing which darlings need to die. Your cooking keeps us alive and well as we both write novels, comics, short stories, podcasts, films while we work, go to school, and raise our boys. Thank you to my Black Caps writing group: Linda (www.lmwhitaker.com), Stephen, Alyssa, I couldn't ask for a better band of merry friends. I am so excited to see what new characters and stories you create.

Thank you to my mom, who read so many versions of this book that she should rightly be listed as an editor. Thank you to Raina, the sister of my heart, who has read this and every one of the last several books that did not make it to publication. Thank you to Derek for saying the right thing at the right time, too many times to count.

And to new readers: THANK YOU for taking a chance on a debut author! I love to hear from excited readers, so please reach out on my website at www.corannaadams.com.

9 798989 691517